Always

Also by Timmothy B. McCann

Until

TIMMOTHY B. McCANN

AVON BOOKS
An Imprint of HarperCollinsPublishers

This is a work of fiction. Names, characters, places, and incidents either are the product of the author's imagination or are used fictitiously. Any resemblance to actual events, locales, organizations, or persons, living or dead, is entirely coincidental and beyond the intent of either the author or the publisher.

AVON BOOKS
An Imprint of HarperCollins*Publishers*
10 East 53rd Street
New York, New York 10022-5299

Copyright © 2000 by Timmothy B. McCann
Interior design by Kellan Peck
ISBN: 0-380-80597-9
www.avonbooks.com

Library of Congress Cataloging in Publication Data:

McCann, Timmothy B.
    Always / Timmothy B. McCann.
       p.   cm.
    1. Afro-Americans—Fiction. 2. Florida—Fiction. I. Title.
    PS3563.C3354 A79 2000
    813'.6—dc21   00-29287

First Avon Books Trade Paperback Printing: August 2000

Avon Trademark Reg. U.S. Pat. Off. and in Other Countries, Marca Registrada, Hecho en U.S.A.
HarperCollins® is a trademark of HarperCollins Publishers Inc.

Printed in the U.S.A.

RRD   10 9 8 7 6 5 4 3 2 1

Be not forgetful to entertain strangers:
for thereby some have entertained angels unawares.

HEBREWS 13:2

In Memory of Dr. Charlene W. Armstrong
1969–2000

Your essence will forever redefine For Always.

Chapter 1

Washington, D.C.
November 7, 2000
NBS News Studio
7:00 P.M. EST

"Good evening, America. This is Franklin Dunlop reporting from our NBS studios in Washington. Tonight we will elect the next American president, and the first president of the new millennium.

"Not since the election of 1960 has a race looked as close and compelling coming down to the last day as this one. The results of our NBS/*New York Times* poll completed last night show only a five percent margin between the leader in the race, Democratic senator Henry Louis Davis the Second of Florida, and Vice President Ronald R. Steiner. Trailing is third-party candidate Republican governor Thomas Baldwin of Arizona, but he is running close in enough states to make things very interesting.

"Davis is the candidate who has had an almost meteoric rise within his party, while Steiner is representative of the compassionate conservative wing of the Republican party. Staunch conservative Governor Baldwin lost the GOP nomination and is running on the Reform party ticket. He has strategically focused his time and money on several key states and is the wild card who could have a significant impact on this election.

"We have much to get into and we have reporters standing by in Atlanta, New York, Miami, Phoenix, Sacramento, and Chicago. When we return, we will take you to a couple of those spots for an up-to-the-minute report.

"Prepare yourself America, for when this night is over, we will walk into history. We will elect either our first African-American president, our first female vice president or the first true third-party candidate in the history of the country. Whoever wins tonight will lead this nation into the third millennium, so stay with NBS election-night coverage. Now to your local station."

Miami, Florida
Fontainebleau Hotel
Presidential Suite

Henry rubbed the crystal of his watch while he gazed at the newscast he had waited for his entire life. As he sat alone in the bedroom of his suite beside a two-olive dry martini, he listened to a dark-haired reporter who compared him once again to an African-American JFK. With his legs crossed at the ankle and still wearing the wrinkled shirt and slacks from the last day of the campaign, Henry could hear his inner circle of supporters in the living room of the suite cheer every time his name was announced. Every positive comment from the television would ignite the chant "We want Hen-ry. We want Hen-ry!"

The first time he had heard the cry, he'd been running for Congress and it had sent tingles down his spine. He had rushed to the phone that night and called his mother, then held the phone in the air so she could enjoy the moment with him. Given the enormity of what was happening on this occasion, the chants had no effect. He knew from reviewing the numbers taken by his pollsters that he was in for a long night. He also knew he carried the hopes and dreams of the staffers waiting for the results in the next room, as well as millions across the country and around the world. As the chants subsided, Henry closed his eyes, cracked his knuckles, and attempted to hold his raw emotions close. Placing the remote on the end table beside him, he said the first of what would be many prayers on a night in which he hoped the last words Franklin Dunlop would say before signing off would be, "Tonight, America, you have elected your forty-third and first African-American president of these United States. President-elect Henry Louis Davis the Second."

HENRY

Hello. My name is Henry Davis, or as my people like me to say, Henry Louis Davis II. I'm forty-seven years old, a member of Alpha Phi Kappa, and a tad under six feet three. I weigh around two-thirty, wear contact lenses instead of glasses and I have a cleft chin. I would like to wear a mustache like my father and brother, but polls say it gives a politician an untrustworthy look, therefore I have not worn facial hair since the Nixon administration.

My eyebrows are expressive—I find myself sometimes making a conscious attempt to keep them straight when I'm hit with a question by surprise—and our brain trust never approves an official campaign photo unless my dimples are clearly evident.

I collect the artwork of Paul Goodnight, my wife and I own a few rare imports in our wine cellar and I enjoy the work of Richard Wright so much I hear music when I read his words.

I enjoy playing basketball. I'd rather hang out with Kobe Bryant and Vince Carter than Tiger Woods, but Tiger has a higher Q rating, so guess who made it into the final thirty-minute television commercial. I have nothing against Tiger whatsoever, but for me basketball is a release, although my people have been on me for the last eight years to play more golf.

As I said before, my name is Henry Louis Davis the Second, and yeah, I know it sounds pretentious, but sometimes in my profession being a little ostentatious is not necessarily a bad thing.

I have an older brother by the name of Herbert. Why was he not given my father's name? When Herbert was born, our parents were not married. That was an act that could have you ostracized in and of itself in the forties. My father wanted to give his son his name, but my maternal grandfather would not allow it. He was ashamed because my father would not marry my mom until he was able to do so financially.

Although my dad was unable to serve in the military he did desire to go to college but could not afford it. As a result, my grandfather would not allow them to see each other until my mom was eighteen and Herbert was seventeen months old.

I know Herbert has made up several stories to explain why he is not named after our father, none of them close to the truth, and although he has never mentioned it, I don't think he has ever forgiven me for having the name Henry Louis Davis.

Last year I was invited to work on a book about the twentieth century that went into a time capsule. The author of the book asked me what year I felt was the most important in the previous one hundred years. Although it was a knee-jerk response, I answered 1968.

I felt that was when the country came out of its pubescence in the areas of technology, medicine, and social issues and was thrust headfirst into adulthood with the realities of what lay ahead.

On a personal note, the first day of that year is etched in my mind forever. I will never forget it for the strangest reason. That was the day I smoked my first joint, although when I was asked about it by Ed Bradley before the presidential debate, I categorically denied it. I gave him the impression that I had never touched, inhaled, or even seen a joint. The *only* way I would ever admit it would be if someone had produced a videotape. After all, the only witnesses that day were my cousins Percy and Johnny, so I felt confident the truth would never get out.

Did I feel uncomfortable telling a bald-faced lie to millions of people and doing what so many people expected of me as a politician? Even though it was my first and last taste of marijuana, the answer is no. Why? Because sometimes I'm convinced that America would like for you to lie to her.

A lie gives us the illusion of moral indignation, and I am sure other countries are perplexed by our system of governing. Was it wrong for me to skim the truth? Possibly, but I was just playing by the rules given to all politicians.

Nineteen sixty-eight was also the year I decided I would one day be president of the United States of America.

It felt good saying the words, "I'm going to be the president of the United States of America." I even knew what year I would be elected. I wanted to be the first president of the third millennium.

At fifteen I formed my first presidential campaign slogan: "New ideas for a new millennium." I liked the word *millennium.*

Why did I set upon a course that would alter the rest of my life? I was in Sears & Roebuck, and while Herbert and my mother were looking for sneakers, I was in the television department. My dad was never big on having TVs in the house. He thought watching a movie would stymie the creativity we would get from reading a novel, so we only had a ten-inch television in the living room and walls of books.

I was watching *Truth or Consequences* when she walked into the department store. As I close my eyes I can still see her in that red miniskirt, black go-go boots, and her hair cut in a short bob. Her skin glowed and I can still hear her laughter. It was a high-pitched infectious laugh that made her eyes close and nose wrinkle. She was with friends, and as the group of girls wandered around the stereos, I got my first opportunity to see her up close.

The thing that took my breath away was the playful, almost mischievous look in her eyes. There was such depth in them. When she looked my way, my breath froze in my chest and refused to melt. I had never seen a person as dark as she was with hazel eyes. Then she smiled at me and walked away.

By the time the girls left the media department of Sears & Roebuck, I was strung out. It seemed that even the air itself had changed color.

I followed her around the store like a stray who had received its first pat on the head. The more I followed them, the more I tried to plan what I would say and the more nothing seemed right.

As I staggered behind the group of giggling females, one of her friends noticed me and tapped her on the shoulder as she pointed in my direction.

I panicked. I was standing next to women's undergarments, and asked the sales clerk how much a boxed set of cotton bloomers was. Although I did not actually see the girls' faces, I think everyone in the store heard them laughing.

I was embarrassed, but as I coyly looked in their direction I noticed that she didn't laugh. She smiled, but she was not laughing, and that was all the encouragement my teenaged heart needed.

Our tour of the store led us through hardware and jewelry down an aisle of white Kenmore washers and back to the television department. In my head I figured out exactly what I wanted to say to her when I noticed a young black man in a burgundy Nehru jacket turning the televisions to NBS. I stopped my pursuit because for some reason Vincent Winslet was on and the six-o'clock news had gone off.

"Hey, bah, turn that ta'vision back!" a white man with a red neck said. The brother never looked his way.

A crowd gathered as the youthful forlorn face of Vincent filled the screen. I felt a tug on my sleeve as I watched him clear his throat nervously. "What's going on?" asked the African rose with a gleam of interest in her eyes. As she stood in front of me to get a better view of the television, I think I said something clever like, "Aba, aba, aba," if my memory serves me correctly. And then both of our hearts fell to the floor of the department store as we heard him say:

"We interrupt your regularly scheduled program to bring you this late-breaking news story. The Rev. Dr. Martin Luther King, Jr., who championed nonviolence and brotherhood between the races, was gunned down on the balcony of his hotel room in Memphis, Tennessee. The lone assailant raced away in a white Ford and is presently being sought. After the thirty-nine-year-old Nobel prizewinner was shot, we are told a curfew was imposed in the city of fifty-five thousand people, forty percent of whom are

Negro. *There has been a smattering of gunshots and bottles thrown at police officers by disgruntled Negroes, and we are told that the National Guard may be called in to restore order if and when needed. Once again, if you are just joining us, the Rev. Dr. Martin Luther King, Jr. was shot in Memphis, Tennessee. As of this time the extent of his wounds are unknown. We will give you more details as they come to us up until the eleven-o'clock news hour."*

The sheer magnitude of the words seemed to push her into my chest. Our leader, our savior, our King, had been gunned down?

I remember when Malcolm was shot, and although it got to me, the pill was not as bitter as this one. Why? Because it had been ingrained in my brother and me at an early age that Malcolm and the Muslims were evil. So it never cut as close to the bone as this did.

"That goddamn nigga. Serves 'em right," a skinny pale man with a protruding Adam's apple said. "Raising all that Cain round here. Where da say da get him at?"

"In Memphis!" a woman exclaimed, with excitement in her voice. "I knew he couldn't get away with that mess in Memphis. I'm from Tennessee and them ole boys up there don't play. Don't fool ya'self."

"Well, ew they tell me they were gonna run dat . . ."

A fat Hawaiian-shirt-wearing man looked around, taking a colored-to-white ratio scan, and noticing it was only me, the girl, and an elderly black lady, finished, "*coon* for vice President if Bobby gets the nomination."

"You shitting me, right?" someone shouted from the back of the crowd.

"I ew wish I were shitting. That's what this 'ere world is coming to. You know how them Kennedys are and how much the nigras love 'um. That's who put 'um in office, ya know. And now 'days a nigra can even vote in ew Miss-s'sippi. Well," he laughed, "at least try, so it would be a perfect match. The Kennedy-Coon ticket!" he laughed.

"Well, from wud we just saw on the ta'vision there, that won't be mush of a problem in a coupl'a of hours," a ruddy-complexioned man said with a chuckle, as he wiped his

tobacco-stained lips with a yellowed handkerchief and wobbled away.

It was at that precise moment, with the girl who I later
learned was named Cheryl in front of me, that I decided no
matter what it took, I would one day become president.

As I watched the reporters give us the update from Tennessee, I wanted to be president because of the comments I
heard around me. My father used to tell Herbert and me
that people were racist because they did not know any better. To me at that age, it meant if they knew a black person
who achieved a position of power, then they might just look
at all black people a little differently. So in my fifteen-year-
old heart, I felt that if I was elected president of the United
States, I could single-handedly end racism. A lofty goal, but
I felt it was totally within my grasp. Einstein had his theory
of relativity, Fleming his penicillin, and I would eradicate a
problem that had infected mankind since Cain and Abel
were just a gleam in Adam's eye.

It was in the spring of 1968. I met the girl of my dreams
and fell asleep that night watching the cities of Detroit, Chicago, and Boston being burned to ashes by the fire of racial
divide. It was a day in which I fell in love and had my heart
broken and even now, when I think about it, I get emotional.

Washington, D.C.
November 7, 2000
NBS News Studio
7:20 P.M. EST

"Now for the latest from the Davis campaign, we take you
to a rain-soaked Miami and Butch Harper. Butch, what's the
word from Miami?"

"In a word, Franklin, it is wet. Actually one might even
say it's monsoonal. We've received almost eight inches of
rain within the last ten hours here in south Florida, and we
are told it has had a dramatic effect on voter turnout. The
National Weather Service has informed us that the storm
clouds will be over this region until two A.M. But it has not

deterred the almost jovial atmosphere tonight here in the ballroom of the Fontainebleau.

"In spite of the campaign loss of seven to ten points in the last three months, there's a sense of real anticipation in the air. The campaign supporters are wearing buttons that read, 'Tonight We Changed the World,' and they sincerely believe that they'll be a party to history. Pop icons Eric Clapton and Kenneth 'Babyface' Edmonds have both flown into town and will be onstage at some point tonight to sing a song they had on the charts a couple of years ago, 'If I Could Change the World.' That tune has been the unofficial theme song of this campaign in the last few weeks as it has been played at every campaign stop.

"So although it's a dead heat for the presidency according to our latest polls, hope is very much alive here in Miami. This is Butch Harper reporting from the Davis campaign headquarters in the grand ballroom of the Fontainebleau Hotel."

Miami, Florida
Fontainebleau Hotel
Suite 1717

"Hail Mary, full of grace," Leslie whispered, and touched her fingers to her forehead, her chest, her left, then right shoulder.

The wife of the candidate stood slowly, rubbed her knee, and sat on the corner of the king-sized bed. With the black lacquer television remote in hand, she flicked through several channels until she found CNN and a familiar face. She'd liked Bernard Shaw, who was a friend of the family, even when he was at CBS, and on this night she needed him to hold her hand until it was all over.

As she leaned back on her pillows and ignored the wrinkles forming in her designer dress, she kicked off her shoes and dug her toes into the thick paisley comforter. It felt good to relax for a moment.

The bedroom of the jasmine-scented suite was completely

dark except for the blue light emanating from the television, and she could hear the supporters in the living room erupt as soon as the *H* in her husband's name was heard. Her administrative assistant had left the suite to meet with her press secretary, so Leslie took a half Valium with a glass of red wine to soothe her mind. She never allowed anyone to see her take medication. Not even an aspirin. No one, except her husband and a physician friend of the family, knew about the Valium, because they remembered '88 and what Kitty Dukakis had gone through. If Henry were to lose, history would point to her as the reason, and she did not want to bring any additional harm to this campaign.

LESLIE

My name is Yvette Leslie Shaw-Davis. I am forty-seven years old, five feet six and a half, a member of Delta Alpha Rho incorporated, *Ooop Skiii*. I attend mass twice a week, and I am a graduate of Georgetown Law.

I weigh just under one-ten, work out every morning with a videotape from our friend Billy Blanks, and I typically wear my shoulder-length hair in a soft flip.

My complexion is what one may call cocoa, and my eyes and nose are nothing special.

I handle the money in our family, and let's just say we're financially well off due to investing in a small Florida-based company when I graduated which is now known as Red Lobster.

I was born in Rome, New York, in the autumn of '53 and we moved to California for my dad's job in '67. He came home one Friday after work and announced to us at dinner that we would be moving, and my mom never stopped sipping her tea.

My brother, sister, and I looked in her direction, and all she said was, eat your food and stop looking at me. Next thing we knew, she was calling movers, and in a week we were in the station wagon headed toward the Pacific.

As we rode through the mountains of Pennsylvania, I realized I could never be a woman like that. The kind of woman who would follow orders without question. The sort of woman who would find an unknown shade of lipstick on a shirt and simply put it in cold water or will herself to believe that men always kept phone numbers folded up in their wallet. That was my mom. Quiet. Reserved. Never going against the grain. I knew that could never be me.

Regarding my name, I've never cared for it. It doesn't seem to flow like other names, such as Eleanor Roosevelt. Her name floats from your mouth like warm air in winter. Or Jacqueline Bouvier Kennedy. That's a name that forces one to say it slowly because one's lips actually *kiss* themselves when they form the words. She didn't have a name. She had a poem.

On the other hand, mine just does not do it for me. Henry's brother told him before our first campaign that my name would sound better if I went by Leslie instead of Yvette. He thought that Yvette sounded too ethnic, which is a code word for black. So I went with it. Now even my husband calls me Leslie.

Henry and I are the same age, and he is the validation that there is a Supreme Being, and that *She* loves me beyond compare. I know this because no other entity could bring so much happiness to someone like me and I know the sole reason She created me was to love Henry.

When I think of the good times we've shared I feel closer to heaven than earth, but don't get me wrong, I'm not a "stand by your man whatever the reason" type of woman, but I can say that I have been blessed with him . . . and Henry was definitely blessed with me.

Henry's eyes are as dark as sapphires and nearly as unforgettable. All it takes is a little sunlight to make him squint, which does not make for the best photographs, but when you see them clearly, it's hard to look away.

The man has never, at forty-seven, had a single gray hair. A producer for *Prime Time Live* in a preproduction meeting asked him to come clean and tell him what he did to his hair. When he was asked that question, I could see Henry get a little agitated. This same producer asked the other candidates about their stance on China or campaign finance. When he got to us, he asked Henry about hair dye and why he, like Oprah, Bill Cosby, and Colin Powell, was considered to be *colorless*.

On the other hand, my hair has been graying slowly since I turned thirty. I did not have a strand of gray hair until the morning of my thirtieth birthday. I looked into the mirror that day and started howling. It was not me looking back. It was Aunt Esther from *Sanford and Son*, in the flesh. Teddy, which is my pet name for Henry, ran down the hallway into the bathroom thinking I'd hurt myself. When he saw the three strands I'd just plucked, he didn't laugh, as I am sure some men would have. He didn't patronize me by saying there were *only* three strands. He understood. He's always like that, although at times it's not readily apparent. Teddy wrapped both his arms around me like a first-time mother holding her newborn, rested his chin on my head as we rocked slowly to unheard music, and said, "I wish you could see you through my eyes."

And then, lowering his voice, Teddy said, "I once heard that angels congregate on the shores of the ocean at sunrise. And that the moment is so beautiful, they could actually hear music in the rising of the sun. Leslie, even if I were one day able to witness such a moment, I know it could never compare to the beauty I've found in you." And then he told me, with his voice as soft as church music and just as emotional, to look at myself in the mirror. As I opened my eyes, for the life of me, all I could see was him. But it seems since the day we met, all I've ever seen was him.

A friend heard me quietly call him Teddy, which is something I rarely do in front of others, and asked me why. Because, I told her, they could have Henry. Henry belonged to the world, but Teddy was all mine.

My calling him Teddy is a curse in a way. I gave him the name because he reminded me of a big, cuddly teddy bear. When he ran for president it got leaked on the Internet that I called him Teddy and he received hundreds of teddy bears from women around the world. As a result, the teddy bear became our unofficial campaign mascot, which he initially felt trivialized the seriousness of his efforts, but I think he soon grew fond of it.

I must admit, and I would never tell anyone this because they would never understand, but a small part of me would like for us to lose tonight. I know the notion is maniacal, and I feel ashamed even admitting it to myself when you think of the historical relevance and social implications, but that's how I feel in my heart.

I hate sharing my husband with the world, and I don't think that's necessarily a selfish emotion. Having him burned in effigy and talked about like a dog in the papers and on the news shows every day is not something I look forward to. Add to that the fact that if we should win, for the next four or possibly eight years I will not be able to sleep peacefully knowing there is someone somewhere just thinking of ways to assassinate—no, let's call it for what it is, *kill*—him.

Saying JFK was assassinated takes the sting off what happened. John Fitzgerald Kennedy was killed in front of the world, and having my husband subjected to that possibility is something I dread.

I assured Henry that I was over the scare of what happened in the parking lot in Omaha, but I will never forget it. I will never see him pack his bags and leave, and take it for granted that I'll see him again. If the security officer had been a fraction of a second slower, there would be no Henry Louis— I don't want to think about it. Damn those tears. So if he loses tonight, maybe, just maybe, we can fall in love. Again.

If Teddy were not a politician, I am sure he would be a history professor, because he is enamored by the subject. I once heard him tell a reporter how important 1968 was to the fight for civil rights. When he thinks of '68 he thinks of the race to the moon, Muhammad Ali, and McCarthy. Ironically, when I think of '68, the first thing to cross my mind is TV dinners. Weird, huh? I told Teddy that once, and I bet he still gets a laugh out of it.

I was not socially aware then. I did not watch the freedom riders get hosed down the streets of Selma like litter. I had no idea that Brezhnev, Khrushchev, and Kosygin were names of people I should know, and while I hate to admit it, my family and I didn't even watch the King funeral processional on TV. In the Shaw household, having pro-colored thoughts was looked upon as harboring contraband. You just didn't do it.

Looking back on my childhood, I realize we were raised *Brady Bunch–Leave It to Beaver*–suburban white. I think we watched *Get Smart* or something the night King's body was returned to Atlanta.

My dad was an interesting character. He was well educated, but inside he felt his skin was his sin. He used bleaching cream every morning just as most people used toothpaste. He used so much of it, it left his fingertips red and the skin on his face raw in places. As I grew older, I felt sorry for him because what he hated *most* was not who he was, but what was done to him by society, yet he never understood that. I think—well, I know—that is what attracted me to Henry. Henry always had a clear idea of himself and what he wanted, and people had to accept him on those terms.

In the late sixties I formulated my mission in life. It was simple. I would move to New York City and become incredibly rich. Doing what? I had no earthly idea whatsoever. All I knew was that I wanted a brownstone on the lower west side, a hideaway somewhere on the coast with a view of the Atlantic ocean, and a Fleetwood Cadillac.

I had a sister by the name of Kathleen and my younger brother is named Myles. I love them both equally, but Myles and I are a lot closer. I don't think Kathleen ever forgave me for doing the unforgivable. That is, being born. She is eight years older then me and was the only child for years. Then I came along and screwed up everything.

My parents used to go to this retreat for the firm's associates and their spouses every August and March in Southern California, and they would leave us home with her. She was a mean bitch. I remember one day getting into this fight with a girl who called me a nigger and being sent to the principal's office. Well, he gave me three licks with the paddle and sent me home early. When I got there, Kathleen was already home.

I was fourteen or fifteen, which would have made her about twenty-three, and she attended a junior college or trade school or something. That day she did not go and was sitting on the couch smoking, which was totally forbidden in the Shaw household. So I just walked in and headed to my bedroom, but before I took one step up the stairs, she yelled, "Where the hell you think you going?"

"To my room."

Without breaking eye contact with the TV, she said, "So you can't speak when you walk in a room?"

"Hey," I said, and continued my march up to my room, still sore from the paddling.

"Stop!" she screamed without looking in my direction. "Put your book bag down . . . on the stairs . . . and come here."

"Come on, Kat, don't start."

She stood up. "Don't start what? Bisch, I told you to put down that bag and come here. Mom and Dad left *me* in charge of this house and I'm the boss. What I say goes!"

I stood there just staring at her and decided the best thing to do would be to go along and get it over with. So I walked back downstairs and stood sluggishly in front of her.

"Okay, you black bisch! I ain't gonna have you back-talkin' me like you do Mom and Dad. You ai got no manners, that's yo problem now. What time does Myles get out of school?"

"I dunno," I said quietly. Then she pushed me backward over the ottoman and my head bumped into the TV. It really didn't hurt that much, but I was just tired of her, the principal, and that white girl I had the fight with, so I started crying and rubbing the back of my head.

I saw a glimpse of a black hand, heard swack and saw whiteness. Before the first tear could fall, she smacked me so hard while I was on the ground it hurt my neck more than my face.

"I done told you, tar bisch, I ai Mom and Dad! I'll hurt

you up in here, girl, you just don't know. I ai nufin' to play with. Now, get your little spoiled black smutty ass up in that kitchen and I want it cleaned from top to bottom. I mean everything! If you leave even one speck of dirt in there, your ass is grass, and I'm the lawn mower."

Still crying softly, I got up and walked into the kitchen. I noticed there were twice as many plates and glasses as there'd been before I went to school that morning. There was no way she could mess up the kitchen like this by herself. There were cigarette ashes *everywhere*, sticky dried sugar on the counter, eggs stuck in a frying pan, raw un-wrapped hamburger sitting in the sink with flies buzzing around, and garbage that had spilled to the floor. The kitchen smelled worse than the boys' rest room I had to clean one time when I was on after-school detention.

I decided to take the course of least resistance and get it all straightened up so I would not have to deal with Kathleen, although I was sure she would make me help Myles clean the yard when he got home as well.

After a couple of hours you could have shot a 409 com-mercial in the kitchen. I cleaned the toaster and all the crumbs under it. I cleaned out the refrigerator, including the brown, green, and yellow gunk in the pan beneath it, and even got on my hands and knees and scrubbed the floor. I really went above and beyond the call of duty because I knew Mom and Dad would be home in two days, and al-though Kathleen would try to take all the credit, I would let them know that I'd done it all by myself.

As I put away the last pot, the door swung open so hard my skirt blew between my legs. With her wide nose and thick lips in the air, she looked around for something, anything, to get mad about. She snatched open the fridge, looked under the burners in the stove, inspected the countertops. She even shook the toaster for bread crumbs. Nothing. Then she smiled at me and said, "I told you to wash *all* the dishes."

Looking behind me to where the dishes were neatly stacked, I replied, "I did."

Kathleen said, "Move out the way, smut slut." She walked to the cabinets and pulled out every dish, bowl, saucer, cup, glass, spoon, fork, knife, and utensil and piled them on the counter. She reached under the sink and proceeded to pull out every pot and pan and added them to the silver and white mound. Last but not least, my dear, sweet sister went over and opened the china cabinet and pulled out all of my mom's fancy china and added it to the stack. Even their wedding china. "You chip one plate . . . and I'll chip yo black ass," she said, then smiled as she walked out the door.

I did not care much for Kathleen after that.

Later that night something happened that I blocked out of my memory for years and years. Actually, the first time I thought of it was when we were on a campaign bus headed to Gary, Indiana.

I couldn't sleep the night after I washed everything in the kitchen, so I got out of bed and went downstairs to get some Tang. When I passed by Kathleen's room, I heard her moaning and groaning and stuff. I knew that her boyfriend had left her a long time ago and I didn't know of her dating anyone else, so being the average fifteen-year-old, I had to find out more.

I quietly opened the front door and walked outside barefoot. I remember the grass being wet between my toes because it had rained earlier, but curiosity had already gotten the best of me, so I kept going. When I got outside her room, I noticed the shades were not drawn as usual, so I moved quietly up to her window, shimmying between a few wet hedges. They grew thick on that side of the house, but I was too close to turn back.

I got about two or three feet away from the window and I could see beer bottles on the dresser and hear the Doors playing on the radio. I moved up a little closer and my mouth opened. I had never seen anything like that in my life. In fact, I'd never even heard my friends talk about such things. I could never imagine two people having sex . . . like this. I walked in on Mom and Dad a couple of times, on purpose, but this was something else.

Kathleen and our neighbor, a Russian immigrant who was at least as old as our father, were going at each other. Except his face was buried between her legs, and her head was between his. As I stood there, something crawled on my leg and I jumped, and both of them held their heads up. To make it even worse, his head was not the only place where he was bald! I immediately ran in the house and up the stairs into my room. As I lay under the sheets, I was shaking, expecting her to open my door and do God only knows what to me. But she didn't. She never mentioned it and I never said anything to Mom and Dad.

The next night she made me and Myles eat frozen TV dinners, saying we had to cut back on "electwisity" as she called it. Myles, who was thirteen, refused to suck on the frozen Salisbury steak, but I didn't say a word.

One day, Dad told Kathleen he'd spoken to a friend and would be able to get her into a four-year university. The following week he and my mother took her to visit a college, and when Myles went to Scouts I had the house all to myself for one of the few times I can remember. How would I celebrate this momentous occasion? Would I raid the refrigerator? Would I call my friends over and play some of Kathleen's Redd Foxx and Richard Pryor LPs she had hid in the basement? No. I went into my sister's room and found a package of Lucky Strikes.

I'd always wanted to smoke and had tried it a couple of times before. The first time it burned my throat and made me nauseous. The next time I just coughed a lot and felt dizzy. But like anything I wanted, I worked hard at it until I was able to fill my lungs just like the ladies in the movies.

That afternoon I heated up my own after-school snack, went in the backyard, took out my smokes, shook the bow out of my hair, and placed my cat eye'd glasses on the windowsill. I sat in our fenced-in backyard and felt as beautiful as Ruby Dee in *St. Louis Blues*. As the California sun shone down on me, I lay on the lounger and felt good about myself. For some reason, smoking made me feel *more* secure and *more* confident, and not a day has passed since that afternoon that I have not enjoyed at least one puff.

Yeah, that's what I remember about '68, TV dinners . . . and I guess Lucky Strikes.

Chicago, Illinois
Four Seasons Hotel Grand Ballroom
7:45 P.M. EST

"Hello, Franklin, and hello, America! This is Judith Finestein in the ballroom of the Four Seasons Hotel just off Lakeshore Drive in Chicago, Illinois. The polls just closed on the East Coast forty-five minutes ago, and these canvassers, supporters, and campaign workers have been in the ballroom for about three hours. The last time I can remember this type of euphoria was in seventy-six in Plains, Georgia, when then-little-known James Earl Carter shook the political process and was elected the 39th president of the United States. Initially no one expected him to win, and a couple of months ago no one thought Vice President Ronald Steiner had a plausible reason to celebrate tonight. But after the well-publicized scandal in the Davis campaign coupled with the successful cross-country 'We're in It to Win It' tour, many people are expecting him to pull off a Trumanesque upset and become the next president of the United States. He has momentum on his side, and in a three-man race with the weather conditions affecting voter turnout in many parts of the country, who knows what will happen?

"If you at home are having trouble hearing me, it may be because, this crowd of supporters are shouting as one, 'I stand. You stand. We all stand, for Steiner.'

"As has been reported on numerous occasions, the race is so intriguing because we could elect either the first African-American president or the first female vice president. We have noticed that this room is packed to the brim with a strong contingency from California. We have also learned from our sources that Republican vice presidential nominee Mayor Sydney Ackerman of San Francisco will break with conventional wisdom and address the attendees within the hour. Her breaking with tradition is expected, since for this team, it has been anything but a traditional Republican campaign."

Carol City, Florida
The Allen Residence

As the newscast played, Cheryl and Brandon sat on opposite sides of the room. She had just told him how she felt and what she had done weeks earlier, and as usual when he was upset, he said nothing. But she had never seen him this quiet. Like a faucet in winter, there would be an occasional drip in his demeanor, but on this night the drips had turned into cold brutal ice. He seemed beyond mere anger. As he dug his fingernails into the leather armrest of the couch, he sat and shivered, and she could feel the white heat of his rage from across the room. While he was a large man, Cheryl never feared that he would get physical, but she had never experienced anything like this before. As he sat with his eyes fixed and unblinking, the thought of domestic violence more than crossed her mind. Brandon's best friend in the Sheriff's Department worked in the black-and-blue division, which was a code name for internal affairs, so Cheryl knew if anything happened to her, there would be no repercussions. As the news reporter spoke in the background, she clenched her hands until her palms turned red in hopes that she, and they, would make it through the night.

Cheryl glanced at Brandon, and when his eyes met hers she immediately looked away. Then as the first exit-poll numbers of the night were broadcast, she heard the front door close. The rain was falling in thick splats and Cheryl jumped off the couch because she could not believe he would just walk out without an umbrella, coat, or anything. But he had. She opened the door as he was standing in the rain searching for his keys, and said, "Brandon, wait! Let me give you my umbrella!" His eyes swept over her like a light from a watch tower over the sea, then turned his attention back to the keys and opened the door to his patrol car. As he sat inside it, Cheryl saw him take a deep breath as if he was attempting to gather his composure. Then the yellowed dome light went off and he looked at his wife, backed out the driveway, and disappeared into the night like a secret whisper.

CHERYL

My name is Cheryl Anne Allen and I have been married for five going on six years. I'm five feet three, a size six or eight, depending on the cut, and I run religiously every day. At one time I blew up to a size twelve, but I cut out red meat and buried a husband to shed it.

My complexion is brown. What shade of brown is irrelevant. I have a nicely proportioned figure, thanks to good genes and watching my diet, and I'm a Cancer, for whatever that's worth. I live in Carol City, a suburb of Miami, and work at one of the largest and oldest hospitals in the area as a nurse with fifteen years under my belt. I enjoy reading, although I don't do much of it anymore, and I am and always will be in love with the man I feel in my heart will be the next president of the United States.

I rarely tell this story to anyone because I don't think people would believe me, but I met Henry Louis Davis the Second in 1968. I cannot even say the year without smiling.

I was riding around with friends one day and they said they wanted to go to the shopping center. This was during the PM (pre-mall) period. So we went to Sears and I was messing with the typewriters. I was looking at the new Smith Corona and all its features when I saw him. He was so cute, and shy as I don't know what. I looked at him and he looked down. The first time he did it, I didn't think anything of it. I walked over to the vacuum cleaners while my friends were trying on clothes, and there he was about ten feet behind me. Now I was getting suspicious. So I walked into the ladies' department to join my friends, and he slowly followed. When I turned toward him he panicked and asked the salesgirl how much bloomers cost. I think I bit my tongue, I wanted to laugh so bad, but my girlfriends were not so polite and burst out so loud I thought we would be asked to leave the store.

That day I remember I was wearing this lavender miniskirt and these powder-blue high-top patent leather go-go boots. I'd gone to the beauty parlor a couple of days earlier and asked Lori to cut my hair just like Diahann Carroll wore hers on *Julia*. So I was feeling *extra* cute that afternoon.

As I walked, I thought I'd give him a show. I slowed down and moved my hips with a little extra pop. Thinking back I probably walked more like Flip Wilson doing Geraldine than Dorothy Dandridge playing Carmen but when I looked back, he was gone. Boy, did I feel foolish because I'd done my best walking for nothing.

I decided to look for him. After all, I had not finished the show. I noticed a crowd around the TV sets and there he was. As I got closer, there was an eerie feeling and I knew something was wrong. This little black lady about my height was crying and so I walked up to him and tugged on his shirtsleeve. He looked around and said, "Hi," and I saw his gorgeous coal black eyes and thick, long, dark eyelashes. And on top of it all, he had this smile that pulled you in like a warm hug. I asked, "What's going on over here?" and he said, "I don't know," then moved aside and motioned for me to stand in front of him.

After we heard the news, I can remember getting a little weak in the knees. I mean this couldn't be true. There was no way that Dr. Martin Luther King, Jr. had been shot.

In my house you never called him Dr. King or just Martin Luther King. It was almost sacrilegious not to say Dr. Martin Luther King, Jr. I could feel Henry tense as these old crackers started saying things and he exhaled so hard I could feel each breath on my head.

About thirty minutes later my friends came in search of me, and when I told them the news they were like, "Umm. Hey, they got some XYZ for sale," or something. No, I did not associate with the *brightest* people in the world.

Henry introduced himself and asked if he could walk with me back to the car. I knew he was torn inside. I could see it in his reddening face. The walk he walked before was nonexistent. I don't know what it was, but I'd seen him shortly before and then afterward, and I could tell that this singular event had changed Henry Davis. Maybe it was his innocence, maybe it was his belief in God, apple pie and the American way. I don't really know what it was since we never spoke of it, but I do know a small part of him died right there in Memphis when Dr. King was shot.

I called Henry later that night, which was the first time I had ever called a boy before he called me. When he picked up the phone I was a little nervous, but I don't think he ever noticed.

"So what are you doing?"

"Nothing," he said. "Just finished watching the news and was getting ready to do my homework."

"Oh, I'm sorry. I could call you back another time if you like."

"No way José. My homework can wait. I was going to call you anyway as soon as a commercial came on." There was a piercing moment of silence as I think we both contemplated what to say next.

"So," he asked. "Do you, ahh, go to Sears often?"

"Go to Sears?" He was so cute. "Only when I need something or when one of my friends can get their daddy's car."

With Henry, after the first few awkward minutes, the conversation was fun. We talked about school and about a lot of things most boys didn't like talking about, although at times I could tell his attention was on the news. We even liked the same TV shows. We both liked *The Dean Martin Show*, especially when Nipsey Russell would be on there rhyming and stuff. He also said he liked Perry Mason. I asked him why since I was not really into it, and he said it was because he was going to be an attorney. I told him that was cool and that I had no idea what I wanted to be. I didn't want to tell him but I wanted to be a cosmetologist at that time. Where I grew up that was as big as I could dream.

Then Henry Louis Davis the Second, at the age of fifteen, laid out this plan that would lead him to the White House in exactly thirty-two years. He'd decided what college he would attend and what law school he would graduate from. He knew what year he wanted to get married and how many kids he wanted and what office he would run for first, second, and everything.

I had friends who were ambitious, don't get me wrong. But Henry spoke at fifteen as if he were an adult and he could actually see it all happening. It was so distinct and clear that even I could see it taking place.

Henry's parents never accepted me. It may have been because I was from a part of town known as Liberty City. At that time it wasn't a terrible place to live, but it was the projects and they wanted more for their son. Looking back, I can't fault them for it, but at the time it did hurt. Henry would get his cousin to drive him to my house after lifting weights with his friend David, and we would listen to Motown records as he *tried* to dance. He would be Marvin Gaye and I would be Tammy Terrell. The only problem was he never could dance a lick, but we had fun until 5:45 when he would leave because, just like clockwork, the bus would always arrive at 5:50. Sometimes he would pass Mom on the sidewalk headed to our house, and I could just imagine him laughing to himself as he walked away.

Then one day for some reason he rode his bike over. Now, he lived in North Miami, and their house was a good ten miles from ours, one way. He said his cousin would not bring him and his parents were not going to be home for a while, so he just hopped on his bike and pedaled across Miami just to see me.

When he came in the house we laughed and talked about nonsense like we usually did. And then we started touching. Just our hands at first. I was sitting on his lap and he was saying these silly knock-knock jokes in my ear. Although I giggled and would occasionally say, "Stop it!" I was loving every moment of it. He then kinda awkwardly tried to move his lips closer to mine. Although he was cute, he never was the most coordinated brother in the world, but I took the hint and brought my lips closer. Then nervously he swallowed and braced himself, as if he were about to jump out of a plane, and brought his lips to mine. As we kissed, we really did not know what to do. It was my first real kiss and felt nothing like I expected it would or should. I didn't know if I should give or receive, so we just sat there with our lips locked waiting for someone to make the first move. As I was kissing him, it felt good . . . but funny, so I opened my eyes and found him looking at me. I didn't even think he knew he was supposed to keep his eyes closed. Henry looked at me with a smile still plastered on his face, and said, "What you laughing at?"

"You, Goofy!" I said.

"Oh, I'm *Goofy* now?" His lips, which were curled upward, flattened as he put his finger under my chin, tilted my head back, and gave me a kiss that was sweeter than any he had given me in my dreams. I felt a burn that went through my veins, and my toes curled as if I were soaking wet and had stuck my finger in an electrical outlet. The hairs on the back of my neck stood up, my tongue felt thick. If he didn't know how to kiss when he walked in the door, he was a fast learner.

At that time I was a virgin and very proud of that fact. I was only tempted once before, but nothing had enticed me to this degree. Somehow he eased me off his lap and onto the floor with my legs open, then positioned himself on top of me, and we lay there dry-humping like I don't know what.

He was heavy and I absolutely loved the force of his weight on top of me. And then I said, "No, no. Let's not do it here." We got up and went into my bedroom upstairs. I was scared to death. I knew we could never get caught, so that was not a problem, but I was scared of him hurting me. I mean he was big, and from what I could tell from the grinding, his thing was big too.

We sat on the edge of the bed, and that was when I remembered I'd left the front door unlocked. So I got up, ran downstairs, and locked it, and as I did so, something told me I was doing the wrong thing. All of a sudden I felt dirty, like some of the other girls in the projects who did things like that all the time.

I thought about Nanette. She and I were the same age and had gone to the same school since the third grade. The year before, she got pregnant and no one had heard from her since.

My dad, God bless him, tried to scare me with that story. He said sometimes when girls are hot and nasty and get pregnant, they are taken to this lady named Big Momma's house to get rid of it, and sometimes she'd dig too deep and the girl died. When he first told me this, whenever I saw a boy, I saw a clothes hanger with sneakers. But Henry was so different from anybody I had ever met in my life, so as I walked back up the stairs into the room, I decided to give myself to him.

As the door closed, Henry looked at me and we met in the middle of the room. I think he wanted to make sure he had that kissing thing down pat. The answer was yes. I stood on my tiptoes as he kissed me softly, gently, and it felt as if we were floating.

Henry then led me to the bed, and as he kissed me, his hand undid the first button on my blouse. I opened my mouth a little wider trying to breathe because I didn't want him to notice how scared I was. I always knew this day would come. I knew it would be someone like Henry. I just never knew it would come so fast.

Henry undid the second button. Now my heart felt as large as an elephant's inside my chest. Every night leading up to this day I would lie on my bed and imagine what he looked like without his clothes. I would see him standing there, nude, and for some reason wearing shoulder pads. I don't know what that meant, but I was about to find out.

He undid the third button and I knew that if he felt as good as he kissed, I was in trouble.

Inside me he unbuttoned the fourth and, with a flick of his thumb and index finger, opened my bra like it was nothing. This was the first time a boy had ever seen my breasts.

"You look so sexy," he said, as I thanked God he had come by today unexpectedly. Otherwise, my bra would have been stuffed with toilet tissue.

"Thank you."

"I can't tell you how many nights I have thought about us together," he said as his thumb grazed the slope of my cheek. "The first time I saw you, I knew I loved you. That's strange, huh?"

Henry had never told me he loved me before "No, No, not really."

"Well, it felt strange to me because I have never met a girl I thought about all the time like I think about you. Sometimes I can't even concentrate on my homework because I'm thinking about how cute you are or how I'm going to get over here the next day."

"I think about you too."

"Really?" he said, with wide-eyed surprise.

"Yes, really . . . silly."

And then he kissed me on the tip of my nose with a smile, and said, "Cheryl, tell me something. Are you a . . . I don't know how to say this."

"A virgin?" I asked with a smile.

Embarrassed, he said, "Yeah. Are you one?"

"Yes." I was so proud to say.

His eyes fell as he lowered his head onto my breast.

"What's wrong?" I asked. Could I have answered the question incorrectly? Could he be looking for a girl with experience or something?

"Nothing's wrong. Can I tell you something?"

"Yeah," I said, and rubbed his face as he closed his eyes like a big baby.

"Doggone, I ain't never told *nobody* this before."

"What?"

Then he looked at me with those dark eyes of his, and said, "I'm a virgin too. Actually, Cheryl, this is the first time I even kissed a girl."

"Really?"

"I'm serious. And I just don't think we should do this. I mean I want to do it so bad it's not even funny. But I think— No, I know I love you. I don't want to look back one day and regret our first time being like this. We've waited this long and I just want it to be—"

"How long do you want to wait?"

"Until it's right. Or at least until it feels right."

How was I ever so lucky to meet a young man like Henry Louis Davis the Second?

After fixing ourselves up, we were just hanging out like teenagers, both happy about the decision inside. That's when I heard the key in the front door. That couldn't be my mom. She could not be getting off two hours early. I went downstairs as Henry stood stammering in the middle of my room, "What, what, who, what?"

"Hey, Momma. How you doing?" I said loud enough to alert my guest to be quiet.

"Whose bike is that outside?"

"Wud bike?" I had to think *fast*.

"The bike on the front porch."

"Oh, *that* bike. I didn't want to bring it in 'cause the tires were dirty. I rode it in the mud and stuff."

My mom's momma-antenna sprung up. *Bong!* "You still never answered me. *Whose* bike is it?"

"Oh. Well, it's Penny's bike. You know Penny who lives down there in building R?"

With a slow, I'm-about-to-catch-your-ass-in-a-lie folding of the arms across her belly, she said, "Since when you borrowing anything from Penny Clark?"

"Well, I didn't want to walk all the way to the store, so she was next door, and I asked her if I could borrow it. She said give her a dollar and I said no but I'll give you a quarter, and she said she had to have a dollar and I said you ain't getting a dollar but—"

"Cheryl? Why are the pillows on the floor?"

"I was down there watching TV." Then I made my move, the move all teenagers are taught in How to Be a Teenager 101 class. I said, "Momma, you not trying to say you think I had a boy in here. Are you?" I looked at her with a puzzled face, my palms open and shaking my head as if I were so disappointed that she had not trusted me.

She did not say a word. She just looked in my direction.

"Well, Momma," I said with a heavy sigh, "first of all, I'm too young to get serious, and even if I did, I wouldn't do *that* in your house. I'd never bring a boy in here."

"So who's that proper-talking nigga always calling here at night?"

"Oh, Henry," I said, and then lowered my voice with a cluck of the tongue. "Momma, he's just a friend."

"Umm." With that she headed upstairs. I did not want to follow her because it would look just a tad obvious, so I turned on the TV and prayed his big butt could hide.

"Ahh, Cheryl," she said, with *I caught you* in her voice, "what is your room window doing open?"

"Doggone, Momma, I was just airing out the room," I said and, then decided that I should go upstairs. Thank goodness he had gotten away.

She was looking around my room, and I noticed her on her knees looking under my bed. I walked in and said, "You know, this is really sad, Mom. I hate to say it, but I done told you I didn't have company. I'm not even courting anyone and look at you. You in *my* bedroom, on your knees, looking under *my* bed? I can't believe this."

I watched my words cut through her. My posture, the tone of my voice, or the words, I don't know which it was, but she looked almost embarrassed for the first time.

"I know, sugar," she said, standing with a soft grunt. "You right. You're a good girl, I must admit. I just had a long day today and, I don't know, I saw that bike out there and those pillows on the floor and just flipped."

As she sat on the bed I went to the window and closed it, looking for Henry but figuring by now he was so scared he was probably halfway home. I hoped he didn't take the bike, because how would I explain it? And if Mrs. Jefferson across the street saw him, I was up the creek anyway. But I didn't have time to worry about that now. I had to deal with my momma.

"So what happened Momma? Why you home so early?"

"I quit, got fired, whatever you want to call it."

"What?"

"Well, I called your dad and asked him what I should do. They are still refusing to integrate that lunch counter at Woolworth. I know I'm just a custodian out there or what have you, but right never wronged nobody." As she spoke, wrinkles appeared in her forehead and at the corners of her eyes, and she looked at me with indignation. "They were supposed to do it two years ago and then they said definitely last year, and now they still are not doing it. It's 1968. If not now, when do they plan to do it? So I told them I was not cleaning up the dining area. If we can't eat there, dammit, we can't clean there."

"Really?"

"Yeah. I called your father before I did it just to make sure we could get by on one income until I could find some day work, if they did what I expected them to do. He told me to do what I felt was right because I had to work there and somehow we would get by. So here I am."

"Well, Momma," I said, sitting next to her, "I'm proud of you."

"Thanks, baby. I appreciate that."

"What can I get for you? I wanna make you queen for the day. I'll run your bath, clean the kitchen, do the laundry, whatever you like. Would you like a Co'Cola or some iced tea or something?"

"Yeah, sweetie, bring me an RC. That would be nice."

I stood and kissed her on top of her partially balding head. I had never been so proud of that little lady as I was at that moment. She looked up at me and smiled, because she knew it.

As I ran downstairs, I looked at the clock, trying to anticipate how long it would take Henry to get home. I looked out the window and saw that the bike was there. He was obviously waiting in the area since he had heard the story about me borrowing the bike. He was so smart, and so fine, so nice, so considerate, so cute, so— And then I heard, "Son, come on out that closet, you're messing up my shoes."

The next thing I knew, I was out the door, on that bike, and riding as far away from that place as I could.

Chapter 2

"This is Vincent Winslet reporting from the statehouse in Phoenix, Arizona, where there's a rally for the much-beloved yet sometimes controversial governor of this state, Governor Thomas Edward Baldwin, or as he is affectionately known in these parts, Governor Tom. The polls here will close in about three hours, and we expect the crowd to increase here in the valley of the sun. Arizona State Police estimates indicate about four thousand supporters have gathered here on Washington Street to support their governor in his bid to become the next president of the United States. As you may remember, Franklin, in the fifties Arizona was considered a Democratic stronghold, and it was not until 1968 that that trend came to a screeching halt with the man viewed by many as the father of modern-day conservatism, one Senator Barry Goldwater."

"What's the mood out there, Vinny?"

"There is a deep sense of patriotic optimism, Frank. As you know, after the Republican convention most of these people never thought they would have the opportunity to cast a presidential vote for their favorite son. Two events have shaped this day. First, the decision by Governor Tom to don the mantle of the party initially worn by H. Ross Perot in the 1992 election. He of course is running on the Reform party ticket and has the full-fledged support of the religious right and what most would call the conservative wing of the Republican party. As you know, the candidate for the Republican party, Vice President Ronald Steiner, lost a considerable amount of his support when he selected the pro-choice mayor of San Francisco, Mayor Sydney Ackerman, as his running mate. We are told."

"Vinny, if you would hold on for one brief moment. I hate to cut you off, but we have the very first election results from our exit polls at ten minutes after the hour.

"NBS News is reporting that the great state of Virginia has gone to Senator Henry Davis of Florida. Repeating, the commonwealth of Virginia has cast its thirteen electoral votes for the two-term senator from Florida, Senator Henry Louis Davis the Second. This is a state in which he campaigned hard and heavy for several months, with former governor L. Douglas Wilder by his side. It is one of the few states in which his numbers have not dropped in recent weeks. With 280 electoral votes needed, the two-term senator from Florida is thirteen votes from making his dream a reality. We will be back with more election coverage after this message."

DAVIS	**13**	
STEINER	**0**	
BALDWIN	**0**	

Fountainebleau Hotel
Presidential Suite

The eruption in the ballroom shook the walls as someone pounded on the door of Henry's bedroom. "Sent'a Davis! Sent'a Davis! Have you heard the news?" the female voice shouted. He did not move from his chair. Hours earlier he'd joined his key staffers in the living room of the suite. Phone calls, telegrams, and faxes from all over the world were being sent to wish him well on the monumental night. After that, he'd asked Marcus to clear the bedroom so he could just have a little time to himself.

As Marcus asked the individuals to leave one by one, Henry noticed he stopped to talk to Joey Wood, his chief of security. Joey, who was rail-thin and reminded Henry of Barney Fife because he seemed to always have had one cup of coffee too many, had apparently refused to leave as Henry watched the two men exchange words. Then Joey whistled with his index and pinky finger in his mouth and a gentleman bearing Secret Service credentials walked over and the words subsided.

While they had had Secret Service protection since the New Hampshire primary and the death threats began, never had they had as many agents as on this night. The agent spoke into the microphone in his sleeve, and the bulge from his magnum was apparent under his black jacket. Soon the Secret Service agent pointed his index finger at Marcus to make his point. Henry's first inclination was to see what was going on, but he resisted doing so because in the last couple of years he'd taught himself to delegate. Thus he allowed Marcus to handle the situation while he returned his attention to the news.

TV crews from all the major networks had asked to set up cameras to watch his emotions as the numbers came in, but Henry had vetoed the idea the previous day. His running mate, with whom he'd had differences in the last weeks of the campaign, had brought a contingent of about thirty people to his door, only to be turned away by his campaign press secretary, Ed Long.

"You mean to tell me," Henry's running mate shouted, loud enough for everyone in his entourage to hear, including a few members of the press, "that he's not going to let me in there? What kind of horseshit is he trying to pull this time, Eddie? You know it's tradition for the candidates to watch this here thing together." Six-foot-five-inch Dirk Gallagher was the stereotypical elbow-grabbing Texan with ostrich boots, barrel chest, slick salt-and-pepper used-car-salesman hair, and matching attitude.

"I know, Governor, I know," Ed said, shaking his head

like Rafiki. Noticing the reporters in the crowd, he then said at a lower decibel, "He and I talked about that a couple of hours ago and he's just dead set against it right now. Maybe a little later on. What we've done is made my suite the reception area for the inner circle."

"Your suite? Why not the big one at the other end of the hall!" Dirk demanded, spilling his drink on a member of the Texas press with a pen poised over a yellow notepad. "We can't all fit in that tiny-ass suite of yours anyways! Why, trying to fit us all in there is like trying to push a porcupine into a—"

"Governor," Ed said into the candidate's chest, "we sorta got the missies in there until things . . . you know . . ."

With a tilt of his cowboy hat, Dirk asked quietly, "Are they still going at it?"

"Well, aha, yeah."

"Well, good! Fuck 'um!" Dirk shouted, and then turned toward his laughing supporters and said, "Listen, guys. There has been a small change, but it's no problem. We have handled more difficult situations with them assholish senators in Austin. So let's just go across the hallway and watch this thing in good ole Ed's room. And Eddie has assured me he *does not* have any cheap liquor in there. Right, Ed?"

HENRY

Nineteen seventy-three. Umm, what do I think of in '73? Well, the obvious answer is Watergate and how this country was awakened and brought to its knees with the reality of what really goes on every day in Washington. On a more personal level, it was the year I lost Cheryl and met Yvette Leslie Shaw.

Cheryl and I dated through high school. I had always told her I was going to Florida A&M and then either Georgetown or Harvard Law. She said she would go to FAMU with me, and so I was just sure she would be there. We never really talked about it much. I played football and made all-city and all-state and a few other all-teams, but she really never did anything regarding extracurricular activities. Why did she not participate more? Just like our choice of colleges, it never really came up.

My mom and dad bought me a car in January of '71. It was a sleek sky blue 1966 Mustang that my dad got an incredible deal on from his boss. My father worked as a medical records administrator but could have been a great salesperson because he was always thinking two steps ahead. After I got the car, girls were almost throwing phone numbers in the windows when I came to red lights.

I never cheated on Cheryl. Was I tempted? Does Ted Kennedy own a black suit? I think any red-blooded American kid would be. This was about the time I started hearing reports about John and Bobby Kennedy possibly having affairs. There was even a rumor floating that Dr. King had had a couple of flings, which I refused to believe, but I did not want a ghost from my past to appear one day with a story of my own indiscretions. I know these thoughts were not typical for a kid that age, especially in the free-sex late sixties and early seventies, but like I said, I knew I wanted to be sitting in this chair, in this room, on this night.

So I was eighteen years old, a star on a state championship football team, driving a new, to me, Mustang. And I was still a virgin. Yes, Cheryl and I had come close on more than a couple of occasions, but we had never crossed that threshold.

To this day my parents have never accepted Cheryl, which, when I look back, I think only made me love her more. After they found out who she was and where she lived, they got to the point where they wouldn't allow her to call the house. My dad even called her mom and dad one night and got into it with them. They wanted the best for me, I know now looking back, but I still don't agree with the way they handled the situation.

And then came the time to select a college. I remember getting this catalog from Florida A&M as soon as it came into the Guidance Department. I brought it to lunch, and after Cheryl and I finished eating our Tater-Tots, I remember pulling out the catalog as if it were a three-carat diamond and looking for the smile of utter joy on her face. But all she said was, "Umm. When did you get that?"

"Today. It just came in!" I was beaming from ear to ear. "I was looking at the campus map. They have the dorms on opposite sides of the campus, but I noticed the football dorm is over here, so—" And then I noticed her crying.

"Cheryl? Cheryl, what's wrong?" She just sat there saying nothing, still looking at the pictures in the orange and green catalog. I slid closer to her, and said, "Baby? Did I say something wrong? You don't wanna live in a dorm? Whatever it is, I'll fix it." As soon as those words parted my lips, the floodgates opened and she stood and ran away. I chased her for a while until the assistant principal blew his whistle for me to stop running and to walk. Then the bell rang and I started to walk back toward my next class. Thoughts ran through my mind like a herd of broncos, because I had never expected such a reaction.

"Hey, Henry, somebody told me you were going to play for the Gators. For real?" Regina Grant asked. Regina was the head cheerleader, and you could always tell she had this thing against wearing bras.

"Yeah, the recruiter called me the other night," I said, looking over my shoulder for Cheryl, "but I'm not going."

"Why not?" she replied, and hugged my left arm. "That's where I'm going. That's where Angela and Joanna are going too."

I was feeling so many emotions inside, but as she spoke, all of a sudden those feelings were taking a backseat to the cleavage Regina had parked on my triceps. Cheryl had beautiful breasts, don't get me wrong. I'd played with them a number of times, but I had not actually seen them since one particular day when we were fifteen. Unfortunately my girl had nothing on Regina D-Cup Grant. I had never felt breasts so soft. It was as if my arm were just enveloped in their uptilted softness, and I didn't want to pull away, although I knew I should.

"Really? All of you going to UF?"

"Yep. In fact, we're going to Gainesville on the thirteenth to look over the campus. There's a lot more to do in Gainesville than in Tallahassee."

"I know, I know, but I've always wanted to go to FAMU. Even as a—"

"Chile, das ole-fashioned thinking. Most colored folk are going to the University of Florida nowadays. They're recruiting colored kids left and right."

When I heard her say the word *colored*, a chill swept over me, and I knew I had made the right choice in colleges.

"Well," she continued as I got to my classroom door, "here's my phone number. If you change your mind, let me know. I would love for you to come up for a weekend. And who knows?" she said, with a suggestive look, a giggle, and a wiggle. "Even if you do decide to go to that nigga school, maybe you could come down and see me on the weekend."

I took the number, smiled, folded it into a square, and went into my classroom. As I sat at the desk, my first inclination was to throw the digits away. After all, she was calling the school I had dreamed of attending my entire life a *nigger* school. Yeah, I wanted to throw the number away, but I was experiencing a sensation in my jeans that created a tingle in my left foot due to a lack of circulation. And I was a little embarrassed to stand up once I was in my seat for fear that I would pitch a tent. The "colored" and "nigger school" talk did not mean a thing to the action below, which could not get the bouncing peach blouse out of its mind.

As I extended my legs beneath my desk and adjusted things with my hand in my pocket, my thoughts went back to Cheryl. I reviewed everything I had said to her as well as conversations from the previous days, and I came up blank. Glancing down at the slip of paper with Regina's number, I wadded it up and shot it in the can just like my idol Clyde "the Glide" Frazier of the Knicks. There was no doubt, if there was any before, as to what I should do. I should attend Florida A&M, pledge Kappa, be elected student body president, and graduate cum laude. But first I needed to find out what was wrong with my baby.

*   *   *

Before the sound of the bell left the air, I was out the
door. Since I always made a point of sitting in the front
row, that was no big deal. I only had five minutes to get to
my next class, and it was on the other side of the school. I
knew if I ran, I could go by Cheryl's class, find out what
was wrong, and get back to my Americanism Versus Com-
munism class before the bell rang.

I was running down the hallway full speed wearing my
football jersey with the big "35" plastered on the back of it.
As I slid and skipped through students, I looked down at
my watch and figured I was making good time. Two or
three football players tried to stop me; one tried to tell me
something about his decision to go to UCLA. It didn't matter, because I now had only three minutes to see Cheryl,
kiss her, and get to class. As I ran down the hallway, my
best friend on the team, David, yelled at me, "Hey, Stang!
Wait a minute!" Most of the fellows in school called me
Stang, which was short for Mustang.

"Can't, man. I'm in a rush. I'll getcha' on the comeback."

He ran up behind me, and said, "Listen man, I need to
tell you something."

I looked at my watch and slowed down. "What, Slick, I'm
in a rush."

"I know, I know, but dig on this, blood." And then he
looked the other way as he got closer. "It's your honey."

"What about Cheryl?"

"Man." And then he looked down.

"David. What's up, man? Something happened to
Cheryl?"

"Listen, jack. You know you my ace boone coon'. But you
don't need to go round that corner."

I just looked at him, because I now knew why she was
crying. As I tightened my jaw and my fist, I just had to see
who *he* was. I walked toward the corner with the other
students coming toward me like salmon swimming upstream, and David hollered, "Stang! Don't start anything. It
might mess up your ride, man. You got a full ride, man.
Don't blow it."

The scholarship offers were the least of my concern as I

turned the corner. I remember how hot it was. At least ninety-five degrees under a tree. I was full of sweat from the run and now my heart was beating like a snare drum.

There she was, standing next to him. Darius Kingsley. Darius was a wide receiver on our team and dumb as wet clay. In fact, this was the first year he was out of special ed, and he and Cheryl were in first-period cooking class together. They were not holding hands, smiling, or anything. They were just standing closer than acquaintances stand. And then she looked up at me.

"Henry? What are you doing here?" The look in her eyes confirmed everything I needed to know.

"What do you mean, what am *I* doing here?"

"Aren't you supposed to be in AVC? You gonna be late."

"What's going on, Cheryl?"

David stood behind me, and said, "Man, cool down. It ain't worth it, blood. Not for some chick."

"It's not what it looks like, Stang," Darius said.

"What does it look like, Cheryl? Since when is this dumb"—I paused for the right word and it just sorta rolled out—"*dumb* motherfucker walking you to algebra?" Neither Cheryl nor David had ever heard me curse before, but no other word seemed to fit.

"Who, who, who you calling dumb!" Darius stuttered with this sinister smile on his face as his eyebrows arrowed downward and he took a couple of steps in my direction.

"He called your punk, short-bus-riding ass a dumb motherfucker!" David said. "You ain't got no business even talking to the chick!"

"You, you, you ain't in this shit!" Darius replied. "So you might wanna find you some business to get into and stay out mine."

"Listen, Stang, let's go, man," David said, tugging on my jersey. "We ain't losing our ride fighting over no damn broad, man!"

Darius dropped his books, spread both arms crucifixlike, bugged his eyes, and sneered, "Yo, David, you really want sum a dis? I been wanting to peel off in yo ass anyway.

You know I ain't scared of your backwoods, musky, seed-of-deodorant country ass!"

As David and Darius traded insults, Cheryl and I spoke with our eyes. It's funny. I guess because we were together so much, our communication went beyond the physical. For only the second time in my life, I saw her tears fall. Those hazel eyes, her full brown lips, and her body were expressionless, but her face glistened from a tear track on her cheek.

I could tell she wanted to say something to me, but she could not. What was it? Did she feel more comfortable with Darius? He, after all, didn't expect anything from her. He wouldn't push her to stay on the A-B honor role. He wouldn't bring her college catalogs and stick them under her nose. He wouldn't insist she start a college fund and save her money while other girls her age headed straight for the mall they had just built in town.

We broke our stare into each other's eyes as a teacher came out of the classroom to quiet David and Darius. I turned to walk away and I heard her plead softly, "Please don't leave, Henry. Please don't leave me. I need—I want to tell you something." But for a moment I couldn't stand the sight of her. I already knew, in a way, what she both needed and wanted to say.

As I walked around the corner, the bell rang, students bolted for their rooms, and I heard the door to her classroom close. As it did, I leaned against the redbrick wall trying to catch my breath. For the first time, something happened to me that had never happened before. My chest burned, there was a white blindness and I couldn't think straight. There were no colors, no noises, yet my eyes were wide open. It was as if I had entered this chasm, and I knew my life would never be the same.

It was not supposed to be this way. I'd planned every detail of my life and this was not a part of it. And then David came by and said, "Listen, man, I gotta get to the coach's office, but we gonna handle this later on. You cool?"

"Hey." I looked at him with not enough strength to crack

even a fake smile, and said, "Yeah I'm cool. I'm cool, man. Get to the gym."

"All right, man. I'll see you after school in the weight room. Hold ya' head up and don't be late this time."

As David ran away, I heard Darius talking to another girl in the hallway. I had too much to lose to waste my time with him or Cheryl if this was the type of guy she wanted to be with.

I walked slowly toward my class, trying to think of an excuse for Mr. Rivers. But as I walked, Darius passed me, and said, "Man, if that's your woman, you better keep that fine ass of hers on a leash, because a brother like me would—"

I waited in the dean's office for more than two hours. They called in our principal, Dr. Langston, and the head football coach to determine the best way to handle such matters since I was an athlete. At that time colleges, especially Florida A&M, were strict about player conduct, and my coach did not want it to affect my ride. Apparently I'd knocked out one of Darius's front teeth and shaken another one loose. I don't even remember the punch, it happened so fast. One minute he was saying something, and the next I was waiting for Nurse Arndorfer in the dean's office holding a wet paper towel around my split knuckle.

Later David told me he had seen the two of them together at a house party. He said he never saw them kissing or even holding hands, but he had noticed that Darius would walk her to all the classes I could not due to my schedule.

When I got home that day, I wanted to call her. I wanted to call her so bad. Because even though it was her who was in the wrong, I felt guilty. For the past three years we had spoken on the phone at least once a day. As I paced in my room, it occurred to me that she and I had never so much as had an argument before. Sure, we had a Romeo and Juliet–like pressure from my parents, but that was a minor thing, because she knew I loved her, and up until that day, I knew she loved me.

We used to say our love was so deep, the word *love* could not possibly define it. That true love transcended four letters. I once read that Eskimos have more than fifty words or phrases for *snow*, because snow affects their lives in so many ways. So it befuddled me how four letters could begin to describe the love for a brother and the love for a job and my love for Cheryl. I felt the word *love* was deficient because I was supposed to use this word to describe just how much *she* meant to me? So we had our own word to describe how we felt. And that word was simply *always*. Because we felt that our love would never die and would last forever. That it would last . . . for always.

When the phone rang, my heart stopped. I remember falling over the couch onto the floor to answer it.

"Stang. What's up, man?"

" 'Sup?"

"Damn, man, you sound like stewed shit. Listen. I got some good news for you. Coach handled that situation. He told Dr. Langston that he would discipline you, because he didn't want you to miss any days from school. He said he would have you run stadium steps and your parents would have to pay to get Darius's teeth fixed."

"Umm."

"Umm? That's all? Umm? You know, they talked that punk out of calling the pigs. If you had a record, you could have forgotten about FAMU. You know how Coach Gaiter is."

"I'm happy, man. I just—"

"Yo, get over it, brother," David shouted. "Like Coach says, either you're the hammer or the anvil. That's life. Deal with it and move on!"

The next day I was at the stadium running the steps and trying to focus on my halfback physique. Coach Niblack sat in the distance watching me but it didn't matter. I felt good running up one row and down the other. I never stopped my conditioning after the season, so I was in the best shape of my life. Up one row and down the other. I attacked the steps as if I were trying to punish them. I wanted to push my body to the limit, and Cheryl out of my mind. Up one row and down the other. Then I did something I rarely did. I pulled off my shirt and tossed it on the bleachers. I knew a few girls from the pep squad were watching and I could hear them making comments, but I never looked back. At this time I was getting more definition in my thighs and abdomen. My chest, which was always large, was now accompanied by a flat stomach and thick triceps. As I ran, sweaty and hot, I had no time to even get tired, I was too busy punishing the stadium and trying to forget Cheryl.

And then I saw her, and almost tripped on a step. I regained my balance and I could hear a couple of the girls giggle. When they did, Cheryl looked around and noticed me running. We had not spoken the previous day, although someone had called the house two or three times and held the phone without saying anything. I'd called her house and done the same thing. She knew it was me. I knew it was her. But neither of us knew how to give in.

As she watched, I continued running. I ran harder, as if the answer to what had happened to our "for always" were buried in the cinder-block steps. Up one row and down the other. Up one row and down the other. I pounded the steps as if they contained answers. I could feel my heart pump acid throughout my body and it didn't matter because I saw her and I saw Darius. I saw them standing closer than close and I saw her tears. I saw her choosing to stay here with him instead of going to Tallahassee with me. And then I sprinted the rest of the way, skipping two or three steps as I ascended to the top. Sweat flung from my arms like a wet mop being shaken outside a back door. Breathing heavily, I finally stopped and gathered my composure, determined that I would stare her down. When I looked in her direction, she was gone.

After school I got off the bus and ran home as fast as I could. Herbert, who came in a distant second, thought it was because I wanted to control the TV. Getting to pick which program to watch on television was the last thing on my mind. I listened to the radio and did my chores and my

homework with one ear waiting for the phone to ring at
all times.

That night my parents went to church, and while I was
tempted to call her, I didn't. I picked up the receiver one
time and held it so tight to my ear I felt my biceps cramp,
then Herbert noticed and asked me what was wrong.

"Nothing," I lied as I returned the receiver to its cradle
and decided that the next day in school I would resolve this
one way or another. I didn't need her and the more I
thought about it I didn't even want her. I had my pick of
any number of females so if our for always was over . . .
so be it. Then the phone rang.

"Hello?" While the person didn't say a word, I did hear
background noise. It sounded like the faint sound of traffic,
but I wasn't sure. My head said "Hang up and make her
call back," but my heart would not allow me to play the
game. "Hello?"

"Henry . . . Henry, I love you. That's all I can—wanted
to say."

I said nothing as I held the phone, trying to form the
words. Previously four letters could not contain our love.
Now four thousand could not share the way I felt. My love
for her was infinite, there was no doubt in my mind about
that, but I didn't want her to know just how much I
needed her.

There was silence until she said, "I know . . . well, I know
what I did was wrong and I'm sorry. I just . . . Henry," she
said with tears in her voice, "I do love you. And I hope you
can still love me too."

Say "I do," say "I do," I shouted in my thoughts. *Say "I
do!" Just say the damn words!* But my stubborn tongue would
not allow the sound to pass my lips.

"You know, Henry, sometimes I wonder if we could have
ever stayed together, because—"

"What do you mean, if we *could* have stayed together?
You quitting *me*?"

Silence. "Let me finish," she replied as what sounded like
a semitrailer blew its horn in the background. "I wonder if
one day I could be the right person for you. I mean, my life

right now is crazy and I don't know if I'll be able to fix it. I don't know . . . Actually, Henry, I can't be the person you want me to be. I can't live up to your—"

"What are you talking about?"

Silence. Then I heard her exhale a deep breath. "Henry, remember when you wanted me to be a cheerleader and I didn't try out?"

"Yeah. At first you wanted to and then you changed your mind. Just like I guess you changed your mind about going to FAMU, like you changed your mind about us."

"I never changed my mind about being a cheerleader!" she exclaimed. Then she gathered herself and said, "And *you* never asked me one time *why* I didn't try out!"

"Because you didn't want to!"

"You never asked me, Henry, never once. Did you know after my mom was diagnosed with diabetes that not a day has passed that I have not had to cook and clean that house? That I could not be in student government because I had to come home and—"

"Why didn't you just tell me? All you had to say was 'Henry I'm not trying out because—' "

"Because you didn't ask, damn it! You never seemed to care. That's why, Henry. You never cared. We spent all our time talking about you, and getting married, and you and children, and you and the election, but we never spent any time talking about me. What's my favorite color, Henry?" Silence broken only by more traffic in the background. "We never spent any time talking about us."

I was tongue-tied. The words hit me like a blunt object across my shoulders, because it was true. It just never occurred to me to ask her what was happening in her world. "So," I whispered, "is that why you're going with Darius now?"

"Henry, this has nothing to do with him." And then I heard a monotone female voice on the phone say, *"You have two minutes."*

"Henry," Cheryl continued, "this is about us. You never asked me if I wanted to go to Florida A&M. You never asked me if I wanted to leave Miami and my parents."

"Is that what this is about? If you don't want to go to

FAMU, we could go to the Bethune Cookman or even the University of Miami. Wherever you want to go, I'll go. Okay?" And then I heard her tears again. I could feel them sliding down her face as I said, "Cheryl, just tell me what can I do to make it right? I'm sorry, okay? Just tell me and I'll do it."

"If the truth be told, Henry, yes," she said with a smile in her tone, "I would love to go to Florida A&M. I would love to go out for Rattlerette when I got there and help you run for student-government president too. It's just not that simple. See—"

"You have one minute left."

"See, I have an aunt . . . in Arkansas who is ninety-five and deathly ill. She has a few kids, but none of them can move in with her. So my momma and daddy want me to move up there to be with her for a while."

"But—"

"Henry, I can't talk much longer. I just wanted you to know that I love you and what you thought you saw, you didn't see. I would never quit you and go with Darius. I would never do that to you. Henry, I've never met a boy like you before. And I mean that. But I'm not going to be the person you need in your life. I just can't. And sometimes we just have to face what is. But I do love you. I really . . ."

The previous smile I heard in her voice was no longer present and I could hear the tears flowing nonstop. I had to say it. If I was going to ever win her back, I had to tell her then. And then this loud truck started honking its horn in the background as I said, "Cheryl? Cheryl, can you hear me?"

"Just barely, Henry."

"Cheryl," I repeated, wanting to make sure she heard me say the words. And then the phone line went dead. There was no traffic. There was no truck horn and there was no Cheryl.

The next time I would see her would be in the spring of '73, exactly two years and one day since she had seen me running up and down those stadium steps. When I saw her, I wanted to hold her, to kiss her, to love her even then, but I couldn't.

"Welcome back. This is Franklin Dunlop reporting from the NBS Studios in Washington, D.C., on election night 2000. Tonight we have our reporters all across this country to bring you the latest news as America travels on a course to elect the first president of a new millennium. So far it is shaping up just as the experts have expected, with Senator Henry Davis jumping out to a sizable lead as all the work he has done on the East Coast starts to pay dividends. For more on the story we will turn to Butch Harper down in Miami, Florida, home of the Dolphins, Marlins, Heat, and possibly the first president of the new millennium. Butch, can you hear me?"

"Yes, Franklin, but just barely. The crowd here is exultant and has almost doubled in the last half hour as the results begin to come in. Although they expected the election to run its present course thus far, as one campaign official told me, it's like a baby. You may already know its sex, but there's nothing like seeing the birth."

"Tell me, is there any concern about the Lone Star State? There was a considerable amount of speculation regarding friction between Davis and his running mate, Dirk Gallagher. Can you confirm that story?"

"There has been friction, Franklin. There is no question about that. Many of us in the traveling press corps detected it as far back as two weeks ago before the last debate when Senator Davis attempted to distance himself from remarks made by the outspoken Texas governor. They have tried to paint the best face on it. I spoke to the press secretary for Senator Davis, Edward Long, about five minutes before going on the air, who said, and I quote, 'When America elected its first Catholic president and a Texan, they, too, had friction, but the country was never in better hands.' "

"Well, thank you, Butch Harper, for the inside scoop. Now we will look at the tote board thus far.

DAVIS	25	███████
STEINER	3	■
BALDWIN	0	

"So far, the races that are hotly contested are in New York, where there is literally a three-way tie for her thirty-three electoral votes, the Peach State of Georgia, and there is a surprising race in a state that at one time looked like a slam dunk for Senator Davis, and that's his home state of Florida. He did not campaign as much there in the last few weeks, and with the scandals swirling around the campaign, as well as torrential rains which are affecting voter turnout in south Florida, the state is a toss-up."

Fontainebleau Hotel
Miami, Florida
Suite 1717

Leslie sat watching the TV, flipping back and forth between her favorite news reporter and a Delroy Lindo movie on Spectravision, and tried to ignore the knock at the door.

Damn, I wish whoever the hell that is would leave, she thought as she blew a puff of smoke in the nonsmoking bedroom. The living room of her suite, which was previously full of staffers, had been cleared by her administrative assistant so Leslie could get a little well-deserved rest. Taking a sip of her diet cola, she swallowed a Paxil and reluctantly asked, "Who?"

"It's me, Vette, open up."

"Oh my God," she said as she jumped off the bed to open the door to the suite. "Myles, how are you!" As the Secret Service agent moved aside, she wrapped her arms around her brother and asked, "What are you doing in town?"

"Baby girl, I couldn't let you go through all of this by yourself! I know I told you I couldn't make it, but hell, Wall Street was there before me and it'll last if I'm away a few days." As they released their embrace and walked into the bedroom, Leslie held his hands and stood away from him.

"Well, look at you. I like that jacket, and you lost those fifteen pounds, didn't you?"

"Yep, and I bought this jacket from this designer in Beverly Hills named Reggie Jenkins. You like?"

"I love," Leslie said with a smile.

"Well, you're not looking too bad yourself."

"Child, please. Don't even try it. I look like crap and I know it. Who let you up here?"

"Sally. She remembered me from that fund-raiser in midtown and got me past security. I told her I wanted to surprise you."

"So where's Vicki and the babies?"

"Hell, the babies are seven and eight. Can you believe my little man turned seven on the seventh of last month? Time flies, doesn't it? They're riding around South Beach and they'll come up tomorrow to meet the *new* first lady."

"God, don't start with that," Leslie said, returning to the bed. "Oh, I'm sorry, can I get you something to drink?"

"Oh, no. Well, maybe a tomato juice, but you don't have to get it. Just point me in the direction."

"Walk back there in the other bedroom, honey, and there's an honor bar. Just get what you like and let the Democrats pay for it. And get something for Vicki and the babies too."

As he stood up, Myles removed his dark blue blazer and rolled up the sleeves of his starched white monogrammed shirt. As he walked down the hall, his voice echoed in the hallway. "So tell me, how does it feel?"

"The truth?" Leslie replied, watching a Carlos Santana video. "The truth is, I have not eaten a bite in the past forty-eight hours. I know I need to eat something, but I just can't hold anything down. I'm running on two hours sleep. My hair is falling out. Need I say more?"

"You're that nervous, huh?" he said from the bedroom as he popped the top of the can.

"Nervous, scared, pissed off, ashamed, scared, betrayed, tired, and did I say scared?"

"Yeah, you did, baby girl," Myles said as he walked over to the curtains and looked out the window. "They call New Yorkers crazy. You know, there's actually a guy in the building across from us wearing dark shades with his head hanging out the window? What's up with that?"

"Yeah, I saw him earlier. It's probably some photographer for a tabloid trying to get an exclusive, so unless you want to be on the checkout stand next week as the *mystery man* in my suite, I'd close the curtains. Besides, the Secret Service was up here a few hours ago and was adamant about keeping the curtains shut."

"My bad. As I was going to say," he continued, reentering the bedroom and sitting beside his sister, "it's gonna be all right. I promise you it's gonna be fine." Then Myles, who was just under six feet with a pudgy frame, squeezed closer to his petite sister and rested her head on his shoulder. He held her as he had so many times as a child, when they watched *Chiller Thriller* together, although she was two years older than he. And then he took another sip of his tomato juice and made himself comfortable by loosening his Windsor knot and taking off his Senegal loafers. "So what's the deal, baby girl? You wanna tell me about it now?"

Looking down and gazing at the floor, she whispered, "Yes. Yes, I want to tell you everything. But please do me one favor."

"Aw, sugar, anything. That's what I'm here for. What is it?" he said, stretching his body and spreading his toes.

Leslie turned toward her brother as her eyes darted back and forth, looking into each pupil. Then she replied in earnest, "Would you please put back on your shoes? Child, your feet still stank!"

Myles laughed so hard he rolled off the bed, and Leslie fell back on the thick paisley comforter, holding her empty stomach to stop it from cramping while both howled as they had in years gone by.

"See. You wrong. You are so wrong. I fly three thousand miles just to console you and you talking 'bout my feet?"

"You flew? Baby, the way your feet smell, I thought you walked here. I mean, honestly, I can't deal with this election,

not eating, and those hoofs. Either put on your shoes or we
drop right out of the election tonight!"

LESLIE

Nineteen seventy-three? Whoa. Let me think a minute. Of
course, '73. That's the year I first laid eyes on Henry. God,
how could I ever forget that? This is how it happened.

I attended school at University of Southern Cal. Although
I wanted to attend school on the East Coast, Dad told me
he would not pay for it, and I certainly wasn't eligible for
federal financial aid or anything, so I decided to go close
to home.

SC wasn't that bad. I got to meet a lot of famous people,
like Haywood Nelson. Remember him from *What's Happening*? He and I were supposed to go out once, but that's
another story. He was a nice guy, though. I also used to
watch, with all the other girls, O.J. and A.D., Anthony Davis,
run around the track there during the off-season. Yes, they
were both very fine and O.J. was very married, but that
never stopped them from flirting.

Anyway, back to the story. I wanted to go to Europe to
study like a few of my white friends' parents let them do
every year. Well, my dad, who always squeezed a quarter
until the eagle screamed, told me no. But he said there was
a lot of this country I had never seen, so if I made straight
A's, he would let me see America any way I wanted to or
go to any school in the country to study for the summer.
Not exactly Europe, but if you knew my father, you would
be very satisfied to get that. So I did the 4.0 and decided
not to go to school that summer. I had a friend who wanted
to visit a few schools on the East Coast to decide which one
she would attend the following spring. Her list was Temple,
Brown, the University of Rhode Island, and Florida State.
Well, I was all for it when she said Temple, because that
was just a hop, skip, and jump from New York City.

At this time I was twenty years old and she was nineteen,

and believe it or not, for some reason we decided to drive across country for this adventure.

Two days later we arrived, checked into the hotel, showered, then she slept for about an hour before heading off to see the campus. I don't know where she got all that energy. When she left, I went for a swim and I saw this guy who worked at the hotel watching me. He was pretty easy on the eyes, but I could not see myself dating a maintenance man. So I finished my swim and went back to the room and I got this call from the really cute and sexy guy at the front desk. He was kinda stocky, but he wore this bush (which is what we called them before Afros), sorta like Haywood's now that I think about it. I think he was a student at one of the universities in town. So this guy was making his supposed courtesy call. And I played along because he talked kinda cute. He had that Mississippi, Alabama, Georgia thing going in his voice, and it sounded sexy for some reason. It wasn't hillbilly twangy sounding. Just made him sound sincere and earnest or something. Anyway, he finished his call and I got a book to read. I had been waiting to read John Updike's *Couples* for some time, but I fell asleep after the first chapter.

The next morning we went for breakfast and everyone in the restaurant knew we were not from out of state when my friend Veronica asked the waitress to show her a grit. When we returned, there was a single rose on my pillow. I thought, *Now, I know this is the South and they are supposed to be hospitable, but this is a little too much.* Veronica, who was a Valley girl before there was such a phrase, put her hands on her hips and said, "So, like . . . where is mine?" In '73 Valley girls were just considered plain old stuck-up rich girls.

"I don't know," I said, still puzzled, and then it occurred to me why *slick* at the counter was smiling so much when we returned from breakfast. I didn't tell her anything as I sat down to inhale the flower's scent and noticed he'd squirted a little cologne on it. Although the smell mixed with the aroma of the rose, it was sensual. The cologne was airy and I couldn't place it. It was an intensely masculine smell with not a hint of sweetness to it, which I have always hated on men. As I enjoyed the fragrance, Ms. Veronica watched, and if my memory serves me correctly, steam was actually coming from the back of her neck and ears.

"Aha, yes, front desk? . . . Aha, yes, can you, like, help me? . . . Aha, we just, like, returned to our room? . . . Yes, 213? . . . Yes, and, aha, we only received, like, *one* fla'war?"

Now, I know I should have stopped her. I know I should have told her I had a good idea who had left this, but I think you can see why I did not. She had her hand on her narrow hips and was moving that index finger in a tight circle as if they were speaking face-to-face. Although her dad was a physician, when she wanted it, the Inglewood in her would come out in a flash.

"Aha, like, excuse me? . . . So, like, how did this fla'war get in here? . . . Aha, excuse me, Jed." And then she looked at me, and said, "I got Jed Clampett on the phone, you wanna talk to him? Listen, Jethro, stop wrestling with Elly May and answer my question. If we would have, like, brought it here, wouldn't I, like, know it, dahhh?" *Click.* "Well, that basically crosses Florida State off my list. I don't think I could live in a state for four years that's this, like, illiterate?"

I was cramping from, like, holding in the laughter.

The next day we went to Panama City to check out the world-famous Florida beaches, and when we came back, once again there was a single red rose. So now I had to tell Veronica who I thought was doing it, and she was not as mad as I thought she would be. Still mad because she had not gotten one, but not as mad.

"So we're only going to be here one more day, silly Billy. Why don't you go talk to him?"

"Talk to him? What would I say?"

"Anything short of 'Let me blow you' is fair game. I do it all the time," she said, painting her toenails pink and green.

"What would you say?"

"Well, first you have to make sure it was him, and then say something like, 'I wanted to personally thank you for the fla'wars. It was very sweet. You are very sweet. Where

I am from, guys are not usually that sweet. I bet you taste sweet.' And then say, 'Can I blow you?' "

Veronica ducked as I threw a pillow at her head while laughing.

At about a quarter to five I nervously headed toward the front desk, because I suspected he would leave about the same time he left the day before, at five o'clock. So I'm walking along, practicing what I am going to say, when this guy passes me. It was the maintenance guy from the day before. The one thing I immediately noticed was how crisply his uniform was starched this time. For some reason, and I didn't know why, I stopped and turned around. He was still walking, but damn, he made khaki come to life.

So I stood there for a moment and it occurred to me why I stopped. It was the cologne he was wearing. He was wearing the same cologne the guy at the front desk had squirted on the flowers. He continued to walk, and I did something I had never done before. I said, "Excuse me, sir?" As he stopped and slowly turned toward me, I said, "I'm just curious, what cologne are you wearing?"

"Do you like it?" he asked with a smile.

My blood stopped. I remember my knees shaking and feeling weak. I cannot remember what I said when I saw those dimples. The next thing I know, he was walking toward me. I looked back at the front desk with a part of me hoping the guy had not left yet and a part of me praying he had.

The maintenance man said low and sexy, "It's called High North. Do you like it?" What was I going to say? He continued, "I usually put on a few squirts in the morning and it lasts all day." Then he smiled and walked away.

I didn't like light-skinned brothers. My mom was fair complexioned and my dad was the bluest of blacks, and even though I am considered dark by most people, I like my coffee straight, but I was smitten by this brother.

As he walked away, I wanted to scream "Come back" or something, but I had no idea what to say next. And then I thought of what Veronica would say. "Can I blow you?"

No, not that. Then he turned, and said, "Ya know, this stuff also smells great on roses."

And that was the day I met my husband. It was May 15, 1973, at about ten to five. I was twenty years old, and I will never forget that day as long as I live.

Washington, D.C.
NBS News Studio
9:40 P.M. EST

"Okay, America, let's assess where we are at this point. I'm told NBS News will be able to make a call in six to eight races within the half hour. Unlike before, I think we will have a few surprises. Right now, Senator Henry L. Davis the Second of Florida has taken a commanding lead in the race and has sixty-four electoral votes. That's sixty-four for the junior senator from Florida. Thus far Vice President Ronald Steiner has only carried two states, for a total of twelve votes. And as we reported earlier, Governor Tom has yet to hit pay dirt, although he was running neck and neck with Steiner in Connecticut and Davis in Kentucky. Now for the latest on the Steiner campaign we will take you back out to the City of the Big Shoulders, Chicago, Illinois, and Judy Finestein. Judy, are you there?"

"Yes, Franklin, I'm here along with this very optimistic crowd of supporters. Although the numbers are not looking promising at this point, it has not deterred the spirits of the supporters. There has been singing and dancing to the sounds of a couple of local bands, and the mood is generally one of excitement. I have with me the Steiner Illinois campaign chairman, Peter Delahouse of Kankakee, Illinois. I hope I am pronouncing that correctly, Peter. Peter—"

"Judy! This is Franklin Dunlop in Washington. Would you please stand by because we are prepared to make calls in several key states.

"America, these are the up-to-the-minute results. We are projecting that Vice President Ronald Steiner will win in the following states: Vermont, New Hampshire, Nebraska, and

North Dakota. NBS News is also projecting that Governor Tom Baldwin will carry the following states: Oklahoma, the Peach State of Georgia, Alabama, and Mississippi. And I just got word that we are projecting a victory for Tom Baldwin in the state of Tennessee. The state of Louisiana was picked up, we are now told, by Senator Henry Davis. So if you are keeping score at home, with 280 electoral votes needed to win, this is what it looks like."

DAVIS	73	████████████
STEINER	27	████
BALDWIN	48	███████

"There is more to come after these messages."

Carol City, Florida
The Allen Residence

With every passing car, Cheryl's head turned away from the television screen. If he were like most guys, she could have located him very easily. He would be at a friend's house or watching the level of beer go down in an uptilted mug at a bar. But Brandon was not like most guys. He worked the midnight-to-ten shift for the Dade County Sheriff's Department as a patrolman, which he had done since graduating from the academy several years earlier. He'd been the top cadet in his class and had a bright future with the force. As she sat, she thought about how decent and kind he had been to her since day one. How he had never asked for anything but her love. How he had handled so easily their twelve-year age disparity and how she should never have told him that deep inside, she was still in love with Henry.

When the phone rang, she hoped it would be Brandon, but was sure it was her mother.

"Hello, Mommy?"

"Hey, sweetheart, how you doing? I bet you scared to death in all this lightning, huh?"

Closing her eyes as she flinched with every white flash across the ominous skies, Cheryl whispered, "No, Brandon's here tonight." With him out in the weather and her not knowing what would happen in the election for some time, she was not in the mood to explain to her mother why he'd left.

"Well, that's good. Did he take off to watch the election results with you?"

"Yeah. He worked hard down at the campaign headquarters making phone calls last week, and his commander told him he could have the night off."

"Henry's gonna win, you know. I had a dream last night about him, running water and those white doves. You know what that means. I saw him on TV dancing with that pretty wife of his too."

Lying back on her pillows while staring into the lightbulb above until she saw blue spots, Cheryl said, "Yeah, Mommy, I know what the doves mean."

"I always did like him. He was such a nice boy. He never called too late or anything and was always so mannerly, unlike that mannish behind Darius. Did you ever tell Henry I wanted a new pair of shoes to replace the ones his big ole feet messed up that day in my closest?"

"Yeah, I did. He thought that was cute."

"I don't know why I need 'um now with both my legs cut off. You know, he's a good-looking thing too. I saw in *The Globe* where he was seeing that girl Nia Long on the side. You heard anything like that?"

"No, Mommy, but I doubt it's true. She's too young for Henry."

"That's what I'm saying. Henry ain't that kinda boy. I'm just glad he got him a cute little wife and I'm glad he didn't marry a white girl. Ain't she black? Black as soot and pretty as a picture with them big ole baby-doll eyes. You know, I don't believe all this mess about pictures of her doing something either. If they had some pictures, they'd of shown them by now. No-sir-ee-bob. I believe them 'publicans behind this to set him up 'cause they know he gonna win. Everybody I know voting for him. And even if I saw a picture, I wouldn't believe it. I saw on *Inside Edition* how they sometimes take a picture and change it around like in the movie *Forrest Gump*. You know that man never seen all them people before, like Kennedy and Nixon and—."

"Yeah. Mommy, did you ever try on that new prosthesis to see if it fit?"

"Child, I'm too old for that. I don't know why they don't just leave me alone. I can't get round here at my age and try to walk again. I told them in therapy that they were wasting their time. If the good Lord wanted me to walk, he wouldn't have taken my legs. Now, that's that."

"Yes, ma'am."

CHERYL

I remember '73 like it was yesterday.

After I left Miami, I moved to Arkansas to help out my sick aunt. Six months later, Darius moved up right after I had the baby. She was a beautiful eight pounds and six ounces, and I named her Sarah Ruth, after my mother. She was born on Halloween eve '71.

I admit, it was hard at first because Darius initially thought I was going to let him live with me and my aunt. So when I let him know he couldn't live there, he found a job, but he didn't keep it very long and then it was in and out of jobs, it seemed, every two or three months. That is, until he got sick.

Darius and I met in my cooking class. He was very popular with all the girls, which really meant little to me. He started coming on strong, which shocked me since he and everybody else knew about Henry and me. I mean, we were together almost all the time before, during, and after school. But one day Darius asked if he could help me with my books and walk me to algebra. Looking back, I should have said no, but I really didn't think too much of it.

There was this party at my friend Penny's house. She

asked me to help her do things like move the couch into the kitchen, screw in the blue light bulbs and the other stuff upstairs. Now, Penny was a big-boned girl, but she always had a lot of boyfriends. It was the way she carried herself, and everybody in the projects knew if she had a party, it was going to be the haps. So the day before the party I mentioned it to Henry, and he said he would *try* to make it. He had just got that powder blue 1960-something Mustang, but he was also working on this major project for student government. In the back of my mind I was afraid he was possibly cheating on me because I heard David once say to him, "With a car like this, Stang, I'd be pulling women like a blind dentist pull teeth." But I tried to ignore those thoughts because I knew how Henry was when it came to school politics.

The night of the party, everyone showed up. I even saw Henry's best friend David walk past our apartment headed to Penny's, but there was no sign of Henry. I wanted to call his house, but his dad never liked it when I called after six, so I waited by the phone for his call, and it never came. The party started at ten o'clock, and by twelve the phone had not rung once. I could hear the party bounce off the sidewalk right up to my door, but I did not want to go without Henry. My favorite song was James Brown's *I'm Black and I'm Proud* and since I was home alone I did the jerk, swim, and monkey all alone. I knew the party would get wild and I've always had this thing about strange guys grabbing me, so going alone was not an option. After all, I didn't want to dance or even talk to anyone else but my Henry. Although it was midnight, I gave him another hour because I knew the party would not stop until at least two or three. But it was no show.

I gave up and started to undress for bed when who knocks on my door? Darius Kingsley.

I had no idea he even knew where I lived. Turns out, he asked Penny, and Penny asked him to do her a favor and come get me.

By this time I had already pulled off my stockings and

was two snaps from rolling up the hair and getting something to eat, but he really looked good.

Mentally, Darius's belt, as my momma used to say, didn't make it through all of his loops, but he always smelled good. Henry never was the cologne-and-hand-cream prettyboy type. But Darius was. He had his nails manicured and painted with clear coat when most guys were wearing leather gloves and flashing Black Power fists. He was wearing this auburn mohair sweater and wore no shirt underneath, and I noticed he had his name tattooed over his heart. In the early seventies, I didn't know any boys who had tattoos. His name was branded on his chest in Gothic lettering just like a marine, and it was a turn-on. He had a 'fro like Linc from *The Mod Squad* and he was working on a little mustache action as well. Darius was not as tall as Henry, nor as cute, and I really considered him to be what we used to call a friend-in-law, because he and Henry were buddies on the football team. I just took his flirting as fun and games.

Well, I went to the party and before Penny could warn me, I drank about eight glasses of spiked punch on an empty stomach. Marijuna was thick in the apartment and the smoke mixed with the black light made the air cobalt blue. It was my first time drinking alcohol, not counting the little corners I would suck out of my daddy's shot glass when he asked me to put it in the sink. I had not eaten since Henry and I ate lunch together, and the room started to move. It wasn't spinning. It moved up and down as if I was hopping. Next thing I know, I was headed upstairs feeling nauseous, with Darius holding my elbow to balance me.

That is how I lost something I treasured so much and saved only for Henry. On the floor in a bathroom. I don't remember lying down on the tile, but I remember the sounds that were made. I remember him trying to find where it was and then pounding inside of it over and over again. As he grunted I refused to make a sound and wondered how this could feel good to anyone. I recall squeezing my eyes closed so tightly I no longer saw black, but colors moving in my head. And I remember him kissing my shoulders over and over again, then he would just lick my shoul-

ders, and I had no idea why he was doing that, but long
after he left, I could smell his rancid breath on me. When
he got up, I was sober. In the darkness I watched him stand
up, tuck himself in, zip his pants, and walk out, proud of
himself. He never said a word to me, as I laid there on the
floor with my panties draped around one ankle and legs
spread. The person who came to my apartment and talked
about how lonely he was after breaking up with his girlfriend was not the guy who got off me. Even his face looked
different. Especially his eyes. The passion, the kindness, the
friendship he displayed was gone. He walked away after
looking at me as if I was not even human, just a thing he'd
been with.

I curled up in the fetal position and knew in my heart I
had committed the ultimate mistake that I could never correct and had nothing else left to offer Henry Davis. I felt as
if I were not even worthy to be with him. Then I heard
Darius call David and I knew soon everyone would know.
On top of that, I found out firsthand that once was enough,
and so I decided to move to Arkansas instead of facing the
shame in Miami.

In May of '73 we were headed back home to south Florida
for a visit. I was tired of feeling ashamed of my mistake
and felt I had served my sentence. The halfway point for
refueling was—where else—Tallahassee, Florida. If I told
him once, I told him a hundred times, "Darius, we can make
it to Lake City on this tank. Let's not stop here. It's too busy
in Tallahassee." Although I think he knew why I did not
want to stop, he stopped anyway. I mean what were the
odds of running into Henry? So we stopped, I stayed in the
car, and put on my shades and the guy filled the tank and
checked the oil.

Henry and I always said we had a connection that went
beyond the physical. Meaning if he was in trouble, I could
feel it, and vice versa. Sometimes it felt we were twins who
conversed through telepathy, often wearing the same colors,
liking the same food and even finishing each other's
thoughts. If he was worried about a test or if I had problems

at home, we each just knew. For us, words were irrelevant. For some reason, I just knew Henry saw me when we were in Tallahassee. We didn't even drive near the campus, but in my heart of hearts, I knew. I could feel him looking at me. Maybe he passed by in a car or maybe he was walking and just caught a glance, but this feeling was too strong to ignore. When we finally passed the Leaving Leon County sign, I felt a sense of relief that I never remember feeling before.

It had been two years since we had seen or heard from each other. I often wondered how close he had come to making his dreams a reality. Was he majoring in prelaw? Did he pledge Kappa? Did he ever run for a student government office while at FAMU? Once I called and asked a student assistant if she knew Henry, but she had a few stray loops also, so I didn't find out much.

As we drove away from Tallahassee, Darius put his soft hand on my knee. It felt consoling in a way. He worked hard after he found a decent job. Sometimes thirteen-hour shifts five days a week. There was never anything I wanted that he did not provide for me or Sarah. After the incident with Henry, Darius was suspended. The coach knew he did not have college potential, so he didn't stick his neck out for him, and Darius just never went back to school again. I think the only reason he played sports is because it was the only place he was treated equally, where he didn't feel like he was a stupid special education student. When coach turned his back on him, he saw no reason to return. His class graduated one month later, but by that time he was working at a burger joint and sending me half his check each month to put into a savings account for the baby.

"I'm hungry," I said as we passed a restaurant.

"Okay. You want sum Kentucky Fried or a ham'buga?" And then for some reason he looked at me and smiled.

"Whatever. You decide, honey," I said, and leaned back and smiled at him. At times he could look so adorable when he smiled. No, Darius was no Henry but he was a good man. A decent hard-working man. The way fate brought him to me was forgettable, but he was now a part of me, and it felt good to be a part of someone else.

So he did this U-turn in the road in Lake City and we headed back to the fried-chicken restaurant. By this point Sarah was getting a little restless from the ride, and when he stopped and got out of the car, I reached in the backseat for her blanket and walked around the parking lot with her. It seemed this child was getting heavier by the minute. And as I turned back and headed toward the car, I looked across the street and there was a powder blue, 1960-something Mustang with the blinkers flashing. He stood in front of it watching me. He did not look angry or upset or surprised. He just looked at me. Like the first time he looked at me, in Sears.

I almost lost it, I kid you not. At first I thought it was a ghost until I realized no ghost could look so good. He looked like he was still playing football, because he had lost some weight. He was wearing an Afro as well as horn-rimmed glasses from all that reading I was sure he was doing. For some reason it looked like he was wearing a janitor's uniform, and that didn't make sense to me. He then broke his stare and looked both ways for traffic as if he was going to come across the street. When there was a break in the cars he looked back at me as Darius came out of the restaurant. When I heard Darius, I literally jumped off the ground.

"You all right, gal?" he asked more countrified than ever. I said nothing. "I got everything you jew'sly eat. Let's go, and don't be greedy. You know how you is." And then he got in the car, grinning what then looked like the most stupid shit-eating, *Hee-Haw* country grin I had ever seen in my life. I looked back across the road as Sarah started crying, and God knows for a split second I wanted to run across that street and beg him to forgive me, if he had it in his heart to do so. I wanted to explain what had happened and how I wanted to be with him and how not an hour had passed, since the day I left, that he was not in my heart. I wanted to say whatever I could to make him love me, touch me, hold and understand me like he did before.

But I didn't. Instead I flung the baby's blanket in the back-seat and sat myself in the front. I did not want this man who'd asked me to marry him and was told no more times than I care to remember to see Henry across the street. As we backed out of the restaurant, he put his hand on my knee. This was the same hand that minutes earlier had brought me comfort. Now all I could think of was the cold tile of Penny's bathroom and being raped. I knee-jerked it away and he looked at me with his eyebrows knitted. I really didn't care as I stared ahead, ready to drink one last eyeful of my first and only love.

"Oh, I know what you think," he said as if he'd just uncovered the mystery of the Jade diamond. "You thinking I want som. Gul please. I gotta drive if you wanna get to Miami before dark."

We pulled into traffic and Darius was scavenging through the bags with his free hand as if they were filled with a carcass and he was a hungry wolf. But I was so close to *him*, I could taste him on my lips. Our car passed mere feet in front of him, and my body screamed but my mouth did not know what to say. And then I watched him get smaller and smaller in my passenger-side mirror and I thought, *The hell with Darius*. I put the baby down, turned around with my knees on the seat, and looked out the back window at Henry Louis Davis the Second. Sarah started screaming bloody murder, but I couldn't hear her. He'd turned toward me and I could feel him say, "I still love you, Cheryl." I could feel him say, "Baby, I understand and forgive you." I just knew he said, "Cheryl, our love is truly for always."

As he eventually disappeared, I laid my head on the back of the seat and matched Sarah tear for tear as Darius kept eating. I just knew he wanted to be with me, even now. I just knew I would never be loved, or be able to love, as much as I loved him, and I knew in my heart that what we shared was as good as it could ever be.

Like I said, Henry and I had something that went beyond the physical.

Chapter 3

"If you felt the earth move, America, it was not from a fault line in California, but from the State of Florida. This just in: Steiner roars back! This is Franklin Dunlop reporting from our NBS News studios in Washington, D.C., where it is eleven o'clock on the East Coast.

"As little as two months ago, Vice President Steiner was the butt of all of the jokes from Letterman to Leno to every hack comedian within the beltway. NBS News is now projecting Ronald Steiner the winner in two states in which he trailed badly as little as a week ago.

"Ronald Steiner will win in the state of Indiana and in the Show Me State of Missouri. He was helped tremendously by a recent endorsement from the six-term senator of that state, Sam Elkhart. Those two come as little surprise. But here is the real shocker: Ronald Steiner wins not only the Buckeye State of Ohio, but also the state of Florida.

"That's right, ladies and gentlemen, you have heard correctly. NBS is in a position to project that Vice President Ronald Steiner has stolen the home state from the onetime leader in the race, Senator Henry Louis Davis. As we reported earlier, after having had a double-digit lead in the state, Henry Davis pulled back on campaigning in Florida and went on an all-out blitzkrieg to do damage control all over the country after the debate. That, coupled with hurricanelike rains, put the state into play. Our sources tell us that Steiner spent an additional million dollars in the more conservative northern portion of Florida last week, and coupled with the decent weather in that portion of the state, it has paid off.

"For more on this story we will go back to Judy Finestein in Chicago. Judy, are you there?"

"Yes, I am, Franklin, and please don't ask me a question, because I could never hear you. There is actually a live marching band in the background as we speak, playing 'Tusk', by Fleetwood Mac. For the moment, the word here in Chicago is *exhilaration*. This place almost exploded when the results from Florida came in. As you said earlier, they expected to fare well in Indiana, Missouri, and Ohio, as well as in the New England states, which they have all but swept. But they thought they had two chances in Florida. Slim and none. And none was looking like the better of the two. They were wrong. They gambled on bombarding only one part of the state with what many considered to be negative Davis ads, thinking in a three-way race they could let the other two candidates fight over what was left. With a little help from Mother Nature tonight, the gamble has paid off in spades . . . I, I mean the gamble worked.

"The ew, candidate's running mate had just left the stage about five minutes before the results were announced, Franklin. When she did, there was not a dry eye in the building—much like the impassioned speech Jesse Jackson gave in eighty-four or the speech given by this vice president, recalling his brother who died the previous year from lung cancer, in ninety-six at the Republican convention. Most observers said, without question, her impromptu address was the best one of the campaign for her.

"I am standing here with longtime friend and adviser as well as Illinois state campaign chairman for the Steiner campaign, Peter Delahouse from Kankakee, Illinois. Peter, have you had an opportunity to speak to the vice president?"

"Yes, I have. He and his wife are upstairs watching the events unfold tonight, and they are very optimistic. It's been a long road here for both Ronald Steiner and Sydney Ackerman, and tonight they are sitting back and enjoying the fruits of their labor."

"That's great, Peter. Tonight, Franklin, the Grand Old Party is rocking. Lee Greenwood is about to take the stage, undoubtedly to sing 'Proud to Be an American.' We are told that his appearance has nothing to do with a debate question posed to Senator Davis, but if you believe that, I have some swampland to talk to you about after the show tonight. They're telling me my time is up, so for now, this is Judy Finestein from the ballroom of the Four Seasons Hotel in Chicago, Illinois, sending it back to Franklin Dunlop in Washington."

Fontainebleau Hotel
Presidential Suite

As soon as the numbers in Florida were announced, the phone in Henry's room started ringing. Since it was the hotel phone, he did not answer. Close friends and advisers knew to call him on one of two cellular phones or on the private line installed for this night, so as Franklin Dunlop and the other three anchormen reported on the upset, they had his undivided attention. Henry broke his gaze from the TV sets and looked over at the ringing phone and then unplugged the cord from the back of it.

Ringgggg . . .

It was the private line. Looking at it on the end table, he quickly debated if he should answer it. What could anyone say now to help this situation? But he had promised his staff that he would be accessible. "Hello?"

"Hello, Senator," he said with church-mouse timdity. "I was wondering if we could come up to chat about what's happening. You know, uh, people down here are starting to talk and what have you about—"

"Talk about what, Ed?"

"Well, sir, that you are sitting up there alone. I think it was leaked to the press that you and Mrs. Davis are not talking, and the rumor is growing that you might be headed for a divorce. I know it's nonsense, sir, but I wanted to quell speculation before—"

"I'm sorry, Ed, you misunderstood my question," Henry said, lowering the volume of the TV as well as slowing the pace of his voice. "When I asked you what you wanted to talk about, I was referring to why we should have a pow-wow at this time. We've spent the last two years talking about the election, the polls, and the other candidates. Hell, Ed, you and I have been talking about this for—what?— four or five years, nonstop, every day? So tonight, with all due respect, I just need to gather myself a little."

"Yes, sir, I understand," Ed replied despondently.

"No offense. I'm not throwing in the towel. We still have a lot of night ahead of us. I feel really good about California as well as Texas, so don't take this move as a defeatist one. I just need a little time to myself to regroup and be at my best. In the event we win this thing, it's gonna be a long night, and in the event we lose . . ." Henry closed his eyes again and said with a smile, "If we lose, Eddie, I don't want to look like a haggard sore loser. Okay?"

"Yes, sir."

"Fantastic. Listen, I saw you on CNN and you did a great job. What time is Herbert going to be on CBS?"

"C-SPAN, sir. Mr. Davis will be on MSNBC and within the hour, I was told."

"Good. Well, if you need me, just—"

"Senator? May I ask you a question, sir?"

"Sure, go right ahead," Henry replied as he put his feet on the couch and leaned back on the hind legs of the chair.

"Why did you decide to read . . . *Forever* last night?"

Laughing, Henry said, "Good night, Ed. I appreciate the call." And then instead of hanging up on his concerned press secretary, he added, "Ed, the author sent me the book. It was really well written and I just happened to want to finish it last night. That's all, okay? Now, go put a spin on this thing so people out there don't get overly worried. Tell the press you just spoke to me and that we're excited about the key states I just mentioned as well as the returns in New York, the West, and Midwest."

"Yes, sir, I'll, umm, I'll let them know."

Hanging up the phone, Henry alternated his attention between the TVs, turning up the volume whenever they showed the electoral maps and turning it down whenever the talking heads would appear. There was a line down the middle and underneath it the words *Splitville* was inscribed. And then on NBC, a picture of Leslie and him together appeared on the screen. *Damn, that didn't take long,* he thought while turning up the volume.

"That's right," the green-eyed reporter with a glint in her eye replied. "My reliable sources inside the campaign tell me that there's heavy friction between the two at this time. Friends who have known them for years attribute it to the tension of the race more so than the recent photos of Mrs. Davis thought to be floating around Washington. Others are concerned that if Senator Davis is elected, we may have our first presidential divorce. I have traveled with Leslie Davis and the thought here is—"

Henry turned down the volume as his brother's face appeared on one of the other TV screens.

"We are here with the older brother of presidential candidate Senator Henry Davis, Herbert Davis. Now, I must say, Herbert, you have been one of the most camera-shy campaign managers we've seen in recent years While the other campaign managers have visited all the major talk shows, you seem to outright avoid the spotlight. Why is that?"

As Herbert began to speak, Henry leaned forward on his elbows to hang on his every word. He noticed the other reporters start to swarm around as soon as the spotlight centered on Herbert, and Henry could tell his brother was uncomfortable being the focus of attention. *You'll do well, Herbert. You'll do just fine.*

"Well, Beth, I have stayed out of the limelight because I, or should I say we, have always wanted the attention to be focused on the problems of this country." Looking into the camera, he said, "We feel this is a race that should have focused on the candidates' ideology and not the prospective parties' ideology. We did not get into this race for glory or for personal gain but to put this country back on its feet fiscally, socially and morally for the twenty-first century and beyond.''

Henry leaned back, absorbing his campaign manager's words. Knowing Herbert did not enjoy being in the spotlight, Henry appreciated even more his speaking to the media, because he spoke not as a senior adviser but as a brother.

A newsman muscled past the female reporter and his elbow hit her in the mouth as he held his microphone stiffly in front of Herbert. "Duke Kilroy, AP! Tell me, Herbert, what is the status of the candidate's marriage? The word on the floor is that they are headed to divorce court after the election, win, lose, or draw, and that Mrs. Davis has had conversations with Marvin Mitchelson. Will you confirm or deny either of those stories?''

Herbert's appearance was unflappable, yet Henry knew he did not want to lie and didn't want to say the wrong thing either. Looking at the female reporter who had been pushed to the side, he asked with a smile, "Are you all right, madam?" After she nodded her head, he looked at the AP reporter and said, "Sir, that is a family issue." And then Henry felt Herbert was looking at him as he said into the camera, "But I can assure you that there is absolutely no friction between my brother and his wife. None whatsoever. These insipid and cruel remarks being hurled by members of the vast right-wing media outlets are unfounded and, on a night such as this, both shameful and appalling. Henry and Les are upstairs now . . . together . . . and expecting wonderful things to happen this night.''

No words he could have said could hurt Henry as much as those. In the Davis/Gallagher headquarters, signs were posted everywhere: "DO IT ONCE YOU'LL DO IT AGAIN.'' It was Marcus's haiku because Henry was fond of saying it in staff meetings, "If you compromise your integrity once, it's a slippery slope toward repeating it.'' He had never known his brother to flat-out lie before. As a tear glistened in his eye, he knew that his ultimate goal had made his brother do something he as a politician had done more times than he wanted to count. His brother, just like other Davis/Gallagher campaign officials, had compromised his integrity in pursuit of Henry's dream.

HENRY

Forever is a novel that was sent to me a month or so ago by its author. Or at least by his literary agent, who was interested in eventually selling my memoirs. I had heard about it shortly after it was published because of the controversial content. The character's life in the book closely mirrored my own. He was from a deep southern state and was voted the most effective congressional representative three consecutive years. He even chaired the same committees I had in the senate. He was an African-American who would run for and eventually win the presidency. Now, this character, whose name was—get this—Donnell Roosevelt Jones, was a cardboard cutout of a president. In part it was degrading because of the way the author had developed the character's wife, Angie. She decided to redecorate the White House, and in the Purple—yes, I said Purple—Room she had one of those clocks shaped like a cat with the tail that wags and eyes that move back and forth. There was a bowl of dusty plastic fruit in their private residence and a little placard that said "May You Be Dead an Hour Before the Devil Knows You're Gone" over her desk. They even had one of those big stereos with a record player and eight-track in it that looks like a coffin in the Lincoln bedroom.

While the author touched on a few serious world problems that this character handled, the book, all in all, was not believable. The worse part of it was the ending. He was the president, and this scandal, not too dissimilar to my own, catches up to him. He tries to stay above the fray, but he has all these people who want him out of the White House. So he is watching his numbers fall, like I have, on the night of his reelection with his family, and suddenly he leaves them, walks onto the front lawn of the White House, and offs himself in the midst of reporters and staff. He says some corny line like, "You want my blood, now you have it," before he dies. The end. I thought it was such a cop-out to use guns and death to finish the novel, but to each his own. When I dug a little deeper, the story told me how some people with very good intentions can be changed in politics. We want the best and the brightest in office, and when they get there we look for the absolute worst in their character, which causes them in turn to self-destruct. Anyway, it sucked, but the author is a really nice kid. I hear they just paid him a million three for the movie rights.

Nineteen-eighty-three. I guess you could say that was the year I started my drive toward being elected president in earnest. Let me back up a little. When I was at FAMU, I ruptured a vertebra during the last game of the football season. They tried rehab, but nothing really worked. So it was a bittersweet time in my life. Yes, I was upset because now I had to get assistance from my parents and work to stay in school, but it was sweet in a way. Because of my size, when people looked at me they would always say, "Damn, I know you play football somewhere." It was a way to say, "Yeah, I did, but, man, my back went out." Don't misunderstand me. I loved the sport. But I knew what my goals were, and even if I had had the opportunity to play pro football, looking back, I would have turned it down and parlayed the attention I would have gained from doing that into a congressional seat.

Know why I love politics? In many respects it is the ultimate sport society has to offer. First you come up through the Minor Leagues (local politics, etc.), then you graduate to the Big Leagues (national politics) and then there's a playoff, (primaries) until you reach the Superbowl (presidential election). Along the way we keep score (polls) and there's bloodshed (scandal) and if you win you're the champion (in office) until the next season.

I met Yvette Leslie Shaw at my job while in college and she was only in town forty-eight hours. Since she lived in California, I knew my work was cut out for me, so I asked her if I could take her out to dinner and a movie. She told me she didn't want to leave her friend alone, but when she went back in the hotel room I got the impression by looking at them through the open curtains that she wanted her friend to come along for security.

I forget what movie we went to see, but I do remember her friend Veronica. I'd noticed both of them a couple of days before I built up the courage to make a move on Leslie, but actually it was Veronica who caught my eye at first. But then I crossed her off my list when I noticed that she would only try to get the attention of white guys or very fair-skinned brothers.

So while we were at the movies, I gave Leslie fifty cents to buy us some more popcorn, and out of nowhere, Veronica starts telling me about her *blond* boyfriend who lived in Santa Cruz, California. She made sure I knew that his eyes were as blue as Paul Newman's and that he wanted her to learn how to surf. Next she starts telling me how much she liked *red* men with curly hair. How she thought *red* brothers were so much finer then white men and how our butts were nicer and our thighs were so powerful looking. She said, just as Leslie returned with the jumbo buttered popcorn, how she had never *done* a red brother but would love to someday. I never told Leslie about that conversation until we were married. When I did, she laughed about it and said she knew. They'd set a trap for me, which is why Leslie kept giving me the opportunity to grab the bait. When I didn't, she knew I was the one. Women are funny like that sometimes.

After Leslie left Tallahassee, we wrote letters back and forth constantly. She sent me a postcard from every city they traveled to, and when they arrived back in California three weeks later, she had twenty-five letters from me in her box. I was sending her two letters a day at that time. I would have given anything to see her smile when she opened the mailbox. She said the day after she arrived home, the mailman came to her door, and when she walked out he smiled at her and said, ''I only have these two letters for you today, but the reason I knocked on the door was to *see* the lady who inspired someone to write so many love letters."

I made a concerted effort to let Leslie know how I felt. I did not want to scare her away, but I definitely wanted her to know that I was interested in her.

Seeing Cheryl the day my car broke down in Lake City stung. It hurt beyond description. But looking at her, I wasn't mad. Why? I guess because when I saw them drive up, and him get out of the car, I watched her with the baby. I watched her kiss and rub her nose against that child's as if everything else in the entire world ran a distant second. And I knew she had found love in a much greater sense then I would or could provide. Watching her with that baby was akin to watching love take the form of flesh and blood. When she got out of the car, I watched her walk back and forth a couple of times before she saw me, and then, well, it appeared we both stopped breathing.

I didn't see cars passing or even feel the wind against my skin. All I saw was an opportunity to make it right. Then Darius walked out and it dawned on me for the first time that it was totally, completely, and unmistakably over between Cheryl and me. It had been years since I'd seen her, but in my heart the thought that we would never be together again had never jelled. I'd heard rumors that she and Darius were a pair ever since he'd left town, but hearing it and seeing it were two different things. As she drove away in that old Chevrolet, I saw her looking back as if kissing us good-bye. And on that day I was finally able to close that chapter of my life once and for all. At least that's what I assumed.

Since I was young, broke, and in college, a long-distance relationship with Leslie was difficult to sustain. We could only afford to talk on the phone once a week. So every Sunday, between six-thirty and eight-thirty, we would alternate calling. It seemed by the time I said, "Hello, Leslie, how are you?" it was time to hang up. In all honesty, my feelings for her were not as strong as they were for Cheryl. I thought that was because Cheryl was my first in most ways. But I worked hard on my grades, and Leslie and I put together a plan to meet for the summer since her father decided not to spring for another cross-country trip for her. I would get an internship on the West Coast or she would get one on the East Coast and somehow we would get together. And it worked. My internship counselor at FAMU pulled a few strings and got me a job in southern California. I got an internship in Paramount Studios Legal Department in L.A., so she decided to stay in town as well and work as a paralegal for a law firm.

It was going to be strange being together that much. Being able to see her, feel her, touch her every day. As I rode the bus cross country, I thought about my first time. Her name was Toni, but everyone called her Li'l Momma.

Shortly, after breaking up with Cheryl I met Li'l Momma on a weekend trip to FAMU. Although she was younger, she was much more experienced. Her tongue darted back and forth like a snake. She started at my toes and explored every inch of my body.

When I went to my dorm room, although I was walking straight, it felt like my hips were still moving round and round. So the first thing I did when I got to the room was to call my Li'l Momma.

When she answered the phone I could tell she was surprised since I had copied the number from her phone without her seeing it.

She told me how much she "enjoyed what happened," but her voice was not the same. We said goodbye but I held on the phone trying to figure out what went wrong. She hung up but the phone was still off the hook. I heard a man say "Who was that?" Must have been her father. "Where he from?" Maybe it was her brother. Then I heard a smack smack smack and grunting sound of a kiss that could only come from her man.

Soon my thoughts of Toni were replaced by Leslie and my biggest fear, which was that the distance was keeping us together and that once we were in the same city, the relationship would fizzle. As I traveled closer to the Golden

State, I wondered if I could ever fulfill this fantasy I had created on the phone.

The first night I was in the City of Angels, she came over to my apartment. To be honest, I'd had sex a couple of times by then with coeds whose names left me as soon as they left my arms. I had never made love at that time, and I really did not understand the distinction between the two. I'd heard women say things like, "I don't want to screw, I want to make love." I'd never understood the true meaning of that until I made love for the very first time with Yvette Leslie Shaw.

Leslie came over, just beating the rain, and brought a couple of books. No wine, no cheese, no candles. Just a couple of thick Russian literature books she thought I would enjoy reading. So I tried to read between the lines. Was she trying to tell me to slow down? That we had all summer? Did she think I was her intellectual inferior? I mean, we'd set fire to the phone lines our conversations were so hot, but was all of that just talk?

I took the books, read the titles, and said thank you. When she was in Florida, I never remembered her smoking. Since we had not kissed, I never got close enough to smell tobacco on her. That night she smelled like she was a brand tester for Phillip Morris. Being a jock, I was against smoking, and even during a time when a lot of people were into it, it was never done in our household. So when I smelled the stench on Leslie, it was a major turn-off, but I think she thought I knew she smoked and I couldn't imagine telling her I had a problem with it. So I learned to live with it and the subject never came up.

Leslie wore these big thick Buddy Holly glasses, and as I set the books down, she grabbed me without saying a word and yanked me toward her, which caused her glasses to tumble to the floor—so hard I thought they may have broken. She didn't seem to care. She kissed hard, but sensuously. Then she pushed me, causing me to fall backwards onto the bed, and she straddled her legs across my pelvis. I was a sculpted two-hundred pounds at that time and she must have been about a buck-o-eight. But she was totally in

control. I'd never seen this side of her. I'd always watched
what I'd written to her because I did not want to offend her
womanhood while all this time she had this freak inside just
waiting to come out. She unbuttoned my shirt so fast buttons popped off of it and bounced off the tile floor like a
broken strand of pearls as she started to taste my nipple in
slow, soft circles. This was the first time anyone had done
that, and as I felt my nipple harden it gave me a tremor.
My eyes were wide open as I looked at the ceiling trying
to gather myself, then I flipped over on top and just looked
at her. In part because of the eroticism and in part to make
sure it was still my Leslie.

As she lay between my legs with just my jeans and her
white cotton panties between her pleasure and my passion,
I could feel her heat. She felt so warm I could hear her
wetness as our hips kissed and she unzipped my pants.

The rest of that night could only be compared to the feeling one would get on a boat. A boat without a rudder. The
waves were crashing all around us, the moon shining so
bright it could be mistaken for the sun, and our bodies were
moving like the edge of the ocean caressing the shore. I
listened to her moans and responded with what she wanted.
When her breathing became choppy and she panted for air,
I could tell I was touching her the way she wanted to be
touched and I would plunge harder. Her face, especially
her eyebrows, gave me direction like an orchestra conductor
would a symphony. When her eyebrows remained flat, it
was a sign to keep moving around until I found just the
right spot. A sharp arch of her brow said I was approaching
a crescendo. When they slowly fell, they whispered, "Oww,
I like it just like that." And an open mouth needed no expla-
nation at all.

On that night everything moved in rhythm. Boom, boom,
boom. Boom, boom, boom. Our bodies met and became one
deep into the night. One, two, three. One, two, three. More
graceful than any moves made by Fred Astaire and Ginger
Rogers. Boom, boom, boom. The curtains shook. One, two,

three. The rain fell. Boom, boom, boom. Was it just an illusion, a storm brewing, or the love within those walls?

And just as I thought it was over, it only improved. In the midst of making love, we increased the pace. We moved faster, and faster, and faster. I dug in because I knew what was about to happen. Leslie braced herself, preparing for the flood. "Do you want me to release?" I asked, not wanting to do it too fast or too slow. She said nothing so I asked again, only louder. This time she cupped one hand over my mouth and the other behind my head and shook my head back and forth. There was no need for words. And then a feeling akin to an electrical current cruised from my head, past my shoulders, through my stomach, and then into Leslie's body. I could feel it radiate through her fingers and toes, and return to my back and lower torso. Leslie froze and then quietly I felt her shake and shiver and then sigh beneath me. I remember my eyes rolling back and I grabbed the mattress trying to gather myself. I felt another tiny explosion and my body jerked and for a second I could not exhale. Then I looked down and my lips softly touched Leslie on the cheek when I heard her whisper, "No. Don't touch me," as she slowly came down the mountain.

This was the first time I shed a tear after I released. I don't know why or where it came from. I just knew it felt good to be in love and to be loved again. It would feel good to fall asleep knowing no matter what was happening in my life, there was someone who loved me . . . only me . . . just for me.

That night was like nothing I'd ever experienced before. The windows were steamed when we entered the second phase of loving. The smell of desire blanketed the air, and I did something I had no idea I was ever going to do this way. At that point Leslie and I had never said the L word. So in the rhythm of our loving I whispered, "Leslie?"

"Yes?"

I repeated her name again, but louder. "Leslie?"

"Yes, baby?"

And then I had to say it one more time at the top of my

lungs. I knew my neighbor would hear, but I couldn't care less. "Leslie!"

"What, baby? What do you want?" she shouted back, with her hands grasping my lower back.

And then I said to the rhythm of the love we shared, "I know . . . you may not . . . really . . . love me yet . . . but tell me . . . you love me . . . please? . . . Just tell me . . . you love me."

I could tell she did not know if I was serious or if this was a part of the moment we shared. I don't think she really cared, because at the top of her lungs she started to yell louder than before. She screamed so loudly the first time, I opened my eyes and watched her with her eyes slammed shut with emotion. Her hair was wet with sweat, and from the excitement of the moment I could feel the deep scratches on my back. The second time she screamed I was worried the security guard would knock his flashlight on the door. By the third scream, I knew this was a wave I should enjoy, and so I allowed the emotions to flow. "Yes! . . . Yes! . . . Henry, I love you . . . I love you, baby . . . I love you so much," she said, and opened her eyes, held my face with her quivering soft hands, and kissed me with a liquid fire that rolled to the soles of my feet.

On that night Leslie and I moaned together and sighed together. We came to life together and died as one. And as we lay there, I knew in the bottom of my heart that I would never make the same mistake twice. I knew I wouldn't and couldn't, ever let her go.

After graduating from A&M, I went on to Georgetown Law and persuaded Leslie to do the same. Leslie was unlike any girl I'd ever dated. She was the only female I knew who was smarter than me in every subject. She made better grades, read more books, knew more facts, and could speak three languages when we met.

After I completed my studies at Georgetown and passed the bar in the state of Florida, I took a job with the DA's office in Dade County, Florida. Leslie went for the money, as I always knew she would. Her grandfather died the year she graduated, and she and her brother and sister split a small fortune. She worked for a firm on Wall Street and bought a brownstone on Striver's Row in Harlem. We'd talked about marriage and we both wanted to be together, but when and where was never decided. From day one Leslie bought into my dream of being president and understood that if this was going to happen, I had to win a congressional seat by the time I was thirty, and that was not going to happen in New York City where I had zero connections. She was making a wonderful salary there, but eventually gave it up to move to Florida.

When Leslie moved here she was used to the fast times of New York and L.A. so Miami, which is more laid-back, was an adjustment. We did not get married immediately. It was not because we were afraid of it, but because there were so many things to get done professionally, and at that time all of our excess funds were going into a campaign saving fund. Most of Leslie's inheritance was invested, and our unspoken rule was that it was untouchable under any circumstance.

While working in the DA's office, I got involved with local politics and worked closely with a city commissioner on an appropriation bill. He was so impressed with me he asked me to consider running for local office. I thanked him for his vote of confidence, but I already had my eyes on a congressional seat. When we announced our campaign, there may have been seven people present. We were not very organized and we financed 50 percent of the cost of the campaign from our personal savings. Fortunately my friend on the city commission endorsed me and we started getting a few stories in the local section of the *Miami Herald*.

I think it was that campaign that affected me the most as a politician. Not because we lost, but because it taught me how to optimize my strong suit, which was talking to people one on one. I remember literally knocking on doors in this neighborhood of Miami that was 70 percent white and 10 percent Florida cracker. I would walk up to trailers with rickety wooden steps I just knew had white sheets with eyeholes in them on the clotheslines in back and I would talk to them just like they were from my neighborhood. What I discovered is that they had concerns about jobs too.

That they wanted to live in neighborhoods where they could feel safe at night and wanted the best education for their kids. Sometimes we would even drink a Pabst Blue Ribbion and I found out that some people who act as if they are the *biggest racists* in the world are actually a little ashamed of their beliefs and can be quite nice when you get to know them.

Two months after the congressional defeat, Leslie and I were married, and six months later Herbert married Doris, whom he hardly knew. They had gone out for about a month and the next thing I knew, they were calling me from the courthouse saying they were going to do it. I remember asking him if he had been drinking. I sped down there and talked to him for about an hour or so, and then thirty minutes later I was handing him this cheap little ring he had picked up for her on the spur of the moment. By this time Herbert was a civil engineer for a company in Lakeland, Florida, and was making good money and I considered him one of the brightest men I knew. But about some things, he has never shown much smarts. Due to her background in corporate debt restructuring, Leslie was accepted by the law firm of Gray, Moiré, Phillips, Lausanne and Hopper. Mr. Moiré was a bigwig in the Democratic party and would always entertain dignitaries such as Walter Mondale, John Glenn, and, back in the seventies, Scoop Jackson when they were in south Florida. When the opportunity came for Leslie to work in his firm, we were elated.

We started preparing for the '84 congressional race as early as the day after the '83 election. We had made a lot of friends during our defeat in 1982 and had come close, but the party did not support us and we ran out of cash coming down to the wire.

In the fall of '83 I quit my job, because Leslie was now making three times the amount of money I made, and it was obvious that if our ultimate dream was to come true in the year 2000, it was vital that we win this congressional seat. In our first campaign I found out the congressman was beatable, because with smoke and mirrors we'd given him a run for his money. This time he was even more vulnerable because of large sums of cash he was receiving from the south Florida sugar industry.

Before the campaign, Mr. Moiré made a few phone calls and scheduled a meeting for me to talk with Congressman Charles Rangel, a few other members of the Congressional Black Caucus, and an important democratic pollster in D.C. While I was in town, Mr. Moiré thought it would also be a great opportunity to interview a few potential D.C. staffers. I felt that was jumping the gun a little, but who was I to question him at that point?

The meeting with one of the candidates to head my D.C. office was at the infamous Watergate Hotel. I sat in the lobby waiting for him to approach since he'd indicated on the phone that he knew what I looked like. Five minutes beyond our appointment time, in walks this kid with a three-day-old beard, jeans, and a sport coat over his navy "Kennedy in '80" T-shirt. This may have been the way they interviewed for such positions in D.C., but he struck out before stepping to the plate. I was wearing my most expensive wool suit at the time and I'd made sure my shoes were spit-polished clean because you just never knew who you may run into in such a town.

We chatted all of three minutes and I told him I would get back with him. And then he said, "Thanks. And please tell Uncle Ron, I'll try to get down there for Thanksgiving this year."

"I'll do that," I said as I shook his hand and headed for the elevator. If he thought I was going to hire him because he knew Ronald Moiré, then he had much to learn about Henry Davis.

The elevator door opened and I walked in excited about a hastily arranged meeting with Ron Brown of the DMC. Possibly it was the history, or simply the thought that the same monuments I saw had been viewd by W.E.B. Du Bois, FDR, and JFK. That the trees that lined Pennsylvania Avenue had watched a youthful Thurgood Marshall come into town with only the hope of equality and the law on his side. But whatever it was, it seemed every waking moment

I was in the District I thought of ways I could effect change. Ways I could make things better for others. And then it happened . . .

A little Asian lady walked to the door of the elevator, saw me, and stepped back as if I were dressed in bold black and white stripes just out on work release. There was an awkward moment as I stared at her and she crossed her arms and looked away, content to wait however long it would take for the next elevator. And then Ronald Moiré's grungy nephew stepped inside the elevator, and said, "Yow, I'm all out of coinage. Can you do me a solid and let me use the phone in your room?"

The diminutive golden pockmarked face lady looked at him, and then me, and back at him again, and got on the elevator. As she did, my shoulders slumped and my heart beat faster, fueled by anger, because as a great poet once said, "I really was not in a mood to be black on that day." I didn't feel like carrying the weight of years of oppression. I just wanted to feel like a man. Nothing more. Nothing less. And respected as such, if only for that one moment. As the elevator door whispered closed, I understood for the first time, the phrase that Bull Connor and other old southern politicians used to say. You can never *legislate* morality.

When I returned to Florida, I hired this young lady by the name of Penelope Butler as my campaign manager. I paid her almost nothing, which was all we'd budgeted for the position, but she'd watched my campaign in '82 and wanted the experience. Penelope came from a very wealthy and important family in the area. The Butler family was one of two or three families one had to know if one wanted to succeed as a Democrat in south Florida politics. She was just under six feet and had green eyes, curly strawberry blond hair, and sun-freckled skin. If the Waltons ever needed another daughter, Penelope would have had no problem earning a little extra cash.

I think it is fair to say that she wanted to work on more than just my campaign. To make a long story short, we went out to a bar for a couple of drinks and the convo got intense after one of our eighteen-hour days, and one thing led to another. Soon after getting into her Mercedes, she kissed me below. I will admit, I was curious, but that does not excuse what I did. It just felt so different being with a white girl. I'd never rubbed a white person's head until I rubbed hers, and it felt funny. Sort of like seaweed on a smooth stone.

After she finished, she drove me home and Leslie met me smiling at the door. In her hands was the very first cake she had ever baked. Or at least tried to bake. It looked more like a heap of chocolate crumbs glued together with chocolate frosting. I played the surprised role, but I had never felt as ashamed as I did on that night. That was in '83 and after going through that, I felt I would never cheat on Leslie again. She was an eighties career woman who always said that domesticity was not her forte. But she was also the chocolate frosting that held me together so many times when things got rough.

I remember sitting in the yard in a lawn chair at midnight with a Bud Lite, looking at the stars, feeling bad about what I had done as I ate a handful of cake crumbs. And then to add insult to my emotional injury, I looked at the full moon over Miami and wondered where in the world Cheryl was, and if she ever thought of me.

Washington, D.C.
NBS News Studio
11:15 P.M. EST

"Hello, America, I am Franklin Dunlop and welcome to NBS's clear, concise, and continuing coverage of election night 2000.

"Once I watched a Bulls-versus-Knicks game in the Garden, and Michael poured in fifty-five points. I was asked by my friend afterwards if I was a fan of the superstar from North Carolina. Being the devoted Knicks fan that I am, I said no, not particularly. He was a great player, but I was a Knicks fan first and foremost, win, lose, or draw. My friend looked me squarely in the eye and said, 'If you don't like Michael Jordan . . . you don't like basketball.' America, if you are not enjoying this race tonight, you just don't like elections. This election night, which started out as predictable as death and taxes, has given us a number of twists and turns already, and it's not even halfway over.

Before we go any further, let's send it out to Phoenix and Vincent Winslet, at the campaign headquarters of Governor Tom."

"Thanks, Frank. The mood out here, if I had to put it in a word, is apprehensive. They are aware that their numbers have slipped a little in upstate New York where they were looking to pull off a Steiner-like upset. The endorsement from former senator D'Amato has not translated into votes thus far. As the minutes tick by, we hear that the governor and the first lady of the state are in their suite with his running mate former Majority Leader Michael Justice, and his wife and children.

"I have with me an adviser to the governor, Reverend Samuel Bellwort of the Christian Family United Coalition. Reverend Bellwort, your opinions on the race thus far?"

"Tonight I feel America still has the choice, as we have been saying for the last three months across this fine country of ours, to get rid of the liberal ideas which have caused the death of morality, and the soul of this country to become infested with pus at its very core. On one hand you have the poster child for liberalism and a proud card-carrying member of the ACLU, Senator Henry Let-Me-Raise-Your-Taxes Davis, and on the other hand you have the vice president with a pro-choice running mate. We have been trying to tell America for the past three months that if the man cannot be counted on to properly lead his ticket, how can he be counted on to lead a nation? This is the message we have been taking across America."

"And apparently so far America has not listened. Back to you, Frank, for more election-night coverage!"

Fontainebleau Hotel
Suite 1717

Sitting in front of the television as the computer commercial came on, Myles asked, "Can you believe him?"

"Who? The preacher guy?"

"Yeah. He has some balls. I'm glad the reporter dissed his ass."

"Child," Leslie replied as she brought the blue flame of her lighter to the tip of a cigarette, "you need to have alligator skin. I learned that years ago. Nothing is off limits. So you roll with it. After all," she said, blowing smoke away from him, "this is the life we chose and that's a part of the game."

"I know, but it would get to me when it's personal."

"Myles, I hate to say it, but if we win, you will more than likely have a camera crew following you to work every day for a couple of weeks. That's just the facts of life in politics 2000. Inquiring minds want to snoop."

"I guess it's something you get used to. I saw this T-shirt in SoHo that made me mad at first, but it was kinda funny. The front said, 'What's the difference between Leslie Davis and God?' and the back read, 'God doesn't think he's Leslie Davis!' "

With a smile Leslie said, "Yeah, I saw something like that in Seattle. That's what happens when you're an intelligent woman. Either you're stuck up or a bitch. There's never an in between. If I sat in the background, baked cookies, and held Tupperware parties, you wouldn't hear that shit. You kinda learn to ignore it.

"In the last few weeks they have done skits on me on *Saturday Night Live, MAD TV,* and the comedians on BET just can't get enough of talking about it. I was a diehard *SNL* fan but we've just stopped watching TV, period. I don't even like watching some of the so-called news programs. On one of them, this guy said, 'I don't want to sound prejudiced . . . but I'm not sure if I want to live in a country with a black president.' To this day I laugh at this, because the first thing out of his mouth was—'I don't want to *sound* prejudiced.' Now Henry and I just read a lot more." Leslie turned away from the TV, looked up at the chandelier, and tried to blow a smoke ring, but failed. "Like I said, though, it's the life we chose. But it's tough living in a fishbowl."

There was a knock at the door. "Who is it?" Myles asked, as Leslie turned her attention back to the television.

"It's me."

"Oh, that's Penelope," Leslie said without looking up. "Let her in for me, would you?"

Walking through the doorway, Penelope said, "I remember you. You're, umm, Dizzy, right?"

"Wrong trumpeter, but close. Myles."

"Yeah, yeah, that's right, Myles. I met you and your family," she said, and rested a stack of files on the coffee table, "at that function in Detroit."

"Close," he said.

"So, chickee poo, what's up?" Penelope said as she stood over Leslie's shoulder and watched TV.

"Nothing. Not a goddamn thing," Leslie said quietly. "Just trying to figure out how you and Ed are going to put a positive light on the Florida numbers."

"That's no big deal as far as I'm concerned. We'll give them some big-picture bullshit and that'll keep them fat and happy until we win the next big state. Have they said anything about Texas or New York?"

"We're looking good in both. In New York it's a dead heat right now between us and Steiner. Baldwin is helping us more than I expected upstate. We've all but won by a landslide in the city. I'm just worried about California at this point."

"Well, Les, I really don't want you to worry about that. Let me and Eddie handle that shit. Talk to me," Penelope said in her best sister-girl voice, and then looked around at Myles, who was over on the couch.

"Oh, I'm sorry. You all need to talk I guess?"

"You're all right," Leslie said as Penelope took a cigarette from her boss's purse, tapped it on her forefinger, and fired it up.

"On second thought, I think I will go out for a breath of fresh air."

"Oh, I'm sorry," Penelope replied. "Don't leave because of—"

"No, seriously, I want to go walk around and mingle a little bit. This is my first time coming to something like this. It looks so much different on television."

"Hey, Myles," Leslie said, "make sure you get your credentials before you leave, otherwise you'll catch hell coming back up here. I have never seen the security as tight as it is tonight."

"I'll be fine. Talk at you later," he said, putting on his jacket and closing the door behind him.

"So what's up? Talk to me."

Without turning from the TV, Leslie said, "That's the second time you've said that. What do you wanna know?"

"The truth. Give it up."

"About what?"

"About you and Henry, Leslie. What the fuck is up? NBC is reporting that the two of you are splitting up after the election. They're rolling out celebrity divorce attorneys on CNBC like that guy Raoul Felder and Susan Aldridge to discuss what would happen to the presidency if the president and first lady called it quits. We have got to make a public statement and we must make it now."

Clicking off the TV, Leslie stretched her body, wiggled her toes, and then dissolved into her chair as her lifeless hand dropped the remote to the floor.

"Penelope, first of all," she said in a low tone, "you're too damn emotional for a white girl." Penelope laughed. "Secondly, we don't have to say anything about this until tomorrow. If we win, we will say it's all bull. If we lose, it won't matter because we will be private citizens again for the first time since I don't know when."

Penelope ran the tip of her finger lightly up and down the pressed crease in her dark gray slacks, and then mumbled, "Goddamn. I don't believe this shit."

"What now?"

"What you just said is if you win tonight, you will stay

together for the good of history . . . but if you lose, it's over. Right?"

"I didn't say that. See now, you're not *reading* between the lines. You just flipped the page over entirely."

Picking up the remote, turning on the T.V., and clicking from Bernard Shaw to Franklin Dunlop, Penelope said, "Not only did you just say that, Les, you just screamed it."

"Damn," Leslie said, walking toward the bathroom as Penelope flicked the channels, "you *think* you know me so damn well."

LESLIE

"What's the significance of the number 9,871? For nine thousand, eight hundred and seventy-one *consecutive* days, Teddy and I have communicated either by phone, E-mail, or letters. He and I have made love, we once calculated, more than two thousand times, yet we have not kissed or even held hands in four days, and today, on the most important day of our lives, we have yet to exchange a single word.

> *Sometimes we are graced by angels*
> *Amongst us here on earth.*
> *With a touch so perfect*
> *It goes unfelt*
>
> *And then they are gone*
> *And when tears dry our eyes*
> *It's a touch we know*
> *We will never feel again.*

Have you ever heard a song that took you back to a place no matter what you were doing or where you were when you heard it? I hear "Here on Earth" by C. Wilhemina and I think of seeing *Saturday Night Fever* for the first time, the oil crisis, and my Teddy in a black tuxedo and red bow tie. I think of his whispering seductively in my ear as we danced unexpectedly on one of the sweetest nights we ever shared.

* * *

When I met Teddy, I must admit I had a few guys on the side who I continued talking to even after we met. I was attracted to him, but it wasn't love at first sight. On our first date we went to see a movie, and he constantly spoke of his dream to be the president to the point I thought he was a little obsessed by the whole notion. It was more than a little weird, but as I sat in the theater squeezing his arm, I knew why he was my Teddy.

That night we watched *American Graffiti,* and as I took my seat after getting some popcorn, I could tell something had happened while I was away. I knew by the way she acted that Veronica my friend who came with us, was up to something. Previously I'd noticed how she stared at Henry's crotch, which I thought was very disrespectful. I started to read her ass on the spot, but I decided not to so I could see what I was dealing with. There's an African proverb that says, "Two steps ahead and you will never fall behind." With that in mind, for the rest of the trip I watched my back and measured my words. When we got back to California, I told her off and she caught major 'tude and since then we have never spoken.

Henry was not, at that point, the only man in my life . . . but he was in *my* life and she'd crossed the line. Years later when Henry told me about the incident, I told him we were testing him. Why? Two steps ahead and you'll never fall behind.

Henry and I decided to go to Georgetown, although to this day I wish I had gone to Yale, and we both graduated with honors. I fulfilled my dream of living in Manhattan, and with my inheritance from my grandfather's estate I bought a brownstone in the neighborhood I'd always dreamed of.

Now, let me tell you how good a salesman this Henry Louis Davis the Second is. He got me to sell the brownstone to Myles, resign from one of the most well-respected firms on Wall Street, and move to Florida so *he* could eventually quit *his* job. And believe it or not, the word *marriage* had not even come up yet, okay? But my thought process at the time was, do I want a brownstone now or the White House later? Yes, he was a little irritating talking about it all the time when we were college kids, but I've always believed in him. I never doubted that one day Henry would be president of the United States. Not even for a millisecond. Now, that's selling.

So I helped out in the campaign and we lost by, 4 percent. Naturally we considered that a moral victory since we were basically novices at the time. That night I was sealing up this box of unused lapel buttons that we could use next time around and Henry walked up to me and said, "Baby Boo, I'm tired."

"I know, so am I. Let's go grab an early breakfast or something, okay?"

Then he said it. My Teddy said, "That would be fine, and I wish I could find a better way to say this." Then he dropped to one knee and continued by saying, "Yvette Leslie Shaw, will you marry me?" And when he said it, he did not just say it. He asked it from the depths of his heart as if there was a possibility of my saying no. The look in his eyes was so pure.

By this time I was feeling light-headed. I mean yes, we had talked about it, but I was not expecting it now. I said, "Oh my God, Henry, yes! Yes, I will marry you!"

He closed his eyes and brought my left hand to his sexy lips and kissed my arm while he was down on a knee. Just soft, sweet, wet little kisses until he got to my finger and he looked up at me all coy and nibbled my ring finger like he would sometimes do when we made love. I closed my eyes and felt him put the entire finger in his mouth, and when it came out, I was wearing this ring. Believe it, or not, since that moment, this ring has not left my finger.

My sister, Kathleen, had gotten married in the late seventies to this Iranian real estate salesman who used her inheritance to invest in a disco. Even in the late seventies everyone knew that clubs like the one they invested in were going the way of the dinosaurs, but I'm told they kept pouring money into it and kept it afloat all of eighteen months.

Both Kathleen and Myles married outside our race, and I have always wondered if it was nature (something that was natural to them) or nurture (my father and his bleaching creams) that made them cross over. A few weeks before Kathleen's wedding she asked me to be her maid of honor, which completely blew me away. After I moved out of my parents' home, I could count the number of conversations we had on the phone on one hand. But I was honored to be a part of her wedding, and she and Ansar would later have three beautiful children. Unfortunately she died of a stroke in her late thirties, and we later found out that Ansar had been able to convince a company to overinsure her. After her funeral, he and the kids went directly to the airport, and I'm told he remarried in less than six months. Last year when we were in Denver for a gun control rally, he came to the hotel, and I told the security guards not to let him up.

In spite of our differences, when Henry and I married, it would have been nice to reach for my sister's hand and have had it there.

In the spring of '83 my firm sent me to Hawaii. Believe it or not, I had to almost break Henry's arm to get him to go with me. How did I get him to come along? I told him that Mr. Moiré knew some key Democrats and that it would be to his advantage to meet them. Teddy replied that Hawaii *only* had three electoral votes and it would not be worth the flight. He actually said this with a straight face. I had to break him down in a way only a sister can break a brother down. By the time my neck stopped swiveling, he was calling around for tour packages in Waikiki.

Once we got there and I finished with my meeting, he seemed to be enjoying himself. He actually went out and played basketball with a couple of the other attorneys attending the meeting, and that made me happy because I have always worried about his health since he works so much. But that night we went to this black-tie gala I was invited to and I noticed he kept looking at his watch. The old I-want-to-be-president-in-2000 Henry had returned. I asked him if there was a problem, and he replied abruptly, "No." I tried to ignore it in hopes that within the next forty-eight hours I could get the other Henry to at least walk on the beach with me before our flight out.

When we left the convention hall I asked, "Do you want to catch a movie?" and he grunted, "I don't care." Then I said, "Well, would you like to go dancing?" With a shrug of his shoulders he replied, "Don't care." I was getting more than a little irritated at this point. Other couples were kissing and caressing, and all I could get ready for was a romantic night researching Polish martial law. Then suddenly as we walked toward our hotel and I swallowed my anger to think of the ultimate goal we passed this little hut with a hand-painted sign in front of it. "That's an idea," Henry said out of the blue.

I looked around and there's this guy on the shore holding a canoe by a string and staring at us, showing a few more teeth than necessary. I had never been in a canoe in my life, and I found out later that night, neither had Henry. But he walked over to the thing and said, "Come on. Let's get in. This might be fun"

Although I was dressed in a designer gown and expensive shoes with tape on the soles, I say to myself, *What the hell.* At least it was better than writing out campaign speeches. So we paddle to the middle of this lagoon and it was dark except for the stars above. All we could hear was the sound of birds nestling peacefully in the distance. That night we talked. We talked about the dream house we wanted to build, and debated how many rooms we would need for the family we were planning. He also looked at me and cut me off in mid sentence to tell me how beautiful I was and I really needed to hear that. Then he paddled for about ten or fifteen minutes, and just as I started getting a little concerned, I thought back to when we got in this thing and remembered Henry had acted as if he'd met the guy before. As I was thinking this I felt the thump of land. Now, we were dressed in our best evening attire and we were now on a tiny, seemingly secluded island. I looked at Henry and said, "What are you doing?" He flashed those dimples at

me and pulled out a bag he'd stuffed in the bottom of the
canoe which contained one of his shirts he always enjoyed
seeing me wear and my bikini. He'd also left a portable
boom box on the island and somehow managed to get four
slices of NY style cherry cheesecake which awaited us in a
box. That night he popped in the C. Wilhemina eight-track,
pulled out a blanket, and we danced shoeless in our formal
black and white attire on a deserted island under the light
of the moon to:

> *Sometimes we are graced by angels*
> *Amongst us here on earth.*

All that happened in 1983.

Oh yeah! The week after Easter of that year, our plans for
a dream house changed. We found out I was barren.

Washington, D.C.
November 8, 2000
NBS News Studio
12:15 A.M. EST

"Welcome back! If you are just tuning in, you have missed
a lot, but hold tight and we will get you up to date momentarily. First we will swing back down to Miami, Florida, and
the irrepressible Butch Harper."

"Thanks, Franklin. I'm here with the press secretary for
Mrs. Leslie Davis, Penelope Butler-Richardson. Mrs. Richardson, we were advised that you met with Mrs. Davis recently. Can you tell us how she is feeling about tonight's
developments as well as the recent reports regarding the
state of her marriage to the Democratic nominee? Reports
from the wire indicate they are just awaiting the results from
tonight before they begin divorce proceedings. Your
comments?"

"First of all, Butch, you and I go back to Tsongas in '88,
and you know me and what I stand for. Let me be very
clear. Senator and Mrs. Davis have opened their home, their

financial records, even their past and present to public scrutiny. But there should be a line of demarcation. In a word, what you all down here have been hearing and reporting is mere gossip, and you know what they say about gossip. I think it was Baltimore essayist H. L. Mencken who said gossip is the common enemy of all decent citizens. It's theater to the souls of fools. So let me give you a few facts. I was just visiting with Leslie *and* Henry in their suite upstairs. All these reports that they are in separate rooms is total nonsense, and after hearing about the imminent demise of their seventeen-year marriage, they asked me to come down here and put an end to these rumors once and for all. As you know, it's been a tough campaign for them, but they believe in the process and most importantly, they believe that if you don't stand for something, you'll fall for anything. They have laid it all on the line for their country and they are standing up for what they believe in and what will help this country get back on its feet.

They've vehemently tried to stay above the fray in regard to personal attacks and they believe that character does count. That's why they have taken the high road tonight and throughout this campaign. But there comes a time, Butch, when you must pull off the gloves and defend your name, and that's why I am down here this morning."

"Mrs. Richardson, Nate Earl, *Atlanta Constitution!* So what-'cha saying is they are *not* preparing for a divorce? That they are *not* in separate suites as has been reported earlier? Marvin Mitchelson's office has not confirmed or denied that Mrs. Davis is on retainer. Can you comment on that story as well?"

"Guys, take out your pens and turn up the volume on the recorders for this quote, because it's something you can take to the bank and deposit. Are you ready? The answer is, no! Did you get that? They have absolutely *no* plans to end their marriage in spite of any *unfounded* rumors you may have heard. There was *no* stress from the campaign on their marriage, and before you ask again, there are no photos. In fact, the campaign has actually brought them closer together, I personally think. They are people just like you and me trying their best to make it through the day, and they are looking forward to moving to Pennsylvania Avenue and being the moral and loving example of all that is good about this country of ours."

Carol City, Florida
The Allen Residence

"She lying like a sack of shit, Momma."

"Sarah, stop it!" Cheryl said to her still-wet daughter, who was drying her Jherri curls while sitting on the couch and occasionally dribbling her ball on the hardwood floor. Sarah had grown up fast. She'd worked for a pillow factory since dropping out of college, and now in her mid-twenties, she had a daughter of her own and visited her mom daily.

"You can tell that ho lying. All them Butlers full of stuff. I wouldn't believe a thing that came out of any of their mouths. They all about straight up flow. Henry getting ready to dump that ho Leslie. As soon as the election is over, he gonna handle his bid'ness, watch and see. Now, what you gonna do about that ignorant Negro of yours?"

Cheryl looked at her daughter with unrevealing eyes. She did not want to lie about her feelings and what she and hopefully the next president of the United States had shared, but this was her daughter and there were some things she did not feel comfortable talking about with her. "Sarah, I've told you a hundred times. I love Brandon. Okay? I really do."

"Cheryl, please," Sarah said, getting up and heading toward the kitchen. "Don't even fake the funk like that. I mean Brandon's cool sometimes, but *damn*, he ain't like that pretty red nigga on TV."

"Sarah!"

"Wud-eva," she said, opening the oven door and allowing it to "pop" to a close loudly. "Listen, you want me to heat up some popcorn or a lil' sumptin?"

Still staring at her daughter in the kitchen looking for

food, Cheryl said, "No," and turned her attention back to the television.

When she'd married Brandon, he was a little younger than her daughter was now. She'd known there would be friction, because Sarah never gave him a chance, but she'd never anticipated this much antagonism.

Walking back into the living room, Sarah looked for somewhere to sit with the bowl of fruit and a bag of miniature Snickers bars from the cabinet. "Cheryl, I'm, umm, sorry for cursing and disrespecting your house and all, I just—"

"Don't sit in that chair!" Cheryl yelled as her rotund daughter began to squat. "I gotta take it to the shop. Come sit on the couch . . . by me."

"Damn, when I make my comeback," Sarah said, returning with her ball in her food-free hand, "the first thing I'm gonna do is buy you a whole house full of furniture and get rid of these sticks!"

As her daughter sat beside her, Cheryl looked at her lovingly as she ripped open the Snickers bag with her teeth. "You want me to cook you something? You shouldn't be eating all that junk while you're in training."

"Naw, that's okay. I got a call," she said, looking at the television, "from a general manager in Italy first thing this morning. They want me to come over there and try out in Madrid."

"Wow. That wonderful! Madrid, Spain?"

"Naw, a Madrid, Italy. At least I think that's what she said. I told them about Greece and that was where I really wanted to play ball, but she seemed to think I'd have a better chance of making it in the WNBA if I spent a couple of years in Italy like Kym Williams and Tammy Jackson did."

"You told her how many years you've been out of sports?" Cheryl asked as she wrapped her daughter's hair around her finger.

"Yeah, they know. They wanted me, remember, when I left TSU, but I wasn't ready for it then. Now with the WNBA kicking, I'm all for it. You got any Red Devil?"

"For what, Sarah?" her mother asked as she looked at what she was eating.

"Dag, Cheryl, you know I put sauce on everything."

"But, Sarah. You're eating candy . . . and fruit."

Stopping in midchew, Sarah looked at her mother as her basketball rolled away, and said, "And your point would be . . . ?"

Cheryl got up and went into the kitchen as Dan Rather came on the screen and said, "Okay, America, these are the numbers you have been waiting for." Cheryl sprinted in from the kitchen, handed her daughter a box of cold leftover chicken and a bottle of hot sauce, and turned up the volume of the TV in almost one motion.

"CBS News is now projecting that the following states will be won by Senator Henry Louis Davis the Second: New Jersey, Michigan, and a big surprise, Minnesota and her ten electoral votes, as well as a state they were doing very badly in, Wisconsin. So let's look at our up-to-the-minute results as they stand now."

DAVIS	127	
STEINER	135	
BALDWIN	112	

"Damn, Cheryl, this shit is tight."

"I know, I know."

"I thought it would be over by now. Wasn't it two, three weeks ago they were saying he had a shot at a landslide or sumptin?"

"I didn't hear that one."

"Well, I'm sure I heard it on *Dateline* or *20/20* or something. Maybe it was on Rikki Lake."

"It doesn't matter," Cheryl said, running her fingers through her hair and leaning back on her sofa.

"So tell me," Sarah asked as Cheryl watched her put a chicken thigh in her mouth and pull out a bone. "How does it feel to have your name in the history books and shit?"

"What are you talking about?"

"C'mon, Cheryl. We both know you *slept with* the brother, and it's bound to get out when he wins tonight. You got a million-dollar book staring you right smack dab in the face. I got a title for you. How's this? *Henry's Hootchie*. Get it? If you don't sell the shit to the press, I will. I'll call Jerry Springer at his mammy's house and tell ev'ythang for enough money."

Cheryl turned up the volume to block out her daughter's voice, switched to C-SPAN as she wondered where her husband could be, then said, "I didn't sleep with him."

As she dropped the empty chicken box on the hardwood floor, Sarah spread her legs, put several dashes of hot sauce on her Snickers bar, and replied, "Like I said before . . . *wud*-eva."

CHERYL

Nineteen eighty-three seems like a million years ago, but it still stands out in my mind. It took me about three years to really get over Henry. The only man I had ever been with was Darius, and for three years I constantly, unbeknownst to him, compared him to Henry Louis Davis the Second. The myth moreso than the man. He didn't walk like Henry. He wasn't as motivated as Henry. He didn't dance like Henry. Although Darius actually danced better, I preferred the herky-jerky way Henry danced. For three years I put him through that hell, and seeing Henry when we visited Florida didn't help. But soon the wounds healed, as wounds sometimes do, and I was only thinking of Henry two or three times an hour. At that point I felt I could get on with my life.

Darius and I were wed on my twenty-fourth birthday. We were married on my aunt's farm in Hope, Arkansas. We had about ten people, thirty or forty goats, and four pigs in attendance. As long as we were standing downwind, we would get a gust of fragrance from the numerous miniature rosebushes she had planted all over the farm in her youth. Unfortunately, for the few seconds when the wind shifted we encountered a not-so-special smell from the pigpen. As the sun set over the mountains on the cool spring afternoon, I looked at Darius. Dressed head to toe in white, he smiled his cute gapped-tooth Huckleberry Finn smile at me, and I felt lucky to have him. Yes, I wore white as my child cried in the background, because I couldn't imagine getting married in any other color. If I could change anything, about that day looking back, I wouldn't.

My aunt, who was almost one hundred at this time, was not able to attend the wedding. She could be so funny at times. Once I asked her about getting a dog and she said no. I asked her a few weeks later about getting a cat and she said hell no. Then I asked her if I could get a parakeet and she asked if I was out of my mind. I asked her what she had against pets. She said she loved pets, but the pets she loved were pigs, goats, possums, coons, and rabbits. She said a pet wasn't a pet unless you could eat it when you got sick of it.

So we had the wedding in the back of the farm, not far from her bedroom so she could be with us. She wore cream and had on these white lace gloves which I kept after the ceremony. She even asked me to "paint her face." So I put on her the same shade of auburn lipstick I was wearing, a dab of rouge, placed a few snips of baby's breath in her hair, and she looked pretty as a picture.

She died three months after my wedding.

After Auntie Eunice died, I found out that she left me the farm and over seventy thousand dollars in her will. Her four children, who lived in the area, divided up about eight thousand dollars. The reason she did that, her neighbor told me, is because I came up from Florida to help her, and they were living in the area and rarely even visited. It was funny—at her funeral, the ones who had seen her the *least* were the ones who hollered and screamed the *most*. I didn't cry one tear, because I had already given her my baby's breath while she could enjoy it.

She had one son she did not have to leave anything to. His name was Jesse, but we always called him Jesse James.

If Jesse visited the house, we almost had to do a cavity search before he could leave. When I say he would steal anything I mean just that. There was a guy in town who had no teeth. All of the kids called him sock puppet and he bought Auntie Eunice's dentures from Jesse.

At sixty years old, Jesse was the family drug addict. Once he and Darius came close to fighting because Darius caught him stealing eggs out of the farmhouse. Jesse finally left and went to New Orleans, and we never heard from him since. We tried to track him down but came up empty, so everyone assumed he'd ended up a John Doe.

Jesse had a son by the name of Jesse Jr. who was the spitting image of his father and about a year younger than Sarah. Since Jesse's girlfriend, for lack of a better word, was no more than twenty and was not able to support their child, I took him in and raised him along with three other foster children. I just felt so uncomfortable with all that money and that big old farm for just the three of us, so I thought I could help others in a way. I always wanted to have playmates for Sarah, but who did she play with? Jesse "Future Felon" James Jr.

I had always wanted a daughter. I always enjoyed wearing pastel colors and doing my hair and wearing makeup, and since Darius was painting his nails when we met, you would imagine that we would have a prissy little daughter. Wrong. She used to whip little Jesse's butt coming and going. She was climbing trees faster than any boys in the area. She could run farther and jump higher. All she wanted to wear was these cut off dungarees and an Ohio Players T-shirt. Every day, all day.

I was concerned about her being so rough and tough, so I talked to her school psychologist. He said not to worry, that a lot of girls just go through this phase in life. So I decided not to worry about her and let her do her thing while I made clothes for the foster children and fixed their hair.

In late '79 Darius quit his job. He'd worked at this job for over eight months, and I thought he would at least get his year in before stopping. In actuality we didn't need the money, because we had no bills and grew a lot of our food right there on the farm. But he came home one Sunday afternoon, dirty as a pig, and walked upstairs. I was sewing and Jesse and Sarah were lying down in front of the TV watching the Cowboys and Redskins game. When he walked in, I said hello, but he kept walking. I thought that was a little strange, even for a sometimes quiet guy like Darius. So I followed behind him upstairs and found him sitting on one of the foster children's bed. As he sat his jaw moved up and down, yet he wasn't chewing on anything.

"Darius, what's wrong?" I asked, standing in the doorway of the room as he sat quietly. He said nothing. So I walked up to him and asked, "Had a rough day? Why are you home so . . ." As soon as I said the words, he stopped chewing and glazed at me and I knew he was unemployed . . . again. I didn't want to make a big deal out of it, because I knew it was the last thing he needed. I reached down to unlace his work boots, and in the blink of an eye Darius kicked me under my chin and knocked me across the room.

I grabbed my jaw hoping it was not broken, and he just looked at me and said nothing as I crumpled to the floor. I didn't want to cry because of the kids downstairs, but the pain radiated in my face like a neon light. Darius tied his boots up and walked back downstairs, and I didn't see him again for two days.

I didn't know how to handle this situation. I wavered between wanting to call to report the assault to wanting to call to file a missing person's report. Believe it or not, Darius and I had never had a real argument. Did we have differences? Of course, but we never flared up at each other. I guess we'd had a way of stifling it until it was all over, and it worked for us. We had been together by this time over eight years, had been married for three, and there was absolutely nothing in this man's character that could have prepared me for what he did. My dad, bless his heart, and mom used to get into it all the time. They would fight with verbal switchblades, which in a way was worse than physi-

cal fights, because my dad could sometimes get brutal and
left emotional scars that took years to close, not to heal but
just close.

One morning at about 4:00 A.M. I felt Darius slide into
bed. I didn't know what to do or think. I wanted to kick
him back or at least give him a nice, stiff elbow to the ear.
And I also wanted to hug him, cry on his shoulder, and tell
him how scared I'd been. Looking back, I think I was closer
to the stiff elbow than the tears. But the swelling had gone
down and I did neither.

The next morning I got out of bed and fixed the kids
breakfast at 6:00 A.M. like always, and before I was finished,
I saw him walking out the door. This was the month of
November and we had a few inches of snow on the ground.
Suddenly I realized he'd walked out without a hat or coat
or anything. Just walked out in his long johns. All the kids,
except Sarah, saw him and burst out laughing as I ran to
the window to see what the hell he was doing. I heard
Sarah, who was not the oldest or even the largest, stand up
and say, "Y'awl best'a shut up before I stick ya with dis
ere' fork." Darius walked out past his truck and my car
toward the mailbox and started peeing. As he relieved himself, he put his hand on the mailbox, held his head back
and really got into it. I went out on the porch without my
shoes, and yelled, "Darius, what's wrong with you? Get
back in this house!" He looked at me as if he were in a
trance as steam came from the earth, finished his business,
shook and tucked himself in and came back to the house.

A week later I did the shopping, and when I returned the
phone was ringing. I dropped my bags and ran to the house
because we didn't get many calls out there in the middle of
nowhere. It was the police department. Darius had gone
into the department store, pulled off his clothes, and started
walking around buck naked wearing a pair of Stacy Adams
and a cowboy hat. That's what the policeman told me. He
didn't use an official-sounding term like *indecent exposure* or
anything. He said, "Ma'am, your husband was in Wal-Mart
buck naked." Or was it "bare-ass necked"?

Anyway, I jumped in the pick-up and sped down to the

police department, assuming that since he did not have a record of any nature, I could bring him home. After evaluating him, they sent him to the psych ward at the hospital for observation.

I found out later that the reason Darius had not spoken much to me was because he had an aneurysm in his brain, which was affecting his speech as well as his thought process. The doctor told me it could have been dormant for ten years or more. That would explain why he was not too bright. He was a nice guy and all, but sometimes you would look at him and you could see that all the lights were not turned on.

The operation on the aneurysm left us almost broke. I had to pay cash for it since he had quit his job and had no health benefits. So after he was feeling better, I sold the farm that had been in our family since the 1800's and moved back to Miami with my husband, daughter, Jesse James Junior, and the foster children.

After returning to South Florida, I was constantly reminded of Henry. There was no way to avoid him. His face was on buses and cabs and he was in my bedroom on TV. At night Darius and I would sit there and I would feed him a little peach sherbet because he'd lost the use of his arms, and whenever the "Henry Davis for Congress" commercial would come on I could see my husband almost cry. Like I said, Darius was always a decent man.

It was about this time I started gaining weight. From stress and excuses, I blew up four dress sizes almost overnight. I could feel rolls on my stomach, the upper portion of my thighs started to turn black, and when I walked a flight of stairs, it felt as if I'd worked out in the gym for an hour. But in spite of all of my physical changes, Darius always looked at me when I undressed like he had the first day he had walked me to class in high school.

Unbeknownst to anyone, I started collecting Henry Davis memorabilia. I had a clipping of him at the dedication of a library, and I had one of him speaking to the state legislature in Tallahassee. But the last one I put in there in 1982 was "Local D.A. Loses Bid to Unseat Congressman Moorehouse." While in Miami, Ronald Reagan took a photo with Moorehouse which appeared in the *Herald* and that was all it took to cement the victory. I could feel the pain as much as Henry did. I noticed he was married to this attorney, but I knew deep in my heart she could not love him the way that I had or the way I was afraid I continued to. Although I was married and could not imagine myself cheating, being in Florida made me want Henry more. After putting the kids to sleep and making sure Darius was okay, I would take whatever dessert was left from dinner and sit on the back porch just thinking of what we had. Then I would look at the moon and what-if myself past midnight.

My mom lost her right leg to diabetes in 1983. It was a tough time for her, with my dad, bless his heart, being gone and all. He'd died of a lung disease the previous year, so I moved my invalid husband and six kids into a four-bedroom house about three blocks from her home. I still had a little money from the sale of the property in Arkansas, and although Darius never knew it, I sent Henry a thousand-dollar check for his second congressional race.

Looking at my life, I decided it was time to make some changes, so I enrolled in Miami-Dade Community College's nursing program. I knew it would take a while, but as the saying goes, the journey of a thousand miles starts with a single step.

HRS came to my aid and helped me find someone to assist my mother while I was at school. Her name was Chianti', her skin tone was smooth and even, she wore thick-as-a-banana dreads with ebony lipstick, and wore Little John Lennon-like glasses. She would assist Mom in going to the bathroom and dressing and sometimes would even cook for her. I used to rush over to help out after doing my housework and getting Darius and the kids situated, but she always had everything under control. So one day she and I were talking and she asked me if I needed any help with my family since I was going to school. Although I wanted to say no, I knew with a little help, maybe just for three hours a day, I could have a much better GPA and spend a little more time working out to get rid of the weight. So I said, "Sure, but when could you do it with your schedule and all?" She said, "No way." She was going to school and had two other patients. But she said her boyfriend had decided at the last minute not to go into the military, and his folks were not too happy with the decision. He had moved in temporarily with her and they needed the money.

Her boyfriend's name was Brandon. He was eighteen, I was almost thirty, and it was the fall of '83.

Chapter 4

"Welcome back to our NBS Studios in Washington, D.C. This is Franklin Dunlop and we will be momentarily taking you to Chicago, Illinois, and Judy Finestein for an update on the new leader in the race, Vice President Steiner. If you are just joining us, after a few key victories in the Midwest, Ronald Steiner has taken a small lead in the race for the White House. He is at present narrowly ahead of the man who has led the race all night and in a way has been leading the race since his party's convention in August."

"If you were not with us earlier, the vice president picked up wins in the states of Missouri, Indiana, Iowa, and Ohio, as well as his home state of Illinois, as expected. But the biggest victory of the past hour has been the Empire State of New York. Yes, the Steiner train has rumbled through the Northeast, and we are projecting New York and her thirty-three electoral votes will be carried by the vice president. The Baldwin campaign, which badly needed to take a major state if it was going to have any opportunity to win tonight, has had little to shout about thus far. The only state they have added to the fold is Arkansas, and we are told they are trailing badly in California, which would be the cornerstone of any chance they would have tonight for a victory. It has not been confirmed, but we are told as soon as the results in his home state of Arizona are announced, Governor Tom will give his concession speech.

"As for the Davis campaign, they are still very much in the hunt and stand an excellent chance of winning tonight. They won a key victory in New Jersey and carried the state of Texas, which was a must-win state after losing in Florida. They have also won in Maryland and Massachusetts. As of this minute the numbers look like this:

DAVIS	172	████████████████
STEINER	174	█████████████████
BALDWIN	118	███████████

"Now, for more on the state of affairs in the Davis campaign, we will go to Gus Edmond, who is standing by with a former Davis supporter in a small suburb of Atlanta, Stone Mountain, Georgia. Gus? Are you there?"

"Yes, I am, Franklin. Actually I am in Marietta and I am with a former Davis supporter who calls herself a Reagan Democrat, Mrs. Agnosia Clay. Mrs. Clay, tell me, how does one go from being a major and even vocal supporter of one candidate to a supporter of the opposition in such a short time?"

"Well, I just had to look at all the relevant facts. First, as a black woman, I think for myself just as many other black people do, and we don't feel obligated to vote for a person based on the color of his skin. I looked at the person he picked for his running mate, I looked at the new role his wife has taken in the campaign, and I also looked at the moral issues that Vice President Steiner pointed out so poignantly in the debates. I come from a family that has always voted Democratic and I have never pulled a Republican lever in my life except in eighty-four, but there comes a time when you have to make a choice as to what is good for America. I asked myself, would America be better off in the hands of Vice President Steiner, who has worked in government for the past thirty years or so and knows the ins and outs, or in the hands of Mr. Davis, who I just don't think is ready for prime time? At least not as ready as the vice president, and in my opinion, now is not a time for on-the-job-training."

Fontainebleau Hotel
Presidential Suite

Turning up the volume of another network, Henry responded to the knock at the door. "Who?"

"Henry, it's me."

Standing up and walking backwards to the door so as not to miss a second of the results, Henry opened the door for his brother.

"Did you see me on TV?" he asked with a wide-eyed puppy-dog look in his eyes.

"Yeah," Henry said, turning to him with a smile. "You did good, man. Really good."

"Thanks. I was nervous as all get out. You see how they tried to get personal with the questions, but I wouldn't let them."

"I noticed," Henry said, sitting back down in his chair with his leg over the arm and looking at his brother, who fell on the couch. "So tell me. What's the mood like down there in the lobby?"

"I don't know," Herbert replied, with a drink in one hand and a fistful of granola in another. "I mean, at first, people were going crazy, but now they're more subdued. Ed and I were trying to determine the mood of the crowd in Chicago and they seem to be a little quieter also."

"Yeah, I noticed that. So you realize," Henry said, looking back at the TVs in front of them, "it's gonna come down to California."

"I was just talking to Willie Brown about that. I hate it, but we still polled well there as recently as Sunday night, so I feel good about it."

"I know. But California scares me, man. It's still a conservative state, and I think a lot of moderates there feel good *saying* on the phone they'd vote for us, but when the curtain closes, they'll find it easier to vote for Steiner."

"I don't know, I got a good feeling about Cally."

There was a knock at the door to the suite. "Who?" the two brothers answered as one.

"It's, aha . . . it's me, Senator. Me and Penelope."

"Let them in," Henry said as he watched another defector, who had transferred from his camp to the opposition, being paraded out by the network.

"Ah, Senator Davis? Penelope and I have some important news to pass on to you," Ed said, and inhaled a deep breath as he rubbed his palms together.

"What's going on?" Herbert asked, chewing his snack as Henry continued to watch the TVs.

"Umm, Senator Davis, sir?"

"Yes."

"Did you hear me, sir?" Ed repeated as Herbert's chewing slowed and his eyes volleyed from the back of his brother's head to Ed and Penelope.

"Henry!" Penelope shouted. "Turn off the goddamn TV, for chrissakes!"

Herbert glared at her as she transferred her weight to one foot while crossing her arms over her large breasts and then composed herself.

Henry reached down blindly and picked up the remote. With a single click, all four TV sets went black. Refusing to look at Ed and Penelope, he asked, "Better?"

"Aha, yes, sir," Ed replied, and put his hand on Penelope's as a clue not to repeat her previous performance.

"So, Penelope? Ed?" Henry asked stealthily. "Do they know who he, or they, are?"

"Know who? Henry? What the hell are you talking about, man?" Herbert questioned, thoroughly confused and about to spill his drink on his indigo blazer.

Silence loomed over the room as each person waited for another's response. And then Penelope snatched her arm away from Ed's grasp, and said, "*Sir*, were you informed earlier?"

Henry's thumb moved back and forth over the remote like a wiper over a windshield. After an elongated pause, Henry clutched the remote in his palm and looked at a square of wallpaper above the TVs. "No need to inform me. You know how it feels to stick your finger in something hot," he said with a sardonic smile, "or have grease pop on you when you're cooking? You know how for just a split second . . . you wonder just how badly it's going to burn? I've lived in that split second for the past six months. Just waiting for the burn. Maybe it's something primitive we have in common with other animals, but it's a queasy feeling you get in your stomach when death is around the corner."

"What the fuck's going on! Who's trying to—" Herbert shouted.

"Hen." Penelope lowered her voice. "Henry, they know who he is, and rumor has it he's in the hotel tonight. We haven't confirmed that with the FBI, but our people tell us he is here. Now," she continued as Ed looked at her, "with the race as tight as it is, for security purposes the FBI and Secret Service would both feel more comfortable with you and Les in a more secure place. They would like to take you out of here, via helicopter from the roof. You can watch the results from—"

"Not gonna run," Henry blurted out with a burst of air and looked at the delft-blue screens of the TVs. "I've waited for this damn moment my *entire* life, and I'm not gonna run and hide now. This is a part of the show."

"But, sir, it's not a cowardly act and it's not running!" Ed replied as the eyes of the room landed on the small flushed man moving his hands like a demonstrative professor. "It's preposterous to stay here. If he has infiltrated this hotel, he may have accomplices. That's what we fear the most, and if he has, then the Secret Service said they could not guarantee our . . . I mean your safety in this place. What they would simply like to do is to—"

"Henry," Herbert said. "Maybe we should consider this seriously. I mean, this threat, unlike the rest of them, could be for real."

Looking at his brother, Henry continued to stroke the rectangular remote and asked, "Are you aware that I have received, according to the FBI, more threats in a week than the other candidates have received during the entire campaign? One agent told me that during my campaign, I've received more level-three threats than the president has received in eight damn years in office!" He closed his eyes to gather his composure, as his Adam's apple slid up, and paused. "I'm not trying to be a martyr, and I know there are more than a few bullets with my name on them." He clicked on the televisions and added, "But I believe in what we have done so far. So if some asshole tries to take me out because of it, I'm a man. So he can . . ." Henry's torso tightened as he opened his eyes, unable to finish the thought.

Ringgggggg . . .

The Democratic presidential candidate picked up the cellular phone, listened a moment, then hung up.

HENRY

I could not wait to turn the calendar to 1993, because that was the year I actually started campaigning for the presidency. It was still seven years away, yet all the pieces were in place. Naturally, whenever anyone in the media asked me if I was running, I never said yes, yet was far from saying no. But in '93 we started targeting key benefactors in each state we would need for our run. My advisers felt we would have to have a minimum of twenty million in the bank or near our fingertips the day we made our intentions known. Planning for that in a quiet manner was not the easiest thing to do, but that was our mission.

I won the seat in Congress in '84 and won reelection in '86. And then I ran for, and won by a landslide, the U.S. Senate seat in Florida in 1988. That was the first time I made the cover of *Ebony* magazine and it was the easiest race I had ever run. The incumbent senator was in his third term and took us for granted. But we did a lot of grassroots campaigning and started the "One Man, One People, One Vision" campaign, whereby we would visit a work site in each county and my staff and I would spend a week working just like the common people. One week in Tampa we worked as ditch diggers for the county, and in St. Augustine we spent three days in an elementary school reading to blind children and assisting the teachers. In Dade County we helped build houses with former President Carter, picked up 60 percent of the major city newspaper endorsements, and at every stop the media coverage grew larger and larger. By the time Senator Griggs noticed us, we'd tied him in virtually every county in which he held a lead, and weeks later we were looking at a possible landslide victory.

In the final days of the campaign, Griggs, who was an old-school cut-and-gut dirty-tricks campaigner, started getting negative in his attacks. With a week left, he went on a campaign swing from the Panhandle of Florida to the Keys, holding airport press conferences where he would blatantly lie about my record in Congress. Once he said I cheated on my law school entrance exam, and another time he hinted that I had been arrested in Little Havana for solicitation. Although his tactics were crooked at best and slanderous at worst, the ink was in the water, and the negative ads worked. We were told by our pollster that our opponent was pulling closer even in my home district.

So on the Monday before the election we decided to take a chance and not play it safe. Griggs was holding a press conference in Fort Myers, and we conveniently set it up so that Leslie would be flying out of Fort Myers to meet me in Panama City for a rally. Just as we had planned, she and Penelope just *happened* to be on the tarmac as Griggs was in the midst of making up another half-truth, and Leslie just stood there with her overnight bag over her shoulder. On the news you could see the look in Griggs's eyes when he saw her for the first time. It's easy to lie about someone with his or her back turned, but another thing to do it face-to-face with a camera and thirty reports looking at you, examining not only the words you say, but also the words you leave out. Griggs then took a chance I don't know if I would have. But then, he did not know the Yvette side to my Leslie.

"Well, well," he said, "it seems we have been *infiltrated* by the Davis campaign."

Leslie stood quietly without expression.

"It appears that while the congressman is off doing *whatever* it may be he is doing today, he sent the little lady to defend him."

Leslie remained silent and continued to hold the garment bag just as rehearsed.

"I think that speaks volumes about Mr. Davis." The next thing Florida saw on *The News at Six* was Leslie walking toward Senator Griggs. When she did so, you could hear the oohs and ahs in the background.

"Sir, my husband did not send me here, nor do I believe he even knows you are here. I am simply flying out of this airport to meet him for a rally. But let me say that my husband and I are saddened by what you have become in the last few days of this election. You, sir, have served the people of this state with dignity for twelve years. Now you have stooped to outright lies and slander, and we have decided to stick to the record. You knew we could not respond to the outrageous statements in the last seventy-two hours of the campaign, so you have resorted to the oldest trick in the book."

I watched on TV while Griggs looked at his assistant, and when he looked at Leslie with the cameras all pointing her way, I know he knew he was in trouble.

"Sir," she continued, "we refuse to allow ourselves to sink to your moral and ethical level. Win, lose, or draw, we will not hang our heads due to anything we have done in this campaign. We only hope that you can do the same."

Griggs stammered, trying to get the attention of the reporters with a snide retort, but most of them continued to focus on Leslie as she looked at her watch, then walked quietly through the crowd and headed for her plane, refusing to take any questions, but taking half the reporters with her.

Needless to say, the ploy worked. The next day, election day, from coast to coast the image of this gray-headed white man debating my wife was on every newspaper in Florida.

He came off looking scared and a part of the establishment in Florida. Leslie looked like a wife defending her husband's morals and dedicated to changing the face of politics.

When I think back to the early nineties, what I think most changed my life was sort of unusual. Rodney King hurt, don't get me wrong. I know the brother made mistakes and may still make more, but I don't think there is a black man in America who didn't see himself, under the lights, getting lynched by the public servants when it was shown over and over on TV. The ending of affirmative action in many states stands out, because I took it as a slap in the face to all of the leaders who had fought and died for the cause. But when a reporter asked me what event in the nineties impacted my life more than any other, it was a day in '91. Actually, the date was November 7, 1991, when Magic Johnson announced he was HIV-positive.

I admit it. Like the ad goes, "I love that game." I watch as many of the Heat and Wizard games as I can when I am in town, but I don't have an obsession with it like some of my friends. I once heard Bob Costas say the game of baseball was *proof* that there was a God, because no man could create a game so beautiful. I would not say the game of basketball is such proof. But Magic was.

I met Earvin and Cookie when they were in D.C. doing a promotion for Pepsi with Earl Graves. I think he and his wife are genuinely nice people. When I heard the news, I was in my office and my AA barged in and said, "You know Magic has AIDS?" I said yeah, I'm sure he does after all that kissing on Isaiah Thomas. And she said, "No. I'm serious. It was on CNN when I was home for lunch." As soon as she said the letters "CN," I was reaching for my remote. By this time the news conference had gone off, so I turned to ESPN, saw Magic's face in a blue suit and designer tie, and I knew it was true.

I guess the reason it affected me so much is that for the first time, HIV had a face. I'd voted on bills regarding funding for AIDS research, but honestly, I'd done it because I'd felt it was a way to help people who were gay or drug users. But now HIV was not black or white, gay or straight, young or old. HIV was my friend, HIV was my hero. HIV was Magic. It was someone I knew, and it brought the issue home to me.

I remember Earvin at Michigan State playing against Bird, as well as his first few years in the pros. In fact, before Magic, I was a die-hard Atlanta Hawks fan. Don't ask me why. But I became a Magic fan. Not Orlando, Johnson. He played with so much passion and love for the game. He played with the same intensity I had in my run for the presidency. A single-minded determination that nothing and no one would ever stop him. He fought the disease with the same fire in his belly. Although people laughed when he said he'd beaten it . . . no one is laughing now. I sent him a telegram as soon as I heard about his condition, and the four of us have remained friends ever since.

I look at Cookie and I see the type of love Leslie and I shared. I can honestly say if it were not for Leslie, I would not be where I am at this time. She was much more than my most intelligent and trusted adviser. She was my friend, my lover, and simply my life when my dream squeezed everything out of me and left me dry. There was one particular time around '93 when the dream was too heavy to bear and I sunk to my lowest point, which I don't like to talk about. But she was there, and she never left my side.

One night I flew to New York to be on *Meet the Press*. It was my first appearance on the show, so I was a little nervous. To make a long story short, I stunk up the place. I don't know if I had an anxiety attack or if the angst of what was on the horizon suddenly came to light or what, but none of my thoughts came easily and I screwed up a number of important facts which normally I could have spouted off easily if someone had awakened me in the midst of my sleep. Although I know he would never admit it, Tim Russert must have thought I had more than coffee in my U.S. Senate coffee mug. Since the show was live, there was no way to edit out my snafus, so when I heard "It's a wrap" and the lights went out, I felt like a clown, minus the big red nose and floppy shoes.

When I came off the set, Herbert looked at me as he would as a child when he knew I had screwed up and was going to get a beating. After accepting a couple of insincere congratulatory phone calls from friends around the country, I got out of the NBC studio and Manhattan as fast as I could.

As fate would have it, there was a mechanical problem with the plane we were boarding in Atlanta and we were forced to wait for another connecting flight. I have always enjoyed Atlanta, so Herbert and I, as well as my advisers Marcus and Wayne, took off for the Underground. I thought getting away for a while would do me good.

When I got out of the limo, we decided that we'd find a sporting goods store and waste time in a restaurant until Herbert got the page that the plane was ready. We walked through the mall and a few people noticed me. This was one time I did not care to be recognized after what had just been televised. But as we were walking, I saw her. This woman who was moving through the crowd toward us was the spitting image of Cheryl. Same complexion and height; even the smile she shared when our eyes met was similar. Marcus noticed her immediately and nudged my forearm as she appeared to be headed our way. When she got closer, everyone in the group, including Herbert, was almost panting for air. Of course, it wasn't Cheryl, but the woman looked exquisite in her leopard scarf, matching gloves, cream vest and skirt, and sling-back four-inch leopard pumps.

"Senator Davis? Right?" she asked, standing in front of me.

"Yes. And you are?"

She reached in her purse and pulled out a card that read:

Alicia Simmons
President, Ole' Dirty South Records

"I'm a political junkie," she said. "I watched you on NBC this morning and I thought you did a wonderful job." At this point I knew she was a BS artist beyond compare. She continued, "You may not have heard of my label, but we produce Chill E and So-So Dangerous, as well as a female group by the name of BWP, which stands for—''

"Bitches With Problems," Marcus, who is Asian, interrupted, and then looked at us a little embarrassed that he'd supplied the name. "My son. He's really into the *rap* thing."

"That's great," she said, looking at him and then right back at me.

"Well, ahh, Alicia, right?" Herbert said, with a gentle tug on my elbow. "We need to finish up a little shopping before we head back to Miami. It was nice—"

Pulling away, I said, "It was nice meeting you, Alicia, and thanks for the card." Herbert was good at his job for the most part, but he had a tendency to be a little overprotective with me and women. There were several incidents in Florida when women had made advances, and he would always cut them off at the pass. But there was a fine line between sheltering and being obnioxious.

Alicia noticed my defiant gesture toward Herbert and continued to talk, although we were walking away from her. She shared with me how she'd started the company and how many acts she wanted to have and how hard it was to get any publicity when you were from the South when most major rap labels were based in New York City. As she spoke, I could not get over her uncanny resemblance to Cheryl, and wondered how she and Darius were doing. I had made plans to attend our class reunion in '91. Although I was receiving national attention, I always wanted to stay close to my friends in south Florida. Unfortunately I and several other members of the Congressional Black Caucus were asked to accompany the president on a trip to Israel, so I was forced to cancel. David, who was living in Oklahoma at the time, went to the reunion and told me that Cheryl had come alone and looked as good as ever.

". . . and that's how we came up with the name of the company," was all I heard from Alicia.

"Well . . . that's very interesting," I said, trying to be polite. "It's always nice to, ahh, see people take chances and live out their dream."

We headed into the sporting goods store as Alicia continued to talk, and Herbert would not get rid of her because of the way I'd pulled away from him previously. Then I heard her say, "And I also want to thank you, Senator Davis, for your vote on SB-91-1037." As she quoted the numbers, we all stopped in our tracks.

"You remember the number for the HIV bill?"

"Like I said," she replied. "I'm a political junkie." And then she lowered her voice to say, "and also, my mom died of AIDS two years ago." As she spoke the words, her body slumped.

"I'm sorry to hear that," I replied.

"It's okay," she added, and then looked at my shoes and then back into my eyes. "For the first time, I didn't say my mom died of AIDS but she *wasn't* gay." As she stood before me, she reached in her purse for something to blow her nose on when Marcus handed me his handkerchief. After giving it to her, I asked Marcus, our bodyguard, and Herbert to go in and do their shopping while I went with Alicia to a corner of the eatery for a cup of coffee.

As we sat there, from time to time people would come up and ask me if I was that-senator-you-know-what's-his-face, but for the most part we were able to talk in peace. She told me of how she'd dropped out of college to take care of her mother and was there when she took her final breath. As she spoke, I was moved, because this was not a doctor testifying before Congress with sterile charts on a tripod behind him. This was a person who had watched the shame of HIV turn into the realization of the disease transfiguring itself into the abhorrent face of AIDS and take someone from her whom she loved. As she spoke, she started to tear up a little more and brought the handkerchief to her nose. At some point I reached across the table to console her by holding her hand. When I did, I saw her open her eyes and look at me differently than before. I immediately returned my consoling hands to my side of the table and leaned back in my seat. I wanted to hug her because she was in so much pain, but sending the wrong message to her was something I could not deal with at this point in my life, personally or professionally.

"Sorry for babbling on and on like that, Senator Davis." I noticed that she kept saying my entire name and title with a look in her eyes that said she wanted me to say, no, just call me Henry. But I'd been down this road before. "So . . . Senator Davis, how's Leslie?"

I paused. The conversation was getting more eerie by the minute. I just could not put my finger on what was bothering me as I answered, "Fine. She's fine. Listen," I said, standing up. "I need to catch up with the guys. Thanks again for sharing that story with me. It really meant a lot. And I will keep an ear out for your—"

"Do you have to leave? *Right* now?" she asked, leaning over just enough to let me know she was braless.

With the words and her cleavage on the table, her intentions clarified and I smiled and said, "Yes," then left her sitting in the corner as I caught up with my staff.

When I entered the Congress, a representative from the Midwest asked me to dinner one night. He'd served with distinction on the Hill for more than forty years and wished to retire. During our conversation I got the distinct impression he was sizing me up. For what, I had no idea. As soon as the appetizer was served, he started giving me advice on how to deal with lobbyists and how to raise money without breaking any campaign finance rules and regulations. By the main course we'd discussed who the real movers and shakers were in Washington politics. Then he looked at me over coffee with these clear green eyes, and said, "Let me tell you, son, the easiest way to win in this city. Remember three things. Talk about the economy. Talk about the press. And if that doesn't work, talk about your competition. *Always* in that order. Always. Forget all that bullshit about foreign policy, because most people cannot find three major foreign cities on a map if you paid them. And as far as your past accomplishments, save them for the mantel at home. No one outside of your publicist and your mother cares. But there are three surefire ways to lose as well," he added. "Women, women, and girls. Most decent people when they get to this level in politics can avoid the temptations of drugs and money. Most," he said with a chuckle. "But with women, women, and girls . . . you're always suspect, given the right time and circumstance. And trust me. This town is full of film and Fotomats."

I'd never forgotten what he'd told me, and used it as my personal mantra of sorts. *Press, economy, competition, women, women, and girls.*

We arrived at Miami International a little past midnight, and I wanted to call Leslie, but she usually went to sleep around ten because she has always been an early riser. So as I drove through the streets of Miami, I was proud that I had done the right thing earlier, but a part of me wondered how after all these years I still had thoughts of Cheryl. Other girls I dated before Leslie were a distant memory. But I could still remember how she smelled like water and soap. I could still feel her touch when we held hands.

When I pulled into our driveway, the enormity of the earlier nationally televised disaster rested on me like cinder blocks. *Did I really forget Castro's first name? And what the hell did I mean when I made the comment about Libya? Oh my God.* So I sat in the car with my forehead slowly thumping the backs of my hands, which were grasping the steering wheel. The house was dark, so she was obviously asleep. I'd had Marcus call from the airport to tell her we would probably sleep over in Atlanta so she could get some rest.

I opened the car door and reached for my briefcase and overnight bag. I needed a meeting with my people in DC to plan a way to get me back in the public eye so the first taste of me for Middle America would not be a lasting one. There was this conservative gathering in Seattle who'd asked me to speak and I had turned them down. But as I searched for my house key I was having second thoughts. As I opened the door and turned off the alarm system, I clicked on the light switch. Nothing happened. *Damn fuse box.* I then picked up my briefcase and out of the darkness came the light from a flashlight. "Aha, excuse me, sir. Umm, where do you think you are going?"

"Hey, Baby," I said, with the first real smile I had felt all day.

"Aha, boo? Excuse me, there's no *Boo* here. This is the Davis residence, and Senator Davis will be staying over in Atlanta tonight. So who are you?"

We had not played games like this in years. When we were younger we would do and try anything. But we had grown comfortable with each other, like most married couples, I suppose. Even though I was tired and my body ached from the long day of traveling and extended layover in Atlanta, I played along.

"I'm sorry, ma'am. I guess you've found me out. I'm a Secret Service agent, hired by the government to protect your husband and—"

"You're lying. He's just a junior senator. He doesn't need protection."

"Oh. Well," I said, walking toward the source of the light after dropping my briefcase and overnight bag in the foyer, "I'm a doctor. I was told that someone at this address needed a little"—I know it was corny, but I had to say it—"sexual healing."

"Be serious," she whispered, as I stood inches away from her nude body lying on the couch. I loved the way she took care of herself, always eating healthy and dieting. I loved the way she smelled. Her scent was so feminine. My Leslie's body suggested flowers, and it was a luscious, erotic, and beautiful scent that always helped me reach my peak. And as she lay there, with her legs slightly apart, my blood rushed as I reached for my collar to undo my tie.

"Aha, excuse me," she said, with the light still shining in my face. "What are you doing? First of all, yes, I'm in need of healing, as you put it, but I already know a doctor," she said, and stood up. "In fact, I married a doctor," she said, cutting off the beam of light and leaving the room pitch dark. "My doctor is sleeping over in Atlanta," Leslie continued, and brought her nude body as close as she could without making contact. "And I must say, sir, you're no doctor."

"Okay, ma'am," I replied in my Billy Dee Williams, *Lady Sings the Blues* voice as I pulled off my tie and brought my lips a hair-width from her mouth. "I must be honest with you. I am a . . . compulsive liar. I do it," and then my lips almost touched hers, "for a living."

"See what I'm talking about? You're even lying about the lies that you're lying about. You must be a lawyer or a politician. Now, come here," she commanded. "That's better." Leslie then grabbed my hand before I could unbutton my shirt. "Listen to me," she continued as her eyes grazed the surface of my face. "I love you, Teddy. Okay? Not for who you are, or what you have done. I love you because you mean more to me than *anything* on this earth, and I will love you until the day I die. And if I am fortunate enough to be given the opportunity by God to love you after I am gone, I'll love you even more then."

We moved slowly as one in the middle of the room to the radio, I held her inside of me, and it pained me to think of ever letting her go again. She allowed her kisses to slide up and down the center of my chest, and as we danced, the radio disc jockey said, "We're sending this song out to Teddy. Welcome home, and remember," he said in a voice that reminded me of Barry White, "today is just a small step backward, toward bigger things to come tomorrow. I love you madly, and that's from Yvette."

As the Bee Gees started to sing our song, she looked at me, and before I could say thank you, she whispered, "I was reading a story about this man who lost his hearing when he was struck by lightning in a field. He had just gotten married and was bitter about what had happened. As he lay in the hospital, he was in complete denial and was against learning sign language initially. So he and his bride made up a code that only they knew. When they wanted to express their love," she said, rubbing the top of my eyebrow with the length of her thumb slowly, "they just did this. So whenever you miss me, or need me, or want me, just do this, and you will feel my love wherever you are."

"I love you so much, girl." That was all I could say. I guess that was not a day for words to come easily to me.

* * *

A month later I got a call at two in the morning from Marcus, who was working on a senatorial campaign in Utah. "Senator Davis, I hate to call you this late, sir, but I called and paged Herbert first. For some reason I can't get in touch with him."

Still half asleep, I rolled over, rubbed my eyes, and said quietly so as not to disturb Leslie, "Herbert's on vacation. What's going on?"

"Well, sir. I don't now how to tell you this without just saying it."

As he said those words no politician wants to hear at any hour and definitely not past midnight, I was sitting on the side of my bed, putting my feet in my slippers.

"We just got back to the hotel in Salt Lake and . . . well . . ."

"Marcus," I repeated, this time from the hallway, "what's going on?"

"Well, sir, NBS *Overnight* is reporting that you had an affair with a twenty-five-year-old model."

"What?" I said, trying to gather myself as I walked toward my office. "They're reporting what?"

"Well, sir, I just caught the tail end of it as I was getting undressed in my hotel room. But this is not the worse part. It's that girl you talked to in Atlanta. Alicia something."

I could not say a word as I turned my television to NBS, which by this time was running the sports scores.

"Also, they mentioned that the story would be running in a major national publication this week."

"Wait, wait, wait," I said to him. "Is it the *Atlanta Constitution*? The *Washington Post*? Did they mention a source?" As I spoke, I could hear Leslie walk up behind me, and ask, "What's wrong?"

"No, they didn't mention a source or name the paper. But as you know, they're connected to *The Globe*, and I've been told that they've run stories based on a feature in that newspaper. Did they not contact you before running the story?"

"Hell no! They would have called . . ." And then I remembered that Herbert was on a cruise ship in the Mediterranean and did not have his pager, nor was there a way to reach him. "Damn."

"Senator Davis? Is there anything I can do?"

"No . . . I mean, yes. What else did they say? Anything?"

"No, sir, that's basically all that I caught."

"Okay," I said, trying to think quickly of the best course of action. But most important was how I would handle this with Leslie.

As I hung up the phone, she sat down on the couch in front of my desk. So? she asked with her eyebrows without saying a word.

"Les, umm. It ain't pretty."

And then my wife pulled out the business card from the pocket of her robe, and asked, "Was it anything to do with this Alicia person?"

There was a long, prickly silence as I looked at the card and then flipped it over to see Alicia's home phone number scrawled in pen, which I had not noticed before. Looking into Leslie's eyes, again, I said, "Yeah. First of all"—and as I said the words, even I didn't believe them—"I never noticed her number on the back of this card, but apparently she went to a tabloid with a story about us having an affair The truth is I hardly even know her."

"So how did you get the card?" she calmly asked.

"We were at the Underground and she came up to all four of us and gave me the card. Then she started talking about her company and her mother, and one thing led to another . . ." I didn't want to even tell her I had a cup of coffee with Alicia, but I saw from Leslie's eyes that she was expecting the worst. "Well, she and I sat in the eatery in full view of everyone, and *talked* about her mom dying of AIDS. And that's all that happened . . ."

Leslie stood up and walked toward the door, then spun around and walked back toward me. She asked, "So since Herbert's gone, who do you know at NBS?"

"Umm, I know Philip Valdez, but he's a producer and won't be in until—"

"No good. We need an editor," she said, walking back toward the door and then again thoughtfully toward me.

"Give me the phone," she continued as she punched *N* on my electronic Rolodex. As she scrolled down to the National Broadcasting Service, she asked, "Did you know both NBS and *The Globe* are owned by Kevin Childs?" Kevin Childs was a South Carolinian majority shareholder in a large tobacco company. He also spent thousands of dollars through his various political action committees in an attempt to defeat me in my last election.

Leslie stayed on the phone for more than fifteen minutes in an attempt to find a major decision maker in the news division of NBS. Finally she reached the night desk senior editor, who confirmed that the source was in fact *The Globe* and asked her if she wanted to make a comment. Being as savvy as she was beautiful, she stated, "On the record, no comment." That was a brilliant move, because if she had just said that they had no right to run the story, her denial of the segment neither of us had yet to see would have given them just cause to run the story again and again. Leslie would have inadvertently become the source of the story. It was almost 3:00 A.M. and Leslie was bubbling like a kettle, clearly in her zone. I hoped in my heart that she really did believe me, but I could tell by the way she spoke to the editor that what had actually happened was secondary to what was being reported.

"And I repeat," she said again, off the record, "that story has no merit whatsoever. The plane was delayed and they talked in a mall. That's all that happened," she continued, looking at me and then again into space. "So if you insist on running that story, all we ask is that you have complete disclosure and add in the body of the text that your source was *The Globe*. And while you're at it, I think next week they're running a story on a three-headed chicken you might want to get a jump on also."

I couldn't believe my ears. All that I'd known all along was inside of her had been given a chance to shine for the first time, and she was brilliant. Before she hung up, she and the editor were actually laughing. I think even he had to get a kick out of the chicken comment. And then she and I sat together without uttering a single word and watched

Overnight, waiting to see if they would run the story again. Although the editor had given her assurances that the story would not run in the four-o'clock segment, I was still afraid we were not out of the woods. I could just hear the anchorman saying:

"Senator Henry Davis's office is refusing comment on a soon-to-be-published account of an improper relationship between the senator of Florida and an Atlanta businesswoman."

So as the reporter gave the headline for the hour, we waited for him to mention my name, and he didn't. I exhaled a sigh of relief, and Leslie, who had to fly out at 6:00 A.M. for a fund-raiser at Disney, stood up and walked out of the room. As she did, I followed her, and said, "Baby. Thank you."

She looked at me and nodded her head as she yawned and returned to our bedroom. In my heart I knew she believed I had more than a coffee with Alicia. Otherwise she would not have held on to the business card. But I'd told her the truth, so I did not mention it ever again. Nor did she bring it up to me.

The next week, in spite of the fact that Herbert returned and FedExed two signed affidavits from Wayne and Marcus as well as one from a lady who worked in the sporting goods store who'd asked him for my autograph, *The Globe* ran the article internationally. *Inside Edition* did a story on Alicia Simmons, and she and her record lable got their fifteen minutes of fame.

Washington, D.C.
NBS News Studio
1:15 A.M. EST

"Okay, America, this is Franklin Dunlop from our NBS studios in Washington, D.C. As we reported at the top of the hour, our sources have confirmed that an assassin has been stalking the campaign of Senator Henry Davis for the past several months, and the FBI is close to making an arrest.

The gentleman in question is this man, Calvin I. Arthur. Arthur, we're told, was hired by or heads an organization whose name the FBI has not been willing to release to the press at this point. But they have released photos. As you can see, Arthur is a Caucasian male in his early thirties, and it is believed that the beard he has in these photos may have been shaved off. He is five feet ten, approximately one hundred sixty-five pounds and has a small scar under his cheek, which, if he is clean-shaven, should be very prominent. We are told that he is a former college athlete and a skilled marksman. The FBI and CIA have been closing in on him for the past three weeks, and we are told tonight an arrest is imminent. We will be back with more election-night coverage right after this message."

Fountainebleau Hotel
Suite 1717

Leslie lay on the bed in silence in the master bedroom of her suite. While the living room was beginning to fill with a few of her close friends and members of their inner circle, she still needed a few moments of solitude. She had called Henry three times within the past half hour, and twice he had hung up on her. The first time he had asked her why she was calling him. The next two times all she heard was the click. So as she lay in a ball, still wearing her dress and panty hose, she checked again to make sure the phone was working. And then Leslie pulled out the first cigarette from her third pack tonight and lit it while feeling an alcohol and valium buzz.

Hearing a knock at the door, Leslie wearily looked at it, and said, "Yes?"

"It's me, open up."

"It's open," Leslie said to Penelope.

Penelope walked in talking on her cell phone. "Excuse me? Of course not. Please, we're talking about a major interview. Jane Pauley called this morning and Barbara wants her for a full hour on *20/20*. So we're not giving an exclusive to a morning show even if it is sweeps week. Call me back when you guys are serious. Bye!" "Les, what's up, girl? You know you can't stay in here all night."

"I know," Leslie said as she sat up slowly and stretched. "God it's been a long day. What time is it anyway?"

Penelope looked at her friend and laid her files and cell on the dresser. As she sat beside her she said, "Les, talk to me."

"About?"

"Don't start that shit!" Penelope said, looking at the clear brown unmarked prescription bottle under the edge of the bed. "I got too much going on tonight, okay, girl? Now, I know there is something you ain't telling me. What's up? What's going on?"

"Aha, Penelope," Leslie said, sitting up, kicking the bottle under the bed with her heel, and rubbing the stress lines in her forehead. "I know you do your job well and that is why you're press secretary. I respect you," she said, looking at her assistant. "But you have a habit of pushing and pushing and pushing until you can get on people's nerves sometimes. Now, I'm sorry to tell you, but tonight I can't deal with your attitude. I mean, I try to overlook it at times, but damn."

Penelope looked at her friend and moved the tip of her burgundy alligator pumps stiffly against the nap of the carpet. "You may be right, Leslie. You may be right. But you know something?" she said, still looking down. "I've given you and that man down the hall one hundred percent of my heart and soul for the past seventeen years. Outside of the two of you, no one, and I do mean *no* one," she repeated, "is more responsible for you guys being here tonight than me, and you know it. Now, I respect you. God knows I respect Hen. And, Leslie," she said, looking up at her boss, "I expect the truth and I will not allow you to disrespect me or my work. I'm damn good at what I do and I don't have to—"

"Who's disrespecting what you do? Why are you taking it like that? Now, maybe it's the alcohol or something, but this has nothing to do with what you do. See, a sista would not go there. This is about you. *You* sometimes cross the line into our personal lives too much, and that . . . is where . . . I draw the line."

"I see," Penelope said, standing up and leaning her willowy frame against the edge of the highboy. "So if the papers all around the country run photographs with you and that asshole in Rome for the world to see, and I have to put a spin on it, it's okay, but *I'm* crossing the fucking line. I understand."

"No, what you should understand is what I told you. And to tell the fucking press the truth that I told you! I have never run from that story or those fucking photos and I won't start now. I have . . . Henry and I have worked too damn hard to get here to lose it over some *bullshit* opportunistic prick looking for a quick payday!"

"Okay, Les. If that's all you want to tell me, cool. I work for you and I'm fine with that. But it would help me to do my job better if I *knew* the whole story," she said, walking toward the door preparing to place a call on her cell phone.

"Bring your fifty-cent ass back here! How, Penelope? How would it help you do *your* job better if you knew the intimate details? Huh? Would you like to know how James and I met? How we went up to the room together?" Leslie demanded, her voice getting angrier and lower with each word. "How we *fucked?* Is that what you're looking for? Huh? Would you like to know the details so it can help you do a *better* job?"

After a pregnant pause Penelope said, "I thought you said you never had sex with him."

Staring through her press secretary, Leslie was speechless. She had never told anyone they had actually had sex, and now the words had fallen from her lips. "Yeah," she said above a whisper. "Yeah, we had sex. Not made love, had sex. Had *fuck*. Whatever you want to call it." And then she took a drag on her cigarette looked away, and exhaled. "I had no feelings for him. I was lonely and it happened and I have to deal with it," she said as her eyebrows fell and a calm came over her face. "But tell me, Penelope," Leslie said, looking at the tip of her burning cigarette once again and then toward her press secretary. "When my husband's *dick* was in your mouth . . . did you love him?"

LESLIE

What do I think of when I think of 1993? It was both the best and worst year for Teddy and me.

The first part of that year was incredible. We were getting a lot of national attention, and Teddy was even featured on the cover of *Time* magazine under the heading "The New Face of the Democratic Party?" To this day he doesn't know how he got on that cover. I met this gentleman who worked for *Time* at an elaborate party given by Ben Bradlee. Colin Powell, John McCain, Tipper Gore, and Secretary of State Madeleine Albright were just a few of the A-list attendees. Teddy was out of town and I was filling in for him. I really didn't like doing these types of functions alone, but I was starting to get used to it. Teddy was elected to the Senate in '88 and we received a considerable amount of attention with the first-black-Senator-from-the-deep-South stories for a while. However, eventually that grew stale and we needed something to rejuvenate our presence outside the state, but nothing seemed to work. Teddy drew up a couple of bills, one dealing with the environment and another regarding Internet regulation, but both were page-three stories, and in no time they were swept under the carpet. We had to do something big and we had to do it fast if 2000 was to be a reality. So when I met James Wolinski at this function, I knew it could possibly be a solution to our problem.

When I first met James, he knew me and I did not know him, which was unusual because the room was a virtual who's who in national politics. I spoke with several senators who were interested in Teddy cosponsoring legislation with them, but not one of them asked him to visit their state to campaign for them. When we first came into office, we would get two or three requests a week to campaign from California to Maine, but that was a thing of the past.

James walked up behind me, and said over my shoulder,

"So where is the first man from Florida?" Yeah, I know it was corny, but I laughed because I was a little tired of talking about polls, politics, programs, and prostitutes.

"I'm sorry," I said. "Have we met?"

"No, we haven't. My name is Wolinski, James Wolinski. *Time* magazine."

I laughed. "The way you said that, I thought you would say Bond . . . James Bond."

"That's funny. Actually, I covered your husband's congressional campaign in Florida in eighty-two."

"Oh," I said, and extended my hand to shake his. "So what part of Florida are you from?"

"Originally I'm from Delphi, Indiana, but I moved down South for a job with the *Tampa Tribune*, which is how I got assigned to cover your husband. I'm living up here now covering the Washington beat for *Time*."

"How nice," I said. A part of me wanted to turn into the dutiful wife of a senator and see if I could get them to run a story on us, and another part of me wanted to talk to him about anything else but politics. And although we could use the coverage, I chose the latter.

James wasn't what I would call a good-looking guy. He looked like a journalist who had ink in his blood and lived for late-night deadlines. His hair was darker than the wrinkles around his eyes would suggest his age to be, and even in a tux he looked disheveled.

We chatted about the D.C. social scene for a while and then he told me about his ex-wife, who was from Manhattan. She was a corporate attorney who worked for Dr. Pepper in Dallas and had always looked down on him because he'd had a child out of wedlock before they met. She would call him "Cooter" because of his Hoosier accent and always thought she was his superior because she'd graduated from an Ivy League school and his degree was from a community college. When I asked him why he married her, he simply replied, " 'Cause I loved her."

This was a party I had not wanted to attend. It was on a Thursday night and my plan had been to make an appearance, shake a few hands, and get home to watch Blair on

L.A. Law. But it was nice to meet a genuine person in this city of fake smiles and even faker intentions. As we parted that night, he thanked me for not mentioning politics or asking him to write a story about my husband or about some charitable affair I was a part of. I think we both enjoyed the change of pace.

Two months later Teddy rushed into my home office like a kid who'd just received a good dental checkup in a Crest ad. "Guess what! *Time* magazine is going to do a *cover* story on me! Not on the programs I'm backing or the class of senators I came in with, but me. A cover! Can you believe that?"

"You're kidding!"

"No! I can't believe it," he said, looking at the pink telephone call-back note with the number of the reporter on it. "I can't believe we're finally going to get some *real* national exposure, and it couldn't have come at a better time. I guess the decision to take the high road and work on all those important issues is finally paying off, huh?" he said, and put the call-back slip on my desk. "I gotta call Herbert and Penelope to put together some talking points for the interview. They'll *never* believe this. Then I'll call . . ."

As he reached for the cordless phone on my desk, I looked at the note, and it was from Wolinski . . . James Wolinski.

After the article ran, we rode a crest of popularity and were the hottest commodity in D.C. Teddy was on morning shows almost every day and talk-radio shows around the country every afternoon for a month. Before the taping of the *Today* show, Herbert and Marcus had posters made up that read "Davis '96," and paid people in the audience ten dollars just to enthusiastically wave the signs when the cameras scanned the crowd. Naturally we had no intentions of running in '96, but we were seeding the ground for a 2000 harvest.

We were given a list of questions Henry would be asked, but when the red lights came on, Bryant asked him anything but the questions we were expecting. A media professional had warned us about this tactic, and actually it ended up working in our favor. Henry was in a zone, and a couple of sound bites from the interview were so effective, they were repeated on *NBC Nightly News* with Tom Brokaw.

After the interview even Bryant commended him on his performance and, much to Teddy's chagrin, invited him to play golf in his charity tournament. Although his golf game is pretty bad, Henry hated to say no, and the possible contacts would not allow him to say anthing but "yes."

It was about this time that reporters started to seriously ask Henry if he had dreams of running for the White House. He had a well-rehearsed stock answer. "If any man, or woman, who has entered Congress says they have never *thought* about Pennsylvania Avenue, I think they're being a little disingenuous. But this country has too many problems for me to think in great detail of such things. For instance, in Kazakhstan it was reported . . ." and then he would proceed to take a world event and simplify it so that a layperson could understand the problem and offer a viable solution.

He once had a rule against discussing world events because this old half-crazy congressman told him he should not, but I convinced him that doing so instantly made him look presidential. Reporters would then take the bait and say right on cue, "Senator Davis, you're sounding more and more like a presidential candidate every day." Which would give him the opportunity to show that smile of his and gracefully indicate that he had the best job title in America and did not see himself making any immediate changes in his career.

And then . . . well, then there was the debacle on *Meet the Press*.

I have known Teddy all of his adult life and I have never seen the look I saw in his eyes that morning. There's a saying, "Never let them see you sweat." Well, America almost watched him throw up, it was so bad.

Some of our friends suggested that he could have been drugged. Even he made suggestions to me in private that something may have been placed in his coffee, which is why even to this day he never drinks anything when he's on the road unless it's given to him by his inner circle.

Personally, I think that is a cop-out. I mean yeah, they kept tabs on a number of politicians and people in show business at one time. But could *they* be out to hurt the chances of a junior senator who had not declared his candidacy? I think he just flopped. It happens. Pavarotti has hit a bad note, The Greatest lost a couple of fights, and Teddy simply dropped the ball. They're all human. It was the most important appearance he had ever made and he screwed up. That's life.

When he got home that night he was a little emotional and acted a little strange, but after I teased him a little to get him in the mood, we made love beneath the stars. It was about 2:00 A.M. and he was very nervous at first. We have a privacy fence, but it is not too private. So after we played a little game, we were kissing in the living room and I undressed him very slowly, took his hand, and led him to the patio. He looked like a condemned man going to the guillotine at first, so I had to relax him.

As he was standing in the sliding glass doorway, I went down on him, and just as I'd expected, he was like putty in my hands from then on. We made love that night until about 5:00 A.M., and then it was too close to sunrise to drift off to sleep, so we talked. At first it was about politics, which I did not mind, but then we started talking about our fears.

"What's your biggest fear?" he asked me.

"What do you mean?"

"What scares you? More than anything else in this world?"

"Uew, I don't know. At this stage in life I guess something happening to my mom and dad? I'm a little concerned about Myles, also, up there in New York, with that old hooker he married. Why do you ask?"

"Umm, nothing. Just curious."

Then I looked at those thick black caterpillar eyebrows, and rubbed one of them slowly with my fingertips as I asked him, "So tell me. What's your biggest fear?"

"That I won't win in 2000."

He said it just like that. That he would not win the presidency of the United States in the year 2000 was his biggest fear. This was the dream he carried with him each and every day of his life, and anything short of it would be unacceptable. Even if he lost in 2000 and ran and won in 2004, I don't think it would bring him ultimate joy.

There's a saying that you should always shoot for the moon, because if you miss, you'll be among the stars. With Teddy, the stars would never be enough. It wasn't life or death for my husband. For him, it was more important than that.

After the *Meet the Press* fiasco, we turned into a national joke. It's said that it's a short motion from a pat on the back to a kick in the ass, and we found out just how short the move was. You could turn the dial to almost any station and hear a Davis joke that week.

On Leno: "The one good thing to come out of this is Senator Davis will be in the dictionary. Yeah that's right. Under the word "duh.""

On Letterman: "Hey, Paul, I hear Regis is leaving *Millionaire*. That's right. He's doing a new show for Fox with Henry Davis, *Who Wants to Tutor a Senator*!"

On *Politically Incorrect*: "But seriously, I kid the stupid!"

Saturday Night Live did a skit with an actor with a huge Buckwheat wig who stood behind the podium, and just kept repeating, "One's a day, I wanna be yo . . . umm . . . lemme see . . . don't tell me . . . Das right. I wanna be yoooo prezy-dent."

After the week of comedic injustice, "Have you heard the latest Davis joke?" was the talk coast to coast. Instead of people walking up to us in restaurants for autographs, they would pass by with pointed fingers and snickers. We would laugh at some of the funnier jokes when others were around and show them how big we were, but when the doors closed, the silence could hurt your ears. I think as much as it pained him, it hurt me more because it was unfair. He was the most intelligent man I knew, yet people were calling him a buffoon. Yes, he set high goals, but only because he wanted to help others. Never for personal gain. If people only knew how many times I'd seen him reach into his pocket and give a person a few dollars because he thought he or she needed it. But the people who watched the comedians taking liberties never knew this. All they saw was the blunder, and we knew we would have to live with that.

And then right after that fiasco, there was a report that he'd had an affair with a young lady in Atlanta. The irony of it all was, if we had not been in *Time* and on *Meet the Press*, it would have been a nonstory. Thus the price of fame.

Let me just state for the record, I believe in my husband and I believe he is faithful. And I even say that in spite of the fact that after his layover in Atlanta, he called me *Cheryl* while we were making love. I've never asked him about that night, nor will I, because I felt it was petty. I know he always has a lot on his mind and I think some women take things like that a little out of context. But having said that, I think any man, in the right situation, will do things he might be sorry for later. Especially when his intentions, character, or intelligence are called into question.

Do I think he had an affair with this Alicia Simmons person? No. Am I 100 percent sure he did not? Not hardly.

At a time when we should have drawn closer, sadly, we divided. For the first time since I'd met him, Teddy started to drink heavily. Scotch, bourbon, beer—if it had alcohol in it, it started to show up in our bedroom. I tried to get through to him, but for some reason he had built up a wall as he tried to resolve how to handle this situation by himself.

The breaking point came when he missed a flight out to the state of Washington for a conference on campaign finance. I knew that was an important meeting and one we had to be a part of. So when I got home and noticed him in his underwear sitting on the couch watching TV, I was dumbfounded.

"Henry? Henry, what are you doing home?" He said nothing. "Henry, the flight left an hour ago. Why are you here?"

"Leslie, I just don't feel too good," he said rubbing his stomach. "I had Penelope call and tell them I couldn't make it."

"You don't what? You don't feel too good? Are you kidding me?"

"Leslie," he said, and rubbed his temple as if he had a hangover, "don't start with me, okay? Not today."

"Don't! Don't! Don't start with you? You just missed a conference that will be live on fucking C-SPAN tonight in which you were going to be the keynote speaker and you say *don't fucking start with me?* Nigger, have you lost your mind!" I had never called him that name before, but I lost it. This was the perfect opportunity for him to redeem himself and he was sitting on the couch watching *Home Improvement* reruns.

Looking up at me with glossy eyes, he diverted his attention to Tim Allen.

"Oh, hell no!" I shouted at the top of my lungs. I wanted to shock him back into reality. "You and this goddamn TV have got to go!" And then I kicked over the television. I don't know where the strength came from because it was a mahogany big-screen TV. But I'd had enough, and the tube in the set exploded. "Poof!"

"What the fuck," Teddy said, and before I knew it, he had slapped me. Before I could hit the floor, my mind flashed back to a hot fall day when Kathleen knocked me over the ottoman. As I lay on the ground, before the pain could settle in, he stumbled his intoxicated body over to me trying to apologize.

This was never going to get beyond our four walls and I didn't want to hit him back. Needless to say, he had never done anything remotely close to this before, and I knew he hit me out of weakness. I could smell the alcohol on his morning breath and it made me nauseous. He was crying like a two-hundred-pound baby, and his hot tears fell on my cheek, which was pulsating. At this point I was still in shock. Everything was moving for us at warp speed. From emerging star, to national embarrassment, to the clean-and-sober *Time* magazine husband, to this Negro sitting around in his drawers putting his hands on me. I struggled to get him off of me by putting my elbow under his chin.

Then I looked down on him as he laid on the floor with

one foot on the couch, afraid it had all come to an end. But even in these darkest of hours I knew my love for him had no limitations.

How many things would you die for? Your mother, your religion, a child? Those are easy. Your country? Your core beliefs? Your career? Those are more difficult. In his weakest moments, Henry was actually dying before my eyes for a dream, and I knew I had to find a way to bring him back. No one else could do this. I'd married a man whom I loved more than life, and that man's dream was to become president in the year 2000. So in spite of everything that had happened, somehow, someway, I'd make it a reality.

Washington, D.C.
November 8, 2000
NBS News Studio
1:30 A.M. EST

"Well, America, with all of the talk about a possible assassination attempt on the life of Senator Henry Davis, we have not given you an update on the election. Here's an up-to-the-minute tally.

DAVIS	174	
STEINER	179	
BALDWIN	126	

"With all of the polling places closed in the continental United States, NBS News is reporting Ronald Steiner will win in the state of Oregon and Governor Tom wins in his home state of Arizona, but it may be all she wrote for the governor, who is running in single digits in the Golden State, and we are told they will be conceding the race within the hour. Now we will go back once again to the Fontainebleau Hotel and our correspondent, Butch Harper. Butch, can you hear me?"

"Yes, I can, Franklin. As you can see, it's much quieter

and there is an almost spectral aura hovering over the ball-room. After the assassin-in-hiding story broke, about half of the attendees left. The mood is mixed with the supporters who have stayed. Half of the individuals I have spoken with believe it to be a hoax, while the other half want to be in this hall, in spite of what may or may not happen with the alleged assassin, to be a part of history.

As a footnote to the story, Franklin, back in 1933, right here in Miami on the night of Franklin Roosevelt's first election, an assassin made an attempt on his life and actually shot Mayor Cermak of Miami. The gunman, Joe Zingara, was standing only a few feet away from the president-elect when a hundred-pound woman forced up his arm and pos-sibly saved the life of FDR. So there is a historical precedent for the fear in the hall tonight."

"Butch, has there been any official response from the Davis campaign regarding any of this?"

"Well, no. Throughout the campaign the Davis spokes-man, Ed Long, has been adamant about addressing issues as soon as they occur. A sort of 'nip it in the bud' approach to campaign management. But that has not been the case regarding this issue. The last time we in the press corps saw anyone from the Davis campaign, it was Penelope Richard-son addressing the prospects of a Davis divorce. So I do not know if their failure to address this issue is a sign that there are serious problems afoot or that they do not think such an issue merits a comment, and they are instead focusing on the numbers."

"Butch, do we know if the Davises are even in the hotel at this time? One report indicated they may have been taken to another spot downtown through a service elevator and into their secured limos, while another reported that an FBI helicopter was seen flying away from the roof of the hotel about twenty minutes ago, escorted by two other choppers. Can you confirm either of those stories?"

"I am sorry to report that I have heard both stories and I cannot confirm either. We were told by one source that the senator from Florida was seen with his wife speeding through downtown Miami in an unmarked vehicle. So as of now we are just awaiting an official word. Possibly the helicopter was a diversion. We don't know at this point."

"Interesting, Butch. One can only speculate as to what the mood is with Mr. and Mrs. Davis after all of the controversy with their marriage over the past few days, losing their home state of Florida, and now this suspected assassination attempt. NBS election night coverage will resume after this commercial break."

Carol City, Florida
The Allen Residence

Cheryl looked at her daughter, who was snoring on the couch, and kissed her softly on the forehead. She was abrupt at times and had made some bad choices in her life, but Cheryl knew so many times when she could not count on anyone else, Sarah was a constant force.

After hearing the latest on the campaign, she didn't want to watch anymore, but like a passerby gaping at a car accident, she could not turn away. She would say another prayer for Henry and then pace the room wondering where her husband was. Then the phone rang.

"Hello?"

After a pause, a dark voice said, "It's me. Can you talk?" Cheryl's heart stopped and she could not breathe as she lowered her body into the love seat in front of the muted television.

"Cheryl? Are you there?"

"Yes. Yes, I'm here. Oh my God, I am so scared for you. Is what they're saying true?"

"I don't know. It's something I can't think about. It's a part of this job and I've prepared myself . . . well, as much as one can prepare oneself for this. I always knew it would be a possibility."

"Henry, I'm so sorry. I'm so sorry things worked out like they did."

"Listen to me. Let's not go there. Things happened and that's that. There is nothing we can do to fix it. I just wanted to call you to say I am sorry. I really don't know why I'm sorry or what I am sorry for, I just know I need to apologize to you. I guess for dragging you into this mess. Reporters are swarming around me . . . I mean Leslie and me, like vultures trying to make everything they even think is happening headline news."

"Henry, you know you don't have to go there. I've loved you before I knew what love meant, so I know you would never intentionally hurt me."

"I take it *Brandon's* not home," he replied after a brief respite.

"No. He, well, he left hours ago and I have no idea where he went. We had a heart-to-heart talk tonight, and you know me, Henry."

"Are you crying?"

"You probably know me better than anyone in this world outside of Sarah and my mother, and you know I won't lie. I just can't do it. He asked me point-blank if I loved you."

"And you said?"

"Henry, I just told you. I can't lie to him or anyone else. I told him yes. And then he looked at me and asked me if I loved you more than I loved him. I told him love is different with everyone and that the love you share for your mom is different from the love you share— Well, then he got mad and asked me again. And I told him—" The tears chased each other down Cheryl's face. "I know I shouldn't love you. I know I don't want to love you. Actually, Henry . . . actually I hate loving you. But I do, Henry. For me, our love is for always." Wiping her nose with a tissue, Cheryl said, "I thought time would erase you from my mind. But the older I get, the *more* I think about us as kids and what we could have been as adults."

Henry held the phone in silence with the noise from the half-full room of staffers in the background.

"Henry, I have wanted to ask you this since we met again. Henry Davis. Do you love me? I mean really love me? I need to know."

CHERYL

In 1993, my world started to change, in many ways for the better. For starters, I got my degree in nursing, which I had worked so hard for. I bought a house in a subdivision of North Miami named Carol City, and Jesse James and the foster children I'd taken care of for so many years all left the nest one way or another. It was also the year Brandon Allen reappeared in my world.

I'd not seen Brandon and Chianti' since Darius's funeral. I knew they'd broken up because she saw me in a line at the bank and told me she was moving to North Dakota with a landscape artist. The last time I'd seen Brandon, he'd had six-inch dreads and a baby face, but now he was a full-grown man with a conservative banker haircut parted on the side and a fully matured body. And it had matured in all the right places.

I was at the swap meet when I saw this man dressed in denim jeans and a knit black turtleneck and vest. He caught my eye because he looked mixed. As if he were half man and half amazing. He moved like a long, slow, tender orgasm as he thumbed through the pants the way only men look for clothes, but I knew there was something about him that was vaguely familiar. And then he looked up, and although he had a mustache, I asked, "Brandon? Is that you?"

His mouth opened, and he said, "Cheryl Kingsley?" He seemed elated to see me as he ran around the long row of irregular pants in my direction. As he got closer, my first inclination was to shake his hand, but it was too late. I was already in his embrace, enjoying his cologne, which lingered in my senses and then disappeared like morning dew. As he released the physical hold on me, he looked in my eyes, and said, "So how have you been doing?"

"I'm doing fine, thank you. I hardly recognized you without the Bob Marley look."

"The Bob Marley . . . Oh, that's right. I had the dreads last time you saw me. Jeez, that's been at least seven or eight years, I guess, huh? I cut them off a while back. I'm with the Sheriff's Department now."

"Really? So you did go into law enforcement after all. Congratulations."

"Yes, ma'am. Thanks. How have you been? How's little Sarah?"

"She's in college now. Playing basketball for Tennessee State, believe it or not."

"Whoa. Good for her. I always knew she had it in her."

As we talked, he told me about his change of plans regarding going into the army as well as his intentions to move back to Atlanta to be closer to his family. The more he spoke, the more I thought of the possibilities. I hated to think that way because I knew a young man like him would see nothing in me, but every now and then I'd catch myself giggling when I had no reason to or getting just a little too touchy-feely when he would make an interesting point. But I loved grabbing his forearm and saying, "Really?" and "Are you serious?" His biceps were as large around as my thigh, and his hands were powerful, although they were as soft as if he'd never done a decent day's work in his life. As he told me of his promotion in the Sheriff's Department, I found myself looking at his lips. They were full, and masculine, and the top one was just a shade darker than the bottom. The more he talked with that sophisticated, slow sexy voice, the more I found myself wanting to . . .

"Don't you agree?" was all I heard him ask.

"Well, umm, yeah. I mean, of course." I wanted to change my panties and if I were Catholic, I would have had to say so many "hail-Mary-full-of-graces," I would have cramped my tongue.

I noticed him glance at his watch, then he looked at me, and said, "I had no idea it was this late. Tell me something."

I stared wordlessly with my lips slightly apart, ready to say yes. There was no way he was going to ask me . . .

"What's the best way to get to Key Biscayne from here? I don't want to run into traffic."

What was I thinking? As I gave him directions, he took out a pen and wrote them on a slip of paper he had in his pocket as a couple of women his age walked by, no doubt jealous, thinking he was giving me his number.

"Cool," he said. "This way I can avoid I-95."

"Yeah," I said as he put the piece of paper in his front pants pocket and even that looked seductive. My nipples itched and I wanted to squeeze my thighs a little tighter as he said, "Well, Mrs. Kingsley, you were *definitely* a sight for sore eyes."

"Same here."

"Are you done shopping?"

"No, I mean, yes."

"Me too. I thought they'd have a few more bargains today, but I guess we got here just in time for the leftover junk. Where're you parked?"

We walked to my car and I found myself once again giddy with excitement. But here I was, a few weeks shy of the big one, and I was acting like a child. I knew he was around twenty-seven or twenty-eight and I knew what he would want an almost forty-year-old woman for. But as we got to my car and he said good-bye, I felt even older than my birth certificate.

Sitting in the driver's seat, I slid in a Maze CD and put on my sunglasses as I buckled my seat belt to "Joy and Pain" and I tried to forget how I'd just acted. I wanted to forget about the fact that the last time I'd had a real date, Reagan was president. I knew my next birthday would be a tough one, but I didn't think I'd be ready for a blue special parking decal. *Check you out*, I thought as I looked in the mirror. *Acting like that over that li'l boy. You ought to be ashamed of yourself.* And then I was able to laugh at the situation. In hindsight, it felt good to feel attractive again, if only at a swap meet. I put the car in reverse and my hand on the passenger-side headrest to back out, when I was startled by a knock on my window. It was him.

"Sorry to bother you, Cheryl. This might sound strange," he said, and then put those husky, thick brown forearms on my car windowsill and squatted. "But I was sorta wondering if you were still in the phone book."

"Yessss," I purred, sorta like a kitten curling around one's leg.

"Cool." Looking down, he said, "Well, if it's all right, would you like to maybe"—then his eyes met mine—"go to dinner sometime?"

"Yes!" is what I screamed inside my body so loud I hoped he'd not heard the sound coming through my pores. "I dunno," is what my lips replied. "Give me a call sometime and we'll play it by ear."

Sarah excelled at three sports. Basketball, the discus, and volleyball. She accepted a hoops scholarship but dropped out because she said she just got tired of competing. I learned later she'd flunked out of school and was living off campus with a guy named Austin.

When she brought him to meet me for the very first time I was talking to Brandon on the phone. By this time we'd gone out for several months and Brandon had just asked me if I would like to drive up to Atlanta with him for the Labor Day weekend. Just as I was parting my lips to say yes, Sarah walked in the door with Austin.

"Brandon, that sounds like a good idea, but can I call you back? Something just came up." As I hung up the phone and looked at the *something* named Austin, I wanted to like him, but I couldn't. He walked into my house as if I owed him money. Looking down at the sofa, he wrinkled his nose up as if he were too good to sit on it and then sat on its arm.

He wore jeans that were pulled down to midthigh, silver on his upper and lower teeth, and a tight white tank top. He had a toothpick in his mouth that stayed in place even when he spoke, and he had what my daughter would describe as a zero. I just called it a bald head. As he sat, he kept massaging the inside of his forearm for some reason as I visually inspected the rubbed area for needle tracks. And on the outside of his arm was a tattoo of something that extended from his shoulder to his elbow; I had no idea what the drawing was. He may have called it art. I called it the aftermath of a flesh-eating bacterium.

To say the least, I was too shocked for words as Sarah

said, "So, Ma . . . this here is Aww-stin." I forced myself to smile, and I must say it warmed my heart to hear my daughter call me anything other than Cheryl for the first time in years.

"Austin . . . it's nice to meet you."

"Yo," he said, and tipped his shiny head. She'd told me just how cute she thought he was one night, but as I sat looking at his slanted eyes and sharp mouth, he looked like a human salamander.

Sarah sat so close to him it was hard to see where her body ended and his began. After staring at him with big doe eyes, she glared at me to keep the conversation going. Grasping for straws, I continued. "Sarah tells me you're in the computer industry?"

"The what industry?"

"No, Ma, I didn't say he was *in* the computer industry," she said, knowing that's what she had led me to believe. "I just said he worked at IBM. He's in the environmental control division."

"Environmental con-what?" he said, looking down on her head. Then he sucked his nasty silver-plated teeth and looked at his nails as he said, "If that what you wanna call being a fuc— I mean if that's got anything to do with a mop and a bucket, then that's what I do."

Sarah tilted her head and widened her eyes as I begged myself not to go off on both of them. Sarah had very few boyfriends in high school. Actually she only went out on one date and went to the prom alone where she got into a fistfight with a baseball player, so I was determined to give him every benefit of the doubt.

"So do you like working for IBM?"

"It's a job."

"I hear the benefits are good."

"It's a job."

I tried once again. "I had a friend who worked there. She said—"

"Like I said." And then he looked at his watch. "It's a job. Yo, Big Baby, if we're gonna make that concert on time, you might wanna get dressed." Before he came, Sarah had spent an hour picking out her clothes and putting on makeup. She even asked if she could try to squeeze her size tens in my size-seven imported leather boots, to no avail. Too embarrassed to even look at me, all she could say was, "Okay." Then walking to her room she said with a sad smile, "But I don't care what you say, I don't look like no Notorious B.I.G.!"

I glared at him as he said, "Sure you don't," with his eyes fixed on my child's behind, and then looked at me, shaking his reptilian face.

When Sarah returned that night, I decided just how I had to talk to her about Mr. Aww-stin. I tried to put my words together carefully, making sure I got my point across without patronizing her. When she walked in the door, I said, "Can we talk?" and she said, "Not now, Cheryl." She proceeded to walk into her room and lock her door; she did not come out the rest of the evening.

The next morning she was in the kitchen eating breakfast and I said good morning in hopes that she would initiate the discussion.

"We broke up last night."

"What happened?"

"I, umm . . ." And then she stared at the microwave pizza on her plate and balanced the Coors can on her knee. "I didn't like the way he talked to you, so I told him to go to hell."

I was astonished. I pulled up a chair, sat beside her, and said, "But why, honey?" knowing all along that I wanted to kiss her for making the decision.

" 'Cause he was in here acting like he was all that and it was just . . . I don't know. Disrespectful and shit, I guess."

"Well, darling, if that's what *you* wanted to do. He seemed like a nice enough kid to me. He was a little abrupt and misdirected, but I'm sure it was because he was nervous."

With a sarcastic smile she said, "Yeah, nervous. That's what it was."

I went back in my room to watch *Good Morning America* because they were running a feature story on a guy from

Miami who was due to be electrocuted and I'd read about the case in the newspaper. Brandon had actually worked at the crime scene and gave me a few of the gory details. Then I heard the phone ring. Before I could reach for it, Sarah was saying hello in the kitchen.

"What? Fuck you! Well, that's yo problem. What? No, see, you don't disrespect me like that."

I was shocked. Had she really quit him because of—

"Nigga, please, that bitch was all over you last night, and no, you were not blitzed. Nobody had to tell me anything, 'cause I saw her. What? That *was* you, fool! How many niggas look like . . . That was you, Austin! I guess now my eyes lying too?"

When I went to Atlanta the following week with Brandon, I was concerned about my daughter and hoped she would be okay while I was away. I felt guilty dating a man only a few years older than she was, and even talked myself out of going more than a few times. But then knowing my daughter, who always had a problem sharing her feelings, I thought a little distance might do both of us some good.

Once in Atlanta, I read in the newspaper about a special taping of *The Phil Donahue Show* in the CNN Center. I wasn't a fan of the show but I noticed that the controversial murder case from south Florida would be one of the topics of the show that week. When I shared that with Brandon he made a few phone calls to friends he knew in the Sheriff's Department and was able to get a security clearance and a couple of complimentary tickets.

Once inside the studio, I was shocked by the number of people who'd actually shown up. Everything looked like it does on the television except the set seemed a lot smaller. The topic that day was the death penalty and we could hear people discussing it all around us as we walked around the multimedia, state-of-the-art complex. In a hot dog line a lady with very dark roots, no eyebrows, and a tight halter top talked about how it wasn't a deterrent to crime. In the bathroom another lady repeated the eye-for-an-eye axiom from the Old Testament. And as we took our seats, a black man who looked like he was in the Nation of Islam sat beside us and told his friend loud enough for all to overhear the percentage of black men on death row. He knew statisically how many black men were executed for killing whites and how many white women were ever put on death row for killing a black man. "Did you know that ninety-eight percent of men on death row for rape are black men who raped *white* women!"

Phil walked in before they started taping. The room was buzzing as a few people said, "There he is! It's him," and all heads turned toward the middle-aged talk-show host with the signature white hair.

"You having a good time so far? You like that seat?" Brandon asked me, thinking I was annoyed by the facts being spewed by the Muslim in the next seat, who then started telling his friend and whoever else would listen just how electrocutions were against the will of Allah.

"I'm fine," I said, looking at the bright lights over the makeshift stage and leaning my head on Brandon's shoulder.

"Y'awll just wait," the brother repeated as he tapped his finger in the air as if he were tapping on a door. "Wait till I get my chance to speak. I'm going to tell them how it tis. You can kill the man, but you can't kill the truth, my brother. Truth lives on. The truth shall never perish," he said, shaking his head and then tapping his fist on his thigh.

I noticed Phil with his wife, Marlo Thomas, on the floor level speaking to a few members of the audience and then talking to his staff. And then from nowhere it seemed, he appeared like a bright light in a tunnel. He was in the midst of and head and shoulders above about five other people and he looked stunning. If Hollywood had directed the moment it would not have been more memorable. For the first time in more than twenty years I saw Henry Louis Davis in the flesh. When he walked out, although he was a senator, he looked presidential. His staffers were talking to him and showing him color-coded index cards, but he seemed more concerned with looking into the crowd. I'd told Brandon I knew him from high school, but I never told him just how well I knew him. As his eye scanned the crowd, he looked right at me, but then his attention was diverted by a lady holding her face and stammering as if he were one of the Beatles.

"Well, look who showed up," Brandon said, patting me on the knee. "Your schoolmate. Can you see him?"

As I moved my leg I didn't want to tell Brandon about the relationship Henry and I had shared because I didn't want him either to think I was full of it or feel I was comparing him in some way to a childhood boyfriend. I also feared that if he knew me as well as I thought he was starting to, when he asked me about him, he'd see just how deep the feelings ran.

"Yeah, I see him," I replied with nonchalance.

"Do you think he remembers you?"

"It's been a while. I don't know." Henry ignored his staffers and started talking to people who were near the stage. A few came over with cameras and asked him to pose for pictures or to sign various objects for them. Then someone in the audience called out his name and said, "Over here." Even from sixteen rows up, I could see this was what he lived for. He went to the young lady who'd screamed out his name and shook her hand as her friend searched for something to write with. After signing his name, he walked up the next row and started talking to people as if he'd known them for years. Women were especially excited to pose with Henry and allowed their husbands or boyfriends to take their picture with the first African-American senator from the deep South since Reconstruction.

He walked up to the fourth level and I was nervous and excited. What would I say to him? I had no idea. I knew he had to go on TV, so I didn't want to startle him, but then I thought, *What if he doesn't even remember me?* As he walked up to row eight, he was halfway up to us and I could feel tumbleweeds rolling in my throat.

"Cheryl, looks like he's gonna come up here, so you'll get to see him again after all," Brandon said with a smile. I had no idea what to do. I started worrying about my makeup, but I didn't want Brandon to think I was trying to get cute for Henry. And then I thought, *What the hell,* and I reached in my purse for my compact. As I flipped it open and reapplied my face, Brandon laughed and said, "Well, check you out." I could care less since he was on mute.

Then the brother from the Nation on my right stood up and said, "Mr. Davis! Senator! My brother! Can I have a minute with you? Can you explain why since 1990, eighty white convicted death row felons have been exonerated! Why the death penalty is just court-sanctioned genocide!" He spoke so loud every head in our section turned to his direction. "Yo! Can I get a minute?"

Henry looked at him with that smile I knew so well and then held up two fingers to indicate that he'd be with him momentarily. Then he glanced at me, or at least I thought he did. As I put my compact away, there was a panic riot in my chest. This man whom I'd fallen asleep thinking about most nights of my life was only four steps away from our level. And then I saw her. I'd seen her on television a couple of times, and while I hated to admit it, Leslie Davis was even more beautiful in person. She appeared to be two or three years older than he, but other than that, she looked like a television reporter dressed in a clearly expensive aubergine pin-striped suit. She called his name with a smile on her face and stepped down two steps so they could speak. Then Henry looked at Leslie's watch as a strawberry-blonde staffer huddled with them. Henry squinted his eyes as he looked in our direction when the Muslim to the right of me stood up again, waving his arms fanatically.

"There you are," Henry said loudly so the brother would understand in the noisy studio. "I'm sorry . . . but I have to get ready for the taping."

"See!" the Muslim replied with a smile. "That's how it *always* is for the black man in America! First to die . . . last to be heard!" As the section laughed, the brother sat down and Henry Louis Davis the Second walked down the stairs holding his wife's hand and my heart almost returned to normal. And then he quickly looked over his shoulder back in my direction, and while our eyes did not meet, I knew he was looking for me.

Phil assumed his position at what looked to be a wooden dinette table, and Henry spoke to even more staffers with index cards before it was obvious he was telling them that he'd heard enough. Then a cosmetician came onstage and started to apply a few more dabs of makeup. As she was finishing, Leslie walked over to Henry, and we all watched as she told her to take off some of the makeup from certain places on his face. Then she looked up at the lighting and assumed the role of Henry Davis's personal lighting director as well. As the light shining directly on top of his head was dimmed, she returned to her seat just moments before the producer gave Phil a countdown.

"Hello, America, and hello, Atlanta!" The large orange portable applause signs beamed, and just as one of the producers had instructed us before the show, we all started to clap wildly. "I'm Phil Donahue and today"—he paused for effect—"we are going to discuss an issue that has been with us as long as we've had taxes. That's the death penalty. As many of you may know, in two weeks Juarez Bechuanas will be put to death in Florida's electric chair. We thank the warden at the Florida State Penitentiary for granting us the opportunity to speak with Mr. Bechuanas live via remote." At the back of the stage and on several smaller monitors for the audience appeared the light-brown freckled face of a thirty-year-old prisoner who faced death. His eyes were closed. Other than the small tattoo of a dagger in a heart on his neck, and the bright orange prison attire, he looked just like the guy next door. However, he sat uncomfortably in a chair with his fingers laced and hands cuffed in shackles bound to a chain around his waist. After a short pause, he smiled and said, "Thank you, Mr. Donahue, for having me."

"I should also explain," Phil added in a deaconlike somber tone, "that Mr. Bechuanas was accosted by several inmates the first year he was incarcerated, and the brutal beating left him blind." As Phil spoke, Juarez looked upward at a light in front of him and for the first time allowed the audience to see his disfigured eyes.

To my right I heard, "You see this man. This is foul."

"We also have," Phil continued as Mr. Bechuanas's face on the monitor was replaced by a curly-headed, olive-complexioned gentleman, "a professor of journalism from Northwestern, Professor David Protess. I am sure Mr. Protess would be proud of the fact that according to the American Bar Association, he and his class have been victorious in more death-row appeals than any other group of individuals in the country. Please welcome Professor David J. Protess." The lights flashed and the crowd gave its approval. "And last but not least, we are also joined by a man who is from your neighboring state of Florida. He was . . ." And then he looked at Henry and asked, "Do you ever get tired of hearing 'the first since Reconstruction' before you are introduced? I know that would drive me out of my com-*plete* mind." The audience chuckled as Henry smiled. "We have as our guest the *distinguished* senator from Florida. Senator Henry . . . Louis . . . Davis!" The crowd clapped loudly as the neon applause light flashed rapidly and a few of his staffers stood in an attempt to incite a standing ovation that did not occur.

"Let's just dive right into this topic, because we have much ground to cover," Phil said, leaning back in his chair and rubbing his palms on the wooden armrest.

Looking at his note cards occasionally as well as the Tele-PrompTer, Phil laid out the facts surrounding the case against, and the appeal for, Juarez Bechuanas. And then he looked up at the monitor, and said, "Mr. Bechuanas, you have twelve days, sir. Less than two weeks before the state of Florida requires you to pay the ultimate penalty for a crime you still claim you did not commit. Please tell us, sir, the facts, and why you think the Republican governor of your state, Robert Martinaro, should grant you a stay of execution."

As he spoke, I watched Henry the entire time. I had no idea what his position would be on the case, but I watched him with an impassive look in his eyes watching the monitor and then with compete confidence, he sat taller, crossed his legs at the ankle, and rested his hands in his lap. From his posture he looked like a cheetah in tall grass ready to pounce on its prey.

Bechuanas spoke to the camera and his eyes moved from down to up just as a sighted person would read text left to right. He spoke calmly and respectfully, as if he'd accepted the fate that appeared to lie before him. "So, Mr. Donahue, suh," the condemned man continued, "yes, I think the gov'na should grant the stay for at least another six months, and then if the facts are not as Mr. Protess and his class say, then although I did not commit these here crimes I've been charged with, at least the process would have run its course and I'll accept whatever happens."

As he finished speaking, the room was pin-drop silent. And then Phil said, "On that note we will be back right after this message." The red light went off on top of the huge cameras on tiny wheels and Brandon leaned over and said, "It's a damn shame."

"What do you mean?"

"I mean I was there the night of the murders. I saw the place and I tell you, it was a weird feeling just standing in that room. Blood was splashed on the windows, even dripping from the ceiling fan," he said as he grabbed my hand more for support than for comfort. "I was never a really religious person before walking in that room. But as I stood in there and saw them put pieces of flesh in the a bag, you felt like it wasn't a person who'd done that. It seemed like the devil himself had been in the room. There was a heat in there even though it was below twenty that night," he said, shaking his head. "The room had this satanic feel to it that . . . it's hard to explain. The way bro is talking up there, I would like to believe he didn't do it, but they found his skin under her nails, his blood mixed with hers in his car, and the murder weapon with only his prints on it. Besides, what no one even talks about is the fact that he signed a confession the day after he was caught. He signed an affidavit saying he committed the murders, but that was before Anmesty International or the ACLU or whatever came into the picture and got the confession suppressed. I ain't buying it. Plus, when you add to that his police record, which was not even entered into evidence, if he don't fry, no one should."

I saw the producer give Phil the countdown. Five, four, three, and with a silent count he waved his fingers down, two, one. After the applause and theme music subsided, Phil looked into the camera and said, "We're back."

Then Phil reintroduced the journalism professor, who seemed to want to talk as much as Henry. He gave statistics of how many men claimed to be innocent in the past years and were put to death who he and his students felt without a shadow of a doubt in his heart were innocent. He brought up each questionable point surrounding the case and why he and his honors class who'd investigated the case for the past two semesters thought that Mr. Bechuanas should not only be given a stay, but clemency as well.

And then there was a pause as Phil looked at Henry and smiled dramatically. "Well, well, well. Mr. Democrat-Senator-from-Florida. This crime was committed in *your* state. Actually, in the district from which *you* were once elected to Congress. You and your democratic brethren and sisters who have supported *every* liberal cause since the creation of your party are typically on Capitol Hill championing the charge against the death penalty. But you are here to tell us that *you* support the Republican governor's decision. I must say to you," Phil said, leaning back and lacing his fingers behind his head with a look of bewilderment on his face, "for a senator with your voting record, sir, and, in all due respect, with forty percent of the individuals on death row being black men just like you, more than a few people around this country are surprised by your view on . . . this . . . issue."

The brother next to me caught the attention of one of Phil's assistants holding a microphone. As the young lady walked toward him he said, "Y'awll just wait till I hit them with this. I can't believe you got a devil fighting for this brother's life and a brother trying to kill him!"

Henry's demeanor was somber and much different from the one the audience had witnessed signing autographs earlier. He turned to the people in the audience and spoke to them as if we were friends invited over to his home for a cookout and the subject just happened to come up.

"First of all, Phil, I'm honored to be a part of this important debate. And let me say from the outset that I've *never* spoken publicly against a convicted person's attempt to get a stay of execution. But I thought and prayed about this case long and hard before making my views public." With those words, Henry stood up and brought his fingers thoughtfully to his lips. As he did, we could see the producer's surprise that he had not remained seated as a crew member with handheld camera ran to a point on the floor to get a better view. Henry continued. "But if there has ever been such a case, this unfortunately is the one, and now is the time to make my opinions known." Henry spoke to the audience of the ills of the death penalty and agreed with the professor that there were many imperfections in the judicial system. He briefed the audience on the mountain of physical evidence against Mr. Bechuanas, including the eyewitness who was a member of the clergy and a couple who worked together throwing newspapers who testified that they saw him in bloody clothes the morning of the murders. As he spoke, I thought back to the first night we talked on the phone and how he always seemed so in command of himself and others.

Then Senator Davis sat back down in front of Phil and told us how Mr. Bechuanas had put his wife in the hospital on seven different previous occasions.

"Seven times," he said passionately. "Seven times this lady was treated for broken bones and lacerations. Seven times the system had an opportunity to save this woman's life. He served time for beating her only once because she would always leave the hospital and bail him out of jail. According to court documents, once he beat her because she bailed him out too late. This woman has already paid the ultimate penalty that society can demand. Why? Because she loved Mr. Bechuanas more than the system or even he loved her and their child.

Something went horribly wrong here, Phil. Seven times," he repeated, then paused. "Tell me, when do you stop beating someone who loves you? Four times? Five times? How about after six times? Well, for Mr. Bechuanas it was the seventh time, because now she's dead.

"The court records show Mr. Bechuanas out drinking on one of the coldest nights of the year. He walked into their two-bedroom apartment and, according to the pastor who overheard the fight, started arguing with his wife. This time he accused her of cheating on him. The autopsy shows he punched her and then he took three bullets, put them into the chamber of his .22-caliber pistol, and placed it at the base of his daughter's skull. After he shot her, he tried to shoot his wife, but the gun jammed. So what does he do? He pistol-whips her to within an inch of her life, although even that was not enough because she was a witness to a murder. So then he did things with a knife that even I cannot repeat on this show."

Phil tried to say something, but Henry was fully in control. He held up his palm and said, "Phil, I'm sorry this happened. I'm sorry that we even have the topic on the table today. But in my opinion, if such laws are going to be on the books, the state has no other recourse but to follow through with its duty. My wife and I," he said, looking back at Mr. Bechuanas's face on the monitor, "will pray that your soul finds peace, sir."

Phil nodded his head and then looked for one of his assistants and a question from the audience. As a man across the aisle from us spoke into the mike, the Muslim near me whispered in the associate's ear and quietly returned to his seat. If Henry had moved this brother, I knew that afternoon he had indeed moved many people across the country and around the world.

Forty-five minutes later the cameras went black, the oversized white lights over the stage dimmed to gray all at once, and people headed for the exits. I immediately looked to see where Henry was going. Would he head back into the audience? If he did, this time I would not let him get away without at least saying hello. But he didn't. As soon as the TV lights went out, he and Leslie were whisked away by their entourage. Brandon held my hand and asked if I wanted him to use his security clearance to get us backstage.

Finally I would have my opportunity to see Henry up close and personal. What would I say to Leslie? What would she say to me? How would Brandon react knowing that Henry and I were more than simply classmates? "No," I replied. "Let's just go."

As we walked through the crowd and a couple of women spoke aloud about how fine Henry was, I thought about the day I'd seen him running the stadium steps. How he ran to the top as hard as he could, full speed, never looking back and never taking a break. With the image of an eighteen-year-old dreamer replaced by one in the present, I knew he was still running full speed to the top and in regard to our for always, he was unfortunately not looking back.

Chapter 5

"This is NBS News continuing election-night coverage, and I am Franklin Dunlop giving you the news on two late-breaking stories.

First, it was leaked to the press approximately two hours ago that there is allegedly an assassin somewhere in the vicinity of the Fountainebleau Hotel with the intention of assassinating the Democratic candidate for the presidency. We must note that the story has not been confirmed by the Davis campaign, Secret Service, or the FBI. This network, as well as others, was advised by very reliable sources that this individual has followed the Davis campaign for months and may have been the party responsible for the firecracker-mixed-with-gunfire attack on the candidate in Omaha several months ago, but we have not had a confirmation of that story as of yet.

"Also Governor Tom Baldwin of Arizona is trailing badly and is at the statehouse in Phoenix to deliver what we expect will be his concession speech. We will send you now to our West Coast correspondent, who has done an exceptional job for us all night long, Vincent Winslet. Vinny, what's the word from Phoenix?"

"Well, Franklin, as can be expected, the mood is somber. The governor's supporters knew if they had any chance to pull out a victory, they had to win in New York and carry either Ohio or Pennsylvania. When both those states went into the Democrat and Republican pockets, they knew for them California was irrelevant.

Now, as you can hear, the crowd is starting to chant "Tom-oh-four, Tom-oh-four!" Obviously an indication that they would like the governor to run in the year 2004. However, I think the chances of that happening at his age of seventy-three are unrealistic. Now I am told that Governor Tom—"

"Vincent, I must cut you off. We have a late-breaking story from—. Judy! Judy, are you still there!"

"Yes, I am, Franklin. About three minutes ago a helicopter was perched on the top of the Four Seasons Hotel, supposedly to take the vice president and his family to another location, and there are reports that gunfire was exchanged. That's right. Gunfire! We do not know if there were any casualties at this time. Apparently an individual or individuals were positioned on the roof and as the vice president and his family came out and got into the helicopter, they were ambushed. The helicopter carrying Steiner's family took off for an unknown destination, and soon after, several police choppers descended on the rooftop."

"Judy, were there clues earlier that this might happen?"

"No. In fact, we here in Chicago were listening to the news reports out of Florida and wondering how that situation was going to play itself out. People here are now speculating that the FBI created a diversion on purpose to throw off the assassin or assassins here. We don't know at this point because that's just a rumor and it is much too early to tell. As I speak, Franklin, a fifth—count it, fifth—helicopter has just landed on the top of the hotel. I am going to try to get outside to speak to the head of the FBI for the state of Illinois if I can. As soon as we have more information, we will let you know."

Fountainebleau Hotel
Presidential Suite

"Excuse me?"

"Do you love me, Henry?"

"Cheryl, you know you taught me the true meaning of the word. To this day I say your name and feel a shiver, and I know I will love you for always. What we shared was magic. But I have—" There was a pounding at the door. Cupping the receiver, he said, "One second, I'll be right out." Staring at the Monet replica on the wall, he continued, "But I have a wife now. What we had was so long ago, Cheryl. Yes, I love you and I always will. But I am *in* love with Leslie." It was the first time he'd said her name that night.

"Henry, open the goddamn door. They think Steiner was shot!" Herbert yelled.

"What!"

"Yeah, they're showing it live on NBS! Get out here!"

"Cheryl, I gotta go. Baby, I'm sorry for coming back into your life . . . and hurting you this way. You didn't deserve this. I love you."

"I love you back," Cheryl said before hanging up the phone first.

Damn. Henry took a deep breath to release some tension as he tried to regain his bearings by rhythmically tapping his fingertips together.

"Henry, come out here, man, this is important!" Herbert screamed.

Sitting on the chair next to his private line, Henry wanted so badly to call his wife. Saying her name was all it took to heighten the longing and to remind him of how wrong he was for torturing her.

"Damn, Henry, would you please come out here! The FBI needs to talk to all of us!"

Henry entered the silent room that was filled with his senior staff and advisers. In the back of the room was Dirk Gallagher and his cowboy-hatted Lone Star contingency.

"Hello, Senator Davis. My name is Agent Mills and this is Agent Haggerty," announced a slender man with long, dark sideburns. "We were asked to give you and your staff a briefing on what is going on tonight." Looking around, Agent Mills asked, "Where is Mrs. Davis?"

"She's in her suite with her brother," Penelope said, looking at both agents and then Henry. "She's not feeling well."

"Ma'am, could you send someone down to get her?" Agent Mills requested. "It's very important that she be here."

Motioning with his hand for Penelope to remain seated, Henry glanced at the larger-than-usual bulge in the agent's jacket and asked, "What's this all about?"

"As I am sure you've been informed by the media, there was an attempt on the life of Vice President Steiner. According to our reports, he was injured. However, at this time he's being rushed to an undisclosed hospital for medical attention. Now. What does this have to do with you? I've been advised, sir, that the threat against you has been upgraded from a level three to a five. We believe Calvin Arthur is in the city, although we do not know at this time if he is in the vicinity. It is our hope that with the extra security, he has aborted his plans. But since they flashed his photo on the news, we've been inundated with hundreds of phone calls throughout the night from people who have seen him, or think they've seen him." For a brief moment Agent Mills broke his Secret Service monotone and said, "The threat, sir, *is* real. Now, this is what we would like to propose. We can get you out of here, into a service elevator and through the kitchen into a bulletproof limo. The route will literally be lined with agents and we can virtually guarantee that you and your wife will be able to get into the limo and out of this place safely."

Weary from the taxing night, Henry leaned against a wall wearing a well-wrinkled cotton shirt with his hands in his pockets jingling coins, and said quietly to no one in particular, "Does the phrase 'be careful what you ask for' mean anything to anyone?" Then raising his voice, he demanded, "Mills. Who is responsible for this? Who's behind these assassination attempts?"

"Sir," he replied after looking at Haggerty, "we're not at liberty to say. I can only tell you the danger is real and is now classified as a level-five threat. I'm sorry. I wish I had clearance to say more."

Henry slowly stroked his eyebrow, and said firmly, "I'm not going."

"What!" everyone in the room gasped collectively.

"Henry, you can't be serious!" Herbert demanded, fearing for his brother's safety. "I know you're brave and all, but sitting in this room like a sitting duck and waiting for whoever or whatever to come in here makes no sense at all! What if he's connected to some terrorist group? They could just run into the ballroom and open fire. You know how those—"

"Ahh, listen here, son," Dirk Gallagher said to Agent Mills. "Get me an extra-large vest and about fifteen more for my folks. And let me know when our limos will be ready. We want to get on the first thing smoking out of this hellhole back to civilization."

"Well, sir," Agent Mills replied after a glance at Haggerty, "we don't want to have a motorcade. That would cause too much attention, so we only arranged for two limos at the back entrance of the hotel. One for you and one for the Senator and Mrs. Davis."

All eyes fell on Henry once again. Henry looked around at the room, then at his brother, and said softly, "Come in here a second."

As the door to the master suite closed, Dirk Gallagher shouted, "Hell, this is his hometown. Let 'em stay. Give us his fucking limo!"

After he walked into the bedroom, Henry went over to the stereo, turned it up loud, and returned to his brother. Leaning close to his ear, he said, "Isn't this Kafkaesque? I mean, is it just me? When has there *ever* been an assassination attempt that was leaked to the press beforehand? When have there been two attempts in one day? Herbert, maybe I am just stressed, but something is going on. I can feel it."

Herbert looked at Henry with his eyebrows drawn closer to each other. "What are you saying? You think it's a set-up? Why would they set you up?"

"Why was King or X set up? Were John and Bobby's deaths coincidences?" he whispered in his brother's ear. "Change is *always* harder than doing the same old thing.

Maybe what we're trying to do is too much for this country to handle."

Herbert looked confused as his brother walked back across the room, turned off the stereo, and opened the door. "Guys," Henry said, "I want a few of my top people to take my limo and get out of here. Ed, you and Penelope are free to go. You can do most of your work from the phone."

"Sir, it would really make us feel more comfortable if you and Mrs. Davis would—"

"Enough, Mills. I'm not going and now I'm extending the invitation to my people."

"Listen, guys," Dirk Gallagher shouted to the agents above the milling voices in the room, "when you're ready to stop *fucking* around in here, just let me and the lady know. We'll be in our suite."

"What a fuck'n ass!" Herbert murmured.

"What did you say to me, son?" The large Texan bristled.

"Fuck you and everything that favors ya!"

"Herbert!" Henry shouted, grabbing his brother's balled-up fist. "He's drunk. Don't sink to that level. Ed, Penelope, find a few others and get out of here."

"No," Penelope said. "I'm here no matter what."

Ed looked at Penelope and then back to Henry. "Sir, I really think you should get out of this place. A level five is as serious as it gets."

"Do me a favor, Ed. Get in the limo and go home to Heather. Okay?"

Ed looked at Henry and back again at Penelope before nodding his head yes. Looking ashamed, he said, "Jeez Louise, guys, I have a family at home, two kids in college, *and* a mortgage. I can't take this chance."

"Ed," Henry said as he walked across the room and placed both hands on his press secretary's shoulders. "There's no need to apologize. You have been with me through thick and thin. Do me a favor. Find about eight or nine more people and stuff them in that thing and get out of here. Okay? Please . . . do this for me," he said with a smile. "It's late and I'm tired, but I think this is for the best."

As Henry walked back toward the inner room, Penelope

and Herbert followed him. "Herbert, do me a favor," Henry said without looking back. "Have someone get some fresh granola up here and turn on those televisions! We've got an election to win. And, Penelope?" Henry said, rubbing his thumb slowly over his thick black eyebrow.

"Yes?"

"Get my wife on the phone. Please?"

HENRY

Nineteen ninety-five. It was the year before a presidential election year and the year after we won reelection to the U.S. Senate. I basically ran unopposed, as a Republican state representative from the Panhandle put up token opposition.

Although I was leading, according to Mason-Dixon's statewide polls, I campaigned harder than I had in my first run for office. This time we wanted to win 75 percent of the vote, which would give us a mandate and thrust the name Davis in the forefront of the presidential hopefuls in 2000.

The Republican candidate was a former TV reporter and played well to the camera. When Herbert negotiated with his campaign manager for a statewide televised debate, Herbert agreed to do something I would have never authorized. My opponent and I were to sit on the stage, with just a moderator who would toss out a subject such as "the economy," and we would have a true debate with no time limits. Two friends of mine in the Senate called and asked why I would take such a chance when I was already leading my opponent two-to-one in the polls. I concealed my concern by telling them I thought this was what the people of Florida wanted to see. Although this format was reminiscent of the Lincoln-Douglas debates and I was honored by my brother's belief in me, Abe didn't have a satellite feed that could send any of his mistakes instantaneously around the globe.

The night of the debate the moderator walked between us and said the two words that made my opponent's eyes twinkle. "Affirmative action." The state representative looked in my direction and began his well-rehearsed response. "As you know, Senator Davis, I have come out staunchly against affirmative action. I think it's absurd and illogical to use discrimination . . . to show that discrimination . . . no matter how it is presented, is wrong. I don't believe you have children, but Fanny and I have a little grandboy who just turned four. I've said from the beginning that one of the reasons I am running for this office is to leave behind a better world for him. One day we will have to explain to his generation why we have government-sanctioned discrimination." And then he paused dramatically and spoke to me while turning toward the camera. "So please explain it to me as if I were a four-year-old. Why do you see the need for such a measure in our country at this time?"

As he finished, there was thunderous applause, although the moderator had advised beforehand that there should be no show of support from the audience. I waited for them to quiet, looked into his eyes, and gave him a respectful nod of the head. Then I turned toward the camera and said, "I thank you for asking that question, Representative Edwards, because it is one of the most important issues facing our generation. I feel the only way to explain it is like this. I am sure you would agree that historically people of color in this country have been disadvantaged in many ways. Let's look at sports since the World Series just ended.

In baseball you have one player from one team facing nine from the opposition on the field. Now, the batter must *earn* his way on base. If he hits the ball and does not make it to first, he's out. Point-blank, end of discussion. But if by chance there is a *tie* . . ." And then I paused and looked at my opponent. "If there is a tie, Representative Edwards, since it was nine players on the field against one in baseball, the batter is viewed as being *disadvantaged* and the tie goes to the runner. The affirmative action laws as they are written will not—and I repeat because this is often overlooked— will not give *anything* to *anyone* who has not earned it. But if there is a tie between two applicants in terms of qualifications, what it does give is an opportunity for women and people of color to simply stay in the game."

When I backed away from the microphone, the applause was so loud there was a squeal in the audio and I knew a mandate was a distinct possibility.

After my victory, I went up to New York City for a meeting with JFK Jr. and the editorial staff of *George* magazine as well as *Newsweek* and *Black Enterprise*. Herbert also made sure he got me back in front of Tim Russert and *Meet the Press*. As badly as I did the last time in town, I did well this time. I was comfortable with the questions and Russert shook my hand afterwards and asked if I could do the show again the Sunday before the next general election.

Leaving Rockefeller Center, I walked down the street and a few people recognized me. A couple even wanted autographs, but in a city so used to celebrities, most people just walked on by.

Then I noticed a lady standing in front of a department store across the street. She moved slowly, and as I saw her scratch her backside, it was obvious she had not bathed in some time. I looked at my watch and saw that I had some time before the limo would pick me up and take me to the airport to fly out to the West Coast. I went to a diner, bought a couple of sandwiches, and walked back outside to find the homeless woman asking a tall blond for money. The lady wore a designer cowboy hat, faded jeans, and had one of those dogs that was not much bigger than a rat with a bad perm, and it was wearing a gold-tone collar around its neck. I realized at that moment that we live in a society where pets are treated better than people. All of a sudden I lost my appetite.

I stood to the side out of the way of the flood of people walking past me and watched as this lady asked each and every individual entering and exiting the boutique for change. As they past, they'd step by as if they were deaf or they would pat their pockets and shrug their shoulders to save their own conscience. As I watched, she must have addressed twenty people, and not one gave her a red cent.

I crossed the street to get a little closer to her. I just wanted to hear what she was saying to these people to cause some of them to make the faces they were making. She looked to be in her mid forties and her skin was pale. Not like a white person who's sick, just a yellowish, white-fish, eggshell pale. She wore a windbreaker over several sweaters, although it was a warm day in Manhattan, and one shoulder of the windbreaker ironically draped off of her like a rich woman's mink, exposing the dirty lining inside of it. She wore Burberry polyester pants, she was barefoot and walked with a limp. Between prospects she scratched her head furiously as if she was trying to get something out of her hair, and when she pulled her fingers out she smelled them. I thought, *My God, how dirty do you have to be to smell whatever is in your hair?*

As I stood at a newspaper stand in front of the store next door so as not to make eye contact with her, I listened closely to what she was saying.

"Sir, I'm sorry to bother you, but do you have a spare dollar?"

"No, I just spent my last buck," the man who wore a silk navy ascot replied.

"Sir, I'm sorry to bother you, but do you have a spare dollar?"

Walking so fast he almost tripped, the next prospect ran out into traffic to hail a taxi.

"Ladies, I'm sorry to bother you, but do you have a spare dollar?"

"Bish, please!" the woman said as she and her friend with a bag full of clothing laughed. "Get your ass a spare job."

"Yeah, take yo po white-trash ass down to the damn welfare office," her friend said with a laugh as they walked away.

And then Henry noticed a blind double amputee in a wheelchair with a tin cup extended and a crudely written sign hanging from his neck that read, "I thank my God every day that you can see." One of the ladies almost walked into him as the other said, "Shit, these muttas coming out the cracks in the pavement today, child. You can *never* find a decent can of Raid when you need it. Can you?"

The homeless woman never changed expression as she

asked the next person and the next person and the next the
same question and got the same result.

"Ma'am?" I said, walking up behind her. "Here's a dollar." She looked at me and her eyes showed a joy I had not
seen in them previously. "I also have an extra sandwich.
You can have it under one condition."

"What?" she said, awaiting the catch to my kindness.

"You have to sit over here with me and eat it."

"That's all? You don't want no head . . . or nothing?"

As the words came out, I was glad I had not eaten, because I would have lost my lunch. "Aha, no. I just want a
little company."

As we sat, I smelled her. Let's just say I can only use a
phrase I once learned from a Kansas farmer. She smelled
like urine in a rusty bucket. But I sat and talked to Ora for
half an hour.

She was only twenty-seven, had no children, but was once
married. She and her husband had had a house in Iowa and
a Chevrolet wagon with wood on the side. They were married for two years, but fell into credit card debt, which eventually bankrupted them. One night she left and came to
New York looking for stardom on Broadway, where she got
involved in drugs. "Tits," as she called them. "I think I
smoked up a little bit of my brains too," she said. She was
very proud of the fact that she had kicked hard drugs all
by herself and was not *tricking* anymore. "I still smoke,
though," she said. "I don't even consider weed tits. But I
ain't crazy. A great man named Oscar Wilde wrote, if you
destroy the thing you love"—she took pleasure from the
surprise in my eyes at her knowing the quote—"the thing
you love destroys you. I know I done destroyed me some
weed, so there you go." And then she looked around for a
potential beggee.

"I shot heroin before I even smoked weed. First time I
was out turning, this bitch came up and asked if I had any
shit. I told her I snorted and then she said she didn't have
time for that. A little while later, I saw her in the alley
shooting it in a vein in her waist. She said all of her other
veins were too messed up. I swore up and down right then

and there I would never do any drug I had to shoot in my body. Well, I got to the point where I shot in my arms, fingers, thighs and then between my toes, and then my waist, and then the only place I could do it was to shoot it in right in my neck. After doing it like that for a while . . . I thought I should stop.

"And I would do enti-thang . . . you hear me? Enti-thang to get a buzz in dem days. I used to trick for Jacksons. That would buy me about two packets and I was using about eighteen or nineteen of dem packets a day. That just tells you how much I had to turn. Sometimes the men wouldn't have a Jackson, so I did it for ten and a few times even five or a Washington. It didn't matter 'cause I had to have dem snaps.

"You know something?" she continued, as she vehemently scratched her head again and then the back of her neck. "I been called so many names, when someone says 'ho,' 'white trash,' or 'cracker bitch,' I look around like it's my name. I guess regular people get upset with that kinda stuff, but I don't. I've had people pour hot coffee on me while I was sleeping in the rain, I have had people spit on me just for the hell of it, look at me and run as if I were a monster or something or cover their kid's eyes as if I were contagious as they pass by me. I used to have feelings; not anymore. That's the first thing you lose when you live on the street." She looked at the entrance of the store as a tall black man came out carrying a tennis racket over one shoulder and a white girl on his other arm.

"You know something?" she said, looking back at me. "I also used to read the Bible. But I don't no mo 'cause I don't see how God could let me go through what I have all these years on the streets. I remember somewhere in the New Testament, I think it was in the book of Matthew, where somebody said to Jesus, 'When were you here?' and he said something like, 'I was there and you didn't feed me. I was there,' " she said with a chipped tooth smile, " 'and you didn't clothe me.' " And then she took a bite of her sandwich and her smile faded as she said, "I was there, and you poured hot coffee on me one morning while I was sleeping

in the rain and burned my face. Yeah . . . I was there, and
you spit on me when I wasn't even messing with nobody."
As she looked at the last bite of her sandwich she said,
"What's yo name again?"

"Louis."

"Louis. Umm, that sounds like some rich-white-boy
name."

"Ahh, I'm not hardly rich or white," I said. "I go to work
every day like everybody—" And then I caught myself.

"You can say it." She smiled at me and then laughed.
"Shoot, I go to work too. I just have more flexible hours."

I laughed not so much at what she said, but her spirit in
spite of her circumstances. She continued as she looked at
the last bite of her sandwich in her hand, "I'm not loco, you
know." As she said that I watched her face change like the
seasons from the smile that exposed her dingy teeth to the
aged one I saw earlier as she was begging for dollars. Looking at me, she said, "You know that, Leon? I'm not crazy.
And I'm not lazy either. People think that when you live
on the streets. They think you just crazy or sorry. But that's
not me. I'm just . . . just unfortunate. I have had some bad
breaks in my life, but you know something? When I was a
little girl, I would see people on the street corners and my
mom would say don't look at him, don't look at her, but
I'd sneak a peek anyway. Maybe it was contagious, 'cause
deep inside, I knew one day, somehow, some way, no matter what happened, no matter what I did, I would be just
like them."

She put the last bite of the sandwich in her mouth and
chewed slowly, closing her eyes as if it were a filet from the
Russian Tea Room. "That was a good sammitch," she said.
"That was damn good."

What could I say at this point? I stood and simply said,
"Thank you."

"For what?" she asked, stuffing the aluminum foil from
our sandwiches into her pocket.

"For having lunch with me." And then before I knew it,
I reached into my pocket and pulled out the first bill my
hand touched, which happened to have a picture of Grant

on it, and handed it to her. I don't know how she responded, because I turned away and ran across the street to the waiting limo.

On the cross-country flight to the West Coast I could not get her out of my mind. In an odd way we were somewhat similar. We both enjoyed the flexibility of our jobs, we both suffered the slings and arrows, and most important, we both knew at an early age what we would be when we grew up. I took out a legal pad and scratched a few ideas, because I was bound and determined that even if we stood on opposite sides of the divide, Ora and I would make a difference. I called Herbert on the airplane phone to discuss a few ideas and he reminded me that bills like that rarely make it through Congress because people like her tend not to vote. They don't have unions, nor do they have lobbyists fighting for them. But I knew if I could somehow connect the legislation to a farmers'-rights bill, I could pound it through with the support of senators in populous states as well as representatives of smaller agricultural states. This idea had cost me $105, but I worked on it relentlessly as I flew to California because I knew in the bottom of my heart that it would save thousands of broken lives. Ora may have stopped believing, but God had put her in the right place at the right time.

A year later I introduced legislation we called the "Helping Hands Bill," to assist people who had fallen on hard times. It would help the farmers in Iowa trying to compete with the corporate farmers who were forcing them out of business as well as the homeless in more urban communities. The legislation was handily defeated by a two-to-one margin because the large industrial farmers had better lobbies then Ora.

But the move helped me in so many other ways. I was asked to speak more on a national level and I was even a part of the Farm Aid concert. In a way, I was bridging the gap between urban America and the heartland, and the motto I'd used in Florida in each of my campaigns, "One People, One Man, One Vision," was starting to pay dividends.

* * *

When I returned home from the L.A. trip, I was tired. I had done fifteen cities, spoken more than forty times, and appeared on twenty-seven television shows, all in a two-week period. We knew it was imperative that we strike while the iron was hot to show America the new Henry Louis Davis, and the results were very encouraging. In the polling we did out West, I was doing better than most other potential Democratic presidential candidates. We were trailing Steiner, but only by a few points, which pleased us since he was from the Midwest and had been a part of three national campaigns.

When I returned home, Leslie was out by the pool. She has this incredibly rich milk chocolate complexion, and when she suns herself she looks like a Hershey bar. I used to like to sit and just watch her sweat. As I walked out to the pool, she looked up at me and said, "Hey." After two weeks, that was it. Hey. I placed my briefcase on the chaise lounge beside her, sat there, and watched her as usual.

"What would you like for dinner?" she asked dryly.

"Are you okay?" Now I'm thinking, did I forget an anniversary? Did I forget to call? Was it a holiday or something?

We talked and she told me she had been feeling a little sick. Said she was having a cycle every two weeks and was having trouble sleeping. She spoke to our friend Dr. Snodgrass and he asked her to visit his office. She later found out she was going through early menopause.

"Aw, baby," I said as I got on my knee and hugged her. I didn't know exactly how to respond. I couldn't say it's no big deal because that would be trivializing it. I couldn't ask, "What would you like me to do?" because I felt I should already know and that might add drama, which was something she didn't need. So I just smiled at her and rubbed my fingers featherlike over her eyebrows as I looked into her sad ebony eyes.

"I'm surprised I have any eyebrows left, I've done that so much in the past week," she said, and moved her head away from my hand. "He told me I need to start doing those Kegel exercises at least once a day."

"What's that?"

"It's not important," she replied, and rolled over.

We had never had any children because she was infertile, and I don't think she ever really got over that. I would watch her when our family members or staff brought their kids over or she saw children in the store dressed in some cute outfit.

There is something about a woman who cannot have children holding a child. There is a look of maternal longing as if something was missing. Some women and men don't want kids. But we really did want children and could not have them. That was all we talked about when we first got married. We would lie in each other's arms after making love and toss around baby names and debate sending them to private or public schools. Every house we bought, we asked the realtor about the school zoning and made sure we had at least one room for the child. For us, adoption was not an alternative. The intellectual side of us said to do it, while our hearts wanted to see our flesh come together in one being. Our chances were slim, but we expected we would have at least four or five more years to hope for a miracle. Now any small chance we had of that happening had come to an end.

She looked at my lips and said to me, "The last few times we made love, I knew something didn't feel right. But I'm only forty-two, so I figured it couldn't be menopause. I ignored it, and while you were away I started getting these sweats and feeling weak, and then came the kiss of death, the fucking hot flashes. So I went to see George, hoping what I felt was happening was somehow not happening, and he was no help at all," she said, putting back on her shades and reaching for a cigarette. "It's official. I'ma old bitch."

"Please, Leslie. Now I think you're going too far. You are beautiful. You don't make *People*'s list of hottest couples in America unless you're beautiful. They would—"

"I made it because of you, Henry!" she exclaimed, sat up, and walked through the sliding glass door to our bedroom. I was speechless. When I came home, I was tired. All I

wanted to do was grab a glass of tea, put on my old raggedy
Norfolk State sweatshirt, and watch the Dolphins game. But
all of a sudden that was immaterial. This beautiful woman
I'd fallen more and more in love with over the years needed
me, and for the first time in my life, I didn't know what
to do.

I made a few calls, then went to our room, where Leslie
was lying on the bed wearing a two-piece string bikini and
a pair of football socks.

I walked in, put my overnight bag on the bed, and took
out the suits as she watched me. I never hang up my clothes,
so she was in awe.

"Henry? What are you doing?"

"What does it look like?"

"Why aren't you letting Kadesha do it tomorrow like you
always do?"

"Why are you wearing football socks and a string bikini?"

Leslie continued watching me as I neatly put away the
last of the blue and dark gray suits and red power ties. And
then I opened another drawer and took out some shorts and
T-shirts.

"Henry, what are you doing?"

"Packing."

"I see that. But where are you going? And why you taking
so many casual clothes?"

"Not I," I said, and walked over to sit beside her. "Not
I. We. *We* are going to Cancún. I just called and the flight
leaves from Miami International in two hours, so you might
want to get rid of those socks."

"We can't go to Cancún, Henry," she said with a smile,
and I could tell she was hoping I had not forgotten anything.
"You have that fund-raiser next week in Charlotte and
you're scheduled to address the governors' conference in
Washington on Tuesday night."

"I just spoke to Herbert. He will be in Charlotte for me,
and Penelope is setting up a direct feed for us in Cozumel
so I can address the governors via satellite."

"Oh my goodness, Henry." She searched for a word and

found nothing was there, so she laid her head on my shoulder and started to cry. "Teddy, I've always felt that I'd shortchanged you in some way. That somehow . . . I wasn't the woman you deserved. That's why I didn't want to gain a pound more than what I weighed the first day you laid eyes on me. I thought if I couldn't give you a child, I could at least give you something nice to come home to." She wiped away a tear with the heel of her palm. "But I still felt that I was not everything you needed or deserved." I could feel her warm tears sink through my shirt and onto my skin. "Henry, if I live to be a hundred, I could never tell you how much I love you, how much I need you, and how much you mean to me."

I leaned away from this beautiful creature God had given me and tilted her head up. "You know something? I could never repay you for everything you've given me already."

After our Mexican getaway, things were a little better, but she was different. I don't know if it was because of the depression from the menopause or her physical body going through so many changes so rapidly, but she was not the same. When we returned I stayed in Miami overnight and then headed out before the sun rose to D.C. and our condo in Arlington. Since we were running two households, usually Leslie stayed in Florida to manage the local senate office and run a couple of small businesses we owned. I would hold down the fort in D.C. Being an African-American, I was very careful about my image. I knew all it would take is a few snapshots of my empty chair during an open Senate debate and people would have me smoking crack in a room with a prostitute in no time.

Several weeks after our Mexican vacation, I came home from Arlington for a fund-raiser for the local Democratic party and found Herbert's daughter at the house. She was about seven years old and her name was K'ren. She had an adorable smile and coal black eyes she got from her mom. She obviously got her curiosity to know everything from our side of the family. As I drove up she was playing with her doll on the front porch. When she saw me she dashed for the car.

"Hey there, pudda! When did you come over here?" I asked, picking her up and spinning her around.

"Last night. Daddy and Mommy had to go out of town. They took Gerald."

As I put her down she said, "Uncle Hen, spin me again! Uncle Hen, spin me again!"

I smiled at her and noticed the curtains swaying. I'd wanted to surprise Leslie, but obviously that plan had been short-circuited.

Walking up the pathway, K'ren grabbed two fingers of my free hand and swung it back and forth. We always loved it when she came over. Herbert and his wife had moved from central Florida when his company had laid him off, and he managed a printing company we owned. Leslie and I always looked forward to K'ren and Gerald coming over because they added a certain vitality to the house. The most painful part of baby-sitting for us would be going out in public with K'ren, or especially their oldest child, Gerald, and having people say he or she looks just like you. Leslie always smiled on the outside, but I know it left a mark.

I opened the front door and saw Leslie look at me and then close her eyes. Lying on the floor was no big deal because we have this bearskin rug I was presented with in Oregon, so I didn't think twice about it. But she looked like she had been sleeping, and I was a little curious about that.

"Hon? You taking a nap . . . with K'ren out there?"

She rolled onto her stomach, and said, "You're here. Take care of your niece."

Now, being abrupt like that is not Leslie's style. But I was tired and thought maybe I was reading too much into it. Then I remembered the changes she was going through, and said, "Oh, well, okay. I'll take her to Dairy Queen. Would you like something?"

"No, I'm okay."

"Are you sure?"

And then my wife looked at me with eyes narrowing in anger, and said, "You know, Henry, I really wish you wouldn't do that. You can be so patronizing at times. Why must I repeat myself to you all the time?"

"What are you talking about, Leslie?"

"Maybe you should get your hearing checked, Henry. I'm serious. Are you deaf or are you asking me to repeat myself again?"

I was dumbfounded as I glanced outside and noticed K'ren jumping rope on the carport. After a moment of silence Leslie said, "Just fuck it!" then she stood and marched off into the bathroom, slamming the door behind her. At this point I knew what the problem was. I'd had a similar problem two or three years earlier and she'd been there for me. So I walked up to the door, took off my coat, and said just above a whisper, "Leslie?"

"Henry, just go away. Can you do that or will I have to repeat myself again and again and again about that too?"

"Leslie, would you please just talk about it?"

"GO AWAY!" she screamed so loud I could feel the thin wood of the bathroom door vibrate.

"Fuck you, Leslie!" I know I should not have come at her like that, but I had to do something to get her attention. "I am not leaving until you open this door. Now, please don't make me force my way in!"

"That's right, *Senator* Davis. Knock the damn door down because you can't get your way. That's so like you."

Obviously my approach was not working. I caught my breath and tried to decide between leaving her in the bathroom drunk or attacking this problem head-on. I chose the latter. "Leslie," I said with a little more decorum, remembering K'ren was still outside. "I'm sorry for hollering. That was wrong and I apologize. I'm not going to force you to do anything you don't want to do, but would you *please* come out of the bathroom?"

"What part of 'leave me the hell alone' don't you understand, Henry? The leave me part or the fucking understand part?"

I sat on the floor with my back perched against the door. There was no way in this world I was going to leave her, so I settled in to wait her out. I sat there thinking about our wedding day, about the time we slow-danced in Hawaii, even back to the first time I saw her at the Days Inn in Tallahassee. We had too much water under the bridge to allow this thing to come between us. If I were an average everyday Joe, I would have suggested she go to an AA meeting or get some type of professional help, but when you're in the spotlight you must give up certain basic privileges most other people take for granted. One of which is getting help when you need it without fear that it will be headline news in the *Enquirer*.

"Leslie?" I said after a few minutes. "I know what the problem is and I just want to say—"

"See, *that's* the problem. There is nothing you can say or do! You are not God, Henry. You can't fix everything. Because if you could *fix* everything, you would *know* everything. And if you knew everything, you would know . . . you would know . . . I don't love you anymore."

I closed my eyes.

"I'm tired of staying together because of the fucking presidency. I look at us, Henry, and all I see is a dream. I don't see shit that's real, just some *illusion* of what might happen someday. I'm tired of *asking* your staff if we can go on vacation or how I can wear my damn hair or where we can go to dinner or if I can have some time this weekend . . . to fuck you! I'm just tired of being Leslie. When you leave I'm scared as hell, Henry. I'm scared, lonely, and miss the shit out of you and can't wait till you return. But you know what? I feel the same . . . damn way . . . when you sleep next to me.

And you know what the really sad part is, Henry? You wanna know the worst part of it all? You can't win! They'll never elect you president. White folk pumping your head up with all of that bullshit and you falling for it. How in the hell you gonna have a black president in a country where black folks can't get *jobs* with companies because of their color? Where Texaco, for God's sake, won't promote Harvard grads? Where niggas are getting burned and decapitated for being in the wrong area of town by crackers right here in Florida? Fuck the polls! I don't care what the damn polls say. White people just feel good saying they would vote for a black person. They're too ashamed to say they would not vote for you, because they know you are the best qualified. But when that curtain closes, trust me, they gonna vote white. All you are doing is paving the way for some other nigger to make it because you . . . will never . . . win!" And then she screamed, "Get . . . away . . . from that . . . window!" Obviously K'ren had climbed up the tree and peeked in the bathroom window.

I sat there with my head in my hands trying to maintain my balance after the body blow of words, and then I stood and headed outside to see if K'ren was all right. I could still hear Leslie ranting in the bathroom. I wanted to compose myself before I saw K'ren because I knew that she'd never heard or seen Leslie like this before. As I walked through the kitchen, I remembered we usually kept treats in the freezer, so I opened the deep freezer in the pantry and retrieved a Mickey Mouse ice cream bar. When I went outside, I saw my niece with a scared look on her face trying to draw hopscotch squares on the Italian marble patio tiles.

I smiled at her and brought the ice cream treat from behind my back. Seeing it, she dropped the large, round, orange piece of chalk and walked toward me. I sat on the lawn chair, and as she took the snack from my hand I saw her eyes were red.

"K'ren?" I said as softly as I could. "Auntie Leslie didn't mean to say that. Okay? She's just not feeling well."

K'ren shook her head and sat on my thigh as she removed the paper from the ice cream. I wanted to say more, but comforting children was never my strong suit. I didn't even feel comfortable holding babies for photo ops. But then my thoughts went back to the love of my life sitting in a bathroom in our home.

If she had only said that I was wasting my time, I could have brushed it off, but it hurt when she said she didn't love me. So I sat there bouncing my heel with K'ren on my thigh. And then I saw a tear fall down her cheek as she bit into Mickey's chocolate-covered ear and moved her head as if she was listening to unheard music.

After about thirty minutes, K'ren was feeling better, so I left her playing with a dollhouse Herbert had dropped off previously and went back inside the house to continue my vigil for my wife.

Walking up to the bathroom door, I hoped she would have unlocked it, but she hadn't. I could hear her softly snoring inside the bathroom. Although I was still dressed in my suit pants, I allowed my suspenders to fall to my thighs and sat on the floor facing the door, deciding to wait her out as I replayed every word she'd said to me in search of the truth behind them. Was I obsessed with the presidency and did she really believe we had no chance of pulling this off? Was this home, the Senate, and what little wealth we'd accumulated our manifest destiny? But most important, I searched for the truth in the comment she made about the *illusion* of winning the presidency keeping us together. Was our marriage, our life, simply form over substance? Confused, I took off my shoes and socks, rolled the socks in a ball and placed them inside a shoe, massaged the ball of my foot, and determined not to leave until my wife was better.

Unfortunately, due to the long day, I fell asleep. Eventually K'ren came in and woke me up with a kiss on the forehead. I smiled at her and she asked, "What's to eat?"

I went into the kitchen and looked for whatever Kadesha had left us for dinner. As I heated the meat loaf and mashed potatoes, I decided that I should wake Leslie, so I walked down the hall and stood face-to-face with the door before pulling back my fist to knock. Just as I did . . . the door opened.

"Henry," she said with a weary sigh, and held the basin to balance herself. She could not seem to find the words she searched for. Instead she looked at me. First just my lips and then my eyes, and still she seemed unable to find the words. Her body swayed slightly as she then folded her arms and opened her mouth to speak, but only air came out.

I slowly pulled her close, secured my arms around her, and said, "Leslie, I love you. You scared me. But I know we can make it through this together." She leaned closer to me and I rubbed her head. "I can truthfully tell you that tonight there is nothing in this world that you can say"—I pulled back and looked into her fire-red eyes—"there are no words you can come up with . . . to make me stop loving you."

My bride leaned on me like a two-day-old baby, and I knew I could never let her fall. After that episode we fell deeper in love than we had ever been.

And then there was the trip to Europe.

Washington, D.C.
November 8, 2000
NBS News Studio
2:00 A.M. EST

"This is Franklin Dunlop on one of the most unusual nights I have reported on or can even remember in recent years. The crowning moment of democracy when America elects her leader for the next four years has been marred with an assassination attempt on the life of its sitting vice president, Ronald Steiner. For more on the story, we swing back out to Chicago and our own Judy Finestein. Judith, what's the latest?"

"Well, Franklin, we can now confirm that the vice president was indeed shot in the melee on the roof of the Four Seasons Hotel. We can confirm that the shot, or shots, I should say, were not fatal and that he is being treated at Lake Shore Memorial Hospital as we speak."

"Judy, the assassin or assassins—what do we know about them?"

"Well, according to our high-level FBI source, the FBI knew of a possible planned assassination attempt in Chicago hours ago, and they attempted to get the vice president and his family to a more secure setting. Why it was not leaked, and the story in Miami was, I cannot say. Unfortunately the ambush occurred as the vice president and his family were boarding Chopper Two on the roof of the hotel. We can now confirm two FBI casualties whose names are being held pending notification of next of kin. Also, Franklin, one of the alleged assassins, one Ulysses Ferguson, was shot and killed by a member of the Secret Service."

"My goodness, Judy. This is indeed an incredible story and it seems to grow more tragic with each report."

"Yes it is, Frank. They have asked the individuals inside the hotel who were here for the election celebration to leave immediately. They are attempting to seal off the area to conduct as much of an investigation as possible under the circumstances."

"We can now confirm that Steiner was shot. Were any members of his family or staff wounded during this devastating occurrence?"

"None as far as we know, Frank, only the vice president. I was just informed that he is in critical condition at this time. We will update you on his condition as the news comes to us. Again, according to our sources familiar with the situation, Vice President Ronald Steiner is in critical condition at Lake Shore Memorial, and the severity of his wounds is still unknown."

"Well, there you have it, America. On the eve of what was expected to possibly be the election of the first African-American president or the first female VP, we have a vice president in critical condition and an election night thrown into chaos. With all of the unusual happenings, we still must elect the next man to lead our country."

DAVIS	195	████████████
STEINER	220	█████████████
BALDWIN	126	██████

Fountainebleau Hotel
Suite 1717

Myles sat in front of the television, switching the coverage from Chicago. "Where's Penelope?" he asked his sister.

"She's down in Henry's room. They paged her for a meeting or something."

"So," he asked as he tossed grapes into his mouth, "do you guys know the Steiners?"

"Yeah, we've known them since we came to town in eighty-four. Ron and Sandy were one of the few Republican couples we socialized with. This was before he became vice president, of course. When they were in the Senate, his daughter was dating this black guy who played for the Orioles, and rumor had it that Ron went ballistic. I don't know what happened, but one thing led to another and they broke up. I don't think Ron and Sandy are racist or anything, but if a photo of his daughter with a big-money, fast-living, nose-ring-wearing baseball player was taken, let's just say it wouldn't play well in Peoria."

"Umm. So Ron's a pretty nice guy otherwise?"

"Ronald? Yeah, he's nice. As nice as you can be in politics, I guess. In fact, when Ron was in the Senate he pulled Henry aside and told him he'd heard some very positive things about him. That's not something a senior Republican senator from the North says to a first-term Southern Democrat. Ron was the first person to mention to Henry that he might want to seriously consider running for the presidency one day. I'm sure he just never imagined the future would come so fast."

"It's a sick world we live in. Steiner's people paid to have those protesters interrupt your rally and tried to embarrass Henry publicly, yet you don't seem to be angry with him."

"You can't hold grudges. Hell, we always hear about Republican dirty tricks. I can't swear that the Democratic party has not done the same thing to them." Leslie rubbed her eyebrow slowly. "This is a blood sport. It's just like basketball or football. You give it a hundred and ten percent for the entire game and when the whistle blows, it's over. When the election is done you kiss, do lunch, and cosponsor a bill or something. If you can't think like that in D.C, you won't make it there very long. I just pray . . . he lives."

LESLIE

In 1995 I received a phone call in the month of July I will never forget. I remember it was July because it was a few

weeks before our anniversary and three months after my
change. You know, into old ladydom. I was watching a
movie in the middle of the day, which is something I rarely
do, even on the weekends. It was my favorite movie of all
time, *Sleepless in Seattle,* and as always, I was crying a little
bit toward the end. But this time it was not because of Tom
Hanks and Meg Ryan meeting and holding hands. It was
because of me and Teddy. Let me explain. All my adult life
I wanted to have a baby, and even after the doctor said we
had no chance of that happening, I held out hope that one
day we would. I always thought it would happen on Valen-
tine's night or one of our birthdays or even our anniversary.
I know it was a fruitless dream, but I allowed myself to
fantasize every now and then. Now this was the first time
that it was not even a *remote* possibility.

I also cried because I missed Teddy. People think that
when you live your lives apart this much, you grow accus-
tomed to not having the person you love around. I never
got used to it. I turned to alcohol after the change and one
day said a lot of things to him I should never have said. I
didn't really believe any of them, but even after being together as many years as we had, I guess I wanted reassurance that the man cared. I knew he loved me, but I didn't
know if he genuinely cared. After my rantings and ravings,
he spent more time with me for a week or so, but soon he
had to go back to D.C. In the middle of my crying jag the
phone rang. It was my Henry bear.

"Hey, hon, how are you?"

"Fine now," I said, and dried my puffy eyes with the
back of my hand. "Are you still in Virginia?"

"No, actually I'll be home in a couple of hours. We
couldn't land in Miami so I'm just outside of Lauderdale."

I sat up straight. "Really?"

"Yeah, but I guess I should tell you that I have a meeting
with a couple of other senators at Camp David in a few
weeks."

"So?" I asked. By this time he was meeting with the president several times a year for one reason or another, so why
was he telling me this?

"Well, it's on the seventeenth. The seventeenth of *next* month."

My heart sank because that was our anniversary and I could not leave town to be with him because of my own obligations. Up until this point, we had never spent an anni versary apart. Our bedroom, which I would not even allow *South Florida Homes* to photograph, had nothing but pictures of us together. There were, of course, our wedding pictures and a picture of us taken in Holland when Henry and several other congressmen were invited to a visit by the prime minister of the country. There was also one taken by Kadesha of Henry and me covered in feathers having a pillow fight. We had a lot of fun that night, but those moments came less and less often. As a couple we did not have many rituals, but we held true to one. On our anniversary we would take the phone off the hook and spend the entire day in our bedroom by ourselves with a bowl of fruit, Teddy's favorite snack food of granola, and a bottle of sparkling wine. That was as elaborate as it got and we loved it. We never allowed a television in the bedroom. For us that was a place for other kinds of entertainment, and we felt if a married couple needed a TV in there, then they had problems. Unfortunately, I would spend this anniversary alone here, on the couch, with only the television.

"Leslie? Are you there?"

"Huh? Yeah, I'm here."

"I'm sorry, baby. You know if it was anything short of the president, I'd cancel, but I can't."

"Teddy, I understand," I replied, and I really did. But it did not make the pill any easier to swallow. "What time will you be home?"

"Well, I'm in the car with Penelope and Marcus now. Maybe around nine?"

"Kadesha is cooking veal tonight. She asked me to ask you what you would like for dinner tomorrow."

"Ahh, that's the other reason I'm calling. I need to go on the road for a couple of weeks. A few congressmen would now like me to campaign for them. I hate to give you such short notice."

"Teddy," I said as the tears began to swell, "I understand. We gotta strike while the . . ." And then I could not finish the sentence. Normally I am not that emotional, but "the change" had changed me more then I was willing to admit.

About a half hour later, Teddy called again. I had just finished the movie and was looking over a list of campaign contributors we should add to this year's Christmas card list, which had grown to over ten thousand people, when the phone rang.
"Hello?"
"Hon, I just have to ask you one question."
"Hey, babe, I'm so glad it's you. Listen," I said, laying down the list, shaking loose my hair, and removing my glasses. "I'm so sorry about the way I reacted earlier today. I don't know what came over me. I was watching that damn *Sleepless in—*"
"Honey, I hate to cut you off, but I'm still in the car and need to ask you another quick question."
"Yes?"
"What's your favorite scent?"
Now, I'm thinking, *How sweet.* He's buying me some perfume before he leaves. Not romantic to ask me, but very sweet just the same. "I wear Moon Dust of Paris."
"I know that, Les. I mean what's your favorite *scent.*"
"You mean . . . like smells? Like wild cherry or lemon or something?"
"Yeah. What's your favorite?"
"Well, ahh, I guess jasmine. Why?"
"Thanks. 'Bye," he said, and hung up. Now, why did he want to know that? I guessed he was having my car detailed or something and wanted to tell the guy what to spray in it. And then the phone rang again.
"Hello?"
"Sorry, I hung up before saying I love you."
I smiled into the phone as the words sank in. "Thank you, baby. What I was going to say before is—"
"Nipples of Venus, right?"
"Nipples . . . of Venus? What are you talking about?"

"Your favorite candy. Nipples of Venus . . . right?"

"Uhh, yeah." Although I thought I knew what he was up to, the way he was doing it had me perplexed.

"Okay, I love you. 'Bye."

I stood there thinking how special he could be at times. About thirty minutes later Teddy called again and asked, "Boxers or briefs?"

I didn't even try to say more than, "Briefs, 'bye."

I walked around our house like a hooker in a convent. I didn't know what to expect or how to dress, but I knew I should take a bath in his favorite scent, which was peach hyacinth. It always drove him wild.

As I was sitting in the tub, I tried to figure out why he was asking me questions I was sure he knew the answers to. If he wanted to give me one of those open-your-eyes dates, I didn't know how he could get into the house and set it up discreetly. But if that was his plan, once again, why call me? This was not making any sense, and I loved every minute of it.

As I dried off, I looked at my body in the mirror and was proud of what I saw. I run five to seven miles a day and I always eat very healthily. Initially it was for Henry the politician because I didn't want him to have some fat woman wobbling behind him. And then I did it for Teddy my husband because I didn't want all those young campaign aides and groupies to get his attention when he was on the road and I was down here in Miami. But now I do it for me. I do it because of the way it makes me feel, and I discovered the more I love myself, the more I love him and the more he seems to love me.

I hate to admit it, but after going through menopause, I was always horny as I don't know what. All he had to do was *act* like he was undressing and my nipples would start to itch they'd get so hard. I just could not get enough of the man. Older women had told me after the change, they didn't want anything to do with a man. *Please!* I wanted to say, *Send him over here.*

I went to my closet to find something to put on. I couldn't wear a negligee because this was his night and it might interfere with what he had planned. I couldn't wear regular clothes like shorts and stuff because when it happened I wanted him to have quick and easy access. So I went to his drawer and got one of his thin red and purple fraternity T-shirts and put it on with nothing under it. Now I was ready for whatever the senator had in store.

As he walked into the foyer, I ran to meet him and kissed him passionately on the lips. He looked at me almost surprised. So this was how he wanted to play, huh? Okay, I was game. I noticed he was a little sweaty for some reason, which turned me on even more. "Sorry, hon. Just missed seeing you around," I said as I took his briefcase. And then I looked for the bag with the stuff in it. He didn't have one. But then again, he's not that stupid. He probably put it in his briefcase, although it was feeling lighter than usual. But that still did not explain why he called and asked me those questions. *Forget about it,* I thought, as he headed for the bedroom after looking at the mail on the end table.

Umm, I got it. He was trying to throw me off. He had already bought the stuff and left it in his closet, and he'll call me in a few minutes to come inside the room. He was so sweet. But after pulling off his shirt and slacks to take a quick shower, he put on everything I hated. Not a tank top, which I always liked seeing him wear, or the neat little Reebok shorts Shaq gave him, which I loved because whenever he would squat, his thing would wink out of the corner at me. No, he put on these holey sweatpants and this ratty Tyson vs. Spinks T-shirt. It has these big holes under the armpit, and he knows I hate it with a passion. He walked back into the living room wearing one black sock and one red, yellow, and green Kwanza sock and sandals, and asked, "How was the veal?"

How was the veal? "I, umm, I don't know. I was waiting on you," I said to him as he walked into the kitchen. *Okay, I got it. He just wants me to ask him.* But I don't want to go there. *Henry Davis, I know you pretty damn—*

"Oh, hon? Thanks for answering those questions for me earlier," he shouted from the kitchen above the sound of cabinet and refrigerator doors opening and closing. "We were interviewing this hotshot pollster and he said that certain voters liked certain traits in candidates. So I asked him for polls he had done for other companies to test him, and in a poll of women from forty to seventy, you did pretty good. You had the correct answer for each one I asked him. Do we have any jelly?"

What the fuck? I was taking a damn survey for old ladies? No, he was lying. I know this man. He was just trying to throw me off. "Well, that's nice, dear. Yes, we have jelly. It's in the fridge behind the milk . . . on the bottom shelf." *What the hell he want jelly for?*

"Thanks," he yelled with a mouthful of food. "Do you want to eat in here or in the dining room?" he said, smacking like a kid.

"Ahh, wherever you like."

"Let's eat in here. No need messing up the dining room for Kadesha tomorrow."

Okay, Teddy, you doing a damn good job. Almost too damn good, I thought, walking into the kitchen with a you-can't-fool-me expression.

As we ate, I watched him chew his food so fast I thought I would have to practice the Heimlich maneuver on him before the night was over. I swear, he was chewing like a camel on crack cocaine.

"Sorry I'm eating like this, boo. I flew right in from Dulles, had a three-hour layover in St. Louis, and all I've eaten today is a handful of stale peanuts. Have you ever wondered why they give you such a small bag of nuts anyway? What's the *deal* with that?"

Who the hell are you? Jerry Seinfeld? Fuck you and the horse you rode in on, Henry, I thought while continuing to smile.

Then he said, "Damn, I almost forgot," and wiping his mouth with the end of his shirt, he walked into the living room.

You asshole, you better do something and do something fast, I was thinking.

He came back with the briefcase. Ahh, the briefcase. I had

forgotten about the briefcase. The very *light* briefcase. He opened it and grabbed the phone.

"Hon, I hope you don't mind. I need to confirm the reservation for my flight tomorrow. I forgot to have the new secretary do it," he said, looking at me.

As I held my steak knife, I realized how *easy* it would be to stab him there on the spot, right between his third and fourth rib. If I got lucky, I'd get a female like Judge Judy who would not have the heart to convict me after hearing all of the facts. I could just hear her saying, "He asked you what your favorite candy was, and your favorite scent, two weeks before your anniversary, and then he planned to leave town? Honey, you were provoked. He got what he deserved. Case dismissed!"

As Henry hung up the phone, he looked at me with veal crumbs sprinkled around his pie hole. "I love you, honey boo."

Fuck you, Henry Davis! "I love you too," I replied with a smile.

Later that night I sat on the love seat in the den pretending to read as Henry watched the Florida Marlins game on television. At around ten-thirty I gave up. Sometimes my overactive imagination would get me in trouble, and this was one of those times. Teddy had given me over twenty years of romance, but he screwed up this time. *I know he still loves me*, I thought as I walked across the room and kissed him on the top of the head.

"Where you going?" he asked, grabbing my hand and looking over the glasses he only wore in the house. For some reason, we both looked down at my hand. It was my left hand and we both looked at my wedding ring.

"I'm getting sleepy," I said, and broke the hold. *Please ask me not to go to bed because you have something special planned for me somewhere in this house.* But who was I kidding? I had been here all day. He didn't have anything in the house or his briefcase.

He said, "I'll be there in a minute as soon as the eighth inning is over."

I smiled and gave him an I-know-we're-gonna-make-love look, and headed to our bedroom. As I turned on the bedroom light, I could no longer stay mad at him. I don't know why, but he was no longer getting to me. I sat in front of the mirror to roll my hair, then I looked at the reflection of our bed. The comforter was pulled back, and he had left rose petals on the black silk sheets. On the pillowcase was a lavender envelope that read, "open me." Inside it was a poem.

> *You read me so well*
> *I know I am not a poet, but you read me so well.*
> *I'll try to write a poem to you, about the way I feel.*
> *You make me smile, you push me to excel.*
> *When others smile on the outside, you smile for me inside as well.*
> *I know I'm not a poet, but Yvette Leslie Davis, you read me so well.*

This was the first time the man had ever written me a poem, and as I held it over my heart, I felt emotions brewing inside. I can honestly say if he had left me a strand of cultured pearls on my pillow, I would not have felt as special as I did at that moment.

Seductively I walked into the den and noticed the television was playing, but the only thing on the couch was the dent in the leather where he had been sitting. "Teddy?" I called. Then I saw another lavender envelope on the television and I knew it was *officially* on. I opened it and read:

> *The coldest place in the house is where you will find the next clue.*
> *And after you find it, ohhh the things I will do to you.*

This was getting good. The last time I remembered being this excited, I was twelve years old and running down the stairs at dawn on December 25. I headed for the fridge to find lavender envelope number three taped to the Smuckers jar.

> *Eat too much of me and people will start to stare.*
> *To find number four open me. I'm on the chair.*

Now, this one threw me until I turned around and noticed his briefcase on the dinette chair. On top of a red and black lace blindfold the next clue read:

> *Take me with you to a very special place.*
> *Tonight I will wrap myself around you,*
> *I will cover your eyes as he kisses your face*
> *And does all of the things you want him to do.*
> *Now walk to the back door to begin this special night.*
> *Look left and right and then stop when you see the light.*

I almost tripped as I headed for the back door. As I looked at our yard, I saw a tent behind our pool. It was illuminated with a purple light, which reflected along with the moonlight off the water, and I could see the outline of my Teddy inside of it. He was posing and casting these slow, sensuous, erotic shadows on the walls of the tent. As I walked closer, I noticed there were piles of beach sand surrounding it. . . .

"Teddy, what are you doing?" I asked.

He turned off the light and turned on the music as I walked into the tent. It was our song.

> *Sometimes we are graced by angels*
> *Amongst us here on earth*

"Happy anniversary, dah-ling. May I have this donce?" he asked in a terrible impersonation of Antonio Banderas. And he asked it as if there were a possibility I would say no. Just like on the night he proposed.

As we danced in a tight C formation, I saw the Nipples of Venus candy and smelled the Jasmine potpourri in the air. When we stopped moving momentarily so he could light another candle, I even saw white rose petals in the sand. "You are just too . . ." I started to say as we began our dance again. "But how? How did you do all of this?"

"Well, I can't take all of the credit. I sent Penelope to the store to pick up most of the stuff and I asked the neighbors if I could borrow some of their kids' sand from their play box and whether the tent could get delivered to their house." He smiled. "Oh yeah, I owe Kadesha fifty bucks for keeping her mouth shut. She saw us out here about three hours ago when I was talking to you on the cell phone and made sure you didn't come out."

When the song ended, he pulled out a surprise from behind his back. It was a pair of cute little sexy purple panties. "How did you know I wouldn't be wearing any?" I said, and put them on, knowing they would be off before the elastic band closed on my waist.

"Well, I guess I can read you too."

"But you asked me," I said, looking at him, puzzled, "if I like boxers or—"

In two strokes he ripped off his shirt and dropped his sweatpants just like a Chippendale stripper. He had on a pair of purple silk briefs that could hardly restrain him. "I'm sorry she bought these so small. I told her I had a thirty-four waist. But it was the last minute and she grabbed a pair of thirties by mistake."

"Ahh, remind me to send Mrs. Butler-Richardson a thank-you card."

And then as the stereo played "Scandalous" by Prince, my Teddy turned me around and put the silk black and red blinder over my eyes and whispered into my ear words I could never forget. "Everything that happened to us yesterday, the good *and* the bad, is now history. Everything that happens tomorrow will always be a mystery." Cupping my face in his large, soft hands, he said, "But today, my love, today is God's gift to us, and that is why it's called the present. There were many times I did not deserve your present, and sometimes I even turned my back on your presence, but you were still there . . . waiting . . . to give it to me time and time again. For being there, Yvette Leslie Shaw Davis, I thank you. I thank you more than words could ever express, because you gave me . . . through all the years . . . the present . . . of you."

As the warmth of his voice in my ear subsided, a breeze of reassurance blew through me and I continued to melt as I heard him squeeze something in his hands and rub them together. My teeth clenched as he paused just to heighten my excitement. Then Henry began massaging my shoulders with the tips of his strong fingers. Slowly and evenly he deeply stroked the tension from my body as he had done previously to my mind with his words. I wanted to collapse on the spot, right on the sand with the little green army fighting men mixed in with it.

The heels of his oiled palms moved in big, deep circles down the edges of my back and then in tight shallow, circles up its valley. I started feeling light-headed from what had happened and what I knew would come to pass when he abruptly stopped what he was doing. "Teddy?" I knew he was there, I could feel his essence, but I couldn't hear him.

Then from nowhere he kissed me on the nose, and I smiled. He kissed me again on the forehead, and unable to contain my joy, I laughed like a teenaged virgin. Then he stopped, and before I knew it, he was behind me again. As he blew softly on my skin, the oil on my back started to heat and I could feel his passion as I said, "Dayuummmm."

Henry kissed me again and again, but now I wasn't smiling because my breath staggered and my mouth formed a large O. He kissed my neck and continued kissing me down to the small of my back. He removed the underwear he had given me and I stood there as this man kissed my tush. His kisses left a trail from my lower back to the top of the divide. Back and forth his tongue slid, concentrating on just that one area. Up and down, round and round. He took his time as if that one spot had a large X on it and was the most important place on my entire body.

He paused as if he were trying to decide just how he would proceed and then he softly kissed the area where my thighs ended and my butt began. I stood there with my legs apart, my eyes rolled back, and my fingers locked behind my head as I tried to imagine what else this man could have in store. And on this night there was so much more to follow.

Later that evening Henry took out a blanket and we held each other under the stars. As I lay there, I wondered why this evening was so much better than previous nights. We'd had surprise dates in the past, but none of them were nearly as exotic and romantic as this one. It was not because, after removing the blindfold, he lifted me onto his hips, and as I held the quivering center pole of the tent, he pleasured himself in me. It was not because of the creative things he did when he held my waist in just the right spot, at just that right angle, with just the right movement and just enough force. That night would always stand out because as we lay on the blanket and listened to the soft wind mixed with the sound of swaying palms and crickets, my Teddy made me feel like I was the only thing in the world that mattered to him. That I was more important than financial gain, his Senate seat, even his bid for the immorality. On that night, unlike any other night we had been together, I felt if I told Henry Louis Davis the Second it was either me or the presidency, he would choose me. That he knew the measure of his success was not in what he dreamed, but holding on to what he had.

Yet the evening could not last forever, and soon dawn broke. A dog started barking, morning light replaced the moon and made a streak across our nude bodies, and that feeling of bliss subsided. As I think back, I realize I've never felt that way since.

We had our first official *unofficial* Davis in 2000 campaign meeting Labor Day weekend in 1995 in a small bungalow in the Hamptons. As charismatic, intelligent, romantic, and appealing as Teddy can be, I think his greatest strength is the ability to clearly see his own weaknesses. He and I both know he is not the best judge of character. In our congressional races as well as the first senatorial campaign, he hired people because they were nice or they needed the job. In the second Senate campaign, I assumed that duty and the campaign sailed along smoothly. We hired his brother as the campaign manager when he moved back to Miami from Lakeland, although most of the major decisions were made by me or Henry. But we needed someone else we could trust and whom we could let into our world without fearing he or she would be tempted by the world of tell-all literature. The Carter administration had had a few, Reagan and Bush even more. But in the nineties it seemed campaign staffers were taking notes on every seemingly insignificant thing that happened, with plans to stay only as long as it took to fill four hundred half-decent pages. We were lucky that with Herbert we knew this would never be a problem.

Herbert married Doris soon after Teddy and I got married, and to this day I don't think she ever loved him. I remember the night Gerald, their eldest, was born. Gerald was a big baby just like Teddy and Herbert. After Gerald was born, Herbert walked out of the delivery room wiping sweat from his brow with his hand. There was a glow on his face as he sat down in his oversized green surgical scrubs and told us about the entire event step by step.

"When I was in there, I was holding Doris's hand and she was gritting her teeth and I was scared to death," he said. "I'd never seen her in so much pain, in so much agony. Then," he said, staring at the paint on the wall just over our heads, "the doctor said the baby was crowning. And I looked and saw the top of my son's head. *My* son. Can you believe that?" Herbert looked at Teddy, and said, "You make love . . . to someone you love . . . and you watch that love grow for nine months. Man, I knew this was going to be incredible, but I never knew it was going to be like this. To watch your wife's stomach swell just a little more each day and then panic no matter how much you tried to prepare when you heard those words." With a smile he leaned back, exhausted, and said, "Hell, I think my water broke too." Herbert looked at us, and said, "Guys, you don't *know* what love is until you have a child."

I swallowed so hard because I wanted one, even then, so badly. I had a baby doll fetish until high school. Not dolls that looked like women. But soft dolls who usually came with a bottle. As I held the dolls I wondered how it would feel to have a child moving and kicking inside of me. We told everyone we were not ready, that we didn't want to have a kid because of this or that, but every time we said it I knew I was lying because just the powdery scent of a baby would make me crumble inside.

After ten years and two children, Herbert and Doris filed for divorce. One night she caught him in a compromising position with a lady of the night when we were on the road at a fund-raiser, and a couple of months later the marriage ended.

I don't think most men would care as much as Herbert did when his wife took their kids, because he was in an almost comatose state for several weeks. He once told Henry that not seeing or hearing from his kids was the closest thing to death he'd ever experienced. Doris was nasty during the entire breakup, once making him clear it with her new boyfriend whether he could get his children for the weekend and even threatening to go to the tabloids with lies about Henry. But the deepest cut came when she didn't allow K'ren and Gerald to see or speak to their father for over a year. In time he was able to function and did a very adequate job for us, but he was never the same after losing those children.

Penelope Butler-Richardson was my press secretary. She and I have butted heads a few times, but I respect her because she will not roll over when I raise my voice. Our relationship can be described as incendiary because we both have something in common. We tend to shoot off our mouth at times and ask questions later. Sometimes the words we use get us in trouble, but they are always from the heart.

We're not friends because I don't mix business with emotions. But many times I think if Henry is the heart of our operation and I the soul, she would be considered the fire that pushes us forward.

It was Penelope who stood up to Henry regarding his image, which was something even I did not do. Henry never wanted to smile in campaign photos, and one time he wore glasses to downplay his looks and to look older. Penelope told him how he should style his hair and picked out conservative, custom-tailored suits for him to wear. She refused to use any photos in which he was not smiling, and soon the Davis Factor was picked up by the press. The Davis Factor was described by one reporter as the phenomenon whereby men saw Henry as a jocular friend, women wanted to go out with him, college kids saw him as a cool older brother, and the elderly viewed him as the son they could brag about to their friends. The Davis Factor was devised on a yellow pad as we were flying to London. As I watched her doodle, I thought the idea was too pedestrian to amount to anything. But now we were riding the idea toward the White House.

After our first congressional victory, Penelope and I were in D.C. looking for shoes that would match the dress she'd planned to wear to Henry's congressional swearing in. I knew next to nothing about Washington at that time, so she drove us to this mall in an urban neighborhood. As we got out of the car, she continued talking as she put the Club on the steering wheel and never acted as if she was at all uncomfortable being a minority in a parking lot where there were nothing but black and brown faces. Then she started to talk about congressional committees, and as she spoke I was thinking, *Is she trying to impress me with her blackness?* While I'd known Penelope for years, even before she joined our campaign, I never knew much about her, so I could not resist the temptation. After she picked up the shoes and we returned to our car, I asked her point-blank. "Penelope, why did you choose this mall?"

"What do you mean? Didn't you see the shoes in that store?"

"No, I saw that. But how many malls with J. Linz stores did we pass to get to this one?"

"Two or three. But I wanted to help out the inner-city stores. You know, show support."

I shook my head. I knew there was more.

"I know what you want to know. You wanna know why I'm like this. Don't worry, you can ask me. God knows I've been asked before."

I remained silent.

"I've always been like this. Even in elementary I mostly had black friends. As I got older, I found out that they call you guys Oreo when you act white. They just call us nigga lovers. My daddy hated it that I was, as he would say, 'infatuated with nigras,' and I think that only reinforced me to do it more. In college you think I wanted to pledge Tri Delta? I tried to pledge a black sorority and they turned me down. That would have really pissed my family off, but—"

"You ever dated a brother?"

The question made her pause and she looked in the rear-view mirror for the answer. "Have I dated a brother?" she said, stalling for a little more time. "I guess it depends on what you mean by date. If you mean *date* date, with flowers and a movie and all . . . no."

"Oh. So you've had a *taste* of chocolate?"

She smiled and said, "Yeah, I guess you could say that."

"Why did you do it? I mean, why didn't you *date* date the guy?"

"Because I . . ." She glanced at me and again at the road. As the traffic merged onto the Beltway she said, "It's a long story, but it could have never worked out."

"Was it because of his job? Your parents? What?"

"No. No, not really. I mean they have this power thing in south Florida politics, but that's where it ends."

"Sooo?"

"So what?" she giggled.

"Check you out Miss Thing. Blushing. You know. Why didn't you find this brother good enough to, as you say, *date* date? Did you cross over to see how it felt for a while, or did you just let go the little ho inside ya?"

Her eyes narrowed and her smile waned. "No, it wasn't like that at all. He was in a relationship at that time, and I don't know if I wanted him because he was untouchable or if I really just wanted to see if there was anything to the myth. The more I think about it . . . I *think* I had feelings for him."

"Really?"

"Yeah. He was deep and honest and just totally the opposite of every man I'd dated before or after. And yes, that includes my husband. But I knew it could never work. I mean, relationships are hard enough as it is, but when you add to that the pressure of the family, being stared at whenever you walk around in public, of sometimes being ostracized by one or both families, and even the way society sometimes treats children who are biracial, it was more than I wanted to deal with."

As I listened to the tone of her voice, I could tell she had feelings for this man, and it brought back to me just how special my relationship with Henry was. How many people could say they were married to their first serious sweetheart, who, in spite of problems, was still their best friend? And then I asked, "Whatever happened to him?"

"You mean the brother?" she asked after clearing her throat and returning her eyes to the rear view mirror. "He moved out of town and is happily married. Life's a bitch, huh?"

Although Penelope was more than qualified for the position of campaign manager, it was already taken, so she asked to be Henry's press secretary, which both of us agreed would be very well suited to her talents. The running joke in the campaign was who would call Mr. Guinness because she had the world's largest Rolodex. Need someone to host a fund-raiser in Gallup, New Mexico? She knew who to call. If you wanted the support of the mayor of Dot Lake, Alaska, I would imagine she not only had his office number but his kid's birth dates as well. The massive file filled with names was a virtual who's who in politics, the arts, and industry. She told me once that she began saving the information as a teenager when celebrities and politicians would visit their home. At that time she wanted to one day become an agent and never knew when the information would be of value. This, together with the fact that she was a brilliant speech editor fact checker and could read a crowd just by mingling with them before Henry went onstage to tell us what issues to stress and which ones to avoid, made her a very valuable component to our plans.

When I initially met Edward Long, I immediately did not like him. I trust my gut instincts and knew I could not be wrong about him. Maybe it was the huge, black supernerd watch he wore, the slight lisp when he pronounced *th*, or his small stature and erudite attitude, but the first impression was lasting for all the wrong reasons. He would speak for ten minutes after you asked him a question, but in fact had said absolutely nothing. As I shook his hand and he left the room, I was ready to file his resume in the circular file when I gave his employment history a second look. He'd worked in the Bush White House as the deputy director for public affairs and in the governor's office as a press aide. He also had network experience with NBS and CNN as an assistant producer. He'd run several statewide campaigns and was familiar with our position on a number of important issues.

I called a friend of ours in the governor's office. And then I called both networks. I even called each of the five references he gave us, and the report was the same. "Edward Long is one of the most meticulous, organized, hardworking individuals I know." I looked at his resume in comparison with the other candidates, and it was an obvious decision for me. Now I had to decide exactly what to do with him. I did not think he and I could connect, and to be honest, the image of him as my spokesperson was not too appealing. I considered him for a position as a policy adviser, but he just did not have the experience needed, so I called up Penelope and told her I'd decided to have Ed work with Henry, and I would offer her the position I had open for a press secretary. There was silence on the phone before she said, "I accept." I told her it was not meant as a demotion, but I just wanted to have the two best people working for us, and she said quietly, "I understand. Will that be all?"

The next day I asked Ed to come to Henry's office to meet him, and they had a cordial conversation. That night after dinner, Teddy told me about a few mutual friends we shared with Ed and that he'd decided to take him instead of Herbert on a trip with us the following week to Kentucky. We were lying in front of the fireplace with a stack of newspapers and watching *Living Single* on TV. When I told him how Penelope had reacted, he didn't respond. I said, "The way you're acting, you would think there was something more to it," and Henry remained quiet. So I rolled over and asked him point-blank without an ounce of anger in my voice while staring him dead in the eye, "You fucking her?"

He looked at me like Sylvester the Cat with his cheeks full of yellow feathers, and said, "Why you ask me something like that?"

Now, I don't know a lot about men since I have spent my entire adult life with just one, but I have a Ph.D. in HLD, and the translation to what he said was, "Damn, I'm busted, let me stall for time to think up a good lie." I asked him again, and he said, "No, Leslie. No, I didn't *fuck* Penelope. Damn."

I rolled back over and looked at the TV on the brink of tears. Her reaction plus the story about the brother she once had feelings for, combined with his answer, led me to believe he had either gone down on her or she had gone down on him. I tried to remember if her middle name was Cheryl and wondered if she was the one he'd called for in the midst of making love. From the way he said it, I knew there was no penetration. He would never outright lie to me, but I didn't want to hear the actual truth from his lips. I never mentioned it, yet I never got over it or fully trusted him again.

Chicago, Illinois
November 8, 2000
NBS News Studio
2:15 A.M. EST

"Welcome back. We have a few election-night results to give you, but first we will send it out to Chicago and Judith Finestein for an update."

"Franklin, the hall is all but deserted at this time. We, and most of the traveling press, are reporting from the parking lot of the Four Seasons. I will say that the FBI, Illinois state troopers, and what seems to be a half dozen other law enforcement agencies assigned to protect the area have been hush-hush about the matter. Few official facts have been given to us. Therefore, rumors are swirling this morning. One rumor was that the shot was fatal, and another indicated that it was merely a flesh wound. The view here is that the truth lies somewhere in the middle.

"I have with me the governor of Illinois, Richard Campbell. Governor Campbell, we are told you were on the floor reserved for the key staffers when all of this occurred. Can you answer any of our questions in regards to the health of the vice president?"

"Unfortunately, since I was not on the rooftop, I cannot. My wife and I were in the presidential suite with Mr. and Mrs. Steiner before they went with the FBI to board the chopper, and before you knew it, we could hear the faint sound of gunfire."

"Can you tell us, sir, if the vice presidential nominee, Sydney Ackerman, was in the suite at that time?"

"No. She and her family were taken out via another route. Actually she never came back up to the suite after addressing the campaign staffers."

"Well, there you have it, Frank. The vice president's condition is still, to the best of our knowledge, critical, and according to the governor, the vice presidential nominee was not in the area when the incident transpired. This is Judy Finestein sending it back to Frank Dunlop in Washington, D.C."

Carol City, Florida
The Allen Residence

After Cheryl hung up the phone, she knew deep inside that what the man she'd dreamed of since she was a teenager had just told her was true. But it didn't take away the bite.

When she turned to look at the television, the first face she saw was Henry's. They were showing a tape of him from the debate. He had just addressed a question regarding his Middle Eastern policy when a few people in the audience booed. After gathering his composure, Henry slowly rubbed his eyebrow, which was a sign to the commentator that the candidate was beginning to crack under pressure. As Cheryl watched, part of her felt betrayed. After all, Henry had walked back into her life. She'd been perfectly content to survive on just the memories from the past. But those feelings of betrayal were soon replaced by feelings of remorse and then respect. She wanted him. There was no need to lie to herself about it. But there was no way that could ever occur. Even if he divorced Leslie, which was the hot buzz on the television tonight, he would never marry a common nurse. He would probably date some starlet or another mover and shaker in the Washington scene. When the rumors regarding photos circulated in the press, for a millisecond Cheryl dreamed of rekindling the distant memory. But as she looked at the phone, she knew *for always* was not only a distant memory but a faded one as well.

"Cheryl, wassup?" Sarah asked, slowly making a fist and stretching her large body on the tiny sofa. "Is Henry the president or what? You first freak yet?"

"No, not—" Cheryl said from her bedroom. "Why must you always be so doggone vulgar?"

"Yo, like Popeye the sailor man, I yam what I yam. Wassup? You not watching?"

"No. I'm, ah, I'm too nervous to watch," she said, lying on her bed leafing through an old issue of *Black Elegance*.

"Too nervous?" Sarah shouted while walking into the kitchen and opening the fridge. "The first man you fell in love with, who might be the next president, is handling his bid'ness, and you too nervous to watch? That's jacked up."

"Don't eat the hamburger!" Cheryl called out, knowing her daughter. "It's for meat loaf tomorrow. Want me to make you something else?"

"Naw, that's awright," Sarah said, and Cheryl could hear her continuing to rummage through the fridge for food. "So, Cee, what's up with Brandon? I thought he was taking time off for this shit— stuff tonight?"

"Don't drink all the Pepsi either!" Cheryl shouted, trying to avoid the question. "In fact, while you in there, make some tea."

"Wud-eva," Sarah said. "So you never answered my question. What's up with your husband? I thought he was going to be here tonight."

"He had to go out."

"Go out. Hell, it's what, three, fo in the morning and he had to go out? Right . . . sure."

Just then the phone rang and on the half tone Sarah answered. "Talk." After a pause, she said, "Well, I'll be dammed, Cheryl. Talk about the devil and he will *definitely* show up, won't he?"

Closing her room door and picking up the phone as her daughter hung up, Cheryl said softly, "Hello?" Brandon did not respond. "Honey, I'm sorry for what I said. I really am. I've thought about it for the last couple of hours and I can see how wrong I was. Please come home."

"Cheryl, don't go there, okay? Do . . . not . . . go there. I deserve more than that from you after all these years!"

"What do you mean?" she asked, sitting on the edge of her bed and scared to death of what he was about to say.

"I've been thinking . . . What I mean is this." He lowered his voice. "Cheryl, I can't live in this man's shadow. I've tried hard to make things work out between us, and to be honest . . . to be perfectly honest, I'm tired."

Cheryl stood and paced the tiny bedroom as she nervously ground her fist into her thigh, trying to think of the right words to say and not to say. "I know you've been patient. You've been patient beyond a fault, and I understand it must be tough. I know how you—"

"Shut up!" Brandon shouted. Cheryl's eye swelled and she was stunned because he had never spoken to her that way before. He apologized and said, "But please don't say it. You cannot . . . even . . . relate to it. Most men have women whose ex-boyfriends are in some other city or they hardly see him. Not me. Fuck, I pass a thirty-foot billboard of your ex-boyfriend every day. I have to watch him on TV every night. I watch him with his wife, his nice suits, living in fancy-ass Harris Hills, and on top of everything else, the man has . . ." And then he paused.

Cheryl closed her eyes for the first time, hearing the pain in her husband's voice.

"And on top of everything else," he whispered, "he has you too."

Cheryl couldn't say a word as she started to cry.

"You know something, Cheryl? When I was a kid, I was always the first one picked for anything we played. If it was marbles, twenty-one, or even high school baseball, I was *always* first team. Even when I graduated the academy, I was in the top half of my class. Will I have to live the rest of my life playing second fiddle to this man's memory? Not to what he was . . . but to what could have been? I can't compete with that, Cheryl. How can I compete with Henry fucking Davis the Second? I can't . . . and I won't!"

"Brandon," she replied barely audible. "Brandon, I'm not asking you to compete with him. Brandon, I do love you. I told you that. And because I love you, I can't lie to you. I have to be one hundred percent honest. Maybe if I would have just lied—"

"And that's supposed to make me feel better?" he yelled into the phone so loud Cheryl jumped.

Hearing his rage and knowing her husband, she said, "Brandon, please don't hang up."

"How would you feel, Cheryl? How would you feel if the man you loved with all of your heart, body, and soul told you he didn't love you? Or at least he didn't love you in the way you *deserved* to be loved? It's a deep hurt, Cheryl. It's a pain I can't even begin to describe. If someone had reached into my body, yanked out my veins, and dragged me down the road with them over cut glass, it would have hurt less than hearing you say what you said to me."

As a steady stream of tears poured down her cheek, she knew she understood much more than he could ever know.

CHERYL

In 1995 I started looking at Brandon more seriously. We got married in August of that year.

I must admit, initially Brandon seemed almost like a child to me. A very fine child, I should add. But then he became kinda like a friend. Someone with whom I could hang out, go to brunch, or see a movie from time to time. But then we made love one night in his apartment, and I must say I was impressed with his maturity and flattered that at my age and with all the female attention I was sure he was getting, he would take the time to be with me.

The day after we made love, I received flowers. He sent me a dozen imported white tulips. He knew that I was really into the hidden meaning of flowers, so he sent the only flower that said "You are the perfect lover." I loved the way he courted me. Although he was young, he was not aggressive or presumptuous. From time to time there were other guys who asked me out and a few I even spent time with. But two hours of them bashing their ex-wives or sorry children was more than enough. One guy even had a grandchild, and that left me feeling a little too close to AARP registration. I'm a woman who will tell you her age in a heartbeat and be proud of it, but I felt twenty years older when I was with most of those men.

I guess that was why Brandon was so refreshing. I knew very little about him. He was not secretive by any stretch of the imagination, but he was always shining the light on me. No man had ever done that. Henry had a one-track mind, and poor Darius . . . well, he didn't have one at all.

Two days before Thanksgiving of '95, I was running to the elevator in Jackson Memorial Hospital, a few minutes late to work. The previous night I had gotten only two hours of sleep, and the bags under my eyes were evidence. Some time back I had I found out that Sarah was still seeing Austin before he was finally sent back to jail. I must say one thing about him, he didn't leave her empty-handed. A month after he was sent up to the state penitentiary for a ten-year stay, she discovered he'd left her pregnant and with herpes. When I found out I was livid, but I was glad that due to his incarceration, he would be kept away from her. So on top of everything else in my life, I was now a grandmother taking care of a newborn with colic while Sarah worked nights in a factory.

As I rode up the elevator, I was thinking about the meal I needed to start preparing for the holiday. Brandon was bringing a couple of friends from the department, and my mom wanted to bring a girlfriend of hers as well. The nice cozy dinner I'd planned for my mother, Brandon, and me had grown to a soft nine, which meant cook for twelve because there would likely be more. As the elevator door opened, I was already tired and I had yet to tend to a single patient.

"Good morning," said Erica, who was one of my best friends on my floor at the hospital. "Another sleepless night?"

"Yeah," I said, walking over to the coffeemaker and noticing it was empty.

She continued her conversation with Stan, one of three male nurses we had in our ward. "So what was she doing when you were taking her vitals?"

"Actually I didn't take her vitals. I just walked in and she was knocked out. I glanced at the chart and I don't remember what Snodgrass prescribed, but she was dead to the world. I mean I'm not into older women, but with her I'd make an exception."

"Yeah, I saw her on the news a few months ago jogging in a five-K for cancer or something."

"Girl is fine as hell. But I heard he was flirting with Vivica A. Fox. You know . . . the sister from *Soul Food*."

"I heard that too, but you know how rumors are always floating about him. At one time they even had him with one of the white chicks from *Friends*. But on the fo' real, Senata is finer than I don't know what!"

I was about to have my time card stamped when I heard the words, and almost time-marked my forefinger.

"I mean," she continued, "you can tell he's a little shy because he was on this show one time and this sister started telling him how handsome he was. He started blushing and

that just made him look cuter. Fine as all outdoors with
those dimples and—"

"You all talking about Henry Davis?" I asked.

"Yeah," Stan said as he reloaded his meds tray. "His
wife's upstairs on the ninth floor under the name Yvette
Shaw. I think it's her maiden name."

As he spoke, I tried to keep my thoughts from showing
on my face.

"She's up there for exhaustion, and they kept her overnight to test for Epstein-Barr."

"Oh really? When did she check in?"

"Early this morning," Erica replied. "Girl, you know half
of Miami claims they either knew him, grew up with him,
or slept with him. Wait a minute, you grew up here . . .
Did you know him?"

"No," I said as I retrieved my supplies to make my
rounds. "So who's her attending nurse?"

"Tina. Why? . . . Mrs. *Married* Lady."

"Please. I was just curious." As I left the room all I could
think about was a way to get Tina to switch patients with
me, even though she and I rarely even spoke to each other.
Switching patients was not common, but if you did have a
patient you could not get along with, it was allowed. Why
did I want to see Leslie? I have no earthly idea except maybe
seeing her would give me the closure that I so badly wanted.
Let's face it, Brandon was the type of man most women
dream of, but I was being held hostage in my mind to the
memory of this eighteen-year-old man-child in shoulder
pads. I think a part of my reason for holding on to the past
was that it was something I knew in my heart I could never
have. Marrying Brandon had closed most of the hole inside
of me; now I needed the job completed. At that moment I
saw Tina walking toward the lounge, and I went in after
her. We talked for three minutes and it cost me two days off.
I think she thought I wanted to sell pictures or something of
Leslie to the tabloids, because she told me any money I got,
I had to split. I just ignored the comment like I usually
ignored her.

Needless to say, the first patient I checked on was Mrs.

Yvette Shaw. As I got to the door I quickly thumbed through her medical records and saw Dr. Snodgrass's notation regarding her early menopause as well as his scribbles concerning the cysts on her ovaries which prevented her from bearing children. As a child, Henry had always talked about having children, and I wondered why they had not had any. Now I understood.

When I walked in the door of the large private room, it was dark due to the blinds being drawn to block out the morning light. I was extremely nervous. Then I thought, *What if Henry shows up to visit her, with me in here?* My second biggest fear was that he would recognize me. The biggest . . . that he wouldn't. Leslie was sleeping quietly and her hair looked like a cheap wig. As I walked over to the bed, in spite of my happiness with Brandon, I wanted to ask her if she knew just how fortunate she was. She probably didn't. Looking at her, I thought, *This is the woman who sleeps with the man I dream about, and I bet she takes him for granted. Bitch.* Then she opened her eyes.

"Good morning," she said.

"Good morning," I replied, methodically and reached for her meds chart to justify why I was in the room.

Looking around to see where she was, Leslie instinctively put her hand up to her head, and said, "My God, I must look a mess. Do you have a mirror?"

"You look fine, ma'am."

"Please." She giggled. "I must look like I have not only mousse but a little bit of *squirrel* in my hair too. Wait a minute, is it time to check me out again? That little white girl just left not too long ago."

"I know . . . Mrs. Shaw. I am just following up." *I'd bet anything she sleeping around on him*, I said to myself.

She looked at me and her eyebrows lowered. "Do you know who I am?"

"Yes," I said, flipping the pages of the medical file. "It says 'Yvette Shaw.' I hope that's correct, because if it's not, we have a problem." I put the file down and abruptly grabbed her wrist to take her pulse.

"Yeah," she said as her eyebrows relaxed and she moved

her head from side to side on her pillow searching for a comfortable spot. "That's me, all right."

As I took her vitals, I noticed her squint at the closed blinds, and then she asked, "What time is it?"

I wanted to say morning, but instead I said "A little after seven."

"What time does breakfast come around?" And then looking at my pin, she added, "Cheryl?"

"They should be on this floor within the next thirty minutes. So you have an appetite? That's good."

"Not really, but I could use some coffee . . . and a smoke."

"The coffee, we can handle," I said with a smile, and then wondered if Henry, too, was a smoker.

She closed her eyes and asked, "Can you open those blinds? I don't know what they gave me last night, but I hate feeling this groggy."

"Seems they gave you a Valium."

"Umm. Well, if this is how they make you feel, I hope he doesn't give me any more."

As I pulled up the blinds, I heard the door crack as if someone was just peeping in, and my heart stopped. If that was him, I had no idea what I would say. Then she said, "Marcus? Is that you?"

"Yes. Is it okay to come in?"

"Sure, I'm decent."

I turned around to find this chubby Asian gentleman who spoke with not a trace of an accent. Actually the only accent one could detect was a tinge of Alabama'nese in his vowels. "So how ya feeling this morning?"

"Fine," she replied, and then looked at me with a smile and said, "except for that little unwarranted no-smoking policy they have in this place."

"Well, you look better," he said. "Had us worried last night."

"I felt like shit. I had a sore throat most of the day, but then I got a headache and felt like I was about to black out."

"I know. All I could think of was not to let anything happen to you on my watch. Henry . . . I mean Louis would have gone through the frigging roof," he said with a smile in his tone.

As they spoke, I busied myself by adjusting the IV and the monitors in the room to justify my eavesdropping. And then he said, "Well, I need to run to the lounge to make a few phone calls. Can I bring you something to—"

"You could bring me—"

"Besides cigarettes."

"Oh, then nothing," she said with a smile as she stretched, apparently feeling the full effect of the medication. As Marcus left, I tucked her bed. "Cheryl?" she asked. "How do you enjoy working here?"

"I like it. The hours are crazy . . . but that just how it is in the medical field."

"I've often wondered about that," she said as she closed her eyes and then yawned. "Why they would have doctors working thirty-six-hour shifts when they're making life-and-death decisions. I mean, air traffic controllers only work six-hour shifts and they get a two-hour break. I guess it's all in the number of people you kill at once, huh?"

"Yeah, the hours are long, but I think it's been done that way forever, so I doubt it'll ever change." I picked up her medical records, preparing to leave, and said, "Okay, Mrs. Shaw, everything looks—"

"Tell me something else," she said, looking at me with sleep weighing heavily on her eyelids once again. "When you were in high school—"

My heart came to a dead stop.

"—did you want to be a nurse?"

"Oh. I mean, umm, no, actually I didn't. I had a sick husband and I nursed him so much I decided to make it a career."

"Umm," she said. "So how long have you been married?"

I could tell she wanted to enjoy not being Mrs. U.S. senator's wife for a while, so I put the files down and returned to her bed. "Actually, I'm a newlywed. My first husband passed away."

She opened her eyes, which appeared fatigued, and looked at me as if she really did care as she said, "I'm sorry to hear that, but congratulations on your marriage. Do you have kids?"

"I have one. Her name is Sarah."

"That's wonderful," she said, closing her eyes with a wistful smile. "That's wonderful. It's good to have kids, isn't it?" And then her voice blew out like the soft light of a candle. Just as I turned to quietly walk away, her eyes reopened. "I'm sorry, this medicine has got me falling asleep. So, Cheryl, when you were a kid, what did you want to be?"

I rubbed the linen of her bed with the tips of my fingers, and said, "Actually what I really wanted to be when I grew up was a housewife. Go figure, huh?"

"Yeah," she replied groggily. "But what you're doing is good too, because you get to help people."

I saw her drifting off and I tried to stop myself, but I could not. I had to continue the conversation. "So . . . are you married?"

Her eyebrows rose but her eyes remained closed. "Yep. Been married now going on thirteen years. We don't have any kids, though. Never found the time, I guess."

I smiled. I wanted to ask her if she really loved him; if she thought he really loved her, but I couldn't keep up the charade, so as her eyes closed, I turned again to walk out the room when the phone rang.

Barely awake, she asked, "Will you get that for me, Cheryl? Please?"

"Sure. Hello?" And it was him.

"G'morning. Is this the room of Yvette Shaw?"

"Yes. She's right—"

"Before you put her on," Henry asked, "how is she doing?"

As he said those words, I knew it would give me the closure I needed. His tone said he loved her and showed just how much he cared. "According to her charts . . . sir, she had a rough night, but this morning she's doing much better."

"Great." And then there was a pause as I prayed my voice had not changed that much in the past twenty years. "Listen, I'm in Texas and I'll be flying back home this morning.

Do you think she will still be there when I arrive about
one o'clock?"

"I don't know, Hen . . . I mean sir. But I can have her
doctor call you." I hoped against hope that he'd not caught
my slipup with his name.

And then he said, "Thanks. Put her on the phone. Oh,
wait," he said. "What's your name?"

I looked at Leslie, who knew he was on the phone, so I
could not lie to him and said, "Cheryl."

"Thanks." Pause. "Cheryl."

I handed her the phone and saw her face light up as if
his voice were the only medication she'd needed. As I left
the room, I heard her call him Teddy and hoped the same
medication would bring me the relief I needed as well.

A week before Christmas, Brandon, who had been promoted within the Sheriff's Department, was invited to a holiday fund-raiser. We rode in his Honda Accord through this
exclusive neighborhood in South Beach named Harris Hills
looking for the right address. As we drove around this corner there was no need to look at the house numbers, because
the split-level home was identified by a row of just about
every luxury car on the market. Dr. Kenneth Jarvis was a
prosperous OB-GYN and held fund-raisers for African-
American causes in his home twice a year. Every black person who was anyone in south Florida was present, and I
immediately looked for—who else?—Henry. This was the
type of function I was sure he would be a part of. But when
I saw Leslie, my heart beat faster. As medicated as she had
been in the hospital, and with me here in civilian clothes, I
doubted she would make the connection, but I wasn't positive. She was having a drink with Susan Taylor, Diane At-
kinson, and several silver-haired rich-looking black women,
and in my gut I had a feeling Henry was somewhere near.

I left Brandon, who was talking to a couple of individuals
from his job, and found a bathroom. I looked at my makeup
in the mirror, and it seemed tired. I scrambled through my
purse for a makeup brush to freshen it up and remembered
I'd left it home. "Damn." I started to search through the

cabinet and found one with the double-G emblem on it under the basin. As I reapplied my makeup and repinned my hair, I thought, *This is the first time I'm going to see him face-to-face in over twenty years.* Unlike at the Donahue show, I was prepared for whatever might happen. A part of me feared that Brandon would not understand why I'd been less than honest with him, but I would explain and hoped he'd not get too upset. As I pinned back the last remaining loose strands of hair, I looked at myself in the mirror. What was wrong with me? Here I was acting like I was in high school and I wanted Henry to take me to the prom. This man was married, very married, and *very* much in love with his wife. I smiled at myself in the mirror, patted my do, returned the expensive makeup brush, and walked out of the bathroom.

"You look beautiful." I was shocked to hear his voice behind me.

"Hello, Herbert, how are you?"

"God, it's been a long time. What, ten, fifteen years now?"

"Try twenty," I said, wanting to ask him the obvious question.

"Man oh man, is Henry going to be pissed that he missed this event." *Damn,* I thought. *He missed it? Wait a minute . . . He will be pissed?* "Yeah, I can't wait to rub it in that you were here. He's in Chicago, or is it New Hampshire? I don't even know anymore," Herbert said, as he took a sip of his drink. "I just know it's someplace cold as hell."

I gave him a "that's nice" smile and saw him patting his pockets.

"Listen," he continued, "if you don't mind, can I get your phone number for Henry? I know he will be happy to hear from you."

Happy to hear . . . from me? "Sure, why not?" I replied with insouciance, praying he wrote down *every* digit correctly and that Brandon would not walk around the corner looking for me.

Our brief chat was cut short when Mrs. Henry Louis Davis called Herbert over to meet a few seemingly important people. Shuffling his hors d'oeuvres to one hand and shaking mine with two fingers of the other, he said, "Duty calls. I'll make sure Henry gets your number. We both thought you were still in Arkansas for some reason."

As he walked away, I thought, *Did he say both? That means my name has come up?* So much for closure.

After Herbert left, I walked into the living room and saw a trail of people headed toward the opposite wing of the house where jazz flowed like liquid velvet. As I entered the den I noticed a four-piece combo performing and a small crowd starting to gather around them. A poet from my old neighborhood of Liberty City who was called Skillet was in the midst of the combo, displaying his words.

"I know I'm a man," he said in a semiscream, loud enough to gather everyone's attention.

> *"What architect drafted the plan?*
> *Is it for me or you to know? Please listen.*
> X *marks the spot, a man's heart stops. Why? Because it drains fire*
> *when it cries.*
> X *marks the spot in a temple, fear not. Why? Because lust burns."*

Skillet then walked across the room and for dramatic effect looked toward the crystal chandelier in the ceiling.

> *"Ask a neighbor, ask a friend. To chronicle the time when.*
> *A man could walk the street. With his head back and feel proud.*
> *Feel proud to be a man, a soldier without pause.*
> *A warrior for the cause. Leader for us all.*
> *In the forties they called him Shorty, or Barry, Wayne, or Sal.*
> *A man unafraid of work, and providing for his child."*

I saw Brandon in the growing crowd. He looked so innocent and I felt bad for a moment because I had not been totally forthcoming with him. But I resolved that I couldn't be, because even now I didn't know what the truth was regarding my feelings for Henry. Brandon looked like a kid at the circus as he watched Skillet spin words into gold. I walked over in front of him and he wrapped his arms around me snugly as he rested his chin on my head, and we listened together.

> *"So you call yourself a man?*
> *Do you know what that entitles?*
> *Do you know from whence you hail?*
> *From what seed you survived?*
> *And for you what forefather died?"*

The combo continued to play Train and the sax soloist was in rare form. The crowd around us grew larger, entranced by the brother we had all thought was a little crazy when we were growing up together in my old neighborhood. His insanity had now come into vogue. As Skillet prepared for his finale, he did a decent imitation of James Earl Jones, cupping a little boy's face as if he were looking out a window, and going a tad overboard in the drama department.

> *"Should I call you a man*
> *because you understand*
> *that an absent father is no father at all?*
> *Therefore I know I am a man,*
> *an impeccable man,*
> *a God-fearing man,*
> *A sober and upright man,*
> *a man with faults,*
> *a man with vision,*
> *A man with a dream,*
> *who has fulfilled his dreams.*
> *An educated man,*
> *a simple man,*
> *a woman's man,*
> *A man's man,*
> *a complex man,*
> *a talented man,*
> *A troubled man,*
> *a black man,*
> *because when my son stands,*
> *He'll be a better man . . . than me."*

Folding his outstretched hand into a fist, Skillet brought it securely over his heart and bowed his head. After a brief pause to make sure he was finished, the now large gathering applauded. Brandon clapped with his hands above my head and then returned them lovingly around my torso, pulling me closer toward him. As I closed my eyes, enjoying this gentle man's gentleness, he kissed me on the top of the head. Brandon had incredible lips. Whatever the man kissed would always feel better and I melted, like chocolate rain, right into his arms.

Brandon spent the rest of the day glad-handing public officials and swooning over the Miami Dolphin players who were there as I tried my best to avoid making eye contact with Yvette Shaw. If anyone had told me three weeks before that I would meet Leslie up close and personal, speak to Henry on the phone, talk to Herbert, have Herbert imply that they have mentioned my name, and take my number for Henry to call me, I would have wanted to drug-test the person. But it all happened in 1995. So when Brandon squeezed my hand while we walked toward his car, I wondered if I'd ever really be over the junior senator from Florida.

Chapter 6

"Welcome back, America. We will alert you as to the latest developments on the assassination attempt on the vice president and his condition, as well as the latest news developments on the reported plot against Senator Henry Davis of Florida. But first we would like to update you on the race for the White House. As you may or may not be aware, Governor Tom Baldwin of Arizona has given his concession speech, effectively making this a two-horse race. As of thirty minutes past the hour, here are the latest results. We are projecting that Oregon with her seven electoral votes will go into the Steiner fold. But the election headline news for this hour is this: Davis Bounces Back!

DAVIS	229	██████████████
STEINER	226	█████████████
BALDWIN	126	██████

"That's right. After sustaining losses in his home state of Florida as well as New York, it was not looking good for the first African-American senator from the deep South since Hiram Rivals. But with victories in South Carolina, New Jersey, and Pennsylvania, as well as the Lone Star state of Texas, Henry Davis is making a strong charge tonight to

become the first president of color in the history of the country. Let's swing down to the Fountainebleau Hotel and our
correspondent Butch Harper. Butch, we are told that the
crowd has returned. Can you fill us in?"

"If I may borrow your headline, Frank, you are exactly
right. When the news was reported that an assassin was in
the building, this place cleared out like a group of young
Republicans at a Greenpeace rally. But a little later after it
finally stopped raining here, we in the press corps noticed
that the crowd actually became larger. It may also have
something to do with the closeness of the race at this time."

"Tell me, Butch. Has there been any official word from
the FBI or any other law enforcement agency regarding the
reported threat on the life of the senator? Was it just a diver-
sionary ruse?"

"There is still no official word. But there are those who
believe, shall we call it, the 'ruse theory.' I have attempted
to get the inside story from several of our key sources, and
as of yet, all we have is speculation."

"Butch, I am going to ask you to hold on for a second as
we swing due north to our colleague in Illinois, Judith
Finestein. Judy, what are the latest developments from the
Steiner campaign?"

"We are awaiting a briefing by Steiner's press secretary,
so I will be quick. Here is what has been confirmed. Vice
President Ronald Steiner was shot twice. Once in the right
shoulder and again in the left leg or thigh. There was a
report floating around that a major artery may have been
severed, causing a great loss of blood and putting him in
critical condition. That part of the story, we are unable to
confirm. But we will keep you posted."

"Thank you, Butch Harper from Miami and Judith
Finestein from Chicago, Illinois. Before we send you to a
commercial break, America, I will remind you that as of this
hour, Senator Davis has a small lead, and we are told he is
running well ahead in Utah and Kansas, and the all-important race in California. We reported an hour ago that the
man who wins the Golden State of California will, in all

likelihood, win the election. All indications thus far point to that being true. We will be back in a moment."

Tension filled the air in Suite 1701 as Henry, Herbert, Marcus, a few other advisers, and media representatives listened to the partylike atmosphere next door and the televised reports from the various news agencies on the ballroom floor.

"California will be good to us, I just know it. The bear won't hibernate tonight. We've spent too much damn money and time to lose it," Herbert said as he slid his foot from his shoe and rubbed his sole on the shin of his weight-bearing leg.

Henry said nothing.

"We're going to win, Henry. We are going to pull this shit off, man. Don't you realize that?"

Henry sat stoically.

"Don't tell me you scared now, Henry," he said, looking at his brother. "All night long when I was scared you were telling me it looked good. We gonna win this thing, man."

"Marcus?" Henry said soothingly.

"Sir?"

"Did they bring up my suit?"

"The one we had in our limo? Yes, sir. Would you like me to go get it?"

Looking back at Peter Jennings on television, he replied, "No. I just want to make sure it's not wrinkled when we make our victory speech." As the words fell from his lips, the tension was lifted by laughter and clapping hands.

Standing in the midst of the gathering, Herbert raised his hands and said, "I just want to say something here and now. Where is the young man from *Ebony?*

A bony man raised his hand from the back of the suite.

"Great. What about the young lady from *U.S. News & World Report?* Is she here?"

"Yes, sir."

"I think we also have a photojournalist from *Life* magazine here. Steven Mizzel?" As his name was announced, the photographer clicked his lens into place and walked toward the front of the room.

"Fantastic. I wanted to make sure you all were here to chronicle this moment. You can feel free now to take as many snapshots as you like, and I appreciate your cooperation in not taking pictures of us earlier." Looking down, he said to his brother, "I've always loved you, man. Always have. I have envied you, coveted what was yours, fought you, fought for you, was embarrassed by you, missed you, been proud of you, and hated you. But more than all of those things," he said, looking at Henry, who had his undivided attention, "more than all of those things, Henry, I've loved you." A collective "aww" went up in the room as Henry stood and hugged his brother.

"Now, sit down!" Herbert said, looking at the room. "The floor is mine. Years ago we were brought here in the bowels of ships against our will. We were not asked to come. We were forced to ride, and I concur with Dr. King when he said, America has not fulfilled its promise to us. And when I say 'us,' I mean all Americans. She's given us a bad check because we are only as strong as our weakest link. But this morning America prepares to take a quantum leap toward making good on her promise."

A few members of the campaign clapped as the photojournalists angled their shots to get both brothers in one photograph. In the rear of the suite a security guard opened the door and tried to look at Penelope's credentials as she stormed through and said, "Goddamn, son! I've been in here fifty times tonight. Move the fuck out my way!"

"My brother," Herbert continued, "had this dream when he was fifteen years old. When he was fifteen, he knew he would not just *run* for president. He knew he would win. In the Davis household the first one to the TV decided the station we watched. We would race each other home after school, to see who would be the one to pick the program. He wanted to watch Huntley-Brinkley, and I wanted to

watch Bugs and Road Runner. Who knows where we would
be this morning if I'd been a step or two faster.

"Throughout this campaign, hell, even before it when he
got the flop sweats on *Meet the Press*"—laughter sprinkled
the room—"I knew he would bounce back. Why? Because
he's the walking, talking embodiment of a winner." Henry
looked down at his lap as Herbert paused to contain his
emotions. "And he will put this country back on course to
fulfill its promise to all of its citizens, white, black, Hispanic,
Asian, and female. All its citizens."

At that moment Penelope walked over to Henry and
whispered in his ear as everyone clapped and smiles of confidence showed where none had existed moments before.
"Guys, gals, I'm sorry to go on like that. I just want to finish
by saying, remember our campaign song. Tonight we will
indeed change the world."

And then the clapping stopped as Henry shouted, "What
do you mean missing! You all can't find Leslie?"

HENRY

Although we'd not made any public announcement regarding our intentions to run, by 1998 all cylinders of the "Davis
for President" engine were moving along at a feverish pace.
In February of that year I released a few of my positions on
issues in book form. Leslie and Penelope wanted me to enti-
tle it *Courage Undaunted*, but thinking that was a little too
self-aggrandizing, I went with the more academic title of
The Courage to Change Vs. the Compulsion to Compromise.

The book spoke of how people from all walks of life had
the guts to change the course of their lives, and some even
changed the history of the world. I also outlined a detailed
plan whereby we could save the rain forest without creating
a monetary crisis for the rest of the world, reduce the threat
of chemical warfare, and essentially end homelessness in
twenty years. To many people's surprise, the 915-page book
spent nineteen weeks at the top of the *New York Times* best-
seller list, and after I did *Oprah* and *60 Minutes* in the same

week, our presidential favorability numbers were at an all-time high. In nearly every historically black college as well as many other major universities across the country, "Run Henry, Run" groups organized. Newspapers around the country ran articles favorable to my entering the race for the good of the country, and people started sending in donations for a candidacy that had yet to be declared.

We put together a presidential exploratory committee and it was determined that we could raise over seventy million dollars over the duration of the campaign, which was much more than even we expected. With this information we planned to announce in Miami around Christmas of '98. Why so early? We wanted all of the potential threats to the Democratic nomination to look at the poll numbers, see how much we had raised for the campaign, and decide it was not worth it for them to enter the race. In every major poll across the country we were ahead of everyone, including Vice President Steiner, by seven to ten percentage points. After the announcement I was literally on the road all but two days a month. Actually I wanted to campaign those two days as well, but Herbert thought it best I spend time with Leslie and get some rest.

In April I flew home to attend Easter Mass with Leslie, and I think Penelope had arranged for every major news organization in America to have a photographer there. Walking down the steps of the cathedral holding hands, we cast the Rockwell image we wanted to present. It was wholesome, it was apple pie, it was Americana. But as we sat in the limo, she sat on her side and I on mine, and we did not say a word to each other. Earlier that day we'd spoken, but not as husband and wife, more like two business partners after a board meeting. We both knew something was happening, but I did not make the effort to correct it. Every moment I was awake I gave the run for the White House every fiber of my being. I ate one meal a day, willed myself to survive on four hours of sleep and as a result the other candidates and our marriage ran a distant second.

*   *   *

One day in May I called home and Leslie was not there. She usually got home around seven and would spend time with her various projects, such as Feed the World and the Sickle Cell Foundation. She was always very predictable. But this time the answering machine picked up. I didn't leave a message. I called again an hour later, and once again, no answer. This was strange. We'd been married fifteen years, and I always knew where she was 99 percent of the time. It was not a jealousy complex, but when you're in the public eye and on the road as much as we are, it's comforting to know where your spouse is in the event of an emergency or if you just feel like hearing her voice.

When I got home that night I asked her if she had done anything special and she said, "No." I didn't want to sound like Detective Friday and give her the "Well, on the night in question" routine, but I did want to know the truth.

"No, I didn't do anything," she said. "I just came home like I *usually* do and watched television. Oh yeah, I did go to the beach for a while to clear my head."

I knew she was upset and I should say or do something to comfort her. But I couldn't. Before I knew it, I'd walked out to the garage. Since we had a limo service donate the use of one of their cars to the campaign, we rarely drove. I saw her Mustang still had the canvas cover on it, and I knew she would never take the time to remove it and put it back on by herself with my car there at her disposal. So I looked in my car and I saw a newspaper on the seat from a month earlier. The same newspaper I left on the seat the last time I drove the car. She could have driven it and just left it there . . . but I doubted it.

After eating dinner, we both went into the den. She sat in her recliner and I relaxed on the sofa. I turned the TV on CNN and muted the sound. As we sat there, we both read books and neither of us said a word to the other.

The next day while I was working in the downtown Miami office, I decided to call her to quell the tension. Herbert had arranged it so I would have an extra day in town, and I did not want to spend the time in the midst of a cold war. I called the house and there was no answer. It took all that I could to block out what I thought might be happening, which was the last thing I needed at this time. My poll numbers were beginning to drop substantially. Before I got in the race, everyone was excited about the possibility of the country electing the first black president. But as soon as I made the official announcement, we noticed the numbers starting to slip. Granted this had not come as a surprise. It happened to Kennedy in '80 and more than likely kept Cuomo and Powell out of the race in '84 and '92. We just never expected an avalanche. And then California senator Chuck Clayburn announced that he was forming a presidential exploratory committee and my surefire nomination was up for grabs.

I worked in my Senate office in Miami that night well past nine o'clock. And that was when I got the phone call on my cellular. "Henry, do you mind if I go to Europe for a few days?"

"Europe," I said, putting down my pen and sliding back in my chair. "What's in Europe?"

"An international women's conference. I was invited by Ann Fudge. You know, the president of Maxwell House?"

"Yeah, I know Ann well. So when is this trip?"

"It's, ahh, tomorrow."

"Tomorrow, Les? You're just going to pull up stakes and go to Europe . . . tomorrow . . . knowing what our numbers look like?"

"Well, I was thinking I could maybe press a few palms over there. There will be a lot of powerful women, and with Clayburn making noise out west, we could use the contributions. You know Penelope will pull out that Rolodex and make sure we get the optimum exposure while we're there."

I listened closely to every word she said, and then asked, "So is Penelope going with you?"

"No . . . unless you want Herbert to allocate the money for a last-minute ticket from the travel-expense fund. I just thought I would leave her here to stand in for me at a couple of events."

My heart pumped like a hot piston and I felt blood trickle

through my veins like lava. Throughout our entire marriage I'd never suspected her of cheating on me, not even once. For the past twenty years, we had been running for the presidency as a team, and it was beginning to take its toll. I could not remember the last time she looked at me like she did when we were first married. I could not think of the last time I saw her come into a room and say, "Baby, you look so handsome." When we were younger, she had once heard a saying that she wrote on a piece of paper and sent to me with a dozen white roses. It simply said, "Whatever you do to get it . . . you must do to keep it." Now that was replaced with drives to the beach without moving the car, late nights in the office, and spontaneous trips to Europe.

So she went to Italy. She got the campaign credit cards from Herbert, hopped on a plane headed to Rome, and the next time I saw her, she was being interviewed with Sheila Jackson Lee by Christiane Amanpour for CNN.

At this point I felt betrayed. I'd had countless opportunities to have an affair and I had said no to them all, from Regina in my senior year of high school to Nancy Bolton, a Miss America finalist. I was often tempted, like when a noted Hollywood actress took her panties off under the table, wrapped them around her hotel key card, and put them in my pocket when I was in Los Angeles for the NAACP Image Awards, but I didn't give in. I've always had a one-track mind. But I thought, as the report from Italy concluded, that made one of us.

Walking over to my desk, I flipped open my personal organizer and punched in my code to access the private numbers. I didn't have a lot of them, but the ones I had were good. Models, Olympic athletes, and a number of actresses. Then I saw a number I had tried to delete so many times before for fear I would have a moment just like this one. Unable to resist, I dialed and closed my eyes as she said, "Hello?"

"Ahh, yes. This is . . . I would like to speak to, ahh, Cheryl? I think the last name is Kingsley?"

"This is Cheryl Kingsley," she replied as if she were pre-occupied. "Who's calling?"

I brought my hand up to the receiver and cupped it. I knew I could still hang up, because even if she had Caller ID, it could not trace this particular line. I tried to think fast. Could I do it? Did I want to do it?

"Hello? Is anyone there?"

I had to do it. But was I ready to open this can of worms? And just like when I was a ten-year-old standing at the top of the thirty-foot tower over a pool, I closed my eyes tight, took a step, and felt myself fall. "Cheryl, it's me. Henry."

I could hear the surprise in her silence, and then she said, "My God. Henry, is it really you?"

Cheryl and I had a lot of catching up to do. I put her on hold and called Marcus and asked him to work on the speech I was drafting for a Democratic National Committee function, then took off my shoes and socks, which is something I never do in the office, and lay down on the couch. I was forty-six and yet Cheryl's voice made me feel like I was fourteen. I explained the best I could why I had never called, but she didn't buy it. She told me Darius had passed away and she had gotten remarried. I told her David died in the Oklahoma City bombing trying to save a child's life and I told her about Leslie. No matter how upset or betrayed I felt, I knew I loved that woman because I could not even hold a conversation without her name coming into it. Cheryl and I packed thirty years of memories and guess-whats into a three-hour conversation.

"My goodness," she said. "Would you look at the time? I've got to go to work in an hour. I forgot to tell you, I got a promotion, but it's on the graveyard shift."

"Congratulations anyway. You know, Cheryl, it's been nice to hear your voice."

"Well, I hear yours all the time," she joked, and then the smile in her voice faded as she said, "You're just not talking to me."

"Let's do it," I said as logic grabbed the words and tried to pull them back into my mouth. But it was too late. "Could

you meet me here tomorrow night, about this time?" I felt
confident nothing would happen since we would be here in
the office, but I felt nervous because if she was half as beautiful as Herbert said she was three years ago, I was in
trouble.

"Ahh, sure, Henry," she said. I could hear the uncertainty
in her voice. In all honesty, I did not want to do anything
else but see her. A large part of what was happening in my
life at that moment was due to her. When the seed first
formed, she watered and nurtured it. I think—in fact, I am
positive—if she had discouraged me in those days, I would
have decided to do something else with my life. She meant
that much to me. So we agreed she would meet me at my
Senate office, and as I hung up the phone, I noticed the only
thing sweating more than my ear was my palms.

I called Leslie, and since she was not there, I spoke to
Ramona Edelin of the Urban Coalition for twenty minutes
before Leslie arrived and retrieved the phone. We spoke
again like candidate and campaign supervisor, and I then
hung up and thought about Cheryl.

The next day dragged, and as the time came for Cheryl
to arrive, I went to my credenza and pulled out a fresh shirt.
There was just something about a freshly starched shirt that
made me feel revitalized. I like it so starched I had to make
a fist to put my hand in the sleeve. As I looked at myself in
the mirror while I knotted my tie, I realized I was excited
about seeing this woman who had meant so much to me.

About an hour before my staff left, my secretary buzzed
me. "Senator Davis? There's a Mrs. Allen to see you?"

I thought, *Who is Mrs. Allen?* then I heard her voice in the
background say, "Tell him Cheryl Kingsley." As I asked my
secretary to escort her back to me, I felt myself getting nervous. I was shocked by my anticipation. I had dined with
kings and heads of state and played cards with the president
of the United States of America in his underwear. But this
nurse, who at one time held my heart by a string, had me
shaking as if I were meeting her for the first time in Sears.

And then the door opened.

*   *   *

Even after talking for more than three hours the previous day, we had so much more to discuss. She caught me up on her life. How she got her degree, how she raised her daughter and three or four foster children, how she fell in love with a younger man, and how she often thought of me.

Looking at me, Cheryl whispered, "I hate to just come out and say it like this . . . but God, you're handsome in person." Coming from her, the words melted in my heart as I responded in kind. She was the only person I could think of, outside of family, who loved me solely for me. The famous women who would leave me their numbers wanted me on their resume and to be able to say, "One night I did this or that with Senator Davis." And that even included my wife. I knew Leslie loved me. But something always told me if I were the manager of the department store at Wal-Mart, she would not have fallen for me. I knew she loved me. But I thought she loved who I might become even more. I could not say that about this lady sitting in my office. I think if I managed that department, she would be giving me display ideas and supporting me all the way.

After my staff left and the voice mail box was turned on, we took a break from talking and I walked to the closet, took out a liter of Sprite and a fifth of rum that was left from an office party, and got a few cups of ice from the refrigerator. I offered her a drink and sat down at my desk to make a quick phone call.

"Hello, Appie? This is Senator Davis. That bill on the floor regarding NASA entitlements? Bill number ninety-eight dash—" And that's all I got out. Cheryl walked up behind me, kissed me on the forehead, and said, quietly, "Thank you for the drink." The first thought to enter my mind before I hung up the phone was, *Drink, my ass.*

Before I knew it, we were full-lock, body-to-body kissing. It wasn't passionate, it was more like a two-backed beast in heat. Cheryl did not look good, she looked extraordinary, and her body was still so nice, so firm. Just the way I liked it. As I backed her against the wall, we kissed and logic suddenly kicked in. Something was wrong. I tried to ignore it as I reached down and pulled her leg around my waist, but I could not. I opened my eyes and released her arms from around my neck. *This is not right,* I thought as she stared back at me. And then I walked over to the window and closed the blinds. Pulling off my shirt and cutting off the light, I was about to finish something we'd started in her bedroom thirty years prior. I was about to make love to Cheryl Anne.

As I returned home that night, I looked at myself in the mirror, and for the first time, my reflection sickened me.

We have a tradition in our marriage. Even though we do not have children, we exchange gifts on Mother's and Father's Day as if it were Christmas. I liked that idea so much that one year on my birthday I bought her a gift and gave it to her at my party. Ever since then we have also exchanged gifts on each other's birthdays. As I stared at myself in the mirror, I noticed a lipstick stain right on the evergreen monogram Leslie had added to the shirt she'd given to me on her fortieth birthday. I remembered her face as she told me it was hand stitched and the only design of its nature around. This one-of-a-kind design was now covered with the passion of another woman.

I went into the laundry room, put some detergent on the spot, turned the cold water on, and dropped the shirt in the washing machine. My shirts were never washed in the machine, but I could not risk this one going to the laundry and the attendant telling Kadesha or Leslie the spot could not come out. So I stood there as the water filled the machine and the dank air of the tiny room and thought about the night Leslie and I had christened this very spot. How we had decided that that night we would give each other at least three orgasms. We'd had sex all over the house and then looked at each other when we heard the washing machine go into its spin cycle and read each other's minds. Leslie got out of bed first and started running down the hallway like Flo-Jo. I was hot on her heels like Carl Lewis. I got on top of the machine, she mounted me, and we en-

joyed our bronze, silver, and gold during the shake of the
second rinse cycle. Now I was using this machine to destroy
evidence of me having sex with another woman.

I went into the guest bathroom shower, not wanting anything from the previous sexcapade to sully the domain of
our bedroom. I turned the water up high, in part to cleanse
my body, in part to cleanse my mind, and in part to punish
myself. I had no hard evidence against my wife. Maybe she
was doing something to surprise me as she did from time
to time. Maybe she was just getting tired of the noose
around her neck. I stood in the shower and cried. It's funny.
When I was in my twenties, I would not cry for anything.
I could attend a funeral on a rainy Christmas Sunday morning and I wouldn't drop a tear. But after I turned thirty-
five, I would cry at the drop of a hat. I could be watching
a telephone commercial and from nowhere, I'd begin crying
because the mother of three girls had broken a meeting and
taken them to the beach. It's the strangest thing. But as I
turned off the water and looked at my reddening upper
body, I wept again. I mean, outright sobbed.

It was 1:00 A.M. eastern standard time, which made it 7:00
A.M. in Rome. I waited about an hour because I knew her
schedule when she traveled abroad. Usually she was up
before dawn regardless of the time zone and she would go
jogging before preparing for various meetings. I sat reading
a book and then I called. And if the air conditioner had
turned on at that very minute, the air from it would have
been enough to knock me off the bed. The sleepy voice of
a man answered her phone.

Washington, D.C.
November 8, 2000
NBS News Studio
2:45 A.M. EST

"This is Franklin Dunlop, NBS studios, Washington, D.C.
According to our exit polls, we virtually have a dead heat

in the now all-important California race. The numbers are as follows: forty-one percent of the electoral vote for Davis, forty-one percent for Steiner, and eight percent for Tom Baldwin.

DAVIS	229	████████████████
STEINER	233	██████████████████
BALDWIN	126	████████

"After having a comfortable lead in California tonight or I should say this morning, Davis is locked into an all-out battle with Ronald Steiner. The Steiner numbers have gone through the roof and he is polling extremely well in his running mate's city of San Francisco and in Orange County. We would like to swing first down to Miami and our friend Butch Harper, who is doing just an incredible job tonight. Butch, are you there?"

"Yes, I am, Franklin. In spite of the latest numbers, the number of individuals here has been steadily increasing. When I spoke to you before, Franklin, the crowd here was swelling. At this moment it is literally standing room only as several live bands have taken the stage. There is an aura of victory hovering over this room tonight. The faces are expectant, apprehensive, nervously tense, yet jubilant as one of their own is one state away from making history. The balloons are out and will be released, I am told, as soon as the numbers from California are in, and both the candidate and his running mate are waiting in the wings for the moment which will go down in the annuls of time. Unlike in most elections, Frank, few members of the press have been allowed on the candidate's floor. The Democrats have rented out two floors in the hotel. The seventeenth floor is where a private party for the inner circle of campaign officials and their families is, and the floor we are on is open to the public. There has been little if any party mingling. What I mean by that is, individuals with the blue credentials like I am showing you are restricted to this floor, and this floor only. The red credentials, which I am unable to show you, for obvious reasons, are for the inner circle and their guests only. Tonight the FBI has been very strict about keeping the reds on their floor and blues on ours. This we are told is merely a standard security measure and has nothing to do with the rumored assassination attempt on the Democratic nominee."

"Interesting stuff there, Butch. Keep us posted. Now we take you to Chicago and Judy Finestein."

"Thanks, Frank. As you know, we are now reporting outside the Four Seasons Hotel. We are told there are a number of individuals wishing to congregate in a nearby park for what they expect to be a victorious celebration. A number of clergymen started a prayer vigil for the vice president, and we noticed a group of Young Republicans holding up his picture and ironically singing the old Lennon hit "Give Peace a Chance." There is a lot going on emotionally here, Frank. We're awaiting the latest news on Steiner, we're now looking at the morbid possibility of us electing our first female president, and we're watching closely the results from California. It has been an emotional night, to say the least, for all parties involved."

"Thank you, Judy, for that report. Now, America, when you return, we here at NBS will be in a position to project a winner in several states and possibly even in California. Whatever you do, don't touch that dial, for tonight one way or another you will see history being made."

Fountainebleau Hotel
Suite 1717

"Henry! Where you going!" Herbert shouted to his younger brother. "What's going on?"

Henry pushed aside the agent in front of him with a firm thrust and rushed out the door, followed by Penelope and several other staffers. As he ran in a zigzag pattern down the hallway like a running back through the crowd, Henry's mind raced, trying to think of a logical place where Leslie could be. As he headed toward Suite 1717, the wide-eyed agent in front of the door looked at the crowd approaching him as he spoke into the transmitter on his wrist.

Henry charged past him and into the room, calling Leslie's name, as if there were a possibility whoever searched previously had somehow overlooked her. "Leslie," he yelled as he trotted into the empty master suite, finding it empty. Then Henry noticed her purse and cell phone beside the bed and froze in his steps.

"What the fuck you mean you never saw them leave? How could anyone get out of this room without you seeing them?" Penelope asked the redheaded, freckle-faced agent.

"Well, ma'am, there were a lot of people in the room at one time. Maybe as many as fifty or sixty. I tried to identify each one, but after a while—"

"Penelope, would you come in here?" Henry yelled as he looked into the hallway and noticed a growing crowd with microphones around his wife's press secretary. Penelope walked into the suite, and Henry closed the door so just the two of them stood in the foyer. "Penelope?"

"Yes."

"Her purse. It's in the room. Her cell is in there too."

"Oh shit," Penelope replied, walking toward the couch and sitting on the arm. "That damn girl ain't going nowhere without her purse or that cell." Penelope pulled her curly hair back from her face with her glasses, removed her clip-on earrings, and as she massaged her earlobe, said, "Henry, what the fuck's going on?"

"I don't know. I don't have a clue."

Penelope slid down onto the couch with her elbows planted on her knees and her palms pressed firmly into her eye sockets.

"Penelope? When was the last time you spoke to—"

Looking up, she said, "Henry, when was the last time *you* fucking spoke to her? I'm sorry to be so crass, but enough is enough."

Drawing a shallow breath and not looking in her direction, he asked, "She told you?"

"That you all have not really talked for two or three days? That you accused her of sleeping with Wolinski? That you believe the photos exist? That you hung up the phone every time she called your ass tonight? Which one, Henry? *Which* one you referring to?''

Henry's squared shoulders became round as he turned in embarrassment toward Penelope, unable to find the words.

"Yeah, she told me all of that. And you know something, Henry? I seriously doubt she has ever told *anyone* the stuff she told me tonight. Not even her brother. When you're in the public eye as much as you all are, it's hard to trust anyone for fear it'll one day be on the best-seller list. I could tell she had not said anything to anyone, because I could see the weight leave her as we spoke.''

Henry walked over to the couch and sat beside Penelope.

"Give me your phone," he said softly. Penelope reached into her purse and handed him the cell. "Yeah, Herbert? Listen, the FBI agent who spoke to us earlier? I think he was the chief or whatever. I want to talk to him personally. Okay. Okay. Great. Do me a favor. Call me back on *Penelope's* cell, okay? Thanks, man.'' Henry leaned back into the cushions and resumed the conversation. "I never meant to hurt her. It just killed me that morning to hear that guy's voice on the phone when I called her. I have never gotten over it.''

"Henry, I have a question for you. Have you *ever* heard of splicing photos? Like they say the CIA did with the picture of Oswald holding the rifle? *The Globe* and the *Enquirer* have made a living by doing it. If there are pictures, trust me, they are not legit. You are the smartest man I have ever known, and I mean that. But can I give you a little unsolicited advice?'' Penelope stared at his profile. "Ever since I have known you, hell, ever since Leslie has known you, you've had one passion. She's a better woman than me because she has accepted that your dream is bigger and more important to you than this marriage. She realizes that's first and everything else is a distant second. But don't you think it gets cold living in your shadow and then getting treated like shit on top of it?'' Penelope paused as the words settled. "Now, you know I love you and I always will. You are a special man. But you've got to trust her and you just can't do her like you've been doing her."

Henry sat silent, absorbing the verbal bashing.

"And on top of everything else, you told her about the time I blew you? What kinda shit is that? You don't tell your wife a thing like that, Henry."

Henry looked at Penelope and whispered, "You told her, didn't you?"

"Hell yeah, I admitted to her what happened. I didn't want to get caught telling her a lie on top of everything else that's going on tonight."

Henry leaned his head back and said softly, "I never told her that anything happened between us, Penelope. I never said a word." Penelope's mouth fell open as Henry answered her cell phone.

"Ahh, Henry?"

"Yes?"

"I don't know how to say this, but I asked several FBI agents for Agent Mills and Haggerty, and they said that Mills was killed three miles from here several hours ago. And they never heard of a Haggerty."

"What are you talking about?"

"I don't know. They all seem to have known Mills, so I don't think we were wrong about the names."

"But they were in the room, . . . what, an hour or so ago?"

"I know. I gave them Mills's description, and no one here could place a man like that. I even told them Mills had sideburns, which I thought was a little unusual, and they said that was against regulations."

Rubbing his fingers through his hair and looking at Penelope's blank expression, Henry said, "So who the fuck was in the room with us?"

LESLIE

If there is a year that I will never forget, that year would be 1998. I screwed up. I screwed up big time. I had an affair, and if I live to be a hundred, I will never forgive myself.

A person will do anything from smoking crack to blowing up a plane if he or she can justify it. I knew I was wrong before he started. I knew I was wrong while he was doing it. And I cried myself to sleep after he finished.

I stayed up half the night crying into the soaking wet sheets. Early the next morning I heard the phone ring, and for some reason, I was mummified. I couldn't move. It was as if a bad movie were playing and I was both its star and watching from the front row. I felt dirty and used like a cheap whore, only I wasn't getting paid. Instead I paid the price with my dignity and self-respect. But when I heard James say very sleepily, "Hello?" I immediately snapped out of the trance. I rolled over and snatched the phone from his hand and bobbled it on the receiver several times before I hung it up correctly.

"What the fuck is wrong with you?"

"I, umm, I'm sorry, Leslie. I was asleep and forgot where I was. Besides, I don't even think it was Henry. Sounded like some white guy. More than likely a wrong number," he said, stretching. "Unless I'm not the *only* white chocolate in your life."

I glared at James so hard I know his pale skin must have burned. He looked back at me and touched my bare arm in a consoling gesture. When his soft, damp, clammy fingers came into contact with my skin, it felt like he was actually touching raw nerves, I jumped so hard. "Listen," I said to him sternly, covering my breast with the sheet, "you have three minutes to get out of here!" Then I walked around the bed with the sheet draped around me and stood by the phone. I'd already planned that I would answer it on the fifth or sixth ring and give Henry an I've-been-taking-medication-that-knocked-me-out-and-this-is-the-first-time-the-phone-has-rung-all-morning voice.

So I stood there with the sheet gathered around me like an Egyptian princess, my arms folded, and my hands balled in tight fists while James stole glances at me as he dressed. As he walked out of the room, I didn't respond to his, "Have a nice morning." I simply eyed the phone, praying it would ring. It didn't.

I took a shower and thought about how I could have allowed myself to get into this situation. I have never had a one-night stand in my life. Not even in college. And now, at forty-six, I was letting some *white* man grope all over me? Had the self-hatred in my father's eyes manifested itself within me, or was James simply an aberration?

When our eyes met the night before, I knew what he wanted. After I had dinner with Alexis Herman and a few mutual friends, I walked alone through scenic Via Vènto, wishing I could share it with the old Teddy, and then returned to the reception being given by the U.S. Embassy.

I was slightly tired but put on my best Senator Wife face, and after I had a couple of drinks to relax myself, James's suggestive looks did not seem so repulsive. But more than the effect of the alcohol, this man looked at me like I was beautiful, as if I were a goddess. In all honesty, it was good to feel wanted again. To feel attractive and desired. Henry and I'd had some shaky points in our marriage and that didn't help this situation. I always try to remember the saying "You get what you give," so I always tried to make Henry feel handsome and intelligent and desired. But it was *never* returned.

I've read books on relationships and I have even listened to the gurus on late-night television espouse their theories on love, loss, and happiness. But I have never heard one talk about how love actually changes. Not that it is better or worse, but it changes the longer you know someone. Henry and I were going through those changes. We had not really made love in almost a year and a half. We'd had quickies so he could relax and go to sleep after staying up half the night dialing for campaign donations or something, but I wanted more. I desired more. I needed romance even after twenty-five years with the man. I wanted him to look at me like he did at that hotel when we were kids and tell me I'm beautiful. When I was nineteen and twenty, I'd hear it all the time. But I could have given less than a damn then because I was hearing it from everyone. That was not the case before I went to Europe.

How did James get in my suite? If you've ever been to

Europe or traveled abroad, you know that after a while you start aching for America. For many people it's a few weeks, for others, a few days; with me, it's a few hours. The first thing I want to know whenever we check into a hotel is if NBS International is in the room and if they had an American menu. While I am not a fan of Europe, I had to get away from Henry for a while. I needed space so the destination was irrelevant. I was used to his schedule. I knew how to handle him when he sometimes came home a little short-tempered or when it seemed the *last* person he wanted to see was me. But recently the entire act had gotten a little old and I needed a break for a few days.

In the lobby of the hotel there was a video desk with a great English selection. James asked if I had a VCR in my suite. I told him yes, and when I did, I noticed his eyes brighten. This was no Desiree Washington situation, because I knew what was going on. After a few drinks, I was a more-than-willing participant, as long as I controlled when and how it would occur.

We talked a bit, then went up to my room to watch an old Richard Gere movie called *Breathless*. James was not nearly as smooth as Richard, but I thought it made everything just that much more enjoyable. He sat on one end of the sofa and I sat on the other with my legs resting between us. I wondered what Teddy was doing. I'd tried to call him several times, but he had his cellular off, which was something I could never remember happening before. I felt James gazing at me while I ate popcorn, but I refused to look at him. All the while I made sure I showed more tongue than I should have as I scooped in the white puffs of corn. I could see him out of the corner of my eye smiling. He had grown a bushy mustache and had the most unusual smile. I could see why he used to duck his head before showing it.

And then it happened. He didn't say a word.

I'd forgotten how it felt for a man to ask if it's okay to kiss you with only his eyes and then bring his lips just inches away from yours and guess if you liked it hard or soft. I'd forgotten how that pause felt when you looked into each other's eyes before allowing your bodies to melt. I'd forgotten how it felt to kiss someone and worry if you were pleasing them before allowing yourself to relax and enjoy it for what it was worth. I rediscovered all of those feelings in Italy, and for those moments, I was taken out of my body. I was taken to a place where I was desired and appreciated, where I was not used as a sedative to sleep better, and where I was beautiful, once again. During the act I even heard him saying, "Oh my God! I can't believe I'm making love to Leslie Davis!" It was as if I was his fantasy come true.

I was drying myself from the shower I took after James left when the phone rang. I forgot my plan, dove onto the bed, and bounced so high I just missed hitting my head on the nightstand as I grabbed the phone. "Hello."

"Good morning," he said softly. "You seem out of breath."

"Good morning . . . baby. No, I just ran to catch the phone. How are you?"

"Fine. You know, I tried to call you this morning, about fifteen minutes ago, actually."

I closed my eyes and clenched my teeth as I said, "Ahh, you did?"

"Yeah, some guy answered the phone. I hung up because I hate getting wrong numbers first thing in the morning. I would have called you back, but Ed called me on the other line. So what's on the agenda for today? Are you going to get your running in?"

When he said those words, I almost cried. I'd been so scared I had gotten caught, but he was not wise to me. What was weird was that when I was home, I know he was suspicious of me, but I wasn't doing a thing, although I sometimes led him to believe I was just so I could get a little more attention. But here I am, half a world away, with the scent of a man still in the damp hotel sheets, the used protection on the carpet, and he was asking me if I planned to jog? Was this a way for him to imply that I was getting old? That I was getting fat?

I told him what was going on, and before he hung up he said, as always, "I love you." But this time when he said the words it felt like a cold ice pick had been thrust between my shoulder blades. "I love you too, Teddy," I said. "I love you too."

Henry is sometimes selfish. I can think of no one with a bigger ego than he has. Deep inside the man could make Don King blush with humility. Henry can also be bullheaded, egotistical, and proud, but I loved him more than I loved myself. And I knew there was nothing I could ever do, or say, to forgive myself for what I had just done.

Sacramento, California
November 8, 2000
NBS News Studio
2:50 A.M. EST

"Good Morning, Franklin, and good morning, America. This is Monica Chan reporting from the statehouse in California. As reported earlier, NBS News has made projections in forty-nine states including Alaska and Hawaii, but as of this moment the race here is simply too close to call.

"Presently, Vice President Steiner has opened up a two percent lead, but it's much too close for either candidate to feel comfortable. If you're curious about the chants behind me, we're reporting from the Steiner campaign headquarters, and this crowd of well over three thousand people are chanting, 'I stand, you stand, we all stand for Steiner.' That has been the battle cry throughout the campaign, but has taken on an added dimension this morning. This is Monica Chan sending it back to Washington, D.C."

"Thank you, Monica, for that report. It has been a long night, America. Now we bring you yet another tragic story. A federal agent named Earl Mills was gunned down earlier this evening. His body was discovered in Miami within the past hour. We've received few other details as of this moment. I can— Wait a minute, wait a minute. I am being told now . . . that Leslie Davis . . . is missing. That's right. The wife of Senator Davis has just been reported missing. Oh my God."

Cheryl sat on the edge of her bed saying a prayer for both Henry and Leslie when she heard a knock at her front door.

She stood up and walked down the hallway, trying to plan what she would say to him. Cheryl peeped through the eyehole, just to make sure, and then she opened the door. Soaked to the bone, Brandon stared at her with a pained look in his eyes.

Cheryl moved aside as he walked through the doorway, leaving muddy tracks on the ivory carpet. As she closed the door, the carpet was the least of her concerns.

Brandon did a military about-face, twisted his lips, held up his head, looked at his wife, and said, "I've thought and thought about it, and, Cheryl . . . It's over. I want a divorce."

CHERYL

It was a fall night in '99 and I was sitting in the car outside my house. I saw Brandon come to the curtain, look out, and then close it. And I remember asking myself, *Why can't I let him go?*

That particular day started at nine o'clock sharp for me. I'd worked double shifts two days in a row and it was a Saturday. The only Saturday I would be off for the next two months. I returned home after four in the morning, and when the alarm clock rang five hours later, I heard Brandon swat the off button with his hand.

Raising up from the bed, I asked, "What are you doing?"

"The clock," he said, still half asleep since he'd worked the midnight shift as well. "You must have set it by mistake."

"No," I said, shaking my head and then sitting on the

side of the bed. I slid my feet into my slippers, walked into the bathroom, and closed the door.

As I washed my face, I heard him ask, "Where you going?" I did not answer. "Cheryl Anne?"

I hated when he called me that, and hoped he'd go back to sleep. As I brushed my teeth, I heard him get out of bed and come to the door.

"Honey? You're off today. I was thinking that maybe we could—"

"I can't. I promised Etta I would come down to headquarters to help them plan for the rally tonight."

"Aren't you on call?"

"I'll carry my pager," I said, walking past him to the closet.

"But I thought you wanted to go to the movies or something today."

"Some other time." I rolled up my panty hose, put my foot in, and did not notice the run until I got them rolled all the way up my hips. "Dammit!" I said as I glanced at the clock, pulled down the hose, and tossed them into a corner of the room beside the wastepaper basket.

Watching me scurry around the room with more vigor than I ever had before going to work, late or not, Brandon sat on the bed. "What's wrong with you?"

"I'm gonna be late, and I hate being late."

"Since when?"

"Since . . . Never mind," I said, retrieving another pair of hose and this time sliding my hand in to inspect them before going to the trouble of putting them on.

Brandon walked back around to his side of the bed, pulled back the covers, and lay between the sheets as he watched me rush around the room looking for the right blouse to wear with a green plaid skirt I'd taken from my closet.

"I can't find *anything* in this place," I said, taking his underwear out of my drawer and tossing them on the floor. "Have you seen my new blouse I bought a couple of weeks ago? I can't find it anywhere!" He said nothing. I noticed the blouse under a bundle of clothes and remembered it was dirty. "Damn!" I then tossed the skirt onto the chair, went back to the closet, and took out an ivy sweater shrug and halter with a matching wool A-line skirt and low-heeled ivy sling-backs. All the time I was thinking, *I hope this is still his favorite color.*

"Why are you so flustered this morning? Just call the campaign office and tell Mariah or Etta you'll be a few minutes late."

"Because I gave them my word!" I snapped back, and then as I stood in front of the closet, I caught myself. I was all excited because of the chance I might get to see Henry. And here I was hoping he would see me wearing green and that I would take his breath away. *I'm pathetic.* But as soon as the thought crystalized in my mind, it faded as I found the cream-colored accessories to go with the outfit.

I put my comb, bobby pins, and brush in my purse with my compact and lipstick and slid my feet into my flats. When I turned around I was startled by Brandon standing behind me. "What are you doing?" I asked, walking around him to get my jewelry. "You almost scared me to—"

"What's up with you, Cheryl? We'd planned to spend this day together, and now you running around here like a chicken with its head cut off. And since when you dress like this to go volunteering?"

I ignored him.

"Is it because you might get to see Davis?"

I walked out of the room and down the hallway toward the garage door in the kitchen.

"Cheryl!" he yelled.

I spun around, and said, "What's my problem? What's *your* problem? For once I am doing something I enjoy, and you make a big deal out of it. You should grow up! And stop acting like an overgrown child. I told you I gave her my word, and I'm sorry, that means something to me. Now, if you must know, I am dressed up today because *USA Today* will be in the headquarters taking photos, and Mariah asked us to all look presentable. Satisfied?" I said with my hand on my hip. "Damn!"

Brandon stood speechless. And then he walked toward me with an apology in his eyes, but I just nodded my head

as if I were disgusted, picked up my pager, put my purse
under my arm, and stormed through the door.

As I drove out of our subdivision, my breathing was la-
bored. I was conflicted as to how I truly felt. Once I assumed
that time and maturation would end the longing. Then I
thought if I saw for myself just how much he cared for his
wife, I could leave the thought of him behind. Now I was
working in his campaign headquarters to bring a sense of
closure to what we had had, to break the bond he held on
me. But it seemed everything I did to free myself only drew
me closer.

One of the AM talk radio stations changed its format after
Henry announced his run for the presidency. They adver-
tised as "The only station in America where you can get all
Davis, nothing but Davis, twenty-four hours a Davis," and
my radio was set to pick up all the news. By this time Henry
was holding off the other Democrats for the nomination.
The only one who had a chance of defeating him was the
senator from California, Chuck Clayburn. It seemed that
Henry and Senator Clayburn were both on the same side of
most issues, and the California senator could not point out
any good reason why Democrats should nominate him to
run in the general election. So he started to get personal in
his campaign. When all else failed, he would talk about
Henry's business ventures or the snafu Henry had made
years earlier on *Meet the Press*. Once he went so low as to
question why Leslie had made a major speech regarding
Henry's foreign policy agenda. After he made that comment,
his polling numbers moved up a little, and so he would
mention Leslie in nearly every speech. The country never
approved of Leslie in polls. She was intelligent, articulate,
and unafraid to take positions that were less than popular.
So as I was driving that day, I heard the reporter ask, "Senator Davis, are you offended that Senator Clayburn has begun
to attack your wife in the last couple of weeks?"

"No," Henry replied. "I am not offended. I think that
when you run for public office, many people want to know

all the facts. But will I attack his wife? No, I will not. But you know"—and then I heard a smile in Henry's voice— "sometimes it seems as if Senator Clayburn has given up running for president and has decided to run for first lady." I burst out laughing.

When I arrived at campaign headquarters, which was dubbed the "Southern War Room," the activity was bustling. My favorite radio station was heard from the speakers in the ceiling, and everyone moved with a little extra vigor due to the big rally later that night. The Davis campaign had initially rented a vacant store, but as Henry's numbers improved, they welcomed more and more volunteers wanting to be a part of history, so they moved the campaign across town to a building that was four times larger. The walls were plastered with Davis/Gallagher posters and assorted bumper stickers. There were mayonnaise jars all around filled with sprinkles, because each time Henry scored a major point on the radio or other positive Davis news came over the air, the inside joke was "Can I get a sprinkle for that one?"

There were college kids all around with red, blue, and purple hair stuffing envelopes and making phone calls for donations. Some of the kids had been pierced in places I didn't realize could be pierced, and many of them wore red shirts with either "Henry's Kids" or "Leslie's Kids" on the back of them.

The Southern War Room manager was an overweight woman named Mariah who had long black hair and who I never, as long as I worked there, saw sit down. As soon as she walked through the door, she would kick her shoes into a corner and march around the room talking to the people in charge of each department. The lieutenant who ran our department was Etta, a twenty-something former Gonzaga coed who dropped out to help in the campaign.

I worked in the correspondence room. Our job was to go through all the mail and see if a donation was included. We would then return the letter with a picture of Henry and one of twenty form letters with Henry's signature rubber stamped at the bottom. What amazed me was the type of letters he would get. Yes, there were a few which used the "N" word as if it were the only noun they knew, but most of the people seemed to adore him. So many hoped that he could in fact change the world. And there were letters that came with the most popular gift, which was teddy bears. They came from all over the world, in all shapes and colors. He also received his fair share of other little extras, such as panties. Some clean . . . others less then new. There were also a number of nude photos, and when Henry said he supported gays in the military, several au naturel male photos came in with notes attached. One of these read: "I have a completely open chamber, Mr. Senator. How about you?"

As I put my purse in an open cubicle, Etta ran in with a stack of papers and plopped them down on the oak conference table, which had everything from a TV and fax machine to a laptop and a cooler on top of it. Etta's close-cropped hair was dyed blond and she had a tattoo of her infant son on one C-cup breast. "Did you hear the news?"

"You mean about Clayburn running for first lady? Yeah, that was—"

"Naw, naw, he made that comment yesterday. Henry's in town, and Mariah just told me he called and said he'll be dropping by since this will be the last weekend he will be in town for a couple of months." She looked me up and down, and said, "Good thing you dressed. I wanted to go home and change, but Mariah is guarding the door, saying we have too much work to get done."

Although I told Brandon I was only dressing for *USA Today*, in my heart I knew he would come by. We still had a way of communicating telepathically after all those years. Lieutenant Etta put her headphones back on as she pulled out a box of mail and gave it to me and a guy she dated named Frank.

I started to open letters and scan each one to see what kind of form letter to send. If they asked where he would be in the next few weeks, they got form letter five. If the writer was a bimbo who included a lock of hair, a nude photo, or a phone number, it was form letter twelve. A request for a position paper received a number one letter.

But then there were always some that fell outside of the norm.

One was from a kid who started by saying how he prayed for Henry each night and knew God would answer his prayers. I noticed that taped to the back of the letter was a rolled-up five-dollar bill. As I took the money off and put it with the checks we'd received, I continued to read.

My name is Melvin Gilman and I am eight years old and I have Sick Cell. I got it from my mom side of the family and every time I get sick she cries for a long-long time. I hate getting sick because I get real stiff and everything on my whole body aches. Even my face hurt. Even my eye balls hurt. Doctors use to tell my grand me-maw that I would never live three years. Then it was five years. Then seven. Now I'm eight and a half. But this time my red blood cells are almost all attacked by the sick cells and they saying I will not make it to nine. For the first time they might be right. I know you will win. I just want to be alive for one day while you are president. I just want to be able to call you President Davis.

The rest of the letter spoke of his hobbies and what he wanted to be if he survived. And that was when it hit home for me why it was so vitally important for this man to be elected president. So many people were hurting in so many ways, and I felt the country needed Henry to begin the process of healing. I looked for Etta and Frank, but neither of them was in the room, so I retrieved the five-dollar bill, retaped it to the letter, and put it in my purse. I would write a letter to him that night and have Etta rubber-stamp Henry's signature on it. And I decided that for the rest of the campaign I would try to block Henry out of the picture and focus my energies totally on the election of Senator Henry Louis Davis the Second.

"Turn to seven! Turn to channel seven!" yelled someone running down the corridor. You could almost hear the TVs in the offices turn simultaneously. As Frank ran in the room to turn on our television, we saw the well-tanned face of

Senator Clayburn. All I heard him say was, "After talking to my wife, friends, and staff, we feel the time is now to—" The next thing I knew, the office was having a massive confetti moment. It was rumored for weeks that his campaign had run out of money, but he was gaining momentum, so this move was unexpected.

As Etta and Frank hugged, I picked up the phone and called home.

"Hello?"

"Brandon, I just wanted to—"

"Yeah, I'm watching NBS now," he said in a somber tone. "I can't believe he dropped out."

"No, I'm not talking about that," I said as I put the tip of my thumb in my ear so I could hear. "I just wanted to apologize for this morning. I'm only functioning on a couple of hours of sleep, but that's no excuse. Sorry."

"Thanks, baby. Listen, if you like, I can bring you something to eat."

"That's okay. Domino's and Pizza Hut handle that, and a couple of soul-food restaurants will be bringing some oxtails and yellow rice down later on. You know how I am about some soul food."

"Umm. Well . . . I'm just sitting here doing nothing. Would you like me to—"

"One second," I said, cutting him off before he could finish the sentence. Thinking fast, I said, loud enough for him to hear me, "I'll be right there, Mariah," and then winked at Etta, who was still cradled in Frank's arms. "Baby, can I call you back later? I really gotta go!"

"Okay, but—"

"Thanks, love you, 'bye!"

As I hung up the phone, I felt bad, but in the event Henry did come down to the office, dealing with Brandon's feelings was not something I could handle.

After I finished an early lunch at my desk, Mariah peeked her head into the office. "Cheryl? Your name Cheryl Allan, right?"

"Yes?"

"Are you going to be able to help us out on Monday?"

"I'll be on call, just like today, but more than likely I can help out. Why?"

"Would you mind picking up Jesse Jackson Jr. and Congressman Harold Ford from the airport?"

"Sure."

"Great." And then she wobbled down the hallway, barking orders to another volunteer. As she walked away I could not believe that a year ago I didn't even know who my congressman was. Now I was transporting some of the most powerful men in the country around in my car. As my pager went off, I heard someone say in another room, "Say, what time will he and Leslie be here?"

"About five," Marcus, who never noticed me, said. "They're at his office now and will make a few stops before heading our way."

As I picked up the phone to call the hospital, I looked at my watch. I had two hours before Henry's arrival.

"Front desk," the husky voice of Brett Shuttlesworth blurted.

"Brett, I just got paged."

"Need you to come in. Alice isn't feeling well."

"So?" I said, trying to think of any way to stall or delay her. "Have you called—"

"Everybody, Cheryl. I've called everyone and I'm off in a half hour and I'm not pulling another double."

I held the phone without saying anything when another cheer went up in the background.

"You down at the headquarters?"

"Yeah," I said, hoping she would show some sympathy.

Then I heard her sigh. "Let me see if Tilton can come in. But I can't promise you anything."

"Thanks," I said. "I really appreciate this."

As I hung up the phone I wanted to turn the pager off in the event Tilton could not fill in, but I returned it securely under the waistband of my skirt so I could feel the vibration and returned to opening the senator's mail.

Lieutenant Etta marched in and pulled up a chair to watch television. I turned around to see what was on and saw

Leslie's face. "Talk about a lucky woman," I heard Etta say
to no one in particular. "I've often wondered how it would
be to have a man like that. Don't get me wrong, Frank's my
sweetie but, I mean, the first time I heard him speak was
on my campus," she said, and narrowed her eyes as she
reminisced. "I knew I had to do whatever it took to get him
elected. My mom and dad had Kennedy. They had Bobby
and Martin. But who have we had since? How many of
them were true heroes? Nixon? Carter? Bush? We don't even
remember them on a first-name basis. Now we got Henry.
Unlike that narcissistic Stanton or chauvinist Governor Baldwin, Henry cares. Not like he's doing it because of personal
gain or ego. His plans are so original and he seems to want
to do this because he would like to leave the world a much
better place than when he first encountered it." And then
she looked at me and said, "Don't you agree?"

"Yeah," I said quietly as my pager hummed. "She's pretty
lucky." As soon as I looked down at it and saw *911 I knew
Charlotte would not fill in and I would miss yet another
opportunity to see Henry.

That night in 1999 I returned home and as the water from
the sprinkler splashed against the passenger side of my car,
I remembered the letter in my purse from the little boy with
the sick cells. I retrieved it and read it again, thinking it
would take my mind off Henry so I could focus on reality.
But then I refolded it and wondered again, why couldn't I
let him go? And for the first time I knew the answer to that
question as Brandon opened the house door with a smile
on his face and walked toward the car. It was because sometimes holding on to absolutely *nothing* . . . is holding on to
something, if it means something to you.

Chapter 7

Cambridge, Massachusetts
Harvard University
Saint Patrick's Day, March 2000

HENRY

Although we were invited to participate, I didn't feel comfortable being a part of the St. Patrick's Day celebration in Boston. I couldn't even imagine a few of those drunk, green-beer-drinking politicians joining me in Atlanta on Martin Luther King Day. But I was invited to address a convention, so I did a book signing at a bookstore in Brockton called Cultural Plus and then I swung through Boston for a photo op.

Of all my visits during the campaign, the one that stands out the most was my invitation to speak at Harvard, probably because I had come very close to attending Harvard Law. I spent an hour or so with a photographer from UPI and about ten or so Rhodes scholars in the JFK School of Government. I have always been enamored of youthful intelligence. College students have been the moral conscience of nearly every industrialized country in this century. From the acts of civil disobedience viewed by the world at Kent State to the lone student staring down the barrel of the armored tank in Tiananmen Square, not only have students asked the rest of society *why?* they've stated categorically *why not?*

After leaving the School of Government, a couple of assistants and I attended a general assembly which was going to be broadcast on the campus television network and possibly picked up by C-SPAN. Backstage, I prepared my notes to make sure I was ready for anything these young, bright minds could dish out.

I thought about Malcolm here as well as people such as George Wallace, Lenny Bruce, and even Governor Jesse "The Body" Ventura. Now the name of Henry Louis Davis the Second would be added to that list.

I was not nervous, because I was in debate form. Every Sunday Leslie, Herbert, Ed, Penelope, and I would go through at least two hours of mock debates, whether I was on the road or not. If I was away, it was done via conference call or an Internet chat room. It was simply crucial. We would review the important issues from the week, the other candidates' views, and we practiced over and over again not just my response but the *perfect* response. We even practiced what the other candidates would say. Herbert used to carry around this sign that read, "Character, Clarity, Correctness," and would put it in a visible place as we rehearsed. In other words, I was graded on each answer based on how well I had done in each of those areas.

As I took my trademark half-jog onto the stage, there were a couple of boos from the back of the audience, but by and large the greeting was warm and enthusiastic. We were warned beforehand that the school had a very large and growing conservative contingent that was possibly planning to disrupt the gathering, but I was ready for that as well. There were a couple of well-thought-out questions regarding America's foreign policy with India and my plans to ensure that Social Security was around when the younger generations needed it. One asked if I suspected the CIA or some other government-backed agency had anything to do with creating AIDS, and how could a satellite read an automotive tag from outer space yet be unable to detect poppy fields in Columbia. "With all due respect, sir, I think that is irrefutable evidence that the U.S. government both created the AIDS virus to get rid of the undesirables as well as assisted South American drug lords for the exact same reason."

After I gave him a very noncontroversial answer, another student asked a very good question in a very bad manner. "Yo, Senator Davis. My name is Tron and I am from the boogy down round bouts Yankee Stadium. It's crazy-go-bananas back there but I'm sure you know the area. My question is this, Money. In his book *Black and White, Separate, Hostile and Unequal,* white Professor Andrew Hacker of Queens College says there's a gulf between people of color and the white oppressive majority which may not be closed unless the *black* man makes a move. Tell these folks the dealio and how the people of color in general, and the *black* man *specifically,* will triumph over the autocratical opinions of the oppressor and take the place in this society which is rightfully his!" The crowd laughed and booed as he sauntered to his seat, dragging one leg behind and clutching himself. I wasn't embarrassed for the brother. Was he out of order in his approach? In a way. But he was being out of order . . . in Harvard. Again I answered his question without making waves or creating controversial sound bites.

And then a young man who looked just like an extra from the movie *Mississippi Burning,* with his slick, greasy, black hair and pocket protector, stood up to the microphone. He did not give his name, nor did he show any emotion as he spoke in a monotone, without taking a breath. "Mr. Davis, do you consider yourself to be an African-American and if so why or why not?"

I'd expected this question to come up in the campaign due to a speech Leslie had made at the Million Woman March. I just did not expect it in that gathering. I leaned into the bright lights and said, "Yes, yes, I am an African-American. Because I am proud to be of African descent and proud to be an American. See, I feel—"

"But why not just call yourself an American?" he shouted as a couple of boos mixed in with the cheers I got for the answer. "Is calling yourself simply an American not *good* enough, sir? Not *good* enough for the man wishing to run this country?"

"You know, I have followed politics in this country, and throughout the world, I might add, for the past thirty-plus years," I said, walking away from the podium and up the stairs with the hand-held microphone toward the student. As I did so, there was a collective gasp in the room. "I have probably watched more tapes of debates, with all due respect, than anyone in this room. So I am surprised," I said, standing about ten feet away from the student, "that people are somehow *offended* when I express my pride in my ethnic heritage. When Ronald Rea—"

"Sir! This has *nothing* to do with Mr. Reagan. Black folks in this country have bent over backward to separate themselves! You want to be given the same rights, yet you subscribe to the tenets of separatism. You got black colleges, a black Miss America contest, black television networks. How can you say all you want is to be a part of the mainstream when *you* keep building walls between us!"

By the time he finished his diatribe, I'd returned to the podium. He was making arguments I'd debated in college thirty years earlier at Georgetown, so I decided to allow the crowd, which was booing and throwing paper balls at him, to handle the situation. I was very proud of the way I'd handled the question because I'd resisted the bait to indignify myself. I wondered how it would be played out in the national media.

The next day I expected to see a videotape of the event on the news, anxious about what spin they would put on it. However, as I clicked from one station to another, it was nowhere to be found, which was curious since by this time in the campaign at least three cameras were usually around to photograph everything I did, short of taking a leak. The next day I got up early for my flight to Baton Rouge and a charity basketball game, and read the paper in the limo on the way to the airport. There was just a small corner article about the debate, which said I made an appearance and spoke to the students, accompanied by a snapshot of myself at the podium. I called Ed immediately to find out what happened, and he said it got buried by a couple of larger stories.

*   *   *

For the next several months Marcus had me booked on any and every talk show we could get on. We noticed that the crowds were starting to grow larger and younger, and the press were there in droves, but the downside to this was that any slipup was seen around the world

One Monday afternoon we had over four thousand people show up at a rally at the University of Minnesota, and it was the first time I saw one of the dirty tricks we suspected the Republican party was responsible for.

Our rallies were always carefully orchestrated events. There were three roped-off sections. Up front about one thousand people who had either worked in the campaign or had given donations were allowed to stand. In the next section there were a thousand individuals who were affiliated with the Democratic party. And behind that section stood everyone else. This was done because when hecklers or other disrupters were in attendance, they were so far out of view they never made the news. But on this particular Thursday out of the corner of my eye I saw a young man who must have brought his costume in a brown bag. How he had infiltrated us, I never found out, but as I spoke, he changed into King Henry garb and held up a sign that read:

Support King Henry the XXXIV

And the back of the sign read:

Because thirty-four times last year he voted to raise your taxes!

Needless to say, he was booed and even punched by a few of my supporters, but then I noticed the King Henrys would show up at almost every rally. Then I noticed signs with my face painted with the body of a chicken attached. There was always a caricature of Leslie with the words hen-pecked on the bottom. This culminated into an incident that occurred when I was doing a press conference on the tarmac of LAX. A guy put on a King Henry hat, and when everyone looked his way, someone threw a pie in my direction that missed badly but caught Marcus flush in the face. I had tried to overlook the stunts in the past, but Herbert ended up pressing charges this time, and that was the last of the King Henrys and the henpecked signs.

When I returned home from the swing through California, the tension between Leslie and me was at an all-time high. My poll numbers after Clayburn finally bowed out went through the roof, yet I could not get a decent night's sleep when I lay in my own bed. I couldn't remember the last time my wife and I had shared a real kiss or a hug or even danced. On a plane to Columbus, Ohio, I asked myself, was it really worth it to win the presidency and lose my wife? As we flew, I thought about the man who had answered her phone that morning in Europe, and I knew the answer was obvious. Frightening, yet obvious.

Los Angeles, California
Los Angeles Convention Center
Democratic National Convention, August 2000

LESLIE

I was asked by Jane Pauley what the most memorable moment of the campaign was for me. It was an easy question to answer. It was in Los Angeles at the Democratic Convention. We'd clinched the nomination about a month earlier and had decided to take a few weeks off to both prepare for the general election and relax, and if we could somehow fit falling back in love in the equation, that would be an added benefit.

We took a vacation to Martha's Vineyard, and the first day we were there, Teddy did nothing but work. He and Ed set up interviews and wrote position papers and talked to the chairwoman of the party about a plank or who would speak and in what order. These things he could have assigned to others, but it seemed as we got closer to achieving our goal, the more difficult he found it to delegate.

I wanted my husband back. I'd shared so much of him for so long, and I knew if we won the election, I wouldn't see him for another eight years. In Rio a diplomat once quietly asked me through an interpreter if Henry could possibly be as good in bed as he looked like he could be when he walked. She even had the nerve to say, "I bet he can really drill you, no?" She meant that as a compliment, but the sister-girl almost came out in me for a split second.

Women often told me just how fortunate I was to have Henry as a husband. I would nod my head in agreement while thinking, *If only you knew how much I wished I had a husband like yours.* A husband who could take you out from time to time to a blues club or who would work on the lawn and shoot hoops with your son. Just a simple everyday Fred-type husband who came home at the same time every evening and who fell asleep with you every night. I know I am fortunate to have Teddy for a husband, but there are nights I wish I were not so fortunate.

The five of us had a meeting to officially select a vice presidential running mate at the convention. The names of twenty-five congressmen, mayors, and governors were written on the chalkboard, and Herbert asked us to choose the top three candidates we wanted on the ticket and the three we didn't want considered.

While no one name appeared on all of our lists in the "would like to have" group, one name appeared on all five "would not consider" lists. It was that name which eventually got the nod.

Richard Albert "Dirk" Gallagher was southern just like us, which did not bring much to the ticket. But he was from the Lone Star State, and no matter how we looked at the numbers, with its diverse racial population, it was the keystone to any victory scenario. We knew if we could lock up Florida and Texas it would be hard to defeat us. He was seen as a moderate, which would help in the heartland, and he was a Purple Heart recipient twenty years older than Henry, so he would give the ticket a few needed gray hairs. The reason we did not like him was that it was thought that he was racist and sexist, but for the sake of the campaign, we decided to put our personal feelings aside.

A few party leaders wanted to block Henry's nomination on the convention floor because he was not the traditional Democrat. He was pro-ecology, yet he was for increases in military spending. He was pro-choice, yet he was against the capital gains tax. When asked if they would vote for him in the fall his polling numbers with white male votes were a little less than 40 percent, yet he polled well over 60 percent of white female and more than 90 percent of African-American and Hispanic voters.

When Henry met with Dirk Gallagher, the air crackled with tension. Governor Tom Baldwin was being viewed as a possible third-party contender, so we wanted to split the all-important white male vote. We figured Gallagher could deliver much of the southwest and possibly help us in California. Dirk had made it clear that he was running in 2004 if we lost and did not want to be a part of the campaign if we did not make an all-out push for victory. He didn't want to be branded as being on a losing campaign. So Henry didn't get into a pissing contest with him. Instead he left and allowed Herbert and Marcus to discuss how we felt we could win in the general election against either Steiner or Governor Tom.

After speaking with him for an hour, Marcus walked out bewildered. He told us the more he spoke to Dirk, the more dead set the governor was against accepting our invitation. Henry folded his arms across his chest, deep in thought for several minutes, as he would do when he problem-solved, and then I overheard him whisper to his key adviser, "Listen closely. This is how you sell a big Texas oil man like him. Keep repeating win-win to him. It's like music to his ears, believe me. Tell him if he runs, and we win, he will be a shoe-in for '08. If he runs and we lose, then he will have lost that racist tag. He'll pick up a number of female and minority voters and he'll win the nomination hands down in 2004."

Marcus returned to the room armed with the new strategy, and after another hour, Henry and I walked into the gray cigar-smoked-filled room. Dirk Gallagher looked at me as he was about to light a Cuban as if to ask why I was there, and the more he stared, the more I smiled at him. He looked down his nose like we needed him more then he needed us. Unfortunately, sometimes in politics that is the case, and on a warm night in August, Henry and I joined hands with him and his wife in the L.A. Convention Center in a sign of solidarity. After we left the stage, we didn't speak to them, nor did they speak to us. We attended a star-studded reception given by Rob Reiner and Steven Spielberg after we left the building, and it was the last time the four of us would ever be in the same room again.

Teddy and I were never the partying types, so although we were invited to several other galas around town, we returned to our room in the presidential suite of the Beverly Wilshire a little after midnight. One reason Teddy did not want to go out was that he did not want to be seen as a part of the Hollywood crowd, which might turn off too many people in the more rural parts of the country.

Henry sat in bed reading a book that had been sent to him about this black man running for president. Very rarely did he have time to read for sheer enjoyment, and as he sat there, I put on one of his T-shirts and no panties, which I knew always turned him on, and sat beside him reading a book entitled *Invisible Man*. On the television his face appeared and he looked up from his book. They showed a sound bite where he was looking into the sea of delegates and then the camera zoomed in on his face.

"Tonight I would like to say, as we stand on the brink of the next millennium, that we can make it right. In Dante's *Inferno*, the great author wrote that man has the ability to make a hell out of heaven, or a heaven out of hell. We have an opportunity to create something of beauty. No, it will not be utopia. But it will be a place called America. A place where—" And that's when I cut off the television. Henry's eyes returned to his book. I think even he was tired of hearing him.

I sat there wanting to touch him, to kiss him, wanting to hold him in my arms and rub his head and tell him that I loved him. That I was there for him. But there was this thick wall of ice that ran down the center of our bed, so I sat there and pretended to read.

I had grown tired of the forced period of celibacy. Not of a physical nature, but of the heart. I wanted to open it to him again, to delve deeply into the passion of lovemaking with the only man I ever loved. But I turned the page and my thoughts elsewhere.

Then I looked at Henry and gently put my hand on his forearm. Teddy stopped reading and our eyes met at my wedding band and then he looked over his reading glasses into my eyes. "I just wanted to touch you, honey. That's all. Don't get so scared." He smiled and turned the page in his novel. I started to roll over and go to sleep as I had done nearly every night before, but I stopped. No, not tonight. Tonight, no matter what, I was going to regain my husband.

So I laid my novel down on the nightstand and slowly reached for his book. As I pulled it away from his hands, he broke his grasp and looked at me with that "I'm not ready for this" look. I rolled up his shirt and kissed him on his chest and I could feel him lean his head back. I kissed his nipples and ran my tongue all over his abdomen, and when I looked at him, he was staring at me as if I'd jumped over a fence and were trespassing on private property. But I was not going to give up, on him or our marriage, so I kissed him again and then my kisses fell below. I had not kissed him below the belt for so long I'd almost forgotten what I was doing. As I continued to kiss him, I noticed there was *no* reaction; however, I was going to be persistent. So I kissed him and caressed him and saw there was still nothing. I kissed him harder and more lovingly. I knew it had been a while, but I thought I knew what to do to get what I wanted. Now I was all out of ideas.

Finally I looked him in the eyes, pulled up his underwear and turned on the television with the remote. As he reached for his book, I picked up my novel as well and as I tried to find the page he clicked off the television and I looked at the screen and in it I saw his reflection looking at me. We seemed to just look at each other via the darkened TV, both obviously wondering what had happened to what we shared. And then he turned his back and said "goodnight."

The next day Henry took off on a campaign swing through Texas, Arizona, and Oklahoma with his running mate. I flew out to a meeting with Dorothy Height in D.C. and then to New York to address the National Council of Negro Women. Penelope had warned me not to do the speech for fear the organization was "too black," but as with most issues of this nature, I made my own decision. Afterward I was sitting with a group of campaign volunteers in the Harlem restaurant Emily's when a call came through on my cell phone. "Hello?"

"Les, Penelope. I just got a call from Courtland Milloy at the *Post*. He put me on the phone with someone who told me there are photos being circulated. Do you know anything about this?"

"What kinda photos?" I asked while eating my lunch.

"I don't know. They are shopping them, and the person I spoke to had not seen them. They're supposed to be of you."

"What about me?" I asked, looking at two photographers changing their lenses in an attempt to capture every breathing moment of my life on film.

"I don't know, girl, that's why I'm calling. Can you think of *anything*? Anything at all?"

Quietly I said, "Well, Teddy and I used to make love outside at night or sometimes early in the morning. But that's been several years. Now we—"

"Les, this has nothing to do with Henry. That was the first question out of my mouth. Now, if you can think of anything, I'll jump in there and try to buy the motherfuckers myself. We got a little play money socked away."

"Penelope, you know me. I don't know of anything anyone could have photographed."

The next day Penelope called me from our Northern war office in Washington, needing me to sign a bank authorization for her.

"What for?"

"Les, it ain't pretty."

"What do you mean?"

"Listen, I don't like talking on cells, you know that. Both Herbert and Ed are flying in on the red-eye. We are keeping Henry *completely* in the dark. Please don't say a word to him about any of this. If you give me authorization to sign checks from the play-money fund, everything will be cool."

"Penelope, I know you don't like talking on the phone, but this is ridiculous. Now, you obviously have spoken to Herbert and Ed about these *supposed* photos of me. Why don't you—"

"The photos are of you and some white man going into a room."

I fell on the bed. How could there be photos of me and James?

"He's holding your shoes and a bottle of wine. The photo may have been touched up a little for clarity, because you can read the room number, and yes, I called, and yes, that was your room."

I was speechless. My first instinct was to lie and tell her it wasn't me. Possibly my head was superimposed on some other woman's body. But she obviously did not want me to be in that position, so she kept talking.

"The photographer was already offered a hundred by a couple of the tabloids, sight unseen. If they see these, they will give him more, *trust* me. Maybe as much as a half. Marcus spoke to him and he's just looking for quick cash. He does not have an agenda nor is he connected to the right or anything. He apparently worked for James Wolinski at *Time* and has been sitting on these photographs waiting for the most opportune time to sell them, and I be damned if this ain't it. Now, I don't know how you guys are looking financially, but if you don't have it, I suggest we take the money out of the travel fund, depending on how much we need, and after the election, and before the accounting, we wire-transfer it back in. That will give you a little more time to sell stocks or whatever to locate the funds."

With my throat dry and a quake traveling from my head

to my toes, I whispered, "Penelope, we can't take out money without it raising red flags."

"Trust me, we can, but if you have a better idea, let me know. I've seen the photos, Les. If we don't want them to hit the six-o'clock news every night between now and the election, we gotta pass the hat, wash cars, hold bake sales, or something to get that money, now!"

Dearborn, Michigan
Joe Lewis Center
Presidential Debate
October 2000

CHERYL

The most memorable event of the election for me came the Sunday of the first debate. Due to the hours I was working at the hospital, I was forced to volunteer fewer and fewer hours to the Davis/Gallagher campaign.

The reason I was nervous was that Henry's numbers were starting to fall as it got closer to Election Day. Initially he tried to stay above the mud that both candidates were slinging at him, but eventually he had to sink to their level and the first negative ads rolled out regarding Vice President Steiner.

Earlier in the week, footage had surfaced of Henry at Harvard. No one had seen the tape before it surfaced on an Internet web site, and an AP writer wrote a story that appeared in papers all over the world. In the article the young man, who was originally unidentified, was quoted as saying, "Is calling yourself an American not good enough, sir? Not good enough for the man wishing to run this country?" The headline for over a week was "Hyphenated President?" The day after the release of the tape, the young man was on *Good Morning America*, the *Today* show, and *The Early Show*, all before 8:00 A.M. Eric King, whose appearance screamed bigot, spoke with a deep southern slur and wore his slick, black, cowlicked hair pulled back and to the side. After his appearance on *Larry King Live*, there was a debate on *Crossfire* as to why the term *African-American* was or was not needed in our society. By that time talk radio caught wind of the story and the national firestorm of debate had begun, and Henry's once apparently insurmountable lead had evaporated.

Two days before the presidential debate, while Dirk Gallagher was campaigning in Atlanta, a reporter asked him if he thought it sent the right message for a presidential hopeful to refer to himself as an African-American and refuse to consider himself as simply an American.

"Well, guys, you know me. I'm a straight shooter. Let me speak for *myself*. My grandpaw died for this country. He was stationed in France and died of mustard-gas wounds. My daddy fought in World War II and Korea and was injured. I, as many of you know, fought in Nam and was imprisoned in the "Hainoi Hilton" for two years. So I don't think anything is wrong with being called an American. Too much of my family's blood was shed to give us the right to say that, and that's all I can say about the subject." When I heard his answer, it was obvious this man was sabotaging Henry's campaign for his own run to the White House.

Henry looked stunning the night of the first and only presidential debate. He wore a wool navy pin-striped suit with an American flag on the lapel and a light blue shirt with a bold striped navy tie. On C-SPAN they showed his wife as she and his key staff people walked into the auditorium and she waved at him for good luck. The moderator was Bernard Shaw. Since Henry had given in on the number of debate stipulations, he wanted to have the moderator of his choice.

Henry smiled often and looked poised and relaxed as he gave his opening statement. He spoke of the America he envisioned and bills he had sponsored in the Senate that would help not only the people of his home state but people throughout the country. As he spoke, his campaign theme of "One People, One Man, One Vision" clearly came to life.

When he completed his statement, the crowd was not allowed to applaud, but there was no need to. He had gotten a hit and was standing on base.

Governor Tom spoke next and he was not very effective. Just as you could tell every comma of Henry's opening was carefully crafted, the governor seemed to fly from the seat of his pants. Then he looked at Henry, wrinkled his lips, and said to the world, "I'm a little older than both of you young fellas. But I will say that I'm just a plain ole ordinary American, a proud American. I am an American today. I will be an American tomorrow, and forevermore will I be an American." A collective gasp coupled with a sprinkling of applause was heard throughout the building as Henry looked him in the eye and smiled that confident smile of his. But I wondered, *Will a smile be enough*?

After the dust settled, Ronald Steiner spoke of his dreams for America, ignoring the bombshell that had just exploded in the building.

The first question from the three-person panel was directed toward Henry. "Senator Davis. Why is it you refer to yourself as an African-American, and not *just* an American?"

"My question to you is this. Does my statement that I am an African-American offend you? And if so, why? No one in this room is prouder of their American blood than I. No, my grandfather did not die fighting German soldiers, but he cleaned a storefront where Americans shopped for goods and services for over fifty years. My dad was not killed or maimed in World War II, but he raised two sons and sent them to college while he later graduated from college after he worked for sometimes eighteen hours on his feet. To me, that's the embodiment of the American dream. This is a great country and there is no doubt about it. Leslie and I have had opportunities to travel abroad and I have been to some wonderful cities, but if I am gone more than three days, there's a burning desire inside of me to return home.

"But by the same token, my ancestors were brought here against their will and helped build what is the most wealthy country this world has ever known, with *free* labor. They were brought from a continent that was rich in resources, had given birth to mathematics and science, and was the cradle of history.

In eighty and eighty-four when President Reagan indicated with pride that he was an Irish-American, it was *not* an issue. When I speak to my friends who are the chairmen of the board for major corporations such as Sony or Hitachi and they say they are Japanese-Americans, there is never any fallout. Italian-Americans wear their heritage on their sleeves with pride. And you know what? They should. Because we have all helped create this vast quilt of dreams which is stitched together with a vision, this place called America. Is it Utopia? No, in fact, it's far from it, but it is a place where our conscience is our guide. A place where courage is our goal and a place that searches for the best in us while ignoring the worst deep within the hearts of others."

Henry's statement was poetic and beautiful and brought a thunderous applause. But I thought it would be the death blow to his campaign.

A week after the debate, Henry was back in Miami. With two weeks before the election, he and his staff were making final arrangements for an all-out blitz of the country. The press reported he and Dirk Gallagher were no longer speaking and that the campaign was struggling to get across the finish line. I was cleaning out a drawer in my room when I found his pager number. He had given it to me after we made sex, not love, and I'd never used it before. In fact, I thought it was lost. But as I sat in front of the television watching this man I had loved most of my life, I decided to call him to tell him I was with him in spirit, if that was any consolation at all.

As soon as my phone rang, I knew it was my Henry.

"Ahh, yeah. This is Louis. Someone paged me from this number a couple of minutes ago?"

"It's me, Henry."

There was silence, and before I could give him my name, he said, "Cheryl. Damn, it's nice to hear your voice."

When he said that, I wanted to faint. He was actually glad I'd paged him. We spoke for about fifteen minutes about anything other than the campaign and neither of us mentioned the less-than-romantic night we had shared. Actually, I spoke to him as if I had not even heard he was running for president. And then I heard a lady in the background calling him for a meeting. "Listen, Cheryl, I really have to run. Do me a favor?"

"Sure."

"Meet me tomorrow night. Leslie's in Missouri and I'll be leaving town the next day and won't be back until after the election. I would really like to see you before I leave."

My heart sank when he said that. A part of me felt like a slut he could bang anytime he wanted. But then I looked at the bigger picture. It was said that Kennedy had a death wish. That he knew there was a good possibility he would be killed in Dallas, but he took chances anyway. Henry was made of the same stuff. A month before, he was in this shopping mall in Nebraska and cherry bombs went off and firecrackers popped, and then the distinct sound of gunfire was heard. Several Secret Service men dove on top of Henry, and I could tell, as I watched live on MSNBC, that he was trying to get them off of him so he could see what was going on. As soon as the shots ended, he gathered himself and told the frenzied crowd he was okay and to be calm because kids were getting hurt. But that was typical of him to think of children moments after shots had been fired in his direction.

When I heard him say, "I would like to see you before I leave," how could I say no and I prayed it did not mean one last time. For the first time I could empathize with Coretta, Jacqueline, Ethel, and possibly even Leslie.

"Sure," I said. "Just tell me when and where." As I hung up the phone, something told me after this we would never be together again.

The next day after returning home at six, I laid out my ivy sweater shrug and A-line skirt and took a nap. When I woke up, I felt physically ill. I didn't want to cheat on Brandon again, but my heart was left with no other choice. I sat in front of the tube watching as much of the election news on C-SPAN II as I could when the phone rang. It was Henry. "Listen, ew, Cheryl. I've been thinking. It might not be such a good idea for us to get together." He went on to explain that he had decided to break our date because if the media got wise to it, he would have even more controversy and I would be forced into a very uncomfortable position. Before he hung up, there was a pause. While I could feel pain and uncertainty in his voice, I could also sense just how much he loved her. Then he said, "Cheryl, I love you. And I will love you . . . for always. No matter what happens, always remember that." With those words he hung up the phone. As I hung up the receiver, I was in shock, and in tears.

The next morning Brandon asked me why Henry Davis's phone number was on our Caller ID box not once, but twice.

Fountainebleau Hotel
Presidential Suite

The master bedroom suite of room 1701 had been transformed into a bunker against the rest of the world. Penelope and Marcus paced the floor while Herbert occasionally glanced at his brother, who lay on the bed with his forearm flung across his eyes. No one knew what to say, so the room was silent. As they paced, sat, and lay in the master bedroom, no one knew what was happening in the election, and for the first time in his life, Henry did not care. Lying on the bed, he repented in his heart for the nights he'd had to write one more speech that really could have waited another day. He repented for having taken Herbert on campaign trips on which his wife had been invited, but he'd thought he could get more accomplished with his campaign manager. Last but not least, he atoned for having been unfaithful to her and for treating her the way he had when he had doubted her fidelity. Closing his eyelids tightly, he tried to block out the worst things that could be happening to her at that very moment. He asked for forgiveness and prayed as he had not in years for her safe return.

The cellular phone rang again, yet no one moved, thinking it was just another member of the press who had padded the right pockets in an attempt to scoop yet another news story on the bizarre morning.

Ringgggggg.

Herbert looked at the others and said, "Fuck it, I'll get rid of them." He listened for a moment. "Yeah? Oh my God!"

All eyes in the room sprang in his direction. It was obviously news about Leslie. Henry leaped to his feet and snatched the phone from his startled brother.

"Senator Davis. Who is this?"

There was silence on the other end, and panic such as he had never experienced before welled in Henry's throat.

"Henry. Henry, it's me. I'm okay. I'm okay."

"Oh my God, Leslie. We were . . . I was so worried about you. Where are you?"

"Teddy, I'm sorry. I'm sorry for making such a big mistake, again. Myles came up to visit me, and to be honest, I may have had a drink or three too many. I was a little upset about what had happened between us, so he asked me to go for a ride to clear my head. The room was packed and I changed into some jeans and put on a baseball cap and shades. He diverted the guy's attention at the door, and before you know it, we were going down in the service elevator through the kitchen and outside the hotel. We were driving around and I heard on the radio I was missing. I never meant to—"

"Les, that's okay. One second, okay?" Relaxing his massive shoulders, Henry smiled at his staff, and said, "She's okay. All right, guys, she's okay."

"Great!" Penelope said, picking up her cell phone to make the appropriate media calls.

"Ahh, Penelope? Put that down."

"What do you mean? We need to call—"

"Just what I said. I want to think this through before we alert the press. Just put down the phone," he said with a smile, "and step back . . . three paces. Okay?"

Shaking her head, Penelope returned the phone to her purse as Henry walked into a corner of the room to talk privately with his wife.

"Les, I was lying on the bed just now and it occurred to me that I have worked my entire life for this night. And I asked myself for the first time, why? Why did I want to be president? So I could help people. So I could mark my place in history. So I could be happy with myself. Well, I have done a lot to help people already. After being the first black this and that, I'll go down in history. But you know something? Even if we win tonight, I wouldn't be happy if I could not share this . . . with you. You're everything I've ever wanted. I just never knew it. Leslie, I have put you through a lot over the past twenty-seven years. All I ask is that you give me one last chance to make it right."

Leslie's voice filled with emotion. "Teddy . . . Teddy, I'm so sorry for what I did. I didn't want to. I mean—"

Standing tall, Henry cut her short. "Honey, we'll talk about it later. I just want to see your face. Where are you?"

"Okay, guys, here's the scoop," Henry announced to his family of workers as he softly clapped his hands on every other word. "Leslie just went out for a ride with Myles. She's okay. She's headed back here right now and is going to try to come back through the kitchen to avoid the press since she has her credentials with her. We'll just wait by the phone in case she calls us with any problems."

Washington, D.C.
November 8, 2000
NBS News Studio
3:25 A.M. EST

"America, this is Franklin Dunlop with an up-to-the-minute report on the ongoing stories of tonight. We are told that momentarily we will have an opportunity to speak with the press secretary of Yvette Leslie Davis. She is on her way down, and will be speaking in our Miami studio exclusively with our very own Butch Harper. The news regarding Vice President Steiner is *not* good. For the first time we are able to confirm the report that the vice president is in critical condition. His running mate, Sydney Ackerman, is at the hospital, and in the event the team is victorious tonight and the vice president is unable to fulfill his duties as president, America will have elected its very first female president. I should also note that Cardinal Edmond Giacomo has been called to the hospital in the event the worst is a reality. Now, if those two updates were not enough for you, this is the latest breaking news. The individual we showed you in the photograph earlier is not the man stalking the Davis campaign at this time. Sources confirmed that the individual in the photo, Calvin Arthur, was killed a month ago in a hunting accident. The FBI estimates Arthur sent over a hundred threatening letters to each of the major candidates as well as the president of the United States during the campaign. For the latest on Vice President Steiner, we'll swing it out to Chicago and Judy Finestein."

"Hello, Frank, and hello once again, America. The mood here is subdued. An hour ago there was singing and chanting, but that has been supplanted by fear now that Chicago's favorite son has been confirmed to be in critical condition. As you reported, Mayor Ackerman is with the vice president's family at this time. We have been advised that they have not watched the returns since this event has occurred. Obviously at this time some things are much more important. Back to you, Frank."

"Thank you, Judy, for that report. Now we will head down to Miami for the much-awaited interview with Penelope Butler-Richardson. As soon as the information regarding California is in, America, we will let you know. Now, Butch, take it away."

"Thank you, Franklin. Mrs. Butler-Richardson, what can you tell us about the story floating around these quarters concerning the senator's wife? Was she in fact missing as was reported by many news organizations about an hour ago?"

"No, she was not. That is why I am down here, Butch.

The rumor mill this morning is working overtime. We've been listening to these fallacious allegations regarding Henry and Leslie's marriage and now this report about her missing, and we have attempted to stay above the fray. Yes, I hate to say it, but this could be racial, because I have never seen other candidates on the most important night of their lives being subjected to such blatant scrutiny. But Senator and Mrs. Davis asked me to visit with you about a half hour or so ago in an attempt to squelch these tabloidesque reports. They are simply not true. In fact, they're disrespectful and, might I say, unfair!"

"Penelope, are you saying that there is *absolutely* no truth whatsoever to the reports that Mrs. Davis was missing from her hotel room earlier tonight?"

"That is exactly what I am saying, Butch. Tonight's race has come down to one state. One state will decide the fate of this country for the next four years. Why or how these made-up stories get started and spread by the media to divert this country's attention is beyond me."

"Interesting. Well, Mrs. Butler-Richardson, I would like to ask you about the photograph. There is a story now that the man who took the as-yet-unpublished photos of Mrs. Davis and Mr. Wolinski in Rome was paid one hundred thousand dollars by you or your office out of campaign funds, and he reportedly sold the negatives anyway for a half million dollars to the *National Reporter*. Can you confirm or deny that story?"

"Excuse me?"

Fontainebleau Hotel
Suite 1701

Picking up the phone on the first ring, Henry, who was looking for a fresh shirt to put on, said, "Hello!"

"Teddy, it's me." Leslie was gasping for breath on the phone. "I can't get in. The kitchen entrance is closed and it's a madhouse down here."

"Is Myles driving the car?"

"No. We're parked on the north side of the building. If you look out the window, you'll see the car."

Henry ran to the window as Herbert shouted, "No! Henry, stay away from the window!" Henry ignored him as he flung it open, but only saw the bright lights of the numerous news trucks below.

"Leslie! Listen to me and listen to me good, okay? I'm coming down there to get you. Get inside the building the best you can and keep your cell phone with you."

"Henry, don't come down here! This place is crazy. Send Herbert or Marcus," Leslie yelled over the background noise. "Henry, people are reacting to the news or something from the television," she continued. "I think the election is over, I think they announced the winner in Califor—California. From the sound of the reaction I think we—"

"Fuck the election. Meet me at the north entrance of the hotel, and whatever you do, hold on to that phone," Henry replied, and allowed the curtains to close. He put on his shoes and, wearing only a white tank top T-shirt and suit pants, bolted for the door with his cell phone in his sweaty palm.

"Henry?" Herbert said softly as his brother exited the room. He then jumped to his feet and followed him. "Henry! Where are you going?" he asked as his brother made his way through the crowd of supporters reacting to the California results.

"Move out of the goddamn way!" Henry yelled as the Secret Service agent moved aside, allowing him entrance into the hallway.

As he ran down the corridor, members of the press were shocked to see him and began snapping photos as they followed. Some even asked "How does it feel . . ." questions to get the first postelection interview, but he brushed them aside. Knowing the elevator would be too slow, he entered the stairwell with Herbert on his heels and the growing press corps in tow.

His cell phone rang. "Leslie! Where are you?"

"I'm in the building," Leslie said as she was immediately identified and slowed by the attendees on the first floor.

"I'm trying to get to you, Teddy. They're surrounding me and I can hardly—"

"Don't worry, baby!" Henry said, descending three steps at a time down the stairwell. "I'm coming down the north stairs. Just do the best you can and I'll be there."

"Okay." And before she hung up she said, "Henry!"

"What?"

"Baby, I love you. I love you so much."

"Love you too. I love you too, Les." Henry continued his rush down the stairs and dropped his phone through the gap in the rail. As he continued to run, he heard the phone disintegrate as it hit the cement floor of the basement. Henry kept running, disregarding his safety, because it was all he could think to do.

As he headed toward the door of the first floor, a security guard held up his hand, but it fell quickly as Henry shouted slowly, "Move . . . the fuck . . . out . . . the way!"

When the door opened, he looked for a mob near the entrance of the hotel, knowing his wife would be at its center. After spotting the mob, he shouted, "Leslie! Leslie, I'm coming," but to no avail. As he entered the ballroom laced with orange balloons ready to be dropped, and followed by a barrage of microphones and photographers, a crowd gathered around him, but he wove through the people like a salmon swimming upstream. "Leslie!" he shouted again while waving his arms, but knew she would never hear him.

"Henry!"

"Leslie! Leslie!" he shouted, hearing her voice for the first time.

And then Herbert, who had finally joined him, shouted over the sounds of the ballroom attendees and clicking photographers, "I see her, Henry. She's over there!"

Then the air was pierced with a woman's scream and a man yelling, "Gun! Gun!" Henry looked toward the sound of the scream as five shots clicked off in the lobby of the Fountainebleau. *Bang-bang-bang-bang-bang!* And then hysteria broke out.

Epilogue

Inauguration Day, January 21, 2001
Carol City

CHERYL

Today we watched the inauguration. I have watched each one of these since 1969 when Henry and I flicked spitballs through a straw at Spiro Agnew during Nixon's inauguration. Now I was watching with Brandon and Sarah.

Let me first say that Brandon and I had a heart-to-heart talk the morning after the election. I told him there was no way I was going to let him out of my life. Period. I think that was what he needed to hear, because as I said those words, I literally saw him relax. He loves me and I know that. There's an old saying that a man's love is a *privilege* and should never be taken for granted. I took Brandon's love for granted in search of *perceived* happiness. No matter how silly it may sound, I always felt in the bottom of my heart that I was just one smile, one phone call, one "I love you" from making all my dreams come true. But those dreams died on election night, and I realized that I could continue to live in the past with the memory of Henry Louis Davis the Second or enjoy the rest of my life with Brandon. With my newfound (and much welcomed) closure, it was an easy choice.

Brandon is slated for another promotion, and I am so proud of him. He worked hard to get promoted several times when opportunities arose and he was passed over.

But he never gave up. He worked as hard as he could to break from the crowd, and in two weeks he will be given his captain bars. I guess Brandon never gives up on anything he really and truly wants, and that's just another reason why I love him more and more each day.

I guess the biggest news of all is, believe it or not, I'm pregnant. Yes I'm forty-seven, yes it's a miracle, and no, I could not be happier. We'd always used protection, but after the election we had make-up sex and, well, suffice it to say we were uncovered for a while, and when I missed my monthly visit two weeks ago, I knew. I didn't know what to expect from Brandon, because he always said he didn't want any kids. So I made him a romantic dinner and sat in his lap last night, and said, "Honey, I got some news for you." After I told him, our foreheads kissed and we both sat there looking at my belly for an eternity.

One could say things didn't work out for me and Henry, but I would disagree. There were times it was tough. I would lie awake at night crying silently because of what I thought I had missed out on. I often wondered what would have happened if I'd never met Darius. Where would I be? Henry took me places in my mind I would have never conceived of if I had not met him. But regardless of the outcome, the reason I know he was the best thing that ever happened to me is that he taught me how to dream, how to achieve, how to laugh, how to cry. Most important, he taught me how to love beyond the surface. He taught me how to love a man like Captain Brandon Royce Allen. I guess God's greatest gift to me was the prayer he chose not to answer, and a love that truly is for always.

Inauguration Day, January 21, 2001
The Davis Residence

YVETTE LESLIE DAVIS

We made a number of magazines after Henry announced his bid for the presidency, but that was nothing compared to the coverage after the shots in the Fountainebleau. If there were a periodical called *Klansman Today*, we would have been on its cover.

The most interesting thing to me about that night was how this man was able to get so close to us in the first place. The man who fired the shots in the hotel was named Abraham Smalls, and he and his accomplice were right in the room with Henry and Herbert. He was a drifter, like most potential assassins, and had fallen into one cult after another. And then after the Oklahoma City bombing, he met this guy from Wyoming named Calvin Arthur. Arthur fed him and clothed him and eventually gave him a new family. This Arthur guy was apparently delusional and felt if he or one of his people could kill the president, he could somehow overthrow the government. It seems there was an internal power struggle and one of his disciples decided to do away with him. Arthur's dream was to kill the president. The man who followed Henry across the country, Abraham Smalls, wanted not only to kill the president, but to assassinate anyone with a possibility of attaining the White House in one gory night. It sounds far-fetched, but he had a well-thought-out plan that the FBI later seized in a one thousand-page journal.

Not only did they find shell casings across the street from our suite at the Fountainebleau, they discovered gunmen in D.C. at different posts, all connected to the militia group Waco 2000. They had orders to assassinate the president, the secretary of state, and the Speaker of the House, among others. After Arthur was killed, his followers buried him yet continued to send out death threats with his name on them, causing the FBI to look for a man who had been dead for several weeks. Abraham Smalls followed Henry, and his accomplice followed Steiner. They killed two FBI agents and assumed their identity to infiltrate the hotels and let in their people. We found out later that night that Smalls had at least five of his militia members in the Fountainebleau Hotel, and the plan was to open gunfire on the campaign workers if they could not get to Henry. Fortunately, when they finally got Henry in their crosshairs, they did not worry about the rest of the attendees.

In a news report on Smalls's life, we found out that he and Henry were the exact same age. He had attended Georgetown the same time Henry and I were there, and he and Henry were both willing to die for what they believed.

When I was a child, my mom told me something I would hear over and over again as an adult. But it never rang truer to me than on election night in Miami. She would say, "No matter what the circumstances, no matter how dark it gets, there is always a silver lining for everything in life." That night when I sat in the ICU waiting area, I looked for that silver lining. I looked at what had happened to Teddy, and I couldn't see it. And then it occurred to me. The silver lining in all of this was that Henry Louis Davis the Second had died. He died there on the floor of the Fountainebleau. And with his death, the man I fell in love with was returned to me.

SENATOR HENRY LOUIS DAVIS II

Today was not as painful as I had expected. In fact, today was rather enjoyable. In accordance with tradition, I was invited to D.C. to sit on the podium as the chief justice of the Supreme Court swore in the next president of the United States, but I took a pass. Yes, we had lost the election by less than a 5 percent margin in California. Actually, across the country more people voted for us than for Steiner, but with the electoral college system, that was neither here nor there. After losing the election, in a way I was relieved. It had been a long journey toward the White House, and I was very proud of the campaign we'd waged. But I don't know if emotionally I had enough to carry me for another four or eight years.

Ronald Steiner recovered enough to take the oath of office. He was brought to the stage in a wheelchair and walked with the aid of his wife and Vice President Sydney Ackerman to the podium. When he did that, I doubt there was a dry eye in America.

Believe it or not, I speak to Dirk Gallagher at least once a week now. Even on conservative talk radio, his sabotaging in the final days was noted. But I hold no animus for him. He's invited me to his ranch in West Texas, and we may take him up on it one day. He's apologized profusely to me in private for his conduct during the election, and I'm told he may even do so on BET and before the NAACP national convention. He would obviously like my support and assistance in 2004, and who knows, I may just be there for him. I don't do grudges.

Herbert was wounded trying to save my life. When the lady screamed, "Gun," he turned and saw the perpetrator. His first instinct was to shield me, which he did, and was subsequently shot in the abdomen. And then it seemed everything moved at quarter speed. My brother was falling to the ground, the crowd divided like the Red Sea, I noticed the gunman was no more than five feet away from me, and then he swung the chrome metal toward my face. I looked down the barrel and into his eyes and saw only rage, but in that split second all the unresolved aspects in my life became clear. In the frenzied atmosphere someone pushed his arm and I instinctively dove toward him and grabbed his wrist. We struggled as the gun fired off two rounds, fortunately hitting no one. Then from nowhere my chief of security, Joey Wood, leaped out, grabbed him around the waist, twisted him around, and the nine-millimeter went spinning like a bottle across the emptying ballroom floor.

As I stood, I saw my brother and ran over to hold him in my arms. We were later advised that since the bullet settled just a fraction of an inch from his spine, if he'd tried to stand, he would have been left a paraplegic. Herbert spent about a month and a half in the hospital and *walked* out to a hero's welcome. The *New York Times*, *Miami Herald*, and *Washington Post* have done several feature stories on him, and the scoop in the beltway is, if he wanted it, he could win my old House of Representatives seat hands down. Right now he says he is not interested, but something tells me the box we kept in the attic with the Davis for Congress buttons may be reopened.

Penelope caught a little heat because, for some unknown reason, she used federal matching funds to pay off the photographer instead of the personal funds as she should have. Yet she has proven to be part Teflon and is now negotiating to do segments on *60 Minutes* for CBS. It is said that presidential politics is always a heads-I-win-tails-you-lose proposition. Because if you win, you sit in the greatest bastion of power in the world. If you lose, you do a talk show or write a book, which brings me to Ed.

I'm told Edward Long is negotiating a seven-figure book deal. He's looking at such a large advance because the book will deal with my personal life and the women who tried to get close to me and my marriage. Marcus told me that Ed originally approached the publisher with a book on the day-to-day events of our campaign from notes he kept in a diary. They were not interested. It hurts a little to find out that he was my Judas, because we trusted this man with intimate details and treated him like family. But this, too, is all a part of the game.

I never heard from Cheryl again after the election, which I think is for the best. For the first time since I was in my early twenties, I have a chance to think, and I wonder what would have happened if I had shown up at that party at her friend's house so many years ago. She would never have gotten pregnant. She probably would have gone to Florida A&M with me. Could she have been the wind beneath my wings that I found with Leslie which carried me to the door-step of the White House? Like I said, I have a lot of time to think nowadays, and sometimes you wonder how one simple act can change your entire life. And in our case, even history.

Regarding the election, most political talking heads point to my handling of the African-American question in the debate as the pivotal reason I lost the race. The night before the debate, everyone in my inner circle wanted me to answer the question differently. But I made the call and suffered the consequences. Afterward in a Gallup poll it was determined that many African-Americans thought I skirted the issue and I did not answer the question *black* enough, while some whites thought I was the reincarnation of Eldridge Cleaver. The most ironic part of all of this was the fact that race was the catalyst that started me on the road toward the White House. As a teenager I thought I could be to racism what Sir Alexander Fleming had been to bacteria. Now those thoughts seem like a million years ago. The sword that was formed to eliminate a problem was used to pierce my political heart.

The event that changed me more than any other was the electrocution of Juarez Bechuanas. To make a long, sad story short, when the case made national headlines, I called friends of mine in the DA's office and they shared with me the "mountain" of evidence against him. After hearing that, I reviewed the trial transcripts line by line and I felt in my heart he was guilty without a shadow of a doubt. But my friends in the DA's office never told me that the DNA that was found was botched because the samples were stored incorrectly that morning. They never told me that Mr. Bechuanas's wife had had an affair with the neighbor who fingered Juarez as the person wearing the bloody clothes, because that was not allowed into testimony. I never knew that behind the scenes the governor was pushing for a quick conviction because he had his eye on running for my senatorial seat. Well, last year one of the students who had investigated the case uncovered evidence that pointed the finger at the neighbor as the person who committed the crime. Now the neighbor, who was a pastor, is on death row. I don't think I will ever wash my hands again without looking at the water going down the drain for blood.

Well, enough of that.

I may have lost the election, but I won a lot more. I now live every day as if it's my last day. I had such a fear of death before and I never allowed it to show. The reason I was scared was that there was so much I wanted to do and I had not accomplished any of it. My entire existence was directed toward living for something in the future, and looking back on the experience, I don't think that was living at all.

People often ask me, now that I'm not even fifty years old and retired from political office, what will I do? Well, I have a new hobby. Jigsaw puzzles. I never imagined it before, but simple things like that are so much fun for me. I'm also working with this young writer on my memoirs. But the thing I am most proud of is the fact that I am starting an organization that will help millions of people in this country. The idea was one that I detailed in my previous book, but now that I am out of politics for the first time since my early twenties, I can actually do something about it. The name of the association will be Educate and Counsel the Homeless. The goal of EACH is to eliminate homelessness in twenty years. How? Well, I noticed that day I met Ora how the store employees would sometimes come out and ask her to leave the front of their store—as if she were just a pile of garbage that had accidentally washed up on their doorstep. So in my plan, store owners would make a tax-deductible donation which would be about half the rate of minimum wage, and homeless people would work in the area of their store. Cleaning signs, sweeping, handing out flyers, scrubbing graffiti, et cetera. The store would receive half-priced assistance and a person whom they could train to be a full-time employee while receiving goodwill and a healthy tax break. The other half of the minimum wage would be contributed by major corporations such as Denny's and Texaco.

In each city where the program is in place, we would find a building that we could refurbish to house all of the homeless individuals in the program. They would pay a very nominal amount each week for rent, and we would require them to set 10 percent of their pay aside for savings. My friend Michael Dell agreed to install computers so people who were once asking for dollars on the street will someday surf the information superhighway. Bill and Camille Cosby, Ted Turner, Donald Trump, and Oprah Winfrey endowed the program substantially, giving us the ability to reward each person who was able to save a thousand dollars with a lump sum of two thousand dollars so they could try to eventually provide their own housing. Most important, the co-ops will be run in many cities by the cavalry of students who once called themselves Henry and Leslie's Kids. They will get experience as well as a strong dose of volunteerism, and the enrollees in the program will hopefully learn work skills from the students. Most important, this program would be underwritten totally without government funding.

A week ago I went to the mall for the first time in more than two years and walked into an engraver's shop. You should have seen his face when I picked up a desk plaque and asked him to engrave "President Davis" on it. "President *Yvette Leslie* Davis," I clarified, because she will oversee the organization and I will be there to support her in any way I can.

Once, when I was attending a fund-raiser for my presidential campaign in tiny Hope, Arkansas, this lady who must have been at least ninety was brought to my hotel room to meet me. She was very dark complexioned and had a loose-fitting partial bridge. She was the mother of Annette Smith, a young lady who was killed during a civil rights protest in Birmingham in the late fifties, and when she was being interviewed once, she told the reporter the one thing she wanted to do before she died was to meet me. When she shook my hand, tears rushed from her eyes and she could hardly speak. I was humbled by the scene and would not allow my photographer to take any snapshots. She wiped her eyes, and said, "Son, you are not here by accident. It was meant to be. My daughter's life was taken so you could fulfill your promise, and I know you will do great and mighty things." She was one of the first people I called to thank for her support after my defeat, and even at her age, she will spearhead another program called the Candlelight Campaign.

The name of the organization is taken from my last speech in the run for the presidency. As I was closing the speech, in my heart I knew I would not win, so I wanted to make the campaign as well as the last 32 years of my life stand for something. I spoke to them about giving back and mentioned that the light from a candle is never diminished when it is shared with another candle's. And in fact at the moment the light is shared it is at its brightest. This campaign will be Marcus's baby and it's an international mentoring program I am sure he will do well with.

I became the first defeated candidate for the presidency to win *Time* magazine's Man of the Year award, for which I felt extremely honored. Since I am still in my forties, I know every four years for the next twenty or thirty years of my life, I will be asked if I have plans to run. I will always flirt with entering the fray, but I've run my last political race. At this point I can effect legislation more with the threat of running than actually reentering the arena. Great and mighty things sometimes come from the most unusual of places.

I have changed my opinion on many things over the past couple of months, but my faith remains firm in one simple fact. In spite of its ills, in spite of the mudslinging, backbiting, egos, and greed, I believe being a politician is the most noble endeavor one can aspire to. The Bible says there is no greater love shown than one who would lay down his life for a friend, and our history is marked by great men and women who knew they were doing that, yet put themselves in harm's way so they, too, could, in one way or another, change the world.

We have a duck pond near our home, and I often find myself first thing in the morning walking down the hill to sit and watch the sunrise there. Sometimes I sit in the grass with the newspaper and fall asleep, and once I woke up and noticed a blanket over me and my wife holding my hand, sleeping peacefully by my side. It's at these moments when I know, no matter what I could or would ever achieve, not one thing could compare to what I already had.

I'm a little sore today. The old back injury from college flared up when I was playing basketball in the backyard with a foster kid we are in the process of adopting. His name is Chaz and he is every bit of thirteen years old. Oh yeah, we also are in the process of having a baby. We are adopting this little girl named Mikila Ruth and we are converting one of the rooms into a nursery. Yeah, that advice of living each day as if it were your last day has indeed changed my world. So in losing the election I won a family. But most important, I won a life, and that's not a bad trade-off.

"Teddy?" Leslie called from the living room. "Are you out there?"

"Yeah," Henry said, sitting beside the pool and staring at the end of the Steiner inauguration on television.

"Look what I found!"

"What?"

"You gotta come in here and see it."

"I can't," he said as he sipped his Coke. "My back is sore again."

"Henry! Please don't make me come out there and get you!"

Henry stood and put his feet in his flip-flops while streching his stiff body. As he walked inside he said, "Hon? Where are you?"

And then from nowhere he heard the static-laced sound of a forty-five on the record player:

> *And it's me you need to show*
> *How deep is your love?*

"May I have this donce?" Leslie asked, walking toward her husband with the rose held between her teeth.

"I love you," he said as he held her in his arms. He took the flower from her and kissed her softly on the lips. "Leslie, I love you more than you will *ever* know. I think . . . no, I know my love for you will last . . . for always."

"For always? That's a wonderful phrase. Where did you hear that?"

Always

Acknowledgments

First and foremost, I thank my Heavenly Father for giving me a measure of talent and allowing me to share it with you.

To the one who taught me that *true* faith is the act of holding on to nothing, until it became something. It was you who showed me how a woman could be both strong and beautiful. And when Dad died, it was you who chose not to meet another because as you said, "I gotta take care of my boys." Thank you Annie Mae McCann for holding on to me until I became something.

To my heart and soul and you know who you are.

To the numerous writers whose shoulders I stand on, I thank you. May the words of Richard Wright, Ralph Ellison, Zora Neale Hurston, James Baldwin, Alex Haley, Charles W. Chesnutt, Paul Dunbar, Ernest Hemingway, Langston Hughes and Chester B. Himes forever ring in our hearts.

To my contemporary brothers and sisters who continue to raise the bar with each release: Lolita Files, Eric Jerome Dickey, Victoria Christopher-Murray, Margaret Johnson-Hodge, Tracy Price-Thompson, Franklin White, Monique Gilmore-Scott, E. Lynn Harris, Van Whitfield, Pearl Cleage, Jacqueline Jones-LaMon, Linda Grosvenor, Connie Briscoe, Grace Edwards, Kimberla Lawson-Roby and Tracy Grant. Your words embolden me to make my best even better.

To friends and family who prayed for me after my loss. Thank you, and the prayers were felt.

To the numerous readers worldwide who sent me S-mail and E-mail. Words do not convey the power to tell you how much it means. I read them all, so keep them coming.

Please continue to visit *TimmothyMcCann.com* to see what is next on the horizon and I trust you will continue to enjoy the ride . . .

Until . . .

Timmothy B. McCann
March '00

Timmothy B. McCann
Fan Club
P.O. Box 357814
Gainesville, Florida 32635-7814